ONE BLOOD

the narrative impulse

ONE BLOOD

the narrative impulse

Ronald Spatz

EDITOR

UNIVERSITY OF ALASKA

ANCHORAGE

❖

Alaska Quarterly Review is a journal devoted to contemporary literary art. It is published twice each year by the University of Alaska Anchorage, an Affirmative Action / Equal Opportunity Employer and Educational Institution.
Editor Ronald Spatz **Senior Affiliate Editors** Richard Chiappone, Robert Clark, Stephanie Cole, Michael Jones **Affiliate Editors** Julia French, Arlitia Jones, Stacy Smith, Tara Wreyford **Contributing Editors** Billy Collins, Stuart Dischell, Stuart Dybek, Patricia Hampl, Amy Hempel, Jane Hirshfield, Dorianne Laux, Maxine Kumin, Grace Paley, Pattiann Rogers **Founding Editors** Ronald Spatz, James Jakób Liszka **Copy Editors** Michael Jones, David Singyke

Subscription rates are $10.00 for one year, $20.00 for two years, and $30.00 for three years. Please add four dollars per year for all foreign subscriptions. Sample copies are $6.00. Back issue prices on request. The editors invite submissions of fiction, short plays, poetry, and literary nonfiction in traditional and experimental styles. Unsolicited manuscripts are read between August 15 and May 15 and must be accompanied by a stamped, self-addressed envelope. Send all correspondence to: Editors, *Alaska Quarterly Review,* University of Alaska Anchorage, 3211 Providence Drive, Anchorage, AK 99508.

Web Site: http://www.uaa.alaska.edu/aqr/

Distributors: B. DeBoer, 113 East Center Street, Nutley, NJ 07110
Ingram Periodicals, 1240 Heil Quaker Blvd., Lavergne, TN 37086
University Microfilms International, 300 North Zeeb Road,
Ann Arbor, MI 48106

Alaska Quarterly Review is listed in *The American Humanities Index* and is a member of CLMP.

Publication of *One Blood: The Narrative Impulse* was made possible, in part, by a Creation and Presentation grant from the National Endowment for the Arts. This special anthology takes the place of Volume 18, Numbers 3 & 4 in the publication schedule.

ISBN 0–9673377-2–0

About the cover:
The midnight sun casts a warm glow over a skiff at anchor in Kotzebue Sound during a lull in the salmon fishing. Cover photo © 2000 Chris Arend.

❖

ONE BLOOD

the narrative impulse

EDITOR'S NOTE

When the King of Sweden awarded Karl Landsteiner the Nobel Prize for Medicine in 1930, a number of things were known about human blood. It appears to be red and is pumped by the engine of the heart. It's a physiological necessity to sustain human life. It takes about five liters of it to run an adult body—less than that and the body becomes enervated and will cease to work. And, although there is only *one* human blood, Landsteiner's serological studies showed that human blood can be classified into distinct groups which are not compatible in combination. His research ultimately led to the important, life-saving application of therapeutic blood transfusions.

No one will win a Nobel Prize by explaining the nature of narrative structures or how narrative genres might be mixed. However, narrative is axial to the vitality and *life* of the mind. The very impulse toward story—the human need to tell and to write, to make meaning and sense of one's existence—is universal. The gift of narrative has distinguished the human species from all others. Just about *everything* we think and dream—fact and fiction—is filtered through narrative. It is a *constant* in shaping our sense of self. It is central to our understanding of human nature. Hence the title of this volume, *One Blood: The Narrative Impulse.*

Yet the pressure to classify and divide is no less in the world of letters. This is ostensibly to ensure that readers understand what it *is* they are reading. Is it nonfiction or is it fiction? Is it true, or is it a product of imagination? Richard Ford put it this way: "One of the principal aspects of a piece of prose writing is: what is its purport? That is to say, what does it ask me to trust? What does it ask us to believe? For me it's important that those lines of fidelity be maintained." (*AQR* Vol. 17, Nos. 1 & 2)

As a companion to *AQR*'s volume *Intimate Voices, Ordinary Lives* (1997), *One Blood: The Narrative Impulse* explores an alternative view. We believe the basic impulse at the core of human narrative renders genre distinction an artifice. Fidelity to this fundamental impulse recognizes the primacy of narrative itself rather than its factuality or fictionality. By choosing not to classify stories by genre, we ignore the boundaries between fact and fiction. Although the purpose of each story is unchanged, the *truthfulness* of the story is enlarged. A story presented in this framework brings the reader closer to the story's heart, closer to its original narrative impulse.

Within this context, the methodology for *One Blood* was straightforward. To unify the presentation, we included only stories of fact and fiction employing the first person voice. Over a two-year period, we received about 3,100 such stories, from which we selected 31. They represent the best cross-section of first person stories submitted to us. Contributing editor Patricia Hampl introduces the collection with an essay in which she places the first person voice in our literary history, and in a more general sense of history. She also touches on issues of voice and genre. She does not, however, provide a tour of the selections. By design, we reserve all interpretation of the stories for our readers.

Finally, as *Alaska Quarterly Review* begins its 19th season, we gratefully acknowledge the National Endowment for the Arts for a Creation and Presentation grant that made possible the publication of *One Blood: The Narrative Impulse.*

—Ronald Spatz

Ronald Spatz is executive editor and founding editor of *Alaska Quarterly Review*. He is Professor and Chair of the Department of Creative Writing and Literary Arts and Director of the University Honors Program at the University of Alaska Anchorage. His writing has appeared in range of national literary journals and anthologies and has been recognized by individual artist fellowships from the National Endowment for the Arts and the Alaska State Council on the Arts. He has also produced and directed short subject films including *For the Love of Ben*, which was broadcast nationally on public television.

FIRST PERSON SINGULAR

Although we are told often enough that we live in the age of the memoir, memoirists are not the only culprits of the personal, now or historically. Lyric poetry, especially in our time, is often implicitly autobiographical. And some of the most compelling fiction in our literature turns instinctively to faux memoir for its narrative mode, adopting the first person voice for wholly invented lives.

The magnetism of that voice—the I rather than the he or she—may be a particular hallmark of American literature. Even tradition-ally, we haven't been a people with a story to tell so much as a lot of "folks" (as Whitman liked to call us) elbowing forward with yet another discovery of "the self." We seem to love and even reverence this thing we call "the self." We love even—or especially—its inca-pacity to lay itself bare perhaps because we know instinctively that if the self could be fully revealed, there would be no such thing as literature.

"Call me Ishmael," the most famous first line in our literature reads. Thus the great novel is launched, its huge bulk poised on the frail pedestal of an intro as casual as any passed off in an airport bar. And of course, the fascinating depths of those three words—*Call me Ishmael*—reside in the paradoxical mystery, and even the willful secrecy, of the self that they betray. OK, we'll *call* you Ish-mael—but who *are* you? But this alone Ishmael will not, or cannot tell. His first person dissolves, as every great artist wishes to do and as Keats knew Shakespeare did, into the work itself.

The inevitable struggle of the first person voice to know itself and also to render experience accurately creates of the first person pronoun an endlessly conflicted—and therefore endlessly intri-guing—character. We trust Ishmael to the last page of that heavy American novel, and yet can we ever say we know him? But that may be the sublime fact of first person narration: that the self is never "found," like a lost sock. Rather, following the classic recipe for spiritual transcendence, in the first person voice the self is effec-tively lost—lost in its material and ultimately, in its form.

No literature is as rooted in the romance of the self as ours is. And we are often scolded for it—or scold ourselves. William Gass performed this hand-slapping several years ago in a *Harper's* essay titled "The Art of Self: Autobiography in an Age of Narcissism." Some of his objections make good, if predictable, sense. There *are* bad, indulgent memoirs—but then there are and ever will be bad indulgent novels and poems, too. Only the memoir (or even the autobiographical impulse), however, is criticized for presuming to exist at all, as if it were somehow an affront to good manners. Only memoiristic writing is employed as an accepted cliché in book reviewing, as in the stock phrase which dismisses a novel for being "merely autobiographical." In fact, the adjective autobiographical almost looks lonely without its little escort modifier—"merely." In other words, we have a classic love/hate relationship with the first person voice: we are drawn to it—and we are embarrassed by it.

But what is interesting in this recent case is that Gass's routine complaint against autobiographical writing did not go unanswered. He had only to wait a few months to get worse than he gave. The counterblow came from James Atlas in an essay accompanying a *New York Times Sunday Magazine* cover story devoted to—of all things—"The Age of the Literary Memoir." (The fact of the memoir being chosen as the subject of a cover story in the *Times Magazine* is itself some kind of cultural barometer about the current status of the first person voice in narrative writing.)

Atlas quotes Gass on the narcissism of the memoir: "Look, Ma, I'm breathing. See me take my initial toddle, use the potty, scratch my sister, win spin the bottle. Gee whiz, my first adultery—what a guy!"

"Point taken," Atlas agrees. "But," he goes on, cruelly, "try reading Gass's bloated novel about a closet Nazi, *The Tunnel*, on which he labored for three decades. Fiction isn't delivering the news. Memoir is."

This battle of the genres is silly, and finally beside the point. Who can say that fiction is not delivering the news? Maybe "the news" is not necessarily what literature is supposed to be delivering anyway. But the rise of the memoir in our times has given a special cachet, and even legitimacy to first person narrative that has affected fiction and poetry as well as non-fiction. Every age instinctively reaches out—and finds—the forms and voices most congenial to its urgent messages. It may be that the peculiar authority of the first person voice, whether found in memoir, fiction or poetry—is the real news in our literary culture, not the false dust-up between the novel and the memoir. The news about the memoir is not that it is somehow overtaking the novel, but that it is now included in the pantheon at all.

Beyond these genre wars, why have so many writers chosen to confine themselves to the limitations of the first person when literature is the one place you can choose to be God—for isn't omniscient narration the greatest tantalizing opportunity of literature? What freedoms reside in the first person voice to make up for this abdication of narrative divinity? For I don't believe, as William Gass and others do, that the rise of the memoir signals the literary equivalent of talk radio or that it is the genre of something called the Me Generation. Perhaps perversely, I don't even think the memoir at its deepest has much to do with confession, and it dies when it betrays the scent of self-absorption.

Maybe the current rage for memoir begins not as a reaction to fiction but as an extension of poetry, the genre our culture claims most to marginalize. How could Americans avoid becoming memoirists when our greatest poem is called "Song of Myself"? For the American memoir of recent years does not have an appetite so much for reminiscence, but rather for witnessing. It is the quest literature of our times, an urgent mid-life inquiry, not an end-of-life counting of personal silver or settling of accounts. Whitman, who stands with Thoreau as the inventor of a peculiarly American kind of speculative first person voice, is right in line with this early middle-age quest use of the genre we see so often today:

I, now thirty-seven years old in perfect health begin . . . he says. Memoir is a young man's—or woman's—business. He also makes the point explicitly about being a witness:

> Backward I see in my own days where I sweated through fog with
> linguists and contenders,
> I have no mockings or arguments, I witness and wait.

It's worth pausing to consider Whitman, that great mixer of genres, in any consideration of the sources and habits of the first person voice. He is the father of it all for American writers, certainly. Whitman was a poet but also a journalist (his prose pieces collected as "Specimen Days" constitute either great reportage or a great diary—or both). Whitman understood his "self" not as the tidy, bundled, post-therapy static identity we tend to think of when we hear the word "a self." Rather, for him, the self was a "kosmos."

Looking to Whitman as a model, we see that the deepest conception of the self in first person narration is not dead-ended in the notion of individualism, but is a galvanizing social and political identity which is rooted in love, what Whitman called "the dear love of comrades." This self is essentially communal, not solitary, expansive rather than interiorized. It is not narcissistic because it is not "about" the self, but about *using* the self—as lens, as filter, as tool. It is the right tool for the job which is the task of rendering the world.

Whitman understood the song of his self was the song not of his ego, but of his being in the world. He knew, as Blake knew, that it was the exact intersection of experience and world that created this instrument called "the self." As a result, his self was not separate, special, unique—it was something far greater: it was part of the All. "Clear and sweet is my soul, and clear and sweet is all that is not my soul," he writes in section 3. "These are really the thoughts of all men in all ages and lands," he says elsewhere in the poem, "they are not original with me." For being our first truly modern poet, Whitman has an ancient's distaste for originality. He made his first person voice sing for the nation, not for himself alone.

In fact, even the apparently self-canonizing opening lines of "Song of Myself" take their buoyancy not from an over-amped egotism, but from a profound sense of communion with others:

> I celebrate myself, and sing myself,
> And what I assume you shall assume,
> For every atom belonging to me as good belongs to you.

The poem is predicated from that third line on the essential unity of life, not on some self-proclaimed specialness. He refuses to be unique but still, he must be singular, he must be "Myself." If he were anything else, a bit of the cosmos would be missing.

He has come upon a discovery, the discovery of all the great practitioners of autobiography from Augustine to Nabokov. Namely, that the real subject of autobiography is not one's experience but one's consciousness. And to reveal one's consciousness is more intimate—and eternal—than to reveal one's experience which is, after all, limited to events, whereas consciousness touches—potentially at least—everything in existence.

> . . . now I see it is true, what I guessed at,
> What I guess'd when I loaf'd on the grass,
> What I guess'd while I lay alone in my bed,
> And again as I walk'd the beach under the paling stars of the morning.
>
> My ties and ballasts leave me, my elbows rest in sea-gaps,
> I skirt sierras, my palms cover continents,
> I am afoot with my vision.

Whitman's choice of the first person narrative voice also allows him quicker, more immediate access to the second person address. Precisely because he crows out frankly that he is celebrating and singing "myself," he is able to call out directly to the reader, directly to "you." There is some kind of fundamental mental health at work here: if I know I'm really me, then I can know you're really you—and in knowing this distinction, I also know our connection and can plunge more deeply into relation. Whitman makes it clear that if a writer—any person—allows you access to his consciousness, he has created the truest intimacy possible, person to person. "I might not tell everybody," he says in section 19 of "Song of Myself" about the depths of his mind and heart he is imparting in the poem, "but I will tell you."

Whitman's use of the second person address here is probably the greatest "dear reader" approach ever made in literature. Even Jane Eyre, Charlotte Bronte's first person narrator who must have helped form the consciousness of every girl who ever read that novel in adolescence, does not call upon us at this level of intimacy when she makes her famous declaration, "Reader, I married him." Charlotte Bronte employs the address for an announcement, and the salutation inaugurates the imparting of a piece of information—pivotal information, but not a revelation inviting intimate relation of the sort Whitman attempts.

Whitman's passionate use of the first person as narrative voice *and* as protagonist is one of the treasures of our literature, one that our narrative poetry and prose still take heart from. Yet do we even know much about Whitman? Doesn't he recede into the glory of his work as Keats said Shakespeare does? We even need the biographers and critics to tell us that he was gay. He is not confessional, in spite of being revelatory; his declarations do not point to himself. His poem is not about a search for a self, but about a construction of a self.

This self is no more "real" than any character in a novel. Like those fictional ghosts, the "I" of the memoir is made of words. The coherence or "realness" we keep demanding of memoir, our insistence on calling it "non-fiction" (whatever that is) all bespeak our wistful desire for clear categories. But the memoirist must invoke Whitman's motto: "Do I contradict myself? Very well, I contradict myself."

* * *

Poets may be closer to the enterprise of memoir than novelists, and therefore lyric poetry reverts to the first person more inevitably than fiction. But sometimes a first person voice in fiction appears that just won't let go of us either, a voice so perfectly wedded to its narrative that we cannot separate it from its story. Nick Carraway in *The Great Gatsby* is such a first person voice. He is for the twentieth century what Huck Finn, a wildly different first person voice, was for the American nineteenth century. Nick is the representative voice of his newly urban, newly rich age as Huck was of his still rural, still pioneer age. Nick Carraway carries forward Huck's incorrigible nineteenth century innocence and grafts it seamlessly onto the will-fully unconscious American might of the twentieth century. He is wholly "fictional" (no one has accused Fitzgerald of "being" Nick), yet no one argues that the book would be improved by the detach-ment of third person narration.

Nick Carraway's bland bond-salesman voice is a world away from Whitman's panting immortal "self." Yet it is impossible to imagine *Gatsby* cast in the third person. The book is all Nick's, pos-sessed of his defeated Middlewestern complacency, vanquished at the hands of the cold-blooded capitalist East.

On the face of it Nick's ownership of the novel is very strange, for he is a minor character in his own book. He just shows up most of the time. Aside from his half-hearted romance with Jordan Baker, a romance no reader cares about (and which it's hard to believe Nick cares much about), Nick doesn't even qualify as a protagonist. Yet, it is important to remember that Nick is writing not a story, but a memoir. He makes it clear—at the beginning, again in the middle, and finally at the end of the novel—that he is narrating his tale not from the source of its action, New York and Long Island, but from back home in the Middle West, from a provincial capital that clearly stands for Fitzgerald's hometown, Saint Paul.

This return home, to the safe center of a newly dangerous Amer-ica, is clearly a defeat. Yet Nick maintains it is a defeat with honor, a moral defeat. But then honor is part of his trouble, part of his conflicted modern nature, for he has become convinced that he is being honorable all by himself now in the cold capitalist world of the novel's action. The elegy that saturates his narration and makes *Gatsby* our greatest lyric novel is not just a lament for Gatsby but for the idea of honor.

Nick is in the dark wood of his own experience and writes his memoir to understand it all, to be able to go forward. Or perhaps—and this is why his return to Saint Paul is important—to go back-ward. The novel avoids being nostalgic because its relation to past action is not sentimental (as nostalgia must be) but rather is elegiac as befits tragedy.

Nick Carraway begins as a Brooks Brothers rationalist, a conventional believer in surfaces. Part of the genius of Fitzgerald's creation lies in Nick's laconic, decent, ever-so-slightly dim-bulb quality. Nick isn't stupid—far from it. He's just complacent—and while he may not know this at the beginning of the novel, he knows it by the end. Here is that complacent, almost priggish voice, which opens the novel:

> In my younger and more vulnerable years my father gave me some advice that I've been turning over in my mind ever since.
>
> "Whenever you feel like criticizing any one," he told me, "just remember that all the people in this world haven't had the advantages that you've had."
>
> He didn't say any more, but we've always been unusually communicative in a reserved way, and I understood that he meant a great deal more than that. In consequence, I'm inclined to reserve all judgments, a habit that has opened up many curious natures to me and also made me the victim of not a few veteran bores.

The self-congratulation and satisfied entitlement are almost comical—only the first person voice could reveal it. Whitman starts with intimacy and arrives at detachment; Nick Carraway begins as a benign snob. The action of the novel and his position as witness compel him to attain intimacy—and a bruised humility—by the book's end. It is his task as teller-of-the-tale that gives Nick not grandeur perhaps, but a presence that haunts the book.

No one else left standing at the end of the action—certainly not Daisy or Tom Buchanan and not Jordan Baker—is capable of telling the story, much less the truth. And just as surely, a neutral third person voice couldn't radiate the great elegiac spirit of the novel. Only the lyric intelligence of an essentially ordinary guy, liberated by the events he has witnessed, could do that.

When Nick talks to the reader in the final meditation of the book, when he is truly speaking from the depth of his first person voice, he speaks finally as an adult to history itself. He speaks from and to memory, as all memoirists do. He turns not to Long Island or New York, not to the action of the tragedy at all, but to a seemingly separate memory belonging entirely to himself as a Minnesota boy:

> One of my most vivid memories is of coming back West from prep school and later from college at Christmas time. Those who went farther than Chicago would gather in the old dim Union Station at six o'clock of a December evening, with a few

Chicago friends, already caught up into their own holiday gayet-
ies, to bid them a hasty good-by. I remember the fur coats of the
girls returning from Miss This-or-That's and the chatter of frozen
breath and the hands waving overhead as we caught sight of old
acquaintances, and the matchings of invitations: "Are you going
to the Ordways'? The Herseys'? the Schultzes'?" and the long
green tickets clasped tight in our gloved hands. And last the
murky yellow cars of the Chicago, Milwaukee & St. Paul railroad
looking cheerful as Christmas itself on the tracks beside the gate.

When we pulled out into the winter night and the real snow,
our snow, began to stretch out beside us and twinkle against the
windows, and the dim lights of small Wisconsin stations moved
by, a sharp wild brace came suddenly into the air. We drew in
deep breaths of it as we walked back from dinner through the
cold vestibules, unutterably aware of our identity with this
country for one strange hour, before we melted indistinguish-
ably into it again.

That's my Middle West—not the wheat or the prairies or the
lost Swede towns, but the thrilling returning trains of my youth,
and the street lamps and sleigh bells in the frosty dark and shadows of holly wreaths thrown by lighted windows on the snow. I
am part of that, a little solemn with the feel of those long win-
ters, a little complacent from growing up in the Carraway house
in a city where dwellings are still called through decades by a
family's name. I see now that this has been a story of the West,
after all—Tom and Gatsby, Daisy and Jordan and I, were all
Westerners, and perhaps we possessed some deficiency in common which made us subtly unadaptable to Eastern life.

Even when the East excited me most, even when I was most
keenly aware of its superiority to the bored, sprawling, swollen
towns beyond the Ohio, with their interminable inquisitions
which spared only the children and the very old—even then it
had always for me a quality of distortion. West Egg, especially,
still figures in my more fantastic dreams. I see it as a night scene
by El Greco: a hundred houses, at once conventional and gro-
tesque, crouching under a sullen, overhanging sky and a lus-
treless moon. In the foreground four solemn men in dress suits
are walking along the sidewalk with a stretcher on which lies
a drunken woman in a white evening dress. Her hand, which
dangles over the side, sparkles cold with jewels. Gravely the men
turn in at a house—the wrong house. But no one knows the
woman's name, and no one cares.

After Gatsby's death the East was haunted for me like that,
distorted beyond my eyes' power of correction. So when the blue
smoke of brittle leaves was in the air and the wind blew the wet
laundry stiff on the line I decided to come back home.

Coming back home is not a heroic thing to do. You're not supposed to be able to go home again. Nick, like all memoirists and all
first person narrators, does not get to be a hero. He gets to be the

one left to tell the tale. That's all. But it's a lot. And it's all voice, this presence left to account for the corpses.

In 1949, just four years after the concentration camps of the Third Reich had been opened—or closed, depending on how you look at the liberation, the critic Theodor Adorno made his famous statement: "After Auschwitz to write poetry is barbaric." [*Nach Auschwitz ein Gedicht zu schrieben, ist barbarisch.*]

No poet can acquiesce to this statement, but it is awkward to dismiss it for what happened in the heart of Europe in the middle of the last century seems to become bigger, not smaller, as time moves away from it. Indeed, what *can* be said of the crimes of Christian Europe against, especially, the Jews and in smaller numbers, but in a hardly less appalling fashion, all those who met with its disdain—the Gypsies, the national patriots, religious and moral critics of the regime, Communists and socialists? Silence has always been the token of respect and also of awe.

But the truth is, the reason the crimes of mid-century do not leave our consciousness and do not fade with time is that many people have gone to extraordinary lengths, even risking death, to be sure that the Holocaust, in all its hideous forms, is recorded in interviews, stories, and memoiristic accounts.

In *The Survivor,* his exemplary study of the death camps in Nazi Germany and the Soviet Gulag, Terrence DesPres speaks of "the will to bear witness" which characterized the lives of his subjects, the writers of these documents. As he points out, "the First World War was the first mass disaster experienced by large numbers of people who were literate and therefore able to leave records. . . . In the concentration camps there was an even wider margin of literacy, and many men and women returned who if not sophisticated were certainly articulate enough to give clear accounts."

DesPres also notes that "when men and women are forced to endure terrible things at the hands of others—whenever, that is, extremity involves moral issues—the need to remember becomes a general response." He quotes Emmanuel Ringelblum who says in his *Notes from the Warsaw Ghetto* that the "drive to write down one's memoirs is powerful. . . . Even young people in labour camps do it." To write one's memoirs in this context was not a literary risk but literally a risk of one's life.

In his study DesPres found evidence again and again, in every sort of situation, of the determination to leave a trace, a written record of events. "All I retained," Alexander Donat, a survivor of the Warsaw Ghetto, Auschwitz and Dachau, later wrote, "was a newspaperman's greedy curiosity, the desire to see and find out everything, to engrave in my memory this Dantesque world." The same was true of Milena Jesenka, Kafka's Milena, who did not live to see liberation but whose goal was to write about her experience.

This recording impulse was not limited to men and women in the writing professions. "While still in the camp," says Halina Birenbaum, "I decided that if I lived to see liberation, I would write down everything I saw, heard and experienced." Primo Levi, whose suicide stunned the world precisely because he was a survivor who had told his tale, may be an even darker proof of this law of the will to bear witness being identical to the will to survive. For having told his tale, having relieved himself of his task, he perhaps no longer could abide the living world, and fell again into the fatal indifference he said he had been lifted out of by a fellow prisoner's reminder that "even in this place one . . . must want to survive, to tell the story, to bear witness."

It is not possible to equate or even compare the experience or the works of the memoirists of the camps with the contemporary memoirists and the rise of cross-genre first person work of the last fifteen or twenty years in America. But the literary culture which these contemporary writers have been born into is one in which these personal accounts of radical suffering have had and continue to have extraordinary power. As readers of these essential works of personal history from the past century's history, we have been given evidence of the astonishing power of the personal voice as no previous generation ever has.

As if to crown this mountain of testimony, popular consciousness has instinctively chosen one work to stand for that whole terrible time, and that book is the diary of a young girl. More than a diary, it was undertaken quite deliberately by Anne Frank as a literary memoir—or a novel, not simply as a personal companion. (Interestingly, she did not make a serious distinction between the genres, and during her final weeks in hiding she began to use the diary to shape a more formally satisfying narrative of the experience. She did not see these changes as lies, but rather as natural allies of the truth.) She understood, as Whitman did, that her personal voice belonged to the world. She may have begun as a little girl keeping a diary, but she became, consciously and with complete understanding of her task, a Voice. She was engaged in this editorial work when the Gestapo raided the hiding place on August 4, 1944.

Anne Frank set about organizing the diary entries, giving the residents of the "Secret Annex" pseudonyms like characters in a novel, rearranging passages for better narrative effect. From the first, she addressed the notebook as a trusted girlfriend: "I'll begin from the moment I got you, the moment I saw you lying on the table among my other birthday presents." [p. 1] A few days later this anonymous "you" becomes the imaginary "Kitty," and the entries turn into letters, giving the diary the intimacy and vivacity of a developing friendship. The growing relationship, of course, is with her own emerging self. As John Berryman said, the "Diary" has at its core a subject "even more mysterious and fundamental than St. Augustine's" in his classic *Confessions;* namely, "the conversion of a child into a person." [Berryman, "The Development of Anne Frank," in *The Freedom of the Poet,* p. 93]

"It's a wonder I haven't abandoned all my ideals, they seem so absurd and impractical. Yet I cling to them because I still believe, in spite of everything, that people are truly good at heart." This is the most quoted passage in the diary, and one whose confirmation of human goodness appalls many readers. Maybe she could write such a line in the relative safety of the secret annex, they say, but would she have said such a thing as she lay dying of typhus in the fetid camp? But this line strikes me as less important than the meditation which follows it.

It is the testament of a committed, already psychologically and spiritually mature writer, even a prophetic one: "It's utterly impossible for me to build my life on a foundation of chaos, suffering and death," she writes. "I see the world being slowly transformed into a wilderness, I hear the approaching thunder that, one day, will destroy us too, I feel the suffering of millions. And yet, when I look up at the sky, I somehow feel that everything will change for the better, that this cruelty too shall end, that peace and tranquility will return once more. In the meantime, I must hold on to my ideals." Saturday, July 14, 1944. Less than a month later she was taken away.

Anne Frank was not simply a little girl who believed everybody was good at heart. She was a writer capable of naming her fate and the fate of the world she grieved for. "I hear the approaching thunder that, one day, will destroy us too, I feel the suffering of millions." It was in the homeliness of her diary and the vision she achieved there that she came to be the voice of the Holocaust.

Knowing the fragility of life as it faces the brutality of racial hatred and rigid ideology of all kinds, feeling the suffering of millions, intuiting one's own imminent destruction—is this what the frail first person pronoun can carry on its back?

We have discovered that we can trust no other voice as completely to tell this tale. If we are looking for another reason to explain the first person grip on contemporary writing perhaps we must look at the power of Anne Frank's equation—that to write one's life enables the world to know its history. We trust the first person now more than we ever did—more than we ever had reason to. It is not a trust literature will let us soon abandon. That singular voice—it not only has the evidence. It is the evidence.

—Patricia Hampl

Patricia Hampl is a contributing editor of *Alaska Quarterly Review.* Her most recent book is *I Could Tell You Stories: Sojourns in the Land of Memory.* Her other books include the memoirs *A Romantic Education* and *Virgin Time,* as well as two collections of poems. Her uncollected short stories have appeared in a wide range of magazines and journals including *The New Yorker* and *Alaska Quarterly Review.* She is Regents' Professor of English at the University of Minnesota and is a member of the permanent faculty of the Prague Summer Seminars.

Ben Brooks

THE WOODEN FLUTE

The place I lived was on a street so narrow, you couldn't fit a car down it. Every time we shopped we had to walk our groceries home, bag by bag, for three whole blocks, from the nearest spot Mother could squeeze the old Buick in. If there wasn't a spot to park she'd leave the car running at the head of the alley and station my sister over the trunk, standing guard, while Mother and I lugged the food down the alley and then up the narrow stairs. The heaviest bags were always the ones with the milk cartons, and I carried those. Mother had enough trouble toting the fruit and vegetables. Each time we wound through the alley she would fall farther and farther behind me, and I would wait for her when I got to the apartment door. She was the one who had the key, and she wouldn't leave the door unlocked between trips to the car. She would stop on the landing below me to catch her breath, looking up at me, her foot raised to the next step so she could rest her bag on her thigh for a second. I can still see that—Mother on the stairs panting, with the grocery bag perched on her leg.

Ben Brooks is a frequent contributor to *Alaska Quarterly Review*. He has published a novel, *The Icebox*, and over sixty stories in literary journals, one of which was awarded an O. Henry Prize. He teaches at Emerson College.

Every time we shopped I resolved not to drink so much milk so I wouldn't have so much to carry the next time, but then as the week went by I'd forget, and I'd drink just as much as I had the week before.

When you walked down our street, and you held your arms out, you could run your fingers along the buildings on both sides at the same time. It was that narrow. I could do that even when I was little and my arms didn't stretch very far. Slide my nails into the cracks in the old walls where the stucco was chipped away. Touching it all at the same time, both sides of the street, made you feel like you were bigger than the whole world, like God. We lived on Calle Miguel de Cervantes, named for the greatest of all Spanish authors, even though Cervantes had nothing to do with where we lived then in northern Mexico. I'm sure Cervantes never even dreamed of Mexico—there was enough to dream about right where he was.

We lived in the barrio section of town, the earliest part, built long before there were Buicks to worry about, where they might drive or park. The barrio was built to fit everything in, and then some. It was tight where we lived, things squished together, but efficient, arranged so that no space went unused. We were packed in, one apartment on top of the next, like rows of tiny fish inside a can, then rows of fitted cans on a shelf, and rows of shelves in a store.

Sunlight never made it down to street level, to where you walked on Calle Miguel de Cervantes. The alley was made of old cobblestones, worn and cracked. It was always dim and cool and dank down there, with tiny lizards clinging to the walls, and dogs and cats darting through to get to someplace warmer, sunnier. The closest I ever saw direct sunlight was reflecting off the windows on the fourth floor of our building. The building had five stories, and we lived on the third, so our apartment got no sun either. It was dim and cool and dank inside, which was all right with Mother since so many of the days there were so hot. She wasn't used to that; she was a transplant. She didn't have it in her system.

* * *

We were the only Anglos in the building, the only Anglos living in the whole barrio. My father was a Mexican, Roberto Alarcon. When Mother was pregnant, he brought her back to his home city from Pittsburgh, where she had met him when she was working the counter in a bakery and he was painting houses. Roberto got hired to paint the trim around the bakery door and windows and gutters.

It was a short-term job, but my mother thought he was so handsome on his ladder. When he stretched high to touch up the paint on the gutters his shirt pulled off his belly, and soon enough I was coming along.

My sister and I were only half Anglo, of course—and the half that was Anglo was actually Irish—and half Mexican, but we were paler than anyone else around. Since my father had left, everyone always forgot about him and figured we were Anglo all the way, like Mother. There was no question about her. Even the neighbors who had known Roberto Alarcon forgot what we were. People treated my mother okay anyway, despite her being Anglo, and despite having had her husband walk out on her. Mother always said, it wasn't as bad as it would have been if we had been the only Mexicans living in an Anglo building in Pittsburgh.

"Think of it that way, Bobby," she told me, whenever I asked why we stayed on in the barrio, or if I said that I wanted to move. "It could be a hell of a lot worse." She wouldn't say it, but I knew she was waiting for Roberto to come back—at least at first she was.

Bobby. I was named for my father, Roberto, but after he left Mother stopped calling me that and started calling me the Anglo nickname for it. I wondered if she would change my name back, start calling me Roberto again, if my father ever returned. But he didn't return—at least not until it was too late—so I never found out what she would have done.

My sister was Megan. She was named for my mother's side of the family, the Irish half.

Then when I was eleven Mother sat me and Megan down on the sofa and announced that she was planning to get married again. She had given up on Roberto. And she was going to have a real wedding this time. Megan was going to hold up her gown while she walked down the church aisle and I was going to carry the wedding bands on a red velvet pillow. There was a new man in the place where Mother worked. He was a good man, somebody who would stay with her this time and be right for us kids. Mother worked in a small factory by the river that made ceramic objects, mostly to sell to tourists. Some of the objects were functional, like bowls and pitchers, but most were strictly decorative. They made lizards and exotic birds, and they had a whole line of ceramic religious objects—Marys and Josephs and baby Jesuses and Christs on the cross.

Mother worked hard, and she came home every day too tired. It was hot where she worked, with the kilns baking all day. Whenever I asked why she didn't do something easier, she'd say the only other thing she knew was bakeries, but it wasn't good for her figure to be in a place like that. She had a sweet tooth. She'd eat too much, she couldn't help herself. Mother was a beautiful woman—did I mention that yet? She had light hair, golden, which was rare where we lived, and she grew it long and thick and curly. Men looked at Mother all the time, even when she was someplace with us children. Maybe that's why they didn't mind that she was Anglo, because she looked so good. The women didn't mind either, because Mother ignored the men's looks and their whistles and all their comments.

She ignored them until Tomás Fernando Santamaría came along, that is. Then she started to pay attention again. Maybe she had decided that eight years was long enough to wait for Roberto to come back to her. Time can do funny things to minds and hearts—it can hone them sharper, or it can rub them smooth.

Tomás Fernando looked at Mother too, but she knew right away that he was a good man, the right one for her, the right one for all of us. So it was okay that *he* looked, she said. He looked at her out of one eye, because that's all he had. The left one he had lost in an accident, when his face got too close to a torch he was holding. Usually he wore a dark purple patch over the scar, but sometimes when Tomás Fernando went out he slipped a glass eye into the empty socket instead. Mother said that he was planning to wear the glass eye to the wedding, because people would be sitting far enough away in the pews that they wouldn't be able to tell it wasn't real. Anyway, we should be thankful that men still noticed her occasionally, she told us, that they still wanted to look.

"Are we going to move to his house?" I asked.

"No," Mother said, "he's going to move in here."

"*Here?*" Tomás Fernando Santamaría's going to move in here? *Where*, Mother? We don't have room for anyone else."

"Don't be smart with me, Bobby Alarcon," Mother answered. "Tomás Fernando lives alone. His place is even smaller than ours. He's got exactly one room. You wouldn't want to live there. Once we're married, he's going to move in here with us." She saw Megan and me exchange a look on the sofa. "Don't worry, it'll be like he was here forever," she assured us. "He'll fit right in. You won't even notice there's another person around."

I couldn't remember when my father had lived there—I was three when he left—and I couldn't imagine another person staying in our compact little apartment. We bumped into each other all the time as it was. I shared a tiny room with my sister. She had the cot and I slept on a mat on the floor. Mother unfolded the sofa every night and slept in the living room. The whole apartment was crammed with stuff—aside from the usual furniture and clothes and toys and pots and pans and dishes, it was mostly ceramic things that filled it up, things that Mother brought home from the factory. Defectives, pieces with chips missing, or with bubbles in the glaze. Now, with Tomás Fernando working at the same place, we'd have twice as many of those ceramic things around. There'd be no place to step, no place to sit, no place to swing your arms.

Mother had never got divorced—of course, in Mexico, that's not so easy to do—so she had to have Roberto declared dead before she could marry Tomás Fernando. For some people that would have been enough to derail the plan, but not for Mother.

She spent every night for a week filling out the papers she needed to make Roberto's death official. She had to document the circumstances under which he had disappeared—as if there had been real circumstances—and declare that Roberto Alarcon had not been heard from, by anyone, in all those eight years. That he was gone without a trace, vanished, that it was no longer conceivable that he walked this earth.

Mother wept while she worked on the forms, perhaps convincing herself that it was all true—that her husband was nothing but bones now, if that even, maybe just powder, dust, nothing—that he had not simply walked away from one life because he wanted to try a different kind. She could picture him going up in flames suddenly, as if by spontaneous combustion, falling over a cliff, tragically struck by a bus, toppling off a ladder, succumbing to poison. Maybe Roberto was dead—who knew at the time?—but Mother did know that death was not the reason he had not come home that first night. She knew, that is, until she started filling out the papers. Then, she wasn't so sure anymore.

Roberto's mother and his sisters and brothers had to sign the forms too, and none of them wanted to. Finally, they gave in though. My mother begged them—and swore that she would never forget Roberto Alarcon, dead or not—so they agreed to sign, as a special favor to her. My grandmother held Megan on her lap while the papers made their way around the room, one sheet at a time, and each of the Alarcons signed each sheet. Grandmother signed the papers last, bending along with Megan over the table. Then it was done. They swore to their signatures in front of a notary, who stamped each one of the papers, and then the judge decreed that my father's death certificate should be written out. As of that moment, Roberto Alarcon was no longer among the living—and Mother was a free woman. She had already done eight years of mourning for him. She could now marry Tomás Fernando Santamaría.

* * *

The wedding was exactly as Mother had pictured it. The ancient church was filled with flowers, so many that the age-old sour smell of the stone walls was overwhelmed by the sweetness of all the fragrances. Tomás Fernando grew the flowers with his own hands in a hillside garden plot outside the city that he shared with several other men. The side of the hill the plot was on faced south, so it got the full strength of the sun, and the flowers that came out of the ground were large and robust. Mother wore a beautiful white gown with a lacy veil across her face, and Megan followed her like a shadow in her own identical miniature gown, holding up Mother's train. I carried the rings and stood behind Mother and Tomás Fernando while the priest spoke to them about the sacred responsibilities of marriage, and blessed them, and declared them as one. Tomás Fernando wore a black suit to church. He stared straight ahead out of his single eye the whole time, not turning his head once to look at his beautiful bride, my beautiful mother.

Then Tomás Fernando moved into the third-floor apartment with us in the barrio. He brought all his things over in Mother's Buick. The four of us, even Megan, lugged boxes and bags and suitcases through the dim alley to the apartment. We made many trips back and forth between the car and the apartment, working like ants stocking a nest. Clothes, hats, keepsakes, a little furniture of his own, a few tools, a wooden flute, and yes, his collection of defective ceramic knickknacks. And then just as I had pictured, we were more cramped than ever.

Every morning Mother and her new husband left for work together at the ceramic factory before Megan and I left for school. Tomás Fernando wore his eye patch to work—he kept his extra eye in a glass on a shelf above the living room sofa where he and Mother slept. He kept water in the glass so the eye would stay clean and smooth and cool and moist, and that wet eye stared down at me and Megan every morning after Mother and Tomás Fernando were gone. It watched us pick our way through the cluttered apartment, finish eating our breakfast, locate our school books, and finally leave for the day so it could have the place to itself. I had a key to the apartment now, so I locked up. I locked the watching eye in.

I was always scared to touch Tomás Fernando's extra eye. Those first months I had dreams about it—the way the eye kept look-out over the empty apartment until everyone got back in the afternoon.

Sometimes the eye turned too sharply to peer in a different direction and it rolled over in the water glass, and then it could see nothing but the blank wall behind the shelf. It got frustrated and would try to scream for someone to turn it back, bulging out of itself, but the underwater eye could not make a sound. In my dream I wanted to help it, but I was too scared to even touch the glass Tomás Fernando kept the eye in—too scared to pick up the glass and shake it and make the eye roll back and turn the right way again.

* * *

As crowded as our apartment was, and as crammed as the building was with apartments—that was how the whole barrio was. People bustled about everywhere, even in tiny Calle Miguel de Cervantes, our alley. There were shops that were no more than holes in walls where shopkeepers stationed themselves in doorways trying to entice passersby inside; mothers and grandmothers pushing babies along in carriages; children chasing each other to and fro, banging into the legs of adults; teenagers puttering by on their motorbikes; girls listening to transistor radios they carried by their ears, brassy songs fading in and out; neighbors talking and arguing about the day's events; men sweeping dirt off the cobbled street around their newsstands and vegetable carts. Everywhere people moved, hurried, lazed, talked to one another, gesturing, shouting. Those were the constant sights and sounds that we lived with.

It all took place in the street below our apartment, every day, and in the other alleys just like ours, the shouts and even the whispers audible through open windows even when the people themselves weren't visible. To see anything at all, you had to hang out the window and look straight down. People always heard something first, then thrust their heads through billowing curtains to carry on conversations with someone down in the alley. But it was different for us, for Mother and Tomás Fernando. They were an exception in the barrio—they were quiet. They always approached home in silence. They held hands when they walked, picking their way through the bustle, looking straight ahead, and they didn't say a word to each other.

Instead of words, Tomás Fernando spoke to his new wife with his wooden flute. It turned out that was how he had wooed her, and it was the new sound we had when he moved in with us. Every afternoon when they returned from the ceramics factory, he played for Mother. Tomás Fernando played simple tunes, melodies so slow his fingers never missed a note—but with a tone so achingly sweet that strangers in the alley below would stop their arguing to cock their

7

ears and listen, and sometimes begin to weep. Tomás Fernando had made the flute himself, out of a thin piece of mahogany which he painted with bright birds and then varnished. There were eight holes on the top side for his fingers and one hole below for his thumb—the holes in just the right places for Tomás Fernando's hands.

Mother loved the sound of that flute, and so did Megan and I. When we were helpful around the apartment, Tomás Fernando would play for us, too. He could get us to do anything that way. The music slid in through our ears and made us shiver. It settled into our spines, where it ran up and down with the melodies like quicksilver. If he asked us to wash the dishes because Mother was tired, we would wash the dishes without complaint. If he wanted us to move boxes for him, we would move the boxes. If he wanted us to do tricks, stand on our heads, we would stand on our heads. While we worked or performed, Tomás Fernando would play. He wouldn't watch us, though, even if we were doing tricks. When Tomás Fernando played his flute he kept his one eye shut, the music working its magic on him as well.

Life was different with our new father—he brought change to the apartment. The eye staring out at us from the bottom of the water glass, the extra clutter that was attached to him, the music of his flute. In the evenings none of us talked much, but we relaxed together in a new kind of harmony. When Tomás Fernando finally said his cheeks were tired from blowing and he put the flute away, Mother often kept the music going, humming out the same tunes that he had just played for us.

* * *

The day that Roberto Alarcon strode through the alley on the way to his old apartment building, all sound in the street stopped—the same way it did when a black cloud formed overhead and suddenly began to quiver with rain. Tomás Fernando Santamaría had just finished blowing his flute, and down below the transistor radios and the arguments had barely picked up again. Then abruptly they ended once more. Upstairs, we noticed it too, without knowing what it was.

Nobody spoke to Roberto as he pushed through the throngs. Men nodded and women looked away, and children, who didn't even know Roberto Alarcon, stared at him as if he were a ghost. He had grown a tangled beard in the nine years that he had now been dead, according to the recent certificate issued by the court, but otherwise it appeared to his neighbors to be the exact same man who had once lived among them—the man who had grown up in the barrio and drifted to the United States and learned a new language there and soon brought home a beautiful Irish-American bride with golden hair that all the men whistled at. In Roberto's hand was a tattered gray duffel bag, stuffed full with his belongings. Later people said that he had heard there was a new husband for Mother, and that he had wanted to see for himself. He smiled wanly at the faces he recognized but he didn't speak either, as if in the place he now was, he could not remember anyone's name.

Mother was clattering pots on the stove, getting supper on, and Tomás Fernando had stretched out on the sofa, his glass eye watching over his rest. When I stuck my head out the window to look at the man with the tangled beard—the man who stopped the sounds of the alley—I did not know it was my father. I had not seen him since I was three, and Mother kept no photographs of Roberto in the apartment. There were pictures at my grandmother's, and also my aunts and uncles had some, but I wasn't expecting my father that day, and the beard changed his face, and besides, I hadn't looked at those pictures my relatives had for a long time.

I watched him stride in through the door below, and then heard his footsteps on the stairs. Outside, even after he disappeared into the building, the sounds of the neighborhood remained subdued. Roberto took the stairs slowly, solidly, settling his foot on each one of the creaky steps before he took the next—as if to prove that he was no ghost. Down below, everyone was staring up at me, but I didn't know why yet.

When he got to the third floor, ours, I heard the stranger turn away from the stairs—I heard his footsteps now in the hallway. I heard them stop by our door, and as they did, I pulled my head back inside from the window. By then Tomás Fernando had sat up, and Mother had moved away from the stove and was wiping her hands on her apron. Megan was the only one who paid no mind to the unusual quiet and to the steady footsteps clacking through it. Though we knew the man was standing there, Roberto did not knock at the door. He waited a moment, then slipped his key into the lock. It still worked, after nine years—things change slowly in the barrio. I watched the knob turn, and then the man with the tangled beard pushed the door open.

When Mother saw who it was that had stopped the sounds of the barrio dead, she fainted. Her eyes fluttered back into her head and her knees turned to water. She fell straight to the floor. Roberto and Tomás Fernando looked at her, but neither one of them stepped forward.

Roberto set his duffel bag down. Tomás Fernando, who had

moved to town and did not know my father, did know a ghost when he saw one. He stayed where he was on the sofa, frozen. The eyeball in the water glass, Tomás Fernando's protector, fixed itself on the doorway where the intruder stood.

Then the man with the black beard tangled across his face, like silk threads that had come unraveled and been thrown into a giant knot, looked over at me. He lifted his hand in a gesture—just an inch or two from his side—and it was only then that I knew who he was.

* * *

They called it mixed blood, but that's not the right name for it. It's not the blood that gets mixed up—it's the head. The blood is just one thing, smooth as cream inside you, thick, salty-tasting—spurting, flowing, spreading to every part of you. Mother might be Anglo, or Irish, and Roberto Mexican, and I with some of each inside, but I am just me and my blood is whole. I am not half one thing and half the other, like two pieces of a puzzle that can be locked together or snapped apart. I am simply what I am, no line down the middle. I contain some of each of them, like anybody combines a mother and a father—it's no different because one was one thing and the other something else. My blood is my own, simple enough, straightforward. Like anybody, my smooth blood comes out red when it bleeds.

It's the head where opposing things gather and fester, the head that splits into two, that is snapped apart and locks back together, the head that gives all the confusion. It's the head that tries to hold more than one thing at a time—all that you think and want and could possibly dream.

Mother's eyes blinked open but she stayed where she was on the floor. My two fathers glared at each other, the old and the new—Roberto from the doorway with his wild skein of beard, Tomás Fernando from the sofa with his one good eye popping out. Then Roberto noticed the second eye, popped all the way out, the one in the glass on its perch above my stepfather, the one watching him back now through those clear teaspoonfuls of water.

Roberto snorted and lifted his head toward the shelf, and he spoke finally. "What's that, then?" he demanded, his voice croaking. "Roberto, what do you have in that jar?" He called me by his own name, my given name. "Marbles?"

"It's not mine," I stammered. "It's Tomás Fernando's. It's not a marble. It's his extra eyeball."

"Tomás Fernando? *Tomás Fernando*? Who is this man you call

10

Tomás Fernando? What's he doing in my house, Roberto? What's he doing on my sofa?" he railed, as if he were not just now showing up after having been gone without a word for nine years.

"*Your* house? You gave up your rights—" Tomás Fernando began.

"*Rights?*" Roberto thundered back. Under his beard the lines in his neck strained. "Are we talking about *rights* now? What *rights* do you have to get comfortable on my sofa?"

Then Mother sat up off the floor finally. She ordered Roberto to come inside, to shut the door behind him and join us. There was a lot suddenly for us all to untangle.

* * *

The barrio, tight and compacted and snarled together and folded in on itself, is the kind of place where everyone knows everything, where everyone knows everyone else's business—or thinks they do. But this universal knowing, this knowing of everything, is an illusion. Our neighbors knew that the dead man had returned home, they had seen him float along the alley with his duffel bag, heard his steps, they knew that he had fitted his key into the lock and opened the door to our apartment, had found his widow at the stove and her new husband on the sofa guarded over by his extra eyeball, and his own two orphans by the window—but then with the door shut again, they could not know what happened next, only guess.

They could not know for certain that Tomás Fernando, in his nervousness—nervous not only about the ghost he was suddenly confronted with, the intruder, but afraid also that he would lose the beautiful wife he had only recently been blessed with, his new family, the apartment—took up the mahogany flute with the bright varnished birds on it and twisted it in his hands while Mother went back and forth between the two men, her husbands, trying to do the untangling. The neighbors could not know that Roberto, incensed at his usurper—the way he sat on the sofa like it was his, and the way his eyeball had found so permanent a home in the water glass on the shelf—reached out and snatched the flute from Tomás Fernando's hands, and in the same motion cracked it over his leg, splitting it in two, silencing it forever. They could not know that this was how Tomás Fernando's true voice got splintered into halves—that this was why he was never able to fit those halves back together. They certainly knew that Roberto picked his duffel bag up from the floor and walked off again, because that part they witnessed—and they knew also that after that day, Roberto Alarcon was never again seen in the city.

Roberto's reappearance and immediate disappearance left not

only Mother, but also the courts, with a dilemma. Since Roberto was vanished again, it was not as if he was there among us—yet everyone had seen him and declared him to be alive, though by proclamation and decree, at Mother's petitioning, the judges had already ruled him undeniably dead. And the widow had subsequently married a new husband at the holy altar of the church. If they now said Roberto Alarcon, formerly dead, was alive again, then they were declaring either a grievous error or a miracle, a resurrection—also that Mother's new marriage was not only illegal, it was a blasphemy. If they left Roberto dead, it was a lie and everyone knew it. My grandmother pushed for the declaration of miracle, while Mother was an advocate of common sense in this matter, of leaving things as they were. Tomás Fernando, for his part, tendered no opinion on that or any other subject. His position in the matter was tenuous. For the first time he felt himself a usurper, and without a voice now to express his anguish, he was lost.

* * *

So it was, caught in the dilemma, that we finally left Calle Miguel de Cervantes, the barrio, as I had long hoped—but then beyond the city altogether, continuing north and east, we even left Mexico. The opinions regarding what should be done about the husbands were too sticky and twisted, and too public—they would not smooth down. Mother and Tomás Fernando quit their jobs at the ceramics factory, and they rode us back to Pittsburgh in the old Buick, packed to the hilt with dishes and toys and clothes and ceramic iguanas and cracked Marys. In Pittsburgh I met my other grandmother and my grandfather for the first time, and all my Irish cousins on my mother's side. Everyone was surprised to see that Mother's Mexican husband now only had one eye—they remembered him on the painter's ladder. Tomás Fernando had to find a new voice and learn a new language, while Mother took work in a bakery.

We got an apartment on a street with sidewalks, a street wide enough that cars actually fit on it, and Megan and I were enrolled in school. The bakery opened early every morning, and Tomás Fernando accompanied Mother there, holding hands, in silence, so until it was time for us to leave for the day, Megan and I were left alone to get ready for school. Alone again, presided over by the watchful eyeball in the glass, Megan made the sandwiches and I packed our lunch bags. We both had keys to the apartment now, because on different days we came home at different times.

Starting with her hips, and then her thighs and her shoulders and her waist and even her cheeks and jaw, our beautiful mother's curves filled out. She expanded in every direction like a dry sponge soaking in a tub of water. She got round, and the indentations between her curves thickened up. Mother was done in at work by her sweet tooth.

Tomás Fernando learned to speak English in Pittsburgh, but he never made himself another flute like the one that had been broken. So it didn't matter which language he used—he was never again able to speak his heart to his once-beautiful wife.

I remained Bobby throughout high school, but then when I went off to college, told my new friends I was Roberto. Roberto Alarcon Santamaría, of an Anglo-Irish mother and two Mexican fathers, one a living miracle sporting a wild beard, and the other with an eyeball in a water glass that watched over us wherever we went—but despite my mixed heritage, I had only one blood inside me. Where I grew up, I told them, you could hold the whole street in your arms at once, touch the world. Anyone could do it, even me. It was possible there for a child to be just as big as God.

Nicholas Montemarano

SHIFT

Don't leave them sharp, he says. I want them smooth. That way I won't scratch myself.

His arm jabs near my face. I cannot hold his hand in place long enough to file his nails.

Have you seen the scratches on my legs? he says.

The closer his arm gets to my face the more his arm shakes. I tell myself I am not going to flinch. I would rather he hit me. I would rather he break my nose.

Your eyelids flutter like butterfly wings, he says. What happened? Did your mommy smack you around?

He looks at his wife in her chair. Do you see his eyelids? he asks her.

She opens her mouth wide, which means inside she's laughing, then she drools on her shirt. He tells me to wipe her chin.

Our little butterfly boy, he says.

She makes the noise I know means she wants something.

Do you want something to eat? Do you want the channel

Nicholas Montemarano's recent work appears in *DoubleTake, Gettysburg Review, Denver Quarterly, Mid-American Review, New York Stories,* and *Scribner's Best of the Fiction Workshops 1999.*

changed? Do you want to take a nap? Do you want to read? Do you want to be moved from your chair to the couch? (She raises her eyes and arches her neck, as if trying to look at the top of her head.)

With a clean towel I cover the bottom cushions of the couch; with a disposable pad I cover the towel. I prop the pillows the way she likes them to be propped. I lift her from the chair and lay her on the towel.

Is there something wrong with the towel? Something wrong with the pad? Did I hurt you? Are you uncomfortable? Are the pillows wrong? Do you need me to help you make a phone call? Do you want me to get the mail? Do you want me to check who's working the next shift? Do you want a clean pair of socks? Something to drink? Something to eat? Back in the chair? The channel changed? (Eyes raised.)

I find the remote control between the clean clothes in the laundry basket.

A channel from one to ten? From ten to twenty? Twenty to thirty? Above thirty? Below thirty?

Didn't you just say you wanted the channel changed?

She wants to be changed, he says.

Is that what you want?

I know what she wants, he says.

I carry her into the bathroom, making sure to keep one arm under her neck, the other arm under the bend in her knees. Her body is approximately three feet long and weighs less than sixty pounds. I make sure not to fold her body. I lay her body gently onto the plastic cushion of the shower bed. I watch that she does not roll off the shower bed and onto the floor. I make sure her leg does not spasm into the wall.

The rubber gloves are found in the glove box under the sink.

I pull up her skirt and pull down her panties. I take off her diaper, fold it so that the wet parts are folded inside the dry parts, and drop it in the small trash can under the sink. I push the diaper down to the bottom of the bag.

Do you want to be washed? (Eyes raised.)

I wait for the sink water to warm.

The wash rags are stored in the wash rag box on the shelf above the sink.

Is the water warm enough?

Better?

Too hot now? (Eyes raised.)

Better?

Now? (Eyes raised.)

I watch her face as I pull apart her palsied legs. When her face tells me I should stop I stop. I wipe the insides of her thighs. When I release her legs her legs snap together.

Do you want powder? (Eyes raised.)

The plastic powder bottle is stored in the storage bin under the sink. She does not like when the powder gets into her eyes or nose. I must make sure to face the opening of the bottle away from her face as I squeeze the powder onto her legs. I watch her face as I pull apart her legs, and as her legs snap together. Her toes curl into the bottoms of her feet.

Do you want clean underwear? (Eyes raised.) A specific pair? (Eyes raised.) Blue? (Eyes raised.) With flowers? (Eyes raised.)

Her underwear are kept in the underwear drawer, where I put them every day after washing and folding them. I look through the underwear drawer, and then through the other drawers.

I can't find them, I tell her. Do you want a different pair?

They're out here in the laundry basket, he says.

She raises her eyes and arches her neck.

I take everything out of the laundry basket. I put everything back into the laundry basket.

I can't find them, I call to her.

He moves his chair closer to where I'm standing, so that the wheels stop just before my feet. He lifts the blue underwear with his unpalsied foot. I know where everything is, he says.

The diapers are stored in the diaper bin under the sink.

I roll her body toward me so that she is on her side. I open the diaper on the shower bed, and then roll her onto the diaper. I pull the diaper around her hips. I tape the diaper, watching her face to make sure I have not taped her skin. I make sure the diaper is secure. I pull her blue underwear up over the diaper. I pull down her skirt. I throw away my gloves. I wash my hands with the soap I use only to wash my hands.

Ready? (Eyes raised.)

I make sure my arm is under her neck, the other arm under the bend in her knees. I carry her into the living room and lay her gently on the couch, making sure the diapered part of her body is above the pad, the pad above the towel. I prop her head and neck against the pillow the way she likes.

She frowns.

Are you uncomfortable? Do you want to go back in your chair? Did I not change you the right way? Are you still wet? Do you want me to start dinner? Do you want socks on your feet? Do you want your hair brushed away from your face? Would you like me to scratch an itch? Something to drink? Time for your pill? The channel changed? (Eyes raised.)

I find the remote control on top of the television.

A channel below thirty? Above thirty? (Eyes raised.) Above forty? (Frown.) Thirty-one, thirty-two, thirty-three, thirty-four, thirty-five, thirty-six, thirty-seven, thirty-eight (eyes raised).

Is the volume okay?

Too loud?

Louder? (Eyes raised.)

I watch her face to know when to stop.

I sit at the end of the couch to fold the laundry.

She makes the noise I know means she wants something. It sounds like the sound I've heard bear cubs make on the nature shows she likes to watch.

The wrong channel? More volume? Do you want pillows under your legs? (Eyes raised.)

I place two pillows under her legs the way I know she likes them.

I sit with the laundry. She makes a bear cub sound.

Something else? (Eyes raised.) An extra pillow under your legs? Too many pillows under your legs? A phone call? Something to eat? Is the sun in your eyes? Do you want to order more books on tape?

Go get the mail, he says from his chair. She wants you to get the mail.

Is that what you want? (Eyes raised.)

I take my time fitting the key into the hallway mail box. I count to one hundred after removing each envelope from the box.

I pretend not to hear him calling me. I light a cigarette. I count to one hundred after each drag from my cigarette.

I stare at the ash at the end of the cigarette, and watch it fall on the hallway rug. With the bottom of my shoe I rub the ash into the rug. When I finish the cigarette, I count to one hundred before going back inside.

He's trying to answer the phone with his unpalsied foot, which is the foot he uses to press the pedal that makes his chair move. He gives up on the phone and moves his chair closer to where I'm standing. One leg looks twice the size of the other.

The phone was ringing, he says. Ring ring ring, and then it stopped, and a few minutes later ring again.

I was getting the mail, I tell him.

Didn't you hear me calling you?

I was told to go get the mail.

You were smoking. I can smell it all over you.

I wasn't smoking.

You're going to start a fire, he says. The other tenants say they've seen you smoking where you're not supposed to be smoking.

Do you want me to open the mail?

He moves his chair closer. His arm spasms close to his face. Junk, he says. Throw it all away. It's all junk.

On the couch she raises her eyes.

I sit on the couch to fold the laundry. I hear her making the bear cub sound. I can see her raising her eyes, arching her neck.

I am trying to fold the shirts the way she likes them folded. Each sock must be kept with its matching sock. If a towel is not clean enough it must be placed in the hamper in the bedroom where dirty laundry is stored.

I can hear her getting louder. Her head is all the way back.

She wants something, he says.

Do you want something? (Eyes raised.)

Are you uncomfortable? Do you need another pillow? Do you want you medication? Are you hungry?

She wants you to make dinner now, he says. (She raises her eyes.)

What do you want for dinner?

She can't answer that, he says. You have to give her choices.

Do you want to order out? Do you want steak? Chicken? Pasta? Fish? (Eyes raised.)

With onions and butter? (Eyes raised.) Do you want me to cook? (Eyes raised.)

He turns his chair to face me. I want to cook dinner, he says.

Right now?

Now, he says. You can fold the clothes later.

I leave the laundry and follow him into the kitchen.

Open the refrigerator, he says. Look out of the way. Let me see what we have.

Take out the fish, he says.

Butter, he says.

Lemon, he says.

Not that one, he says. That one's too dry. Get a fresh lemon.

Throw the other one away, he says.

Onion, he says.

Get a better onion, he says. One without so many nicks.

Don't throw that one away, he says. Put it back in the bag.

Get a can of green beans.

In the other cabinet.

Chop the onion.

Make sure you chop it small enough.

Crybaby, he says. Run the water.

Melt some butter in a pan.

A lot of butter, he says. Use the big pan, the black one.

Enough.

Not so high, he says. Do you want to burn it?

I hear her making the bear cub sound. I continue to chop the onion.

Chop it smaller, he says.

The music that means a television show is ending. Her bear cub sounds get louder.

She wants something, he says.

I imagine slicing off the tip of one of my fingers and being rushed to the hospital. The butter in the pan begins to crackle.

Go see what she wants, he says.

As soon as I finish, I tell him.

She sounds like she needs something right away, he says.

I have onion on my fingers, I say.

She wants something now.

My eyes are burning, I tell him. I can't see anything.

Crybaby, he says. Breathe through your mouth.

What about the butter? I ask him.

I'll keep an eye on it, he says.

What if it starts to burn?

Go see what she wants, he says

I'll be there in a minute, I call to her. She gets louder. I walk into the living room and show her the knife. I'm chopping an onion for your dinner, I tell her slowly. I have onion on my fingers, and my eyes are burning. It's very difficult to see. Could you please wait until I finish one thing before you ask me to do another?

Her cries get louder; she frowns and looks at the television.

You'll have to wait a few minutes before I can change the channel, I tell her.

Her lips curl into a frown I know means she wants me to do it now.

Do you want me to finish making dinner, or do you want me to change the channel?

Change the channel if that's what she wants, he says in the kitchen.

Okay, I say. If you want the remote control to smell like onion.

I love the smell of onion, he says.

A channel above thirty? Below thirty?

It's one or the other, I tell her. You either want a channel above thirty or below. Which one is it?

Maybe she needs to look it up, he says, and she raises her eyes.

Look it up in the back of the newspaper, he says. It's over on the table with yesterday's mail.

I find the television listings page in the back of the newspaper. I hold the page in front of her face, and point the blade of the knife at the first program listed. I slowly move the knife down the page so that it passes over every program listed at seven o'clock.

Did you see the show you want to watch?

Is it on later? (Eyes raised.)

Do you know what you want to watch now? (Eyes raised.)

I throw the newspaper across the room and onto the table where I found it. She frowns and her arms shake; she makes the bear cub sound.

Do you want me to change the channel now?

She wants to find her show in the paper, he says.

Do you know what time the show is on?

You want me to go through every page until you find it? (Eyes raised.)

I bring her the paper from where I threw it. I turn to the page that begins with the program listings for seven-thirty. I watch her eyes. Bits of onion are falling from the knife onto the floor. She looks at the knife and frowns. I'll pick it up later, I tell her. Do you want the page turned? (Eyes raised.)

I turn the page and watch her eyes.

The butter, he says in the kitchen. Hurry up and turn off the heat.

I'll be there in a second, I tell him.

Hurry up before it ruins! he says.

I drop the newspaper on her chest, the knife on the newspaper.

With his foot he is trying to turn the knob that controls the heat. His leg shakes and the pan falls from the stove.

Her cries in the other room are louder. She is going to die. If right now the channel is not changed to the channel she wants, and if right now she does not find the program she wants to find in the newspaper television program listings, and if the increasing volume and intensity of her cries are any indication of what is going to happen in the next few minutes, then certainly, she is going to die.

Fuck fuck fuck fuck, he says.

I pick up the pan and place it in the sink. I run water into the pan until the pan steams. I use a towel to wipe the melted butter from the floor, and then a wet rag to further wipe the floor, and then a dry rag to dry the floor, and when I am finished I place the towel and the used rags in the hamper in the bedroom.

Melt some more butter, he says.

Use the same pan.

That's too much butter.

I turn the heat under the pan to high.

That's too high! What do you want to do—burn it again?

I turn the heat to low, so that there is only the flicker of a blue flame under the pan.

She has not stopped making her noise in the living room.

Come back, he says. That's not going to melt it.

In the living room she is watching the knife on the newspaper on her chest. I turn to the last page she was looking at. Her eyes reach the bottom. I turn to the next page. Her eyes reach the bottom. I turn to the next page. I am willing to turn every page in every newspaper. I will not feed her her dinner, nor give her her medication, nor prepare her for bed, nor will I run into the kitchen to save him from being burned by hot melted butter, nor will I pull down his pants and hold in place the plastic container he urinates into, nor will I leave this apartment, until she finds the television program she has been trying to find.

Look out for the butter! I hear him saying.

She makes her bear cub sound and looks toward the kitchen.

Have you found your program?

Do you want me to stay here until you find it? (Eyes raised.)

We're going to have a fire, he says. The butter is coming over the top.

Do you want me to stay here until you find the program? (Eyes raised.)

Can you hear your husband in the kitchen? (Eyes raised.)

Would you like to see your husband burn himself?

Can you smell the burning smell? (Eyes raised.)

Do you want the building to burn down?

Do you want every person in this building to die?

Would you like to explain to everyone why your finding the television program you want to find is more important than the lives of the people in this building?

Go ahead and explain. I want to hear why.

Tell me why your finding the day and time and channel of this television program is so important that you're willing to risk hot butter falling on your husband and maybe a fire burning this entire building and all the people in it down to nothing.

Go ahead and tell me. I'm waiting.

Hurry up and get in here, he calls to me.

I'm not going to move from this spot until you explain why your television program is more important than everything else in the world.

I look into her eyes until she looks away.

Now, I'll ask you one more time. Would you like me to stay here until you find the program?

Do you want me to go into the kitchen and turn down the heat? (Eyes raised.)

Are you sure? (Eyes raised.)

Hurry, he says. Where are you?

The program that's on the television now—is it good enough for you? (Eyes raised.)

Good. I'll let you know when dinner is ready.

I've been calling, he says. Take it off the heat.

I run water over the pan. Steam rises into my face. I find another pan in the cabinet under the sink and set it on the stove.

No more butter, he says. Use vegetable oil.

Finish chopping the onion.

Put the onion in the oil.

Add some black pepper.

More.

That's enough.

Stir the onion. Use the wood spoon.

Write that we need more butter.

Butter, I write on the shopping list held to the refrigerator by a magnet.

Keep stirring, he says, and I then I hear her making her noise.

Skin the fish, he says. Make sure you get all the bones. I almost choked on a fish bone the other night.

Watch the onion, he says. It's starting to brown.

Get all the skin. Use the sharp knife. The smaller one. In this drawer, he says, and points with his foot.

I run the water to drown out her cries. I run it so hard that it bounces off the burned pan and sprays onto the floor.

Turn that down, he says.

Not that knife. The smaller one.

Watch the onion, he says.

I can hear her through the water and the sound of his talking. I walk into the living room with the smaller sharper knife. I turn the volume knob on the television as far as it can be turned, and then I turn it back the other way. Her mouth is open, her eyes closed. I can see the shape of her eyes moving beneath her eyelids, her neck arching, as if she is trying to see the top of her head—that part of her head just below the skin of her scalp, below the hair I wash every morning with two kinds of shampoos. I see the wet of her teeth. I see the clump of her eyelashes. I see the wrinkles under the powder on her face; the hairs at the openings of her nostrils; the lipstick I wipe from her lips before she eats.

Watch out for the sink, he says. It's about to overflow. You've got the drain blocked with the dirty pan.

Where are you? he says.

Where were you? he says.

I lift the pan and the water disappears. I set the pan on the counter on top of a dish towel.

You better put the fish on, he says. The onion is ready.

Get off that last bit of skin.

Right there where your left hand is.

You've got the knife pointed right at it.

Right there.

Over here, he says, and points with his foot.

Hurry up and get the fish in the pan.

First more oil.

A little more.

Stop stop stop. That's too much.

Dump some out into the sink.

Never mind. Leave it alone. Get the fish in there.

Watch that you don't pin the onion underneath. Make sure the fish is on the bottom. That's it. Make sure the onion gets all over the fish.

Watch that the fish doesn't burn. Only a minute on each side.

She's calling me, I tell him.

Don't leave the fish.

It must be an emergency for her to be calling me like that, I say.

Flip before you go.

Look out that it doesn't break.

Careful!

Get the onion all around.

Don't go yet.

But she must be having an emergency, I say.

Cut the lemon in half.

Squeeze it over the pan.

Watch the seeds.

Squeeze harder. Get it all in there.

Now the other half.

Get the seed that fell into the pan.

Right there, on top of the fish.

Right where you've got your finger.

Watch out that it doesn't fall into the juice. Someone could choke on that.

I really should see what she wants, I say.

Get the seed out of there. Do you want someone to choke?

From the way she's carrying on, I tell him, it sounds like it could be life or death.

It's right where your hand is.

I'm sorry, I tell him. I don't see it.

Just pick it out and throw it away.

I really should check on her before it's too late.

Take the fish out of the pan first.

From the way she's carrying on in the other room, I explain to him, it really does sound like it could be a literal case of life or death. I really think it must be something much more important than a piece of fish.

Just take it out of the pan. It will take five seconds.

I don't want to break it up, I tell him.

Then at least turn the heat off.

Now take it off the burner.

I'm sorry, I tell her when I reach her. I'm sorry for not getting here sooner, but I was busy frying the fish. Do you need me to call 9-1-1? Are you choking? Are you having trouble breathing? Chest pain? A pain in your side? In your head? In your neck? A pain somewhere else? A cramp? Something in one of your eyes? A burning sensation?

Come back in here, he says. The fish is sticking to the pan.

Let me ask you again, I tell her. I know it must be something life or death. Are you choking? Trouble breathing? Chest pain? A pain in your side? In your head? Your neck? Somewhere else? A severe cramp? An excruciating burning pain in your eyes, or somewhere else? Should I take out the medical emergency book and go through it page by page? That way you can raise your eyes when we come to whatever life or death emergency you're going through that made you call me and carry on the way you did when I was busy frying the fish, and squeezing lemon over the fish, and trying to find a seed that dropped into the pan.

Should I get the book?

Do you want something else? (Eyes raised.)

Do you want the channel changed?

Is that what you want? Don't be afraid to tell me.

Do you want the channel changed? (Eyes raised.)

Let me do that right away for you, since it must be an emergency. A channel above thirty? Below thirty? (Eyes raised.) Below twenty? (Eyes raised.) Below ten? (Eyes raised.) One, two, three, four, five, six. (Eyes raised.)

Is this what you want? The end of the news? (Eyes raised.)

This fish is no good, he says.

That's okay, I tell him. We're out here watching the weather report. Something about tomorrow's weather is life or death. Maybe you should forget the fish and come in here.

If you take it out of the pan now, he says, we can still eat it.

Let me turn up the volume, I tell her.

I turn the volume knob on the television as far as it can be turned.

Turn that down! he says. What do you want to do—bust my eardrums?

I can see in the shape of her open mouth the sound that means she wants something.

Turn it down! he says. Someone is going to call the cops that's so loud.

This is very important, I say. We really should hear this.

My ears, he says. I'm going to call the cops if you don't turn that down.

I watch him trying to press the speaker-phone button with his foot.

Tonight will be a good night for stars. Tomorrow will be hot and humid. The high temperature record for tomorrow's date, set more than forty years ago, may be broken. Tomorrow will be an unbearable day for anyone with allergies. The air will be heavy. A fifty percent chance of an evening shower. Tomorrow night the sun will set one minute earlier than it will set tonight.

Get the phone cord out from around my foot, he says.

Do you want me to help you call the police?

I want you to turn down the volume, he says.

Is that better?

Lower.

Lower?

Turn it off, he says. My ears are ringing.

Now my foot.

Watch out for the phone.

Now you'll have to make something else for dinner, he says. With his foot he presses the pedal on his chair that makes his chair move into the kitchen.

Open the refrigerator.

I hear her making the noise that means life or death.

I leave the refrigerator door open and go into the living room. I ask her does she want to be moved, does she need to be changed, does she want the television on, does she want the window open, does she want the hair brushed from her face, does she want the fan moved closer, does she want to make a phone call, does she need more pillows under her legs, more pillows behind her head, a clean pair of socks, an itch scratched, something about dinner. (Eyes raised.)

You know what you want to eat? (Eyes raised.)

Something in the refrigerator? Something in the cupboards? Do you want to order out?

What else is there?

She wants the fish, he says in the kitchen.

Is that what you want? (Eyes raised.)

Do you want it in the food processor? (Eyes raised.)

Extra black pepper? (Eyes raised.)

Is the fish okay with you? I ask him.

If that's what she wants, he says.

I divide the fish into two portions with his portion slightly larger than hers. I pour some of the sauce onto his fish—carefully, so that none of the sauce runs off his plate and onto the counter, and off the counter and onto the floor. I empty the can of green beans into a small bowl, and cover the top of the bowl with plastic wrap. The microwave timer must be set for two minutes. I blend her portion of fish to the consistency of oatmeal cereal. I cover her fish with the rest of the sauce.

The microwave makes the sound that means two minutes have elapsed. I touch the green beans to make sure, and then divide them into two portions with his portion slightly larger than hers. His green beans must be placed next to but never on top of his fish, and both the fish and the green beans must be topped with a generous amount of salt. I blend her green beans to the consistency of split pea soup; her green beans must be placed in a bowl that is not the bowl holding her fish. She likes her fish and her green beans topped with a generous amount of black pepper.

In the living room, I position a snack table between where her chair is and where his chair will be. I set his plate and her bowls carefully on the snack table. I cover the seat of her chair with a pad. I make sure to lift her gently—one hand under her head, the other hand under the bend of her knees—and place her into her chair. I bend her legs and arms the way she likes. I make sure her head is secure in the head rest that extends up from the top of the back of the chair. I fasten a clean towel around her neck with a safety pin so that the towel drapes across her chest. I drape a second towel over the first. I drape a pad over the towels. With a wet paper towel, I wipe the lipstick from her lips.

After he moves his chair into the living room, I make sure the snack table is equidistant from his chair and her chair. I fill his plastic drink cup with cold water, and insert a fresh straw into the straw hole in the top of the cup. I fill her plastic cup half with ginger ale and half with cranberry juice. Her cup must be covered with a special cap, which has an opening small enough to prevent liquids from flowing through the opening too quickly. I tie a bib around his neck so that it drapes over his shirt.

I feed her a spoonful of processed fish. I feed him a forkful of fish. I hold the next piece of fish at his lips until he stops chewing and opens his mouth. When she opens her mouth and raises her eyes, I feed her more. I wipe the sauce from his chin. He asks for more salt; she asks for more pepper. I wipe the corners of her eyes.

Don't give her so much at one time, he says. What, are you trying to kill her?

Give her a rest, he says. She can't take so much.

She moves her mouth and arches her neck, and I wipe the tears from the corners of her eyes.

Give her some more, he says.

Not so much!

Take that away from me, he says. I don't want any more. The fish is too dry.

The beans are no good, he says. Throw them away.

If she coughs food onto her chin and onto her chair and onto her ankles and onto the television screen, her chin and her chair and her ankles and the television screen must be wiped clean.

I worry every time she eats, he says. One of these days—who knows?

Give her small bites, he says.

If I give her only small bites, I tell him, it could take an hour, maybe two, to finish eating.

She loves eating, he says.

If it takes an hour to finish eating, I explain to her, I won't be able to get you into bed in time to finish everything else I have to do.

She opens her mouth.

I place a spoonful of fish in the back of her mouth. I use the roof of her mouth to help scrape the fish from the spoon. Some of the fish falls out of her mouth and onto her chin. I spoon the fish back into her mouth.

Her neck arches, her eyes roll back. Her face turns redder than the red it already is. She is trying to look at the top of her head.

I'm sorry, I tell her. Was that too much?

Her mouth makes the silence I know means she is choking.

Is she okay? he says.

Are you okay? he says to her.

Make sure she's breathing!

She asked you not to give her so much!

His voice fades; the room becomes quiet. I stare at her mouth, then her neck. Through the skin of her neck I can see the food clogging her windpipe. Then the windpipe is gone and I can only see the clump of food.

Through the disposable pad and the two towels on her chest, and through her blouse and through the skin of her chest, and through the tissue and bone below the skin of her chest, I can see her heart beating. I can see bits of food on the shiny parts of her teeth. I can see the rough part of the back of her tongue. Below his shirt, and below the skin and tissue and bone of his chest—his own heart. Below my own, my own. As if everything else in the world has been erased, I see three hearts suspended in the air, beating.

Do something, he tells me. Get behind her chair and pump her stomach.

She's going to stop choking, I say.

This is worse than usual, he says. Reach your fingers into her mouth.

What are you doing just standing there? he says. Make her breathe.

She's going to breathe, I tell him.

Call for an ambulance! he says.

Give her a minute, I say.

Use your fingers, he says. Go get a rubber glove if you want.

She's going to be fine, I tell him.

He tries to press the speaker-phone button with his foot. The phone cord wraps around his foot. His leg spasms and pulls the phone to the floor.

She's going to be okay, I keep saying, and I'm watching the three hearts suspended in the air.

You're crazy, he says. Crazy crazy crazy.

She's going to cough it up, I say.

Now the hearts are gone, and I see only her windpipe suspended in the air above where her chair used to be, above where the floor beneath her chair used to be. I see the processed fish trying to fight its way up through her windpipe.

She's going to die, he says.

It's only been a minute, I hear myself saying. This is going to be fine. Everything is going to be fine.

The food shoots up through the opening at the top of her windpipe and lands on the floor. Above the floor is her chair, and sitting in her chair is her body. There are three heads in the room. Six eyes, six arms, six legs, six lungs. Six lips, three upper and three lower. There are three hearts. There is skin covering the three hearts.

Is she okay? he says.

Ask her is she okay, he says.

Are you okay? he asks her.

Would you like something to drink? I ask her.

Do you want anything else to eat?

So I can start the dishes, and then get you ready for bed? (Eyes raised.)

Good, I say. Now I can finish everything I need to finish before I leave.

Crazy, he says.

Get my foot loose from this cord, he says.

Pick up the phone. Put it back where it belongs.

Through the aftersounds of her choking, I hear her making the sound I know means she wants something.

Give me my pill, he says.

Pills are stored inside a small locked metal box in the kitchen. Even if the sounds of her carrying on increase in volume and intensity so as to indicate a life or death situation, and even though neither he nor she is physically capable of opening the metal box, or unscrewing the cap of a pill bottle, I may never leave the unlocked metal box unattended. I push his pill through the foil backing of the pill pack and into a tiny paper cup, making sure the pill does not touch my hands, making sure it does not come into contact with any food, or any other medications, making sure it does not fall onto the floor, or even touch the kitchen counter. I log the pill as taken in the medication log book. I push another pill into my hand, and put the pill into my pocket. I log this pill as contaminated and disposed of, with the date and time of disposal written clearly. I count the remaining pills, and write the total in the appropriate place with my initials under the number.

Did you drop another pill? he says.

What do you mean another?

You're always dropping pills.

When was the last time?

I know you, he says.

I think someone hit you on the head too many times.

They did, he says. The workers over at the state home. They gave it to me all the time. I would ask them for something, maybe a cracker, or a drink of water, or for them to take me to the pot, and they would ask me what, what, what, and then they would beat me.

Do you want your pill?

I think *you* want my pill, he says.

Do you want it with water?

Why don't *you* have it? he says. It will stop you from shaking.

I'm not shaking.

Sometimes I see you shaking, he says.

Open your mouth.

I hold the cup steady, and make sure the pill drops into his mouth. I hold the straw where his mouth can grab it. When it appears that he cannot swallow any more water without taking a breath, the straw must be pulled from his mouth. If the straw is not pulled from his mouth, he will cough water onto his shirt.

I hear her making the sound I know means she wants something.

He coughs water onto his shirt; his palsied leg kicks.

Did you swallow it?

His hands spasm with each cough. Water spills from the corner of his mouth onto his chin. I wipe his chin and wait.

Did you swallow? Or do you need more water?

I got it, he says through his choking.

Do you want more water?

No more, he says. Go see what she wants.

Do you want the television turned on? Are you in an uncomfortable position? Do you need your head moved? Your arms? Do you want something to drink? A pain in your chest? Do you need to make a phone call? Do you want to be changed? Do you want me to clean you up? (Eyes raised.)

I removed the pad from across her chest and use the pad to wipe any spilled and coughed up food from her face, lips, and chin, and from her clothes. I use the first towel to wipe any food not wiped by the disposable pad, the second towel to wipe any food not wiped by the first. I carry his plate and her bowls, his cup and her cup, his fork and her spoon, to the kitchen sink, where they must soak in hot water.

She wants something else, he says.

I hear her, I tell him. Do you think I don't hear her?

I was just making sure, he says.

I'm not made of rubber, I tell him.

He's not made of rubber, I hear him telling her.

Through the sound of running water, I hear him say to her, He's our little butterfly boy.

I spoon her leftover processed fish and mashed green beans into the garbage disposal and watch everything sucked down into the hole. I stopper the drain. I squeeze dish soap into the empty sink. I fill the sink with hot water. I place one of her bowls under the water and count to one hundred. Her other bowl under the water, and I count to one hundred. His plate under the water. One hundred after dropping each fork and spoon and knife and plastic drinking cup into the sink. I place my hand at the bottom of the cloudy water. I can feel the soap working its way into the skin of my hand. I lower my face to the surface of the water. I press my lips against the water, and then push my lips, and then my nose and eyes, and then the rest of my face down under the water, and then my ears. I tell myself I am going to count to one hundred. I make myself count slowly. I hear ten in my head. Twenty. I imagine him sitting in his chair behind me, telling me I will not—cannot—keep my head under the water for one hundred seconds. I hear forty—the water pressing against my eyelids. Fifty. I imagine everything sucked down into the garbage disposal, the bowls cracked into pieces, the plate broken into pieces, the cups melted and sucked down, (sixty), the spoon and fork and knives sucked down, my hair and eyelashes and eyebrows and nose and lips and ears and the skin of my scalp and the tissue and bone under my skin, (seventy), all of it broken apart from me and sucked down into the garbage disposal, until my eyeballs are alone, (eighty), floating in the cloudy water, (ninety).

Bring her to bed, I hear him saying.

I rub the soap from my eyes, and use the dish towel hanging from the refrigerator door handle to dry my hair, my face, and inside my ears.

She wants to listen to her book before going to sleep, he says.

Where are you? he says.

Are you alive in there?

Where were you? he says. I've been calling. She wants to listen to her book.

Does she ever listen to any other book?

She wrote the book, why shouldn't she listen to it?

She didn't write it.

I saw her write it, he says. Five years it took her to write that book.

She had a ghost writer.

Shut your mouth, he says. What do you know?

I know enough to know that—
Take her to bed, he says.
Wash her good, he says. Between her fingers.
Her hands won't open, I tell him.
Don't be lazy, he says. Pull them open.
Don't pull too hard, he says.
And make sure she listens to whatever book she wants to listen to, he says.

I carry her with one arm under her head, the other under the bend of her knees. I lay her on the shower bed. I pull off her socks, and then I pull apart her legs and pull down her panties, and then I unbuckle her belt and pull down her skirt, and then I pull her blouse over her head, and then I pull her slip over her head, and then I remove her earrings, and then I place rubber gloves on my hands, and then I unwrap her diaper and slide the diaper out from under her. I remove the pin from her blouse and place the pin in the pin box in the bedroom. I remove the belt from her skirt and hang the belt from one of the hooks in her closet. I bring her socks and panties and skirt and blouse and slip to the hamper in the bedroom.

I use a warm wet cloth to wipe near her eyes. I wipe her nose and around her mouth. I wipe her lips. I squeeze the wet of the cloth into the sink and wet the cloth again with warm water. I wash her neck and chest and stomach and under her arms. I pull open her hands and wash between her fingers. I wash her legs and feet and between her toes. I squeeze out the wet of the cloth and wet the cloth again. I wash between her legs. I roll her body toward me and reach around her to wash her back. I roll her body away from me. I place a towel over her face and spray deodorant under her arms.

I finger inside my pocket. My lungs feel heavy. The skin of my face is pulling. I crouch. I press my finger against the side of my nose. I count to one hundred.

I remove the cloth from her face.

I wrap a clean diaper around her hips. I watch her face to make sure I do not tape her skin. I wait for the water to warm, and then I wash my hands with the soap I use only to wash my hands.

Do you want your favorite nightgown? (Eyes raised.)

Is it clean? (Eyes raised.)

I find her favorite nightgown folded on the bed. I fit her head through the bottom of the nightgown, and then through the hole on top. I pull the nightgown down. I bend her arms into the sleeves. I carry her to her chair and lock the chair in place. I brush her teeth with her tiny toothbrush. With a wet cloth, I wipe her lips and where the toothpaste has run out of her mouth. I show her her face in the mirror.

I wheel her chair into the bedroom and leave the chair at the foot of the bed. I lift her with one arm below her head, the other below the bend of her knees. I cover her side of the bed with a pad, and lay her on the pad. I prop her head and neck against the pillows the way she likes.

She makes her bear cub sound. I make sure the tape of her book is still inside the tape player.

Is it on the right side? (Eyes raised.)

Do you want the volume higher?

Something else? (Eyes raised.)

Are you hot? Are you cold? Do you want socks on your feet? Do you need another pillow behind your neck? Too many pillows? Do you want to be under the blanket? Do you want the window opened? The fan pointed at your face? Something about the tape? (Eyes raised.)

A different tape?

You want me to listen? (Eyes raised.)

I have to fold the laundry, I tell her, and then I have to wash the dishes.

I carry the laundry basket from the living room into the bedroom. She is making the bear cub sound.

I know you want me to listen, I tell her. But I have to fold the laundry.

She frowns to mean she is disappointed, to mean if she does not get what she wants—if I do not hear what she wants me to hear— she will not stop making the sound I know means she wants something.

I'll listen while I fold, I tell her.

I became aware of sounds coming through the ceiling, a woman's voice on the tape says. *Screaming, crying, groaning. Human animal sounds.*

Each sock must be stuffed into its matching sock; each pair must be placed in the sock drawer.

The food was tasteless. They shoved it into my mouth. When the food fell from my mouth they thought I was being difficult. They smacked me and shoved more food into my mouth. "Poor birdy," the nice ones said at me. Or: "Poor little girl."

She makes a sound I know means she wants me to listen.

I fold his shorts, then his pants, and put them in his dresser. I button the top buttons of his shirts, and hang them in the closet.

There was a woman hunchback, and a girl who slammed her head into walls, and two girls who wouldn't stop reaching inside their diapers, and a girl who had to be put into a straitjacket, and two girls who had to have boxing gloves put on their hands, and a girl who would not stop screaming, and then there was me. I had braces on my legs. I raised my eyes to say yes, and people said, "Poor birdy." Or: "Poor little idiot girl."

Hurry up, I hear him calling from the living room.

I'll be there in a minute.

Hurry up!

I'll be there in a minute.

I blocked out the sound of the screaming by thinking of other things. We were allowed one hour every day to listen to the radio. I liked the commercials.

I have to go, he yells from the other room.

I'll be there in a minute.

Hurry hurry hurry, he says.

This woman used to wrap her legs around her neck. She tied herself up into knots. They called her: "Monkey."

I'm going to have an accident!

Give me one minute.

Fluid had enlarged her head to several times its normal size. She looked at me from her bed, and I raised my eyes.

I dump the rest of the laundry onto the floor. I sit on the floor. I press my finger against the side of my nose. I count to one hundred. I make sure the towels are clean, and then I fold them.

I'm about to have an accident!

I could see snow outside the window. My parents used to wheel my chair out into the snow. I used to like the cold of the snow on my nose.

I only have to fold a few more things, I call to him.

I don't want to have an accident!

There was one girl who understood. She slept in the next bed. One night we heard footsteps, and I looked at her and raised my eyes. She knew what that meant. It meant: Here he comes. Here comes Stony Hands.

You're going to have to clean up the mess!

I wanted to talk about my baby brother. How much I missed him. How much I wondered what he was doing that very moment at home with my mother and father. I looked at her teddy bear and raised my eyes. I tried to raise the pitch of my voice to make it more like a baby sound. She understood. She knew I was talking about my brother.

Can I lower the volume?

Not even a little bit?

I hear his chair slamming against the bathroom door.

I'm going to break it down, he says. Do you hear me? I'm going to break it down.

On Thanksgiving I was allowed one small piece of turkey and some cranberry sauce.

Where have you been? he says. Didn't you hear me calling?

I was taking care of something.

Get me on the pot, he says. I'm about to have an accident.

I had dreams of running and skating. I had dreams of playing with dolls.

I close the bedroom door. Through the door I hear the sound I know means she wants something. I hear, faintly, the voice of the woman speaking on the tape.

I position his special bathroom chair so that the seat of the chair is over the toilet seat. I move his wheelchair in front of and facing the toilet. I lock the wheels and unfasten his seat belt.

Hurry, he says.

I pull his pants to his ankles; I pull his underwear to his ankles.

Jesus Christ, he says.

I lift him with my hands under his arms, my face pressed against his chest. I make sure to bend my knees. In one quick motion I pull him up from his wheelchair, turn him around, and drop him onto the seat of his bathroom chair. He leans into the wall beside the toilet. His palsied leg kicks at me.

Stop flinching, he says. My leg isn't going to hurt you.

I strap him into his bathroom chair, and then push his wheelchair out of the room.

Take off my pants and my underwear, he says. I'll have a shower right after this.

I bring his pants and his underwear to the hamper in the bedroom.

One of the girls fractured her skull. They gave her a helmet. "Let me out of here!" she used to yell at me. "I'm cracking up! Let me out of—"

Let me know when you're finished in there, I tell him.

Through the bathroom door, I can hear him groaning. I can hear his body thrashing against the chair, and the chair smacking against the wall. Through the bedroom door I can hear her bear cub noises.

In the living room I sit in the chair I usually sit in—the chair I have never witnessed anyone have an accident on. I finger inside my pocket. I close my eyes and begin counting to one hundred.

Hey, I hear him calling, I'm ready now.

I'm all finished, I hear him say.

Hello out there.

Where are you?

Are you out there?

Later: Hey, I'm calling you. I'm ready now.

I'm all finished on the pot.

Hey, he says. Hey hey hey hey hey.

Where the hell are you?

Hey butterfly boy! Where are you?

Do you hear what I'm saying in here? I'm calling you!

Later: What the hell is going on out there?

Where are you?

I'm just sitting in here.

What do you think I'm doing in here?

I know you hear me calling you!

I'm going to tell how you like to drop pills!

Do you hear me?

Do you hear what I'm going to tell?

Later: Come on!

What are you doing?

I'm going to have sores on my bottom!

Do you know what you're doing to me?

Please, he says.

I stand up from the chair. I open the apartment door and slam it shut. I knock on the bathroom door.

Are you finished in there yet?

I'm just sitting here!

Are you finished?

Yes yes yes. Of course I'm finished. I've been calling you.

I open the door and see him leaning against the wall. There is a crack in the seat of his bathroom chair.

What took you so long? I ask him.

I've been calling!

I couldn't hear. I was out in the hallway. I was putting the second load of wash into the dryer.

My bottom is sore, he says.

Do you want me to wipe you? Or do you want to just take a shower?

Wipe me first.

No no no no no. That's too sore. Use the wet wipes.

No, he says. It's too sore. Put me in the shower.

You broke your chair.

I know, he says. You'll have to wrap some tape around it.

I pull his shirt over his head. I pull off his socks. I place his shirt and socks in the hamper in the bedroom.

I loved her because of that. She was the only one to look at me that way. She would sit next to me on my bed and watch me raise my eyes.

I removed his glasses and put them on his dresser.

She would ask me yes or no questions. She had been married twice, and she had been to Florida, and she sat with me and told me things.

I pull the shower bed from the shower area; I wheel his special chair into the shower area.

I brush his teeth and watch him spit the paste on his chest. I pour mouthwash into his mouth and wait for him to spit on himself. I turn on the water. I hold my hand under the shower spray hose.

Too cold, he says, and his leg kicks out at me.

How about now?

Jesus, that's too damn hot!

Now?

That's nice, he says. That's how I like it.

I place rubber gloves on my hands and squeeze shampoo onto one of the gloves.

Rub, he says.

Through the closed bathroom door and the closed bedroom door, I hear her making her life or death sound.

Rub it in good, he says.

Not so hard! he says. You're hurting my neck!

Take it easy! he says.

She's calling me, I tell him. Do you hear her?

Rinse, he says.

I'm going to see what she wants, I tell him.

Rinse first, he says. Don't leave me like this.

Listen to her, I tell him. That could mean something serious.

Rinse my hair, he says. She probably wants her tape turned to the other side.

Maybe I should check on her, I tell him. I wouldn't want her to hurt herself carrying on like that.

Get it out of my eyes! he says. Hurry up and wash it out!

Right after I go turn over her tape.

It's burning my eyes! he says. Where are you going?

Water drips from the gloves onto the floor. Water on the bedroom doorknob.

Do you want the other side? (Eyes raised.)

Water on the tape player, and then on the tape.

Water on the play button.

I always received an honest answer when I looked into her eyes. I never cried when she fed me. She was like a miracle to me. All the time we used to have laughter episodes. We used to tell each other—

Jesus Christ, he says. My eyes!

Look up, I tell him. Keep your eyes open.

Don't walk away like that any more!

She didn't write that book, I tell him.

Sure she did, he says.

Just like you cook your own dinner, and do your own laundry, and wipe your own ass.

I did so cook dinner tonight!

Then I guess you ruined it, I say.

Don't be late tomorrow, he says.

What?

Don't be late, he says. This morning you had us waiting twenty minutes.

It wasn't twenty minutes, I say.

Wash me, he says.

Under my arms, he says.

Inside my ears.

Between my legs.

Save my bottom for last.

I know, I tell him.

Don't forget between my fingers, he says.

I know, I know.

I know, I know, I know, he says.

Easy on my bottom, he says.

Watch it! he says. That's too hard.

She wrote that book, he says.

She sat in her chair and made noises, and someone else wrote it.

Rinse, he says.

You're all rinsed.

Rinse it good, he says.

I dry his hair, then his body. I spray deodorant under his arms. I move him from his bathroom chair into his wheelchair.

I find his pajama bottoms in the pajama bottoms drawer.

I was fifteen at the time, and I wanted to prove I possessed a personality, like a well-trained dog doing tricks.

His socks in the socks drawer, his bed shirt in the bed shirts drawer.

Through the window I watched a squirrel run across the grass, and I was sad.

I put clean socks on his feet. He leans forward, and I pull his bed shirt down over his head. He pushes with his good leg, and holds up his body long enough for me to pull his pajama bottoms up to his waist.

I find his glasses where I put them on his dresser, clean them with glass cleaner, and put them on his face.

From the wink she gave me, and from the way I raised my eyes, we knew we didn't have to worry.

I push his wheelchair into the living room. I wash and dry his bathroom chair. I wash and dry the toilet seat. I flush the toilet. I dry the shampoo bottle, and the floor, and the plastic cover of the shower bed. I bring the used wash cloth to the hamper in the bedroom.

He said "I do" and I raised my eyes.

I spray the bathroom. I bring the used towels to the hamper.

After so many bad days, that was one of the best days of my life.

I would like to write something, he says. Maybe my own book. I would like to write about all the terrible things I've gone through.

She is making the sound I know means she wants something. The walls have disappeared, and I can see her heart pumping in the bed.

Maybe I would write about you in my book, he says. About how you don't come right away when I call.

Maybe I'll write something about you, I tell him.

What would you write?

I would write how your body shakes.

I would write about your eyelids, he says.

I would write about the way you groan when you're on the pot.

I would write how you like to drop pills, he says.

You're not going to write anything, I tell him.

Neither are you, he says.

Then he says: What would you really write about me?

I would write how you like salt on your food, I tell him.

What would you really write about me? I ask him.

I would write how you like to drop pills, he says.

When was the last time you wiped my ass? I ask him.

That's not nice, he says. Sometimes you're not a nice person.

I'm sorry.

I would wipe your ass if I could, he says. I would do a lot of things.

I said I was sorry.

I just remembered, he said. You never finished filing my nails.

You can finish them now, he says.

Don't look that way, he says. It will be easy. They're nice and soft from the shower.

Get a file from the bathroom, he says. In the cabinet above the sink.

What are you waiting for?

Don't look at me that way, he says. I never did anything to you.

I look into the bathroom mirror.

I turn the knob of the sink.

I reach into my pocket.

What are you doing in there? he says. How long does it take to find a nail file?

I know what you're doing in there, he says. I know you. I know.

I cup my hands under the water.

Edra Ziesk

IN CAMP

Summer. Early morning. The sidewalks are bluish and chill, the cool cocooned around the secret hot heart of the day.

Girls are waiting for other girls: Margaret, Mary, Karen, Ann; Mary, Karen, Ann, Margaret. A shyness, a quickening, a fibrillation, an adjustment.

Boys heave trunks. Parents fuss with the duffel bag zippers. The sidewalk is sour and cool.

Girls crowd up the bus steps. Somebody loses a shoe. Somebody yells, Hey! We are glinty teeth, hair whips, laughs like hiccoughs.

The bus heads north. Heat hovers inches above, a product of the yellow of the bus.

Camp. We have been going here for three years or eight years or ten.

We are anxious for sameness.

The lit pink dust of the parking lot.

The field, a vast scoop, sunken in the way of a room.

Edra Ziesk's first novel, *Acceptable Losses*, was published in 1997 by SMU Press. She has received fiction fellowships from the New York Foundation for the Arts and the NEA. This is her second appearance in *Alaska Quarterly Review*.

The mountain that rises behind the field. The casino on top of the mountain abandoned intact: tables; chairs pushed out or in; a surprised clock.

The things we forgot or remembered.

Are we in the same bunk? somebody says.

Somebody says, Where else?

Somebody says, It's ours!

Somebody says, Where else?

Mary, Margaret, Karen, Ann.

We check for our names, carved into wood with Swiss Army knives, butter knives, straight pins, pens. The day of the carving comes back.

We finger the names like blind girls.

We unpack. Straight pins fall into the slits of the floor.

Tank tops, chest-pocket T-shirts, jeans, cut-offs (cuffed or frayed), spray deodorants lined up on top of the cubbies. The caps are initialled in pink or in black, although we use one another's toothbrushes, hairbrushes, chapsticks, combs.

We sleep in the right-angled bunks breathing across the protractor angles.

We are always late. Counselors shake us in the morning, pinch, pull off the blankets. They yell, Breakfast! They yell, Move!

Slap of bare feet, slamming of cans back on top of the cubbies. Combs slapped flat in back pockets: rattails, picks, colored combs we spent time choosing in the 5-&-10's where we come from. Shopping, we told our mothers, and went with other girls: we did not see each other in the winter.

You! we said at the bus stop. You! Shyness passed. Girl, girl bubbling under.

We braid each other's hair. Finger each other's clothes.

Can I . . . ?

I love . . .

Really . . . ?

To keep . . . ?

Make parts with the colored combs, make braids, fingers walking each other's scalps. We examine each other's faces, pulling skin with our thumbs. Pretty, we say to each other.

Attractive.

You'll grow into your looks.

We are late to breakfast, late for this or that. The counselors herd and prod, are a distant buzz: bees butting against screens. We are slow. We cross the hot field, eyes closed against the glittering green, the glittering white. We walk touching shoulders, a chain of blind girls, turning our heads from the ballfield, where there are boys.

We do not play.

At least sit and watch! say the counselors already tired of herding, of prodding. Their clipboards say SPORTS! in this time slot.

In the sun?

With those boys?

Baseball?

With those boys?

We meander: arts & crafts, swimming, shop. We make things with feathers and tiles. Lanyards, lanyards, cutting boards, necklaces made out of peach pits. We suck the pits clean, sand them, rub them across the creases and flats of our oily skins.

We wear leotards to swim in the cold leechy lake, our nipples tacks, plucking at the bubbled wet fabric behind.

Somebody drowned here, a boy, years back: most of the other girls weren't here then. The water, the pines. A cigarette. Somebody's blink. The plastic plates. Each fork, each spoon. Everything had that drowning in it.

We smoke in the pines that ring the lake, hands cupped for ashes, the brown needles sticky and sharp underfoot. We click our lighters on, off; turn each other around and around and burn off the leeches.

The counselors are tired.

Boys are elsewhere.

We hear them shouting on the ballfield, coming or going, stubby voices thrown by the mown bowl of land. We hear their voices raised above the sing of the band saw, the smell of cut cedar and pine. We keep our backs turned to the jostling, boy-pitched racket in the dining hall: the clatter of plastic plates and cups and the tin pour of silverware: the knuckles and elbows and knees.

Baby-boy boys some other girls held hands with in the dark.

Some other girls kissed.

Some other girls went home with lanyards, cutting boards, hickeys.

We did not. We were censorious. Those boys: dirty underwear, fingernails, teeth.

We pledged allegiance to Dave, who drove the truck, whose sweat was slippery, clean. Whose T-shirts fit at the shoulders, then hung.

I brought Dave to these girls: a full cup.

Look! I said last year. Look, I said the year before.

I have bided my time. I have waited through Dave's other girls, girl after girl, Dave-ready. I have had fortune cookies: Great romance awaits.

A boy felt like the future.

* * *

Look! Karen says. She has a hold of my hair which curls as it dries in spite of pains to get it to stop: juice cans, irons, products that smell like old eggs.

Don't touch it, she says. Her breath is a tickle. Hold still!

One curl rolls in her palm. She picks another apart.

Look, she says again. Two!

Spontaneous combustion, Mary says.

We bend at the knees and the elbows: Karen, Mary, Margaret, Ann.

Mary's hair is a sheet.

Margaret's long and wooly.

Karen's is newly short: a shock, a change, a betrayal.

Dave's last summer's girl was long and straight-haired, yellow and blue. She curled in the palm of his hand.

We are at the lake: still or again. We have been here for days, each day the same day, the heat incandescent and fixed: a headache. A shimmer at the top of the mountain.

Salt pills. The stick and drag of wet suits. We eat at the water, meat sandwiches slapped together by sweaty cooks. Fruit with the chill gone.

The counselors flip on spread towels. The cooks come and go in their whites. Only the lifeguards seem busy.

Dave stops by for a swim. The truck idles at a distance. He is serious amid splash and laze: arm-over-arm, goaled, out to the float and then back.

On the fourth hot day, I follow. Stand and head for the water to the coax pat shoo of the other girls.

I leave them like water.

Step past the place of the drowning. I swim out, conscious of the stroke pull stroke of the muscles of my arms, of the drowning. I am afraid to look down. There are white splashes, sparkle, dim noise from the shore. I can see Margaret: a dark triangle, two dark stars under the wet yellow skin of her suit, visible even from here.

Of course I will tell her. We speak to each other of smells and stains and discolorations. Touch. Live in each other's damp, named the same.

We say, Attractive.

We say, Ruined.

We say, You'll grow into your looks.

I kick, swimming backwards. Margaret recedes, she blends: a pebble, a speck. I am out of the range of hearing.

Out here there is the slap of the water against the float. There is the float's own musical sound.

Somebody's breath, somebody's passing. Out to the float, touch, turn, go back. Under the water his body is luminous: algaed green at the sides, a wet yellow-white down the center.

Isn't it great . . . ?

Don't you love to . . . ?

Me . . .

I do . . .

Things I could say, things I don't.

Mouth teeth water tongue.

Out to the float, touch, turn, go back.

Margaret is still on the shore. I breast-stroke in. She grows: a speck, a thread, a #2 yellow pencil.

I think: Margaret will like that. "Pencil thin."

Dave gets out. Stands next to Margaret, catching his breath. His shorts wetted to black. The sun a white slide on his back. I bump on the muddy bottom.

Margaret: a dark triangle, two stars. The lumpy kinked droop of Margaret's hair.

How was it? she calls. I'm too lazy to swim, Margaret says.

Nice, I say, a girl who is not. Who swims. Dave swims. I smile Dave's way. I still think a word makes a difference.

Well, Dave says. The truck awaits. Girls, he says. Smiles, turns, goes.

Margaret pinches my arm. The next time, Margaret says. Get in there faster!

* * *

And then it is raining. Heat gone in an absolute way, as if there was warring.

The grass smokes.

Flounces of mist up the mountain, like skirts.

Everything's damp.

Wood swells: the door frames, the windows.

Everything puddles and stains.

Drips.

Drips.

Drips tick onto the tops of our deodorant cans. Our wet sneakers twist on the wet grass.

Cutting boards, peach pits, lanyards, lanyards.

They make up things for us to do in the dim halls that ring the field. Inside the smell of must, mold, infrequent use, we play kickball, we make bunk banners, we square dance with other girls. The boys are elsewhere. Shouts cough out from the shoe-smelling gym.

At night there are movies, held hands, kisses and hickeys.

We are late for breakfast. We are late for shop.

One wet day in the middle of the wet days the counselors ask Dave to drive us into town, to do laundry. He buckles the tarp on. We sit in the back of the truck in the hooded dark, knees up, raincoats tucked, girls, laundry bags: dark greens, dark blues. Saucers of water collect on the top of the tarp, dish-deep.

We bring a picnic: damp potato chips, sandwiches, green juice, brownies sent by Margaret's warm mother.

The laundromat: a warm whir we can't wait to get to.

Dave waits outside in the truck. The paper of his cigarette is spotted with wet. He eats bought food: pre-packaged, pre-cupped. Margaret brings him a brownie.

I stay inside, scraping paint specks off the glass door with my nails.

Margaret's fingers are hooked on the truck's rolled down window.

Margaret, whose hair is wooly. Whose body drops down, a plumb weight, a plum, a rise and a dip. Whose name could turn itself over in somebody's mouth.

What's Margaret doing? Karen says.

The window's steamed up. My fingers squeegee.

Mary says, She's talking up Ann!

She's talking up Ann! Karen says.

There is a cut just under the nail of my thumb.

A brownie, a thank you, a goodbye: how long could that take?

I watch Margaret's mouth: wait for it to stretch into the shape of my name.

Although she is far.

Although she is turned.

Although "Ann" is a name you can keep in the front of your mouth and ease out: lips teeth tongue hardly moving.

I look to see if Margaret's mouth says "wash" or "washing machine."

Cigarette smoke hangs outside the window of the truck like white laundry.

Margaret's hair is unravelling. Margaret's braid is mingy.

What I hate is my name.

Soda? Margaret says when she comes in.

Share? Margaret says. I'm parched.

It is chilly outside. Wet. "Parched" is not in this weather.

I say, Sure.

I say, Your hair! I have my comb out. It is distinctive, my comb. It has been called a Caribbean blue. Much admired. So Ann.

Margaret turns to be rebraided.

I say, Those brownies!

I say, Thank your mother for us!

I say, We'll all get fat! Though that's only a danger for Margaret. The rest of us are flesh, gristle, knobs of bone.

My fingers are braiding. I hold the comb in my mouth.

I say, I was here before any of you.

* * *

The rain goes, though it is grudging. Nothing ever dries. Clothes, mildewed and stiff from hanging outside, crack when we dress. We don't go back to the laundromat. It has turned cold. The end of summer insistent.

My mother sends a postcard: so hot you could fry an egg on the sidewalk! I think about it, as if the message is specific, is personal: my mother, an egg. It is hard to picture. We wear jackets and sweaters. Collars of jackets turned up.

We are going camping, the end-of-summer trip. The counselors' faces are hilarious masks: camp almost over, though there is this still to get through. Two days of vigilance, two days of energy. Two days of fires, of cooking, of WASH IT, DRY IT, PUT IT OUT, PICK IT UP.

Rhode Island! they say with hard smiles. Time must have been spent over maps.

Dave drives. A white long-sleeved shirt with the cuffs rolled.

His arms! Karen says. Those veins! Don't you love that?

There is a girl noise from the other girls: Margaret, Mary. A rising; long e's.

At the campfire, light pinches our faces to pink.

It is always dark, camping.

There is always a fire, trees a looming dark green at the edges; sky an India ink. It is never fully black. That is a myth. That is a ghost story.

There is a hung-over ashy smell in the mornings.

This part goes fast. You know. A white shirt, a dipping away. His back, followed by another back.

Her sleeping bag, watched. Her sleeping bag, empty.

There are pine cone scales in her hair when she comes back. For her to take home in a matchbox.

We both pretend to be sleeping.

People stir, people are stirring: Mary and Karen, voices high-pitched.

I pretend to be washing: a bucket, a stream, cold sharp at the wrists.

Mary combs Karen's hair.

Karen is wearing my sweatshirt.

Somebody says, Where's Ann?

I do a rain dance. Rain or a plague of mosquitoes or black flies. We have to go back a day early.

The counselors sleep in the cab of the truck. Margaret sleeps in the back. Margaret's eyelids are violet.

A breeze, a change, a shift, an unravelling.

I return her sandals.

I return her barrettes.

I say, I believe I have something of yours.

She watches me do things. Not talking.

I do not think she sees him again: ask Mary, ask Karen. Wanting to know is an itch under ten nails.

* * *

The mornings turn frosty.

We wouldn't mind gloves.

We wouldn't mind hot toast.

The days hold no heat in the way of water in a cupped hand.

The counselors are absent.

Girls finish up: cutting boards, boys. The boys can't stop playing baseball.

We say, Write!

We say, Call!

We say, SATs!

A drowning, a boy, a boy, a haircut.

On the bus back we are subdued. Boys scuff and echo in the back: a lonesome, boy sound. We say goodbye with our fingertips.

The bus pulls up. Heat huffs from the sidewalk. Parents stand: chickenish necks hinged upwards.

Everything's slow: our standing, our bending, the movement of the parents' necks, our getting off the bus. A girl, a girl, another girl. Mothers finger fresh hickeys.

I see my mother, awkward, pale, wearing pleated cotton. She squints at each girl off the bus: face? knees? clothes? She is peckish and worried, her movements double-time to our slow tramp.

She is afraid she won't know me.

Alexai Galaviz-Budziszewski

1817 S. MAY

My sister and I used to pan for gold. We used to squat along the curb of May Street, with the frying pans our landlady, Betty, would let us use, and we would sift and pour through the water that flowed from the fire hydrant that our upstairs neighbor, Joe, would open up whenever it was especially hot out. I can remember scooping up mounds of grit from the gutter and turning it over and over in small seesawing circles, convinced that I would one day strike it rich. I suppose, in all our days of panning, if Delia and I had turned in all the glass we collected, all the bottle tops and all the can tabs we found, we might have become millionaires, but probably not. Still, as we made up our separate mounds of would-be valuables, depositing our finds in coffee cans labeled gold, silver and diamonds, filling each one up with bottle tops, can tabs and broken glass, respectively, we thought of how we could one day buy a mansion for my mother, a Jaguar for my father, and how we could leave our apartment to our Uncle Pepe, who slept in our pantry along with the chiles and *frijoles*.

I don't know where, on the south side of Chicago, Delia and I got the idea to start panning. It did not seem instinctual, not like I

Alexai Galaviz-Budziszewski's work has appeared in *River Styx* and *TriQuarterly*.

later realized looking behind my back every few steps was—something inherently Southside. But we panned for gold nonetheless, devoutly, often consuming entire afternoons, sifting through the cold water that flowed like swift moving streams down the gutters of May Street. Eventually, our panning became so routine that, when Joe from upstairs would crack open the fire hydrant on those hot, sweltering days when the humidity weighed upon our heads like torture, Betty, our landlady, would simply leave the pans we used outside her first floor apartment, and the moment Delia and I were allowed out, we would race down our apartment building's steps, scoop up our pans mid-stride, and burst out onto May Street, where we would take up our positions along the running water, and begin to sift and pour.

Until our panning, the main attraction on such hot days was to watch the older kids play in the huge domes of water they would create with the pumps. In what for me was an utter mystery until well into my youth, I used to wonder, every winter, what old tires were doing wrapped around all the fire hydrants. Then, early one summer, I caught the older kids of my block wedging a board between our fire hydrant and tire, and I realized, suddenly, the ingenuity of the kids in my neighborhood.

There were contests to see which blocks had the highest domes, the widest fans of cool Lake Michigan water raining upon their street. In this department, our block, May Street, was supreme. While there was never any organized contest, no official measurements, no professional rating system, whenever someone would walk down to a store on Eighteenth Street past the neighboring blocks, he would always return with vivid, detailed accounts on how the "Dudes" over on Allport or Throop, "got one that's *fucking huge*," and here he would hold up some random, gargantuan measurement with his hands. These words seemed to spark something in the residents of my block. When they heard them, they would all inherit the wide, bright eyes of the story-teller, and it would seem suddenly as if there were some greater purpose now, something for everyone to band together in—defeat of a neighboring block. So Joe from upstairs would be called, and he would come charging out, barefoot, in his cutoffs, squinting at the exhaust of the cigarette dangling from his mouth, carrying the heavy, iron pump key—the tool which allowed him to open the hydrant—and he would slowly, professionally, crank up our water pressure, inflate our dome of water even higher. The valves would creak, beneath the sidewalk the water lines would shudder, everyone would wonder when Joe was going to stop, and finally he would, and a cheer would go up, and Joe would retreat back upstairs, where I'm sure a Sox game and a six-pack of tall-boys were waiting for him.

I felt quite proud that Joe, the miracle worker, he who could feather a pump's water pressure just enough to give us the most beautiful fire hydrant creations ever, lived in our building. For the most part, though—and this is a side of Joe that tends to be overlooked—Joe spent the majority of his waking hours drunk or high. He would have loud parties that ended up in fist fights at three A. M., people falling down our three-flat's stairs, creative insults being slung in the stairwell, bottles being thrown on the front sidewalk. At times, Delia and I would be wakened by Joe's scuffles, and we would look out our front window to see Joe out there either pounding on or being pounded by some similar-looking heavyweight. My father would call the cops (if Betty downstairs hadn't already) and things would be settled. Joe would crawl back upstairs, we would crawl back into bed, and all would be forgotten. It was routine. The way things were. Joe gets loud, someone calls the cops, Joe apologizes with a sincere, smiling face to my mother and Betty the next day. It was an unverbalized arrangement, how we survived.

At times, when summer was in full swing, and the pump contests unofficially underway, the block just down from us, just across Nineteenth Street, would try to outdo us with their own fans of water. It occurs to me now that we really had no name for these fans of water. All one had to say was "Man, look at *that* one," and it was obvious to all those listening that another oasis had been spotted, another reprieve in our neighborhood's desert of concrete. To stand beneath one of these great formations, within its massive dome of water, was to be in a completely different world, secluded, excluded, soundless except for the roar of the rushing water. Even the kids standing right next to you could not be heard. Though you could see that their mouths were moving, that they were screaming just like you, they could not be heard. The test was to see who could stand to be beneath the dome the longest. And then, upon exiting, the most excruciating task of all was to become real again. You would run to someone, the first person you saw, and start bragging about how great it was to have been beneath the dome so long. Or, if you were younger, as I was, you would run full speed to your mother and act as if you had just performed some great feat of courage, some act beyond human comprehension, like the scaling of a monstrously high chain-link fence, the rescue of a baseball from a dog-infested yard, anything to get some kind of reaction, some kind of confirmation that you were there, that people could hear you and that you could hear them. At any one time during those summers, there were hordes of lost individuals, newly escaped from the great domes of water, running around frantic, trying to reestablish some sense of *being* in the real world.

From where our pump was, the kids down the block looked like miniature figurines, pet people running about, yapping, like wind-up toys. They were our block's biggest rivals, and they had their own Joe, a fat man who would walk out with a pump key and turn up their water pressure whenever dominance needed to be established. Often, their routine, their unspoken challenge, was to turn up the pressure of their pump and wait for a response from us. Then Joe would come out, determined, nonchalant with confidence, and the domes of water would begin to rise in battle. Their group would cheer when theirs got higher. We would cheer when Joe got ours higher. The valves would screech; within our cracked sidewalk the pipes would moan like the hull of a sinking ship. We would cringe at every turn of Joe's wrench. Inevitably, at least from what I remember, Joe would feather out just enough water pressure so that we never reached our breaking point—the point at which our board snapped in half and shot out across the street with enough speed to kill someone. For this reason when our battles with the next block began, everyone left the area of water flow and fell in behind Joe, where we could cheer in safety.

We always won. The block down from us had a history of shoddy pump construction. The minute theirs would give, they would all yell in disappointment. Sometimes, a little voice could be heard echoing down the block, "Next time, assholes, we'll get you next time." And they would set to building their dome up once again—runners sent off in search of new boards, water pressure inched back up to a respectable level. Joe would accept congratulations, restore our pump's normal flow, and everything would resume, things back to normal: kids running in and out of the water, experiencing sudden losses upon entering and desperate struggles upon exiting.

* * *

There was a layer of grit settled at the bottom of these gutters, and possibly, this is what sparked the idea to start panning. Maybe at some point one of us had scooped up a handful of this grit and suddenly discovered diamonds and precious minerals. Maybe one of us had looked at the other with the astonished face of a scientist who's just made an inadvertent discovery—a face of excitement—a face filled with the feelings one tries to quell by saying, "Wait a minute. I need to try this again." And maybe we did try again, and came up with more jewels and riches, and soon this prompted us to start panning, like early Californians—ghetto Forty-Niners.

At first, we must've looked like fools, Delia and I leaning over the curb, sifting through the heavy till of the gutters. But soon we became pioneers, and it was not long before the other kids of our block began prospecting as well: Little Joey from the apartment building next to ours, and his sister Genie, were out there. Marcos León, the son of the corner grocer, joined in, and even Peety, the eight-year-old pool shark, whose father owned the corner tavern, began panning as well. I seem to remember Delia saying to me once, "They're taking all our gold," but I am not sure if this is actual memory. Though this seems like something my sister would have said (she was the more enterprising of us two), it seems also that Delia and I almost never spoke while we did our panning; rather, we just squatted there, focused intensely on the task at hand.

Gold was, of course, the most sought-after of the precious commodities we panned for. But often we found diamonds and silver as well. Delia, when she would come across those rare green diamonds (shattered pieces of a Seven-Up bottle) or those blue ones (who knows what these were from?), would hold them up to the sunlight and squint like a jeweler; then she would plunk them in the appropriately labeled coffee can and grunt, as if saying to herself, "Damn, now *that* was a good one." I, on the other hand, often skipped over the diamonds and instead focused on the gold—those gold-colored Seven-Up bottle caps, preferably the ones with the red 7UP insignia still visible on them. But Delia, glitter queen that she was, went for the diamonds, the glass, and always had Band-Aids on her fingers because of it. This became a precautionary measure for her after a time, and I am sure that if my mother had ever found out what was happening to all the Band-Aids, she would have forbidden us from ever prospecting again. As it was, though, my mother had no idea, and Delia would wrap her fingers and dig in, pulling up colored glass, holding it to the sunlight, and occasionally, looking over at me with the sparkle in her eyes that I came to understand as my sister daydreaming about what she would do with our fortune.

We discussed our plans late at night in the bed we shared. Much to the disgust of Delia, my ideas on what we would do with our fortune focused more on family matters: how a move up to a mansion might benefit our other family members—Pepe moving out of the pantry and taking over the apartment, and my cousin, Chuey, who often slept on our kitchen floor when his wife kicked him out, moving into the pantry. There were other ideas as well: how we might purchase a van for my Uncle Max, so his chile-delivering business could prosper, how we could pay for my Aunt Chachie to go to medical school and guarantee ourselves free medical care for the rest of our lives. These were all even trades, I figured, arrangements that would in some way benefit each one of us. But Delia had different ideas—ideas that seemed more along the lines of what millionaires might really do with their fortunes. "A pool," she would say as we lay there in the dark. "For the back of the mansion, we *have* to have a pool. And a dug-in one, too, like they have in 'The Beverly Hillbillies.'" And when Delia would say this I would imagine her eyes lighting up like they always did when she thought of such amazing things. At times, there in the dark, I turned to see if the walls on her side of the bed had actually begun to glow.

The apartment we lived in on May Street was a reflection of the street itself—small and cramped. It was for this reason that Delia and I slept in the same bed, shared a room with my parents, and why my Uncle Pepe slept in our pantry. I suppose, if we had all sat down and thought about it, someone would've come to the conclusion that, "Gee, this apartment is too small," but of course, the thought never entered our minds—or maybe it did. Maybe it was always there, lingering. When I would fall asleep on my uncle's mat in his pantry/bedroom and he would kick me out because there wasn't enough room for the both of us. When we had to turn our mattresses up so that my parents' party guests wouldn't spill beer on them, or singe them with cigarettes. When my cousin Chuey would come over, drunk, kicked out of his own apartment up the block, and he would fall asleep face down on our kitchen floor, deep and comfortable, and Delia and I would eat cold cereal and watch Saturday morning cartoons as he slept there, at our feet, snoring, moaning, gyrating his pelvis as if having nasty dreams. There were no problems then. It was all routine.

And maybe our entire block felt the same. Maybe the entire neighborhood, with its towering church steeples, its neon signs, its liquor stores all tossed together in one big concrete mass; maybe everyone who lived there felt the same problems. So much so that the crampedness, the density, was just another "understood," like the humidity during the summer, like the fact that Joe or any of the other drunks or dope addicts might need the cops called on them, or the inherent feeling that we needed to get into pump battles with the people on the next block. The truth, though, is that *I* never felt it. The fact that I could hear Little Joey's parents, in the apartment building next door, arguing about how Joey's father saw other women, never entered my mind. The fact that my parents screamed about what was happening to all our money then turned around and made discreet love on the other side of our bedroom wasn't a bother. I noticed, but mostly I didn't. Mostly at night, when all the families in the neighborhood would get to arguing and sex, I would lie with Delia and talk about fortunes, about pools and about great schemes that would affect each member of my family forever. All these things, these feelings of crampedness, these feelings of being locked down in close quarters, simply were. They were undeniable facts that fell so far back in the mind one could sit on his front stoop and drink a cold beer, or, in the case of the younger kids on the block, sit on the curb and pan for gold.

Back then, it seems, there was something more romantic about living in a ghetto, poverty, with too many members of your family; or maybe I was simply too young to have made an honest distinction between what was real: the gunshots, the suspicious fires, the deaths, and what was fake, or imaginary: the precious jewels, the gold Delia and I used to strike in the gutters. I've tried explaining out loud to myself that any person, any child, with imagination enough, need enough, to turn chips of broken glass into diamonds, bottle tops into gold, certainly has enough imagination to reverse the entire situation of his youth, turn it all into a fairy land of low-riders, loud radios, sexy women with long dark hair, short-shorts and deep, red lips. But the fact remains that May Street was a place where I saw drunken men brawling to the death, I saw wives get beat by their husbands, I saw children get hit-and-run by cars and then watched those cars get chased down by neighbors and the drivers get beat into bloody pulps.

Early one summer morning Delia and I were awakened by my parents and told to get out of the building. I remember distinctly the smell of smoke, the sound of sirens and the distorted chatter of police radios. I remember also, distinctly, being convinced that someone had set our apartment building on fire, and thinking to myself, what did we do? and running through a list of possible reasons why someone might have wanted to burn our place down—*Has my father been cheating on my mother? Did Joe mess up a drug deal?* As I ran down the stairs, led by my uncle, followed by Delia and parents, I remember thinking also, that something *must* be saved, that a dog or cat must be rescued. And though I am sure I got this idea from some TV commercial for fire alarms, or some newscast of a suburban rescue of a cat or dog, some middle-class situation far removed from the reality of May Street, I still felt there was something I needed to save.

When we got to the front of the building and turned to look in the direction of the flames we saw that it wasn't our building that was on fire, but the building behind, and with faces of relief, each family from May Street's row of apartment buildings stood looking with glassy eyes, at the flames shooting up from behind our building. I still wondered what needed saving, but of course, there was nothing.

Betty was already out there, hard at work, oblivious, sweeping the cascading soot into the gutter, the soot that kept falling over the places she had just swept. And Joe was out there as well, undoubtedly thinking up some way with which to snag one of the pump keys the firemen were using. I remember when word was passed that it had been "Li'l China" who had set the blaze. That he had done so in a jealous attempt to get back at his ex-wife for seeing another man. I remember also the gasps that sounded from everyone but Betty, who was too busy sweeping her sidewalk, when it was further discovered that Cookie, China's ex-wife, and their three kids, had not been able to escape the flames, that they had all died. It was in this instant, especially, this milling around of all the neighbors, the good-looking women revealed in their curlers and eyebrowless faces, the kids in their Loony-Tunes pajamas, the fathers, like mine, in their shorts, shirtless, bare, that I remember hearing all the phrases that made up my youth, and surely Delia's too. "Who was it?" "Did they catch him?" "Did she die?" "Damn, the kids too?" And all these phrases were dealt with sincere concern, delivered in honest sincerity. In the eyes of all those neighbors, looking up, you could see the flames, and you could see also that, just as Delia and I thought about fortunes while we panned for gold, our neighbors were thinking about Cookie, her kids, and even China, who was now, it was reported, in custody. They could see flames rushing through their own apartments, engulfing their own families, and they could see perfectly how the cops had beat China once he was caught, "because any father who kills his own kids would definitely get his ass beat by the cops." And somehow, though China's deed was inherently wrong, it was obvious that everyone there could fathom it completely. In light of China, the death of Cookie, in light of all those other deaths—the unnatural, from bullets or suspicious fires, and the natural, from old age or heart attack—in light of all this, the families could band together, the neighbors could all come together and say, "Damn, the kids too?" and shake their heads with some common understanding, some relief in the thought that they had dodged yet another bullet, then say good night to each other in common courtesy, and retreat back to their apartments, like nothing could be done, like life was simply an arrangement, the cards had been dealt and you had to play.

Eventually, after the fire was quelled and the fireman had given the all-clear, my family climbed back up our stairs. By that time the sun was coming up, and my father asked us if we all wanted to go out onto the back porch, which faced east, towards a Lake Michigan masked by skyscrapers, towards a sunrise that would bring the usual heat wave, and towards the charred buildings which had been affected by the blaze. We stood out there, Delia, my parents, my uncle, and I, looking at the burnt remains, inhaling the deep smell of seared wood, basking in whatever coolness the early morning offered. We looked at the wet streets, the buildings dripping with black, sooty drops of water, and I suppose we were searching for something. As the sun came up, and the morning mist began to burn off, I looked down the long rows of porches that stretched off into infinity on each side of us, and saw each family, arms entwined, looking towards the sunrise and doing the same.

Keith Regan

I WAS EVEL KNIEVEL

In 1986, the year my father gave me "total control" of the Beachway Batting Cages, it rained almost every day during May and June. By July Fourth, beach sand had become oatmeal. Brown seaweed and grayish foam choked the Atlantic. Mosquitoes bred on the mini-golf course and a thin green slime coated the boardwalk.

By then, economy and changing tastes had reduced Steeves Family Amusement Center, which my grandfather founded in 1948, to a single arcade, a T-shirt shop, the batting cages, the nine-hole mini-golf course and a go-cart race track. The mama and papa Ferris wheels, frozen forever by rust, and the wood-framed rollercoaster, shut down by a state inspector in 1978, cast ominous shadows on the parking lot. My family still owned a dozen cottages up and down Salisbury Beach, most rented year-round by the men working on the Seabrook project and the rest filled from Memorial Day on with Canadian vacationers and beach bums.

We were, my mother reminded me when I asked for new hockey skates or a Walkman, just hanging on. And the rain made things extra slippery.

Keith Regan has recent work in *Beacon Street Review.*

According to my father, total control meant that after I paid him twenty dollars in weekly rent, any profits I made on the cages were mine to keep. We'd struck this deal in April, after I revealed that I'd been offered a job at the Grand Banks Bird Sanctuary that paid $2,000 for the summer. "I'm offering you a chance to make five, maybe six grand," he said holding his hands wide to show how far the possibilities stretched. To my fifteen-year-old ears, it was sweet music and I shook his weathered hand to seal the deal.

I kept my new business open as much as I could—on weekends all spring and then every day once school let out in mid-June. Up by six, I packed myself a lunch and made the short walk from our apartment above the arcade across the beach road to the chain-link fortress of the batting cages. I swept what water I could out of the batting areas and made sure the rubber home plates were firmly in place. I checked each machine, putting in a single token and standing behind the fence while it whirred to life, creaked into motion and whipped the balls against the cushioned backstop, a satisfying, wet smack.

After I repacked the wire baskets hung on the machines—two took the rock-hard imitation baseballs and one the spongier softballs—I went inside the booth to sit and wait. I drafted a list of rules, made up some posters advertising the batting cages and offered discounts to people who could answer Red Sox trivia questions. I organized an elaborate bookkeeping system to track my customers by age and sex. And I waited.

During those rainy weeks, my most reliable customers were the ironworkers building the Seabrook nuclear power plant. By then, ever-changing groups of them had been living in my father's cottages for three years, arriving in road-battered cars with Texas and California plates and leaving without notice, often in the middle of the night. They worked eighteen-hour shifts at the plant, which had begun to take shape across the open marshes to the north of the beach: a giant sphere that would hold the main reactor.

Five or six of them came to the cage together, usually late in the morning and always carrying a heavy bag of beer. One of them would slide a twenty through the booth window and they'd take turns smashing balls inside the fast cage. They never wore batting helmets and, by drinking beer, smoking inside the cages and swearing, broke at least half of my rules each time. But I didn't say anything—their thick, tattooed arms kept me quiet. So did their money.

I soon found they would pay me extra for little favors. If I walked two blocks south and bought a tray of Emilio's pizza, I'd get a ten-dollar tip. Running across the street to see whether the door at the Tic-Toc Club had been unlocked yet earned me five bucks.

My grandfather urged me to hock, to stand in the street and shout at people as they walked past: "Ten balls for a dollar. Who's going to try the batting cages?"

I told him I'd rather go broke.

He shrugged, then hunched over on the homemade walking stick he took everywhere, asked if I'd ever heard about the time he hocked Frank Sinatra into playing ring-toss until he'd spent eight dollars to win a big white stuffed bear worth fifty-five cents. It was in the 1940s, when the Starlight Ballroom booked world-class acts and brought droves of well-dressed people to the beach, where they strolled under a full moon. To my grandfather, every night before 1954 involved a big, full moon, a perfect sea breeze and Frank Sinatra.

Only Hurricane Carol left a more vivid impression on his memory. Winds shredded the roof of the Starlight and pounding waves slammed the wooden piers beneath it until it succumbed. A photograph in his bedroom showed the pummeled nightclub being pushed the rest of the way into the sea by a bulldozer. Bye-bye Frankie.

My father began to worry for real in July, after the stalwart Fourth of July failed to attract any crowds. He called a family meeting to discuss the crisis.

My mother didn't attend. A protest. What made us think we could change the weather? she asked. "Typical men," she said, answering her own question as she prepared for a long walk along the beach.

She paused at the door and looked back to the table, where the rest of us had gathered. She was just 19 when she had me and was still slim and feisty fifteen years later. A baseball cap hid her eyes and a rain poncho fell to her knees, her bony legs poking out beneath. "What makes you think anyone wants to come here?" she asked. Before she went out, she asked, "Have you looked around lately?"

I had. To me, even then, the beach looked used up, like empty gas cans lying by the roadside. It had served its purpose, entertaining families and giving teenagers a place to buy cheap souvenirs and have their first flirtations—things that no longer seemed important to people in the '80s. We had become a joke, my mother said, and the punchline, the last word, was the nuclear plant taking shape five miles north, across the flat marshes, like a bigger, better amusement park.

My uncle Leo got the meeting rolling by suggesting we buy commercial time on Boston television. "Maybe Arlene's right," he said pointing to the door, where my mother's presence seemed to linger. "Or maybe people forgot we're here."

He offered to star in the commercial himself as the King of the Arcade. I could picture him, big and round with a full beard and mustache, in a big purple suit, holding up a mini-golf club in a regal pose. "I could do my pinball trick," he said.

My father laughed. "That'd be an X-rated commercial."

Aunt Carol, Leo's wife, punched him in the arm. "This is serious," she wheezed. "Can't you be serious for a minute?"

My grandfather cleared his throat. Patience, he said, is what we needed. He told us about the summer of '64, when things were so cool and damp that no one even thought about the beach. "We survived," he said, pouring the last of his beer into a glass. His arms and face were weathered dark, his hair white with brown streaks I attributed to his pack-a-day cigarette habit. I worried he'd tell us the entire story: How his father had bought the land during the depression, before a road even led to the beach, for a dollar an acre. How they hauled in fill on horse-drawn wagons and killed mosquitoes by setting the marshes on fire.

But my father didn't wait. He ran his hand over his short-cropped hair then held up a finger to get our attention. "We need something special," he said. "Something big."

I spoke up and everyone seemed a little surprised. Most of them thought I hated the family business—probably because I'd said just that the summer before. I had wanted to go to hockey camp at Lake Placid, but was told there was no money and that I was needed to run things. I spent that summer making change, sweeping sidewalks, imprinting T-shirts with suggestive slogans and plotting escape.

"Maybe we need to spruce things up," I said. "A little paint, maybe." I didn't say what my friends had told me: That no one wants to hang out in a depressing place; they could stay home and do that.

Everyone nodded but kept quiet.

My father frowned. "That's a good thought, Andrew," he said. "But I had something bigger in mind."

He got up and went to the desk in the corner of the family room. He came back with a rolled-up poster. He turned his back on us again and unfurled it. Then he held it up. It showed a man clad in white leather wearing a red-white-and-blue helmet jumping over a tractor trailer on a red-white-and-blue motorcycle.

"Evel Knievel," I said. I'd seen the poster in the arcade downstairs. You could win it with 1,500 Skeeball coupons.

My father grinned. He sat down and told us that he planned to woo Knievel to the beach to make a jump. It would be big enough, he figured, to save most of July and all of August—the best we could hope for at that point.

I laughed, thinking it was a joke. Leo shook his head and crumpled up the commercial script he'd been scribbling. My father could be persuasive and although we all questioned his business savvy in private, no one doubted his authority in public. He'd been to college, which put him one up on everyone else at the table, and he had the complete support of my grandfather, who shrugged his approval when we all looked at him.

"Do what you must," he said.

We all helped draft a letter that my father sent to the address at the bottom of the poster. When the meeting was over, I went into my bedroom and fell asleep. I dreamed that I was Evel Knievel and that I had come to save the beach. I revved my motorcycle and took off and flew high over everything. Beneath me, the beach lights flickered and people gasped in awe. And as I flew, things glittered like I'd never seen them, like neglect's dank coat had been stripped away. I soared all night—I never landed.

While we waited to hear from Evel, things continued to go badly. I had little business at the cages and many of the people who came I had to let play for free. Police officers—the beach station was just behind the cages—selectmen and other important town officials. In between, bored teenagers and men in their twenties, eager to prove their athleticism remained intact, trotted through the cage, rarely spending more than two dollars each. I had stopped keeping track of things in my book, but according to the math I did in my head, I had made less than $500 and the summer was half over.

One afternoon, while I read a story in the newspaper about the herds of reindeer that would probably die as the radiation cloud floating out from Chernobyl reached Finland, I heard someone flip-flop up to the booth. I looked up to see a girl about 18.

"Um, do I have to wear a helmet?" she shouted at the glass, as if it was soundproof.

I stood and pointed to the list of rules behind me, holding my finger steady beside number one.

"But do *I* have to?" she asked again, a little whine in her voice.

She glanced at the selection of dingy helmets on the rack, their foam insides hanging out in shreds.

I came out of the booth and offered her the best batting helmet we had. It was blue and someone—maybe me, I can't remember—had put a magic-marker B on the front. Unlike the others, the foam lining still had some spring to it. "Try this one."

She took it in her hands and examined it as if it was an artifact. It was a cloudy morning, but she was wearing those Blues Brothers sunglasses that were big then, a faded tube top and cut-off jean shorts. She put the helmet on and smiled. "Ten tokens, please." She held up a bill. I scrambled back into the booth and slid the gold coins through the window.

She went into the softball cage and tried to put all ten tokens into the machine. I had been meaning to put up a sign about that. The machine jammed, but she tried to act natural, taking a few practice swings and stretching her legs. Finally, she came back to the booth. "It's broken," she said. "Can I have a refund?"

I glanced up at my No Refunds sign but decided not to point. I went around to the back of the machine and flipped it over to automatic. "Let me know when you're finished," I said.

Her stance was awkward, not athletic. She held her elbows at right angles to her body and the bat wobbled high over her head. She didn't swing at the first two balls, which bounced off the padded backstop and danced around her feet. On the third one, she dropped her elbows and swung just enough to tip the ball straight up in the air. She ducked and held a hand over the helmet, like everyone does. The ball landed right next to her.

I figured she'd quit then, but she stood back in. The next three balls she fouled off to the right, making the fifteen-foot wall of chain link quiver. Before long, she was hitting them straight. I went back into the booth and listened. The machine whirred, the ball ejector flapped loudly. Then a brief second of silence before the dink of the ball off aluminum. It went on for nearly an hour.

"I think I'm done now, thanks," she said when she came to the booth. I came out to take the helmet from her and she thanked me again. "I had fun," she said, as if I'd taken her on a date. "Maybe I'll come back tomorrow." She left but reappeared a few seconds later. She stooped down to talk into the money slot and told me her name was Carla. She stood up straight, smiled and waved goodbye.

The letter from Evel Enterprises arrived a few days later, on a Monday. I hadn't opened the cages yet and was inside the arcade, trying to improve on my best score on Missile Commander when my father began swearing so loudly upstairs that the floor shook. It distracted me enough that I lost four cities, each of them vaporized in a noisy mushroom cloud.

My father came down the secret staircase behind the Skeeball machines and popped through the trap door. "A friggin' form letter," he said, handing it to Leo. "Can you believe that."

Evel performed only limited stunts, the letter said, and earned a minimum of $250,000 for personal appearances. "Thanks for being a fan of the greatest daredevil of all time," it closed.

My father fumed. He used his key to get a free game of pinball on the Dr. Wizard machine, the one with the loudest bells and the air horn that belched when a ball dropped past the flippers. He kept the first ball in play for five minutes, slamming the flippers and nearly bouncing the machine off the ground. He let the second one go right past and over the bleating of the horn said he was going to collect weekly rent checks.

Every Monday, he drove his pickup truck along the sand-covered streets, knocking on the flimsy doors. It saved stamps, he said. It took him just about all day but only because he stopped to talk to just about everyone and always had his toolbox handy if something needed to be fixed. The cottages were, by then, being held up by habit, my father said. Most had been built after the Second World War by my grandfather and his friends. Floors creaked. Windows and ceilings leaked in heavy rains. Porches titled to one side.

When he returned that night, it had started to rain again. During dinner, he announced that he'd found the next best thing to Evel Knievel. His name was Dan Jensen and he knocked on the metal screen door as my mother was clearing the table.

He had a shaved head and a goatee and wore a denim jacket with Dan the Man sequined onto the back. He was huge, towering over my father and taking up half the kitchen when he sat. We left them alone to negotiate and before long, we heard the clank of beer bottles that signaled a finalized deal. Dan the Man would attempt to jump over twenty-two bumper cars arranged end-to-end in the Steeves Family Parking Lot on July 15.

We had 100 posters printed and I spent one morning on my bike, tacking them to telephone poles along the beach road and on into town. I put one up in the batting cage booth. Carla, who by then had been coming every day, sometimes just to hang around and watch me work, asked about it the next morning.

"Dan the Man?" she asked. "What happened to Evel Knievel?"

"Retired."

"Oh. Is this guy good?"

"Sure."

"Well, he looks creepy." Carla stooped to look at the picture on the poster. "Hey. I think I've seen him around."

"Maybe he's scouting the area."

She gave me a pursed-lip looked that said she didn't believe me and then slipped a five through the slot in the window. "I think I'll try to hit the little ones today." She waited for me to bring her the batting helmet and then stepped into the fast cage.

"Be careful," I said through the fence. I had stopped pretending not to watch her by then and had even felt brave enough to coach her from time to time. She intimidated me, but I had been practicing—talking to myself in the mirror, working on deepening my voice and standing up straighter. She had an easy, comfortable way of moving through the world, as if anything that happened would be just fine and I wanted to know how she did that.

The fast cage had a quirk: The first ball always came out low and inside, a shin-splitter. I warned Carla, who stepped back to let it pass. "Thanks," she said. She stepped forward and took a couple of easy practice swings. Then she spun her head to wink at me and as she turned back around, the second ball was coming right for her. She managed to get the bat up in time to deflect it, but it still caught her in the face. The helmet rolled away and her sunglasses spun across the concrete. She crumpled to the ground.

I ran down the pathway between the cages and shut the machine off before it could fire any more pitches. By the time I got back, Carla was standing. There was no blood but a red welt on her right cheek, pocked with the fake stitches of the fake baseball.

I opened the cage and gathered up the helmet and her bat. She went and sat on a bench on the sidewalk outside the entrance. I ran home and got her some ice inside a towel.

"I feel pretty stupid," she said when I handed it to her and asked if she was OK.

"Happens all the time," I lied.

Carla spent the rest of that morning inside the booth with me. I didn't know two people could fit in there, but got used to her warm presence quickly. Her breath felt cool against my hot neck and her hair brushed over my shoulder more than once. I avoided eye contact, afraid of what might happen.

I let her add Rule No. 11: Keep Your Eyes On The Ball. I offered to buy her new sunglasses, but she said she didn't need them anyway. "Sun?" she asked and we both laughed. Before she left, she asked me if I was going to the big jump.

We agreed to meet there—she had the night off from work. I

told her there'd be fireworks afterwards. "Maybe," she said. She pecked me on the cheek before letting herself out of the booth.

My father hired some of the Seabrook workers to build the ramps for Dan the Man. They used a pickup truck to line up the bumper cars in the parking lot, a painful scraping sound bouncing off the buildings. A truck brought plywood and two-by-fours. The men hammered and sawed for two full days and when they were done it looked like this was going to happen. Dan painted the ramps red and white himself on a hot afternoon. He took his time, pausing often to step back and look.

The night before the jump, we had another family meeting. Again my mother walked out on us, this time just shaking her head, as if that said enough.

We ran through the details. We'd send some of the summer help into the crowd before the jump with fliers and free passes. When the time came, my father would introduce Dan the Man and then step back and let him do his thing. As soon as the jump was over, Leo would signal for the fireworks to start.

At 11, while we were silently watching a news report about the polar ice caps becoming radioactive, Dan the Man arrived, staggering drunk, asking to talk to my father in private. They went up the stairs to the roof deck, which had a view of the entire beach from the nuclear plant to the north to the Merrimack River to the south.

When they came down, Dan wore a pained expression. "Go get some sleep," my father said, slapping Dan's jacket. Sequins cascaded to the floor, nestled into the carpet fibers.

"He'll be OK," my father said when Dan had gone, though no one asked. "He'll do fine."

The next morning, my father got up from his coffee a dozen times to look out the window onto the strip. I know what he wanted to see: Lines of cars, a traffic jam, people already clamoring for Dan the Man and his death-defying act.

But I now know what he must have seen that morning through tired, worried eyes: An artifact from a time before highways led to Cape Cod, when spending a summer day or weekend or week in Salisbury seemed like a good idea. Did he wish my grandfather was dead, so he could sell it all and move someplace drier, away from the 4 a. m. squawks of seagulls and the salt air that clung to everything metal? Or did he, just for a moment, believe that this day would change things?

That morning, I couldn't tell. To my fifteen-year-old eyes, he seemed in control, still capable of anything he attempted. He rubbed his forehead and sipped loudly from his coffee mug, letting out a long sigh, a breath so deep I felt it across the room.

Outside, weak sun poked through streaky red clouds over the ocean. I hosed seagull crap off the batting cage fences and lined up the bats and helmets. I emptied the coin boxes on all the machines and swept out the entranceway. It was still early and I was fidgety so I walked toward the beach. The garage door to the arcade was half open. The games bleated and dinged, more like warnings than the siren calls they were supposed to be. At the back of the arcade, Leo was playing Skeeball, something I'd never seen him do. Through the tunnel of flashing, beeping games, I watched him hit eight straight fifties, the smooth wooden balls whooshing up the ramp and falling with a thud. Lights flashed, bells sounded and the machine spat out a long curl of tickets.

"Ringer," I said.

He turned and grinned. "I'm saving up for the TV." Our favorite inside joke. On a shelf over the machines was an empty Sanyo TV box. To get it, you needed 150,000 tickets. Even if someone played as well as Leo, it would take nearly 800 games to win the set, which had been in my bedroom since I was nine. At fifty cents a game the $200 TV would cost the best player twice that much to win.

Leo folded the tickets over and put them into the pouch of his apron. "Strange day," he said, looking out. From the back of the arcade, dark and cool, the day looked brighter than usual. "I thought it would rain."

"Not today," my father sprung up through the trap door. "No rain today." He sped off into the arcade, circling past every machine to make sure they were all working. He pushed the door the rest of the way up, stepped onto the sidewalk, turned around and looked up at the faded sign that said "Penny Arcade." He fished in his pocket, pulled out a quarter and approached the Truth Teller located just inside the door. That machine had always frightened me, probably because it contained the realistic head of an old Gypsy woman. Lady Truth sprang to life when the quarter rattled into place. The head moved almost imperceptibly up and down, as if nodding off to sleep. Then the tiny ticket carrying the fortune was spit into a tray. My father reached down for it, read it, shook his head and tore it in half.

By late afternoon, the beach was noticeably busy. Cars lined the Beachway and people marched past the cages with purpose, their eyes and imaginations focused on the beach ahead. But some had stopped and all three cages were full when Carla arrived around noon.

She announced that they had decided to close the restaurant for the jump, then stay open extra late afterwards. "If he makes it, everyone is going to get a free drink," she said.

I told her he'd make it as if I believed it. I remembered what Dan the Man looked like the night before, his eyes big and glassy, his big body moving nervously. I apologized to Carla for the cages being full. She shrugged and said she might hang around for a while anyway. She went around the booth and watched the kids in the cages, their fathers shouting advice with every swing. She spun back around and said she had to go and she jogged away.

By eight, the Beachway was packed with spectators. People hung off the twenty-foot fence around the parking lot. Others had climbed up onto the rollercoaster, only to be shooed away by the police and my uncle. A line had formed at the cages and I enforced a two-token-per-person limit to keep things moving. In between customers, I stuffed cash into my shorts pocket, eager to get home and count it all.

A sound system my father had set up near the jump site played loud heavy metal—Dan the Man's choice—and the crowds had begun to fill the Beachway, setting up lawn chairs and pulling cold beer from coolers. The sun had started to set across the marsh but milky daylight still hung over everything.

At eight-thirty, Carla appeared at the booth.

"Andrew," she said, bending down to talk to the slot. "This is Greg." Standing beside her was a lanky 20-year-old, a prototype right-handed pitcher. He wore the same sunglasses that Carla had and I almost laughed at him.

"He came down from Portsmouth when he heard about the jump on the radio." Carla smiled up at him and then looked down at me. She must have seen the disappointment in my eyes, because she softened her own just enough to tell me she was sorry.

Greg slid me a twenty. I counted out four tokens. "Keep the change," he said shrugging, looking at Carla out of the corner of his eye. He scooped up the tokens and left the sixteen dollars sitting in the tray. I looked at it for a long time before taking it back and cramming it into my pocket.

After listening to Greg connect with every ball shot at him, I locked the cages at quarter to nine and found my way through the crowd to the barricade near the jump ramps. I waved to my father, who was pacing and didn't see me, then ducked under the yellow tape and ran between the hot spotlights. I stood near my father for a long time before he noticed me.

"He's not here," he said to me finally. When I looked puzzled, he said: "Dan the fucking man is not here."

Leo had already been sent to find him. His cottage had been cleaned out and his motorcycle was gone. My father paced some more.

It was after nine then and people had begun to chant "Dan the Man" in unison. At least a thousand people lined the beach road, a sea of unfriendly faces. People had climbed the fences around the batting cages for a better view. Others had gotten inside and were trying to make the machines work. For the first time, I knew my father would be the last Steeves to entertain people at the beach. I felt a tinge of regret for what I would eventually do, but when I looked at my father, he looked at me with sorry eyes, the kind of look Carla had just given me. The look said he knew he had disappointed people in front of me. That he was sorry for disappointing me.

My father signaled to Leo to start the fireworks and when the first trio of red-white-and-blue sparks exploded over the marsh, the crowd let out a collective groan. My father took me by the arm and pulled me back, away from the crowd and into the shadows behind the spotlights. We met my uncle and grandfather behind the old amusement park entranceway and stood there, watching.

For a second, I turned to look at the ramps and tried to remember the mechanics of jumping from my dream, when it seemed so easy, a matter of floating on air. How had I forgotten about gravity? I could no longer imagine how it could work at all.

Pete Duval

REAR VIEW

I drink nine and a half glasses of Chardonnay in the bar at the Hyatt. Now I am behind the wheel of my brother-in-law's Nissan Pathfinder. Near a building in Denver with zebra stripes and no windows, I pull to the curb. We are lost. The building is a strip club letting out because it's two o'clock in the morning. Nearby, the door of an idling charter bus welcomes dazed patrons. Three people are staring at me—two men and a woman between them. I think she is smiling. She walks over to the car. Can we give them a ride downtown? she asks. Keeping her face in my field of vision is a challenge, like talking to a balloon in a breeze. I ask her where Pete's Kitchen is. Pete's Kitchen? she says. She seems relieved. It's right on the way. I turn to my brother-in-law. I see him once, sometimes twice a year. He is a lawyer. We live in different states. He confided to me an hour ago at the Hyatt over a game of nine-ball that he has never masturbated, not once in his life. I asked him if he was serious. He told me he was. I told him I could not keep my hands off myself.

He says to let the three people in. The three people get in.

My brother-in-law is married to my wife's sister. He and I are still

---

Pete Duval's work appears in *Ascent, Chelsea, Grain, Northwest Review,* and *Sonora Review.* His story, "Still Life," won the 1997 World's Best Short Story contest.

what some people might refer to as young men. But those people are fewer and fewer, and once my brother-in-law told me he hoped he had not already fallen prey to a form of *insidious domestication*. He used those words, his eyes a little moist. It was another late night. We had stayed up playing Scrabble. It was Christmas Eve. The in-laws were asleep. There was a blizzard. We were on the way to the river-boat casino in Rock Island, Illinois, where we would lose several hundred dollars and my brother-in-law's eyes would grow moister still. But maybe it was only *accommodation*, he was saying, maybe just a *temporary accommodation*. Jesus! he said, I made wheat bread last weekend, in one of those white appliances! But the way in which he tells me to tell these people to get into his Nissan Pathfinder tonight is his way of letting me know he knows I know we are really at core still open, *radically* so, to whatever raw contingency crass hap is apt to dish up. Tonight we are not mortgage holders. We are not fathers. Stretching out before us is not a life spent on the telephone in beige-carpeted offices during the cool of the day, leaving only after dark. We are noir heroes. We are drifter existentialists. We are in Denver for our other brother-in-law's wedding, ten hours hence.

The people slide into the back seat, and I pull away from the curb. The Pathfinder shows 2,532 miles. It is the newest vehicle I have ever driven. The man sitting behind me leans forward. He has his arm around the woman's neck beside him. Yo, he says, I own these.

It is not immediately apparent what he means though I can smell his breath, an aroma of peppermint schnapps and jalapeños.

He says, These are my titties.

My brother-in-law looks at me. I look at my brother-in-law. He keeps what hair he has left close-cropped. He looks like a lawyer. The top of his head is sunburnt and shiny. Behind us the man is pinching the woman's breasts now with both hands and jimmying his stubbled chin into the crevices of her neck. She writhes and she slaps at his hands. I can see it all in the rear view.

I made twenty bucks a pop tonight dealing sneak peeks at these titties, the man says. Over four hundred bucks. He reaches into his breast pocket. See this? he says. He holds a roll of bills with a thick elastic band around it up to the light.

The man on the other side of the woman slurps drool back into his mouth. Get your sneak peeks at these sweet teats, he says. He may have an accent or he may have a speech impediment. We glide past a closed-out Caldor's and a weedy lot with an overflowing dumpster. Stray greyhounds stand around chomping garbage. The mountains are invisible somewhere. My wife sleeps in a king-sized bed back at the Hyatt. She is drifting away from me, toward dawn.

Where are you boys from? the woman asks. The complex glare from store windows and the street lamps moving over us play hide-and-seek with her facial features. I try to concentrate. All I can tell is she has blonde hair.

He's from Iowa, I say.

There's nothing there, says the guy with the accent. 'Cept a fuckload of corn. He is shaking his head. He is breathing loudly through his nose.

Sure, I say, he's an officer of the corn.

Fucking stupid, says the titty provender.

The woman leans forward with her hands on the head rests. What's your names?

I'm Bob and he's Jim, my brother-in-law says. It is a lie.

Oh fuck you guys, the woman says. You're full of shit.

I look at my brother-in-law. He does not look at me. He is recovering from a cringe. His shoulders are slumped. His eyes are round and worried. Everything about him asks, What have we done?

Fuck you fucking liars.

But why? I say. We are stopped at a red light. A Cadillac from the 1960s traverses the intersection in front of us.

Piss-poor, she says. You can't lie any better than that?

Common enough names, I say.

Yo. The titty proprietor leans forward. Yo. You guys want to see these titties?

I wait. Then I speak. I speak for myself and I speak for my brother-in-law, this attorney who has never masturbated. No, I say, that's all right. I angle onto the main thoroughfare. I am trying not to hurry. The street is almost completely void of traffic. Hey, we're cool.

The woman laughs. You guys ain't cool, let me tell you.

There is a short silence into which the drooling guy snickers. These fucking guys, he says, slapping the back of my brother-in-law's seat.

No, but really, says the titty provender. You want to see them?

I look into the mirror. We're all set, I say. I crank as much gratitude as possible into my tone. We're doing just fine, I say.

For free, he says, in exchange for your refreshing hospitality.

The woman hears what is playing on the seventies music radio station. Hey, Jim, she says, turn this up.

I turn it up.

No, louder, she says.

I turn it up louder. Chaka Khan is singing *Tell Me Something Good*. I can not help but to dig the funky riffs. In eerie falsetto, the woman sings along:

> *Your pro-blem is you ain't been loved like you should.*
> *What I got to give will sure 'nough do you good.*

The drooler seems to be playing air bass. The other man is pounding the door handle to the beat. They are breathing in and they are breathing out, fast, just like Chaka's backup singers in the song, a breathy chorus.

Jesus, that's good, the provender says. But no, really, I want to treat you guys. In the rear view mirror his head is haloed, his uncombed hair glistening with the white headlights of a following car. I do not say anything.

Don't go making me mad by refusing my generosity like that, Jim. Hey, Bob? Come on, are you telling me you don't think she's fine? I mean, look at her.

The woman preens, her lips in an exaggerated pout.

I look at my brother-in-law. He does not look at me. I have never been to Denver before.

I'm offering you a twenty-dollar free gift right now—forty, really, when you think about it—and you're snubbing me. You're saying fuck you. I mean, are you guys for real? Help me understand something here.

The drooler hacks up some phlegm. He rolls down his window, spits into the breeze, rolls it back up. Fucking Jimmy and Bobby, he says. Ingrates.

I am not sure what to say, so I say, We would, but we're married.

The back seat of the Pathfinder explodes with laughter. You're married? says the woman. So? We're married, me and him—not to each other. Her eyes glow in a bright rectangle of reflected light. She has her arm around the administrator of her womanly trust. We're all married, she says. Everybody's married. See this asshole here? She slaps the drooling man with the back of her hand. He snickers. He's married too—you should meet his wife. Don't be thinking that saying you're married is like some magic wand you can wave at us to stop us from busting your balls.

OK, I say. I do my best to laugh. I hear what you're saying, I say. My brother-in-law does not move. Faint waves of nausea have been lapping up against me for some time. It is the wine. We are a mile up. I realize the need for air. I roll my window down and begin to swallow mouthfuls of humid air.

What's the matter, Jim? the woman asks. You don't look well.

Look, I'm going to ask you fuckers one more time, says the provender. You want to see my titties here or not?

I wait. I wait some more. I wait another second. Then I speak. Well, I say, all right, let's see them.

Show time, he says, rubbing his hands together. I watch in the rear view as he reaches behind to unhook her bra. I watch the woman settle herself in the seat, toss her hair, and lift her shirt up to her chin, a white Nirvana concert T, and there they are, what the hoopla has been about: her small bare breasts strobed by passing street lamps, her nipples gray-green in the straining light.

Look at that, the provender says. Just *look* at that.

I feel nothing.

Hey, Bob? he says. What do you think? My brother-in-law's damp forehead is pressed to the Pathfinder's passenger side window. He has shut his eyes. His neck is sunburnt. In the light an artery there is jumping to the rhythm of his heart. Bob, says the titty provender, I'm not going to ask you again, Bob. You don't know what you're missing. Hey, asshole, the world is passing you by.

Jennifer Carr

PHOTO BY THE BED

Your mother hands me photos from your childhood like a test. "Which one is Alec?" she says, tapping the edge. I study the faces of you and your twin, both round, both framed with dark hair, eyes squinted with smile. Your face is almost wider, your nose not quite as long, but what clues me in is that you're always leaning forward. You're the one reaching for the camera, or ready to jump from the frame. You have three minutes and forty-five seconds of seniority on this earth, and you knew it even then. I pick you successfully and the day continues, Easter or birthday, the day continues.

When she visits, she picks up the frame on the nightstand. In the picture, your father is laughing. A beard, John Lennon glasses, a bandana pushing back his hair, then dark. He is a man with two young boys, a man that does not yet know the pain of his wife's affair, the pain of growing to be the father of only a house. His own parents will be dead in two years. He is the age we are now.

In the picture, you stand with your twin in front, five years old.

Jennifer Carr's work has appeared in *Prairie Schooner, Fish Stories, The Nebraska Review*, and *Columbia: A Journal of Literature and Art*.

You're both wearing those striped railroad caps we all wore—I was wearing too, five hundred miles and seventeen years away. She hands me the picture, and this is no test, this is the photo by the bed. I point to you and your mother shakes her head, points to your brother. You nod in confirmation. "No," I tell her, then immediately quiet, frightened I've been loving the wrong face, searching the wrong face, searching the one in the white shirt these years for signs of you.

Alison Dunavan Clement

SALT LICK

My sister, Evaline Fooshee, is an old maid and old maids are not like other women. Old maids think about sex all the time—from lack of sex, they think about nothing else and thinking of nothing else, they notice it even if it ain't there and if it *is* there, why they smell it out, like dogs, with their noses in the air. Sniff sniff.

And Evaline, from lack of sex, from being an old maid, from being alone and knowing she always will be alone, it is her destiny to be alone, from those things, she has turned secretly mean. Nobody can see it but me. In Palmyra you get stuck with what you were. What you were is all you are and all you'll ever be. So Evaline, she is stuck with being nice and nobody but me will ever see different.

Evaline has her eyes on Mama's handyman, Billy Roebuck, and she will do what she can to try and get him. She don't understand how guys like Billy, they don't go for horsy, sweet girls even if those girls *can* cook a fine chicken dinner. You can go down to the store and buy yourself a chicken dinner, if a chicken dinner is what you want. They got other kinds of appetites.

Alison Dunavan Clement's work has appeared in *High Country News* and *The Sun*. "Salt Lick" is excerpted from her novel, *The Queen of Palmyra*.

Evaline won't leave me be. If I am at Mama's house, she is right beside me. If I am inside, she is there too. If I go out, she is next to me. One day I set out from Mama's to go to Aunt Babe's Cafe and Evaline won't take no for an answer but she has to go too. She brings along her little dog, Foxie.

"We all like Billy Roebuck," Evaline says, walking along.

"We sure do."

"Billy Roebuck is a good worker," she says. He works two jobs, one for Mama and the other for Aunt Babe.

"Yes, he is."

"He's a nice-looking man too," Evaline adds.

"No mistake about that."

"Course, looks aren't everything."

"No, they're not," I agree.

"Beauty is as beauty does."

"You're right there, sister."

Evaline isn't looking at me while we walk. She's watching Foxie, who's running ahead of us and going down alleyways and coming back and running up people's porches and hiding behind their shrubs. She can't take her eyes off that dog.

"A town like this one," Evaline says, "people find out anything that happens."

"In this town," I say, "people know more about you than you know your own self."

And she laughs, but it is a nervous laugh. She throws another stick for Foxie and Foxie chases it. She stops to look at Mrs. Runel's cherry tree.

We're at the edge of town now and there is the highway and, across it, I can see Babe's Cafe. I can see the sign and Billy's truck parked out front, with all the windows rolled down. I don't say nothing now, I am hurrying to get there. Evaline is walking behind me.

The parking lot at Babe's is full. I open the front door and hear Evaline, behind me, talking to Foxie, "You sit, girl!" and we go inside.

It's lunch time and all the tables are taken, but we don't sit at the tables anyhow. We walk on by the tables saying, "Hey there!" because this is Palmyra and everybody knows everybody else in Palmyra. It's hot inside, even hotter than outside, and everybody is talking loud and smoking cigarettes. The windows are open and you can hear traffic going past on the highway outside.

I sit at the counter and Evaline sits next to me. We've got summer skirts on and no stockings, sandals, and blouses without sleeves. I can feel the heat from my thighs, where they lay close to each other. I can feel the heat from my arms, where they touch against the sides of my body. And the heat on the back of my neck, and the wetness there, where my hair hangs down. Everywhere that anything touches, it's hot and wet.

I lean my naked arms on the counter and look across the room at Billy Roebuck. Billy is standing, kind of slouched, with the yellow, tobacco-stained wall behind him, and Lester Egree across from him with a plate of eggs, leaning forward, trying to get what Billy's saying. His face like it must be a joke, ready to laugh. I can hear the sound of Margery Johnson's voice on top of all the other ones, the trucks going by on the highway outside. I can smell cigarettes and fried bacon and hamburgers.

"I'd like a chocolate malt," calls Evaline, and Billy moves over to us.

"I got something for *you*," he says to me, and he goes through the swinging doors and into the kitchen. When he comes back, he's carrying the biggest piece of pie you ever saw and he sets it on the counter. Everybody in Aunt Babe's is calling out they want something, but he's ignoring them. "Lemon meringue," he says.

I pick up the fork to take a bite and, while I open my mouth, Billy's standing there, watching. My lips close over the pie and I can taste the lemon on my tongue and all the time Billy's looking at my mouth.

Someplace Margery Johnson's voice is yelling, "Can't nobody get a refill around here?" but Billy doesn't move. He's acting like I'm the only one in the whole restaurant, him and me. Like Evaline and Margery Johnson and all the rest of them are someplace else, instead of yelling out how they want something.

I run my tongue over my lips.

Billy's still watching my face.

I can hear Margery. "Goddamn it, Babe, you better get some help around here!" she's yelling so Babe can hear, clear back in the kitchen.

"Billy!" whispers my sister and Billy looks up.

"Right," he says, looking around, and then he walks away and starts giving people coffee and taking their orders, refilling their waters, handing them plates of food, while I sit, eating my pie. I pat my mouth with the edge of my napkin and then I look down at the print my lips have made on it. I slide the napkin across the counter and leave it there so it's the shape of my lips in red, looking up at Billy.

"He's a good-looking man," says a voice behind me, and I twist around on my stool to see Mavel Runels and Eliza March standing behind us.

"He sure is," says Evaline.

We all turn to him now, as he moves towards us with Evaline's chocolate shake. He isn't like nobody any of us have ever seen. He stops in front of us and slides the shake to Evaline. He is busy but he isn't hurrying.

Mavel and Eliza are standing behind us, with dollar bills in their hands. Billy sees the money and he starts writing in his little notebook, adding up their food.

Mavel leans in between me and Evaline. She says, "You are one *hardworking man*," and she bats her little eyes. "I see your pickup down at the Fooshee's house day and *night*, seems like."

Before Billy can answer, Evaline jumps in, "I never seen a man who could do the work Billy Roebuck can. Oh, and Mama—she's got him working like a dog."

Billy tears the bill out of his little pad and hands it over to Mavel. He is smiling like he has a secret they don't know and, even if he told them, they still wouldn't get it.

Mavel's got her eyes fixed on Billy and her smile is stretched from one side of her face to the other. "Must be hard to work in the dark," she says. She's got her red lipstick on.

Mavel feels me looking at her. I'm looking at her lips, how she's used a brush to make them bigger than what they are. She can feel my nasty thought and now she twists her face around to mine.

"You sure aren't spending much time at your *own* house, Lucy," she says to me.

"Lucy is such a help to Mama," says Evaline, but they know better than that.

"Must be hard to keep up a house as big as the Bybee house." Mavel smiles at me with her big yellow teeth. "All that dusting!"

"And you never there to do it . . . " throws in Eliza.

"There's the garden . . . " says Evaline, but Mavel interrupts.

"I heard," says Mavel, bending forward even more so now we are looking at the tops of her white breasts, "that your mother-in-law is throwing a hissy fit!"

"You're not keeping that house up, is what everybody is saying," says Eliza, quickly. "They say you're always at your Mama's house. You and Billy Roebuck, both!"

"You know how people talk," says Mavel.

Nobody says nothing. Evaline and me are turned in our seats. Billy is stopped in front of us. The girls, Mavel and Eliza, standing behind us, Mavel tilting forward, showing off her little breasts. It's like a game of freeze and someone has called out, "Freeze!" and that is how we each wound up. I've got a fork full of lemon meringue in front of my face and my mouth just starting to open. I could get myself a low-cut shirt and push my breasts up, if I wanted, if I needed to show off like that, I could, I'm thinking, but I don't. Only reason I don't is I don't want to.

But Evaline is not thinking of Mavel's breasts and she laughs a phony laugh and tosses her hair back like she is being casual and she says, "They can't stay away from my cooking!"

I can hear people in the diner shouting, calling out articles of food or names of condiments but we ignore them.

"You know it's the way to a man's stomach," says Evaline, and she reaches across the counter and sets her hand on Billy's arm. And Billy, he doesn't shake it off. He doesn't look surprised but he stands there, calm, like he ain't surprised by that hand, creeping like an old snake on him. Maybe it's been there before, is what his face says.

Mavel and Eliza are just shocked by the notion of my sister, Eva-line, setting her hand on the arm of someone like Billy Roebuck. You don't go doing that out of the blue, they are thinking. They stand there, pale and outraged. Evaline Fooshee! Of all the people! Well, they are thinking, *this goes against all reason.*

And when it is too much for me—when I can't bear it and I start to open my mouth to set them straight, Evaline's other hand travels over to my leg, secretly, and gives it a pinch.

"Billy, would you bring me and my sister a BLT, split in two?" Evaline says, smiling, and fluttering her eyes, and he turns back to work.

"Too bad he don't have any prospects," says Mavel, once he is out of earshot.

She is dying of jealousy because of that little hand of Evaline's touching his arm. She is dying, but it is for the wrong thing.

"Or good family, neither," adds Eliza.

If they could only see what me and Billy do together they would lay down on the floor of Babe's diner and they would just stop breathing. If they could see what my hands have done. If they could look at my mouth and tell where it's been. Oh, they would curl up and die. And I think to myself it is like I have won the Miss Universe contest but I can't tell nobody about it.

Mavel and Eliza finally leave and it is just me and my sister, together, saying nothing.

I eat my pie. I smash it up with the fork so it is all mushed together, flat and yellow, and I eat it. Evaline, beside me, drinks her chocolate shake and she doesn't say a word. We don't look at Billy when he walks by us. We look straight ahead.

Finally I say, "If you got out more, Evaline, maybe you really *could* find yourself a boyfriend."

But she doesn't answer.

"Lot of girls don't get married until they are even older than you are, but you can't find a husband staying at home."

"I don't care about getting married," she says.

"Sheila Garber didn't get married until she was thirty-two."

"I'm not worried."

"Look at Cheryl Lee, how she got married and her with that big nose."

"From the look of other people's marriages, I might be doing myself a favor staying single," she says.

"You just keep telling yourself that," I say, licking my fork.

Evaline picks up the menu then and sets it on the counter in front of her and she starts reading it, like she hasn't seen it a million times before. I ignore her. I eat my pie slow now and I look around. I look at all the people in Aunt Babe's and it is like they are strangers and not people I walked among all my life.

"You don't really think he likes you," I say, low. "You don't *really* think so."

I wait but she doesn't say what she thinks. She leans forward like this is the good part of Aunt Babe's menu and she can't miss a word of it.

I poke my fork in my pie. It is flat and all smashed together. "It may be true for some men that the way to their heart is through their stomachs but . . . "

"Would you shut up!" she hisses. And Evaline never says a thing like that so I do shut up, I shut right up.

Evaline has got to the end of her shake now and she makes little slurping noises, getting the last of it, and I start to say to her how she ought to go easy on the milk shakes—think of Mama, I start to say—but I stop myself. If she wants to wind up looking like Mama, then let her go ahead.

Billy brings the BLT to us, on two plates, but he doesn't look at me when he does it. He walks off and he starts doing the next thing. He has got a white T-shirt on and his hair wet with sweat brushed back from his face and he has got a apron on and in his back pocket, a rag for wiping down counters. His back is to us and I'm watching his neck and I'm thinking how it's like a salt lick somebody has left in the woods and I'm a little deer, just come up on it.

Pretty soon some people come up, Raymond Huff and his

cousin, they come up and start talking to us and for one second Evaline forgets about me. I sit smiling at them, next to Evaline who is smiling too, and I see, from the corner of my eye, Billy going back into the kitchen, the doors swinging shut behind him.

"Excuse me, I have to use the rest room," I say, and I follow after him.

Billy's in the kitchen, talking to Aunt Babe. She's standing at the grill. She's got about two dozen eggs on that grill, all cooking at once, and when she looks up to see me, she jumps in surprise.

"I came to use the rest room," I say. The rest room is through the kitchen. I can see the door from where I stand, but I don't move towards it.

Aunt Babe looks from Billy to me and then back to Billy again. She doesn't know what to do.

"Billy," she says, looking at him, searching his face.

Billy looks back at her and then she wipes her hands on her apron, takes the little note pad Billy is still holding in his hand, and goes out through the swinging doors.

I know what he's going to tell me. He's going to say I can't behave like this. I'm going to ruin everything. I can't make a scene in public. What will everybody say. But I'm sick to death of thinking of everybody else and what they will say.

"Hey," I say, which is like saying hi or saying hello when you come from Palmyra. We say hey.

Billy looks over at the grill at all them eggs cooking away. He moves over to them now, and picks up the spatula, and I move with him so we're both standing at the grill. The heat is coming off it and the smell of eggs and grease.

"Billy," I say, just to feel the feel of it in my mouth and he looks at me, at my mouth and then at my eyes and then back down at all the eggs, their yellow yolks sticking up, staring right back at him. He starts flipping the eggs over, one and the other, the next one, the next, all in a line, and he doesn't break a one.

"You ever had a dream that's so real you can't tell it from the truth?" I say.

I'm watching his chest how it moves up and down with his breathing and how now it's moving like he's been running, like he's been lifting heavy things, like he's really working hard, instead of just holding a little metal spatula and flipping eggs over easy, and I know he's breathing like that because of me and my breathing is the same.

He looks over at me and he's going to say for me to go on out now. I lean forward to hear him, over the sound of the refrigerator and the stove and all the little motors in there, and the sound of the eggs, cooking. I lean forward. He's going to say everybody out there is waiting. Everybody out there will know. They're watching the clock. Everybody in town will hear. And then he shuts his mouth again.

He sets the spatula down and looks at me. He looks at one thing at a time: at my eyes, at my forehead, at my mouth and then he takes his hand and brushes the hair back from my face where it's fallen, and looks at me like he hasn't seen me before and he puts his finger on my lips and traces their outline, first one and then the other, and he slips his fingers into the side of my mouth where it's pink and warm, and I taste the salt from his finger and he kisses me but he doesn't take his finger away but kisses me over it and when he pulls his mouth away the finger is still there only now he moves it from the side of my mouth down to the bottom and he traces my line of teeth and then the line of my jaw and then his hand moves to my hips and pulls me towards him and I fall forward into him and we stand like that, with our hands moving back and forth on each other and I can't tell where I'm touching him and where I'm touching myself and I begin to sob, that's the only word for it, sob, big gasps of sobs and tears and I'm saying, "Oh, oh," and the door flies open and it's Aunt Babe but I can hardly understand that: that now Aunt Babe is here. She's shoveling the eggs from the grill as fast as she can. They're burnt on one side. I can smell it.

"Damn it, Billy. Damn it," she's saying but whether it's about the eggs or me, I can't tell.

Joshua Braff

MAGGOTS IN THE RICE

Uncle Lloyd says he spent two tours in "Nam" and that's why he's allowed to sit in front of the TV all day in his flannel shirts and long johns, yelling out prices on the game shows and slurping from a soup bowl like he's alone. He told me someone named Charlie put a grenade in his flak jacket and if he hadn't had the balls to grab it and toss it like a hook shot, he'd be eating his soup through a tube in his neck. Mama says her brother's always been a storyteller but I've only known him since Tuesday. He does have a scar that circles his pink left ear and darts down his cheekbone in jags near the dimple in his chin. It's purplish-red and deep and I can see the thread marks of the stitches that once held his face closed. He showed up late at night, past two A. M., leaning on our squealing intercom and saying "Ho, ho, ho" like a drunken Santa Claus. Lulu got scared, started rockin' back and forth and moaning like she does while Mama waited for him to climb the five floors. "Shut your mouth now. It's just my brother Lloyd," she told us, squinting from a deep sleep, clutching her satin bathrobe closed with her fist.

Joshua Braff's work has appeared in *New Voices in Poetry and Prose*. This is his second appearance in *Alaska Quarterly Review*.

Before Uncle Lloyd showed up that night, it was just Lulu and me. And Mama, of course. Our couch is a pull-out so me and Lulu had room to sleep and move our legs around without bumpin' each other all night long. But now we're in Mama's room, like a can of crushed sardines, and I can hear the TV late at night and my story-tellin' Uncle Lloyd giggling at the mumbled monologues, picking at the hard dead skin on his ugly toes. In the morning I'll walk out there just like the last two days and the TV'll still be on and Uncle Lloyd will be breathing heavy, sleeping with his chin dropped wide. When I turn the set off he'll blink his eyes awake and make a sticky sound with his lips and dried out tongue. "I want that on, Lorna," he'll groan before he yawns and turns his back to me, scrunching his knees to his chest like a fetus in a jar.

Lulu won't sleep if I'm not next to her and Mama won't let her in bed with her 'cause she pees while she dreams almost every night. Lulu wears a diaper even though she's twelve but Mama says it leaks and hates the rubbery smell of the elastic that's supposed to keep the pee locked in. Mama scrunches her nose, says the diapers smell like "vomit on a Twister board," makes her throat tighten up when she hears them crinkle. Just talking about it gets her forehead hot and makes her pat her pockets for her smokes. Lulu only needs them for bed but nothing gets Mama as mad as Lulu does. When my sister gets crazy, starts bitin' her hands or rocking and moaning like she will, Mama's lips turn white and stiff and her chin juts out. I always look for one blue vein in her neck that looks as thick as cable wire, like it's gonna pop and soak us all with her boiling blood. I tell Mama to calm down in my softest voice but know better than to touch her. I tell her that Lulu can't help it. Remind her every time. Mama usually leaves the apartment. She heads off for dollar shots at Tino's, comes home late and happy, whistling out of tune. I'll hear her fumbling her keys outside the door and when she gets in she'll say, "Sleepin'?" as she passes by me and Lulu on the pull-out. I fake sleep, thinking she'll be quieter and not wake Lulu if she has no one to talk to. But she'll sit down on the end of the bed anyways, start apologizing for all her ranting and the things she wished she didn't say. I breathe steady and easy like a person really sleeping. But I listen. I listen to every remorseful word. And the gentle-kind tone she uses just after Tino's last call.

Mama keeps a Betty Boop shot glass tucked inside her panty drawer, along with a fifth of Beam she calls Uncle James. When she's done confessing she'll kiss us both on our heads before going in her room. I listen for the twangy sad tunes from her record player and just know she's got Betty out, filling her to the rim. Mama says Lulu makes her drink more than she wants to but I think blaming Lulu is wrong. I want to tell her that Ms. Tamms says that Fragile X is something you inherit and the mother of the child is the carrier, the one that passes it on. But Mama says she feels sick whenever she hears the word retardation. She made me promise that if anyone asked, we'd say Lulu got sick when she was a baby. I've heard her tell it like we practiced a hundred times. Spent two weeks in quarantine. Doctor said she'd die. Slept in a bed of ice. A miracle she's alive. A miracle. When Mama's music ends, the needle bumps softly in the very last groove of the album side. It means she's sleeping, and I can sleep too.

With smelly Uncle Lloyd in town, me and Lulu sleep on the floor at the foot of Mama's bed. The first night it reeked like dust and dead mice down there. I mopped it up in the morning and almost gagged at how black the water turned. The next night I wrapped me and Lulu up in every blanket I could find and Mama let us drag in the rug from the living room that she says comes from China. She told me the man that gave it to her was as rich as the Pope and once gave her a necklace made of violet rubies and some dangling earrings that matched. She says they got stolen the day she gave birth to me but I can tell when she's lying 'cause she's says "It's true" over and over and nods her head too much. I guess the man who gave her the rug was either Troy or Gill, or the one with the rat-tail mustache who said I looked like Pocahontas and laughed 'til he coughed. But I know better than to pry too hard. I keep my guessing to myself.

Mama gripped my shoulders the night we brought the rug in her room and stared into my eyes. She told me it was the only thing she had that was oriental and that if anyone pissed on it, she'd go fuckin' crazy and have to kill us with her hands.

"I ain't gonna pee on it, Mama."

"I mean *Lulu*, Lorna. I mean your *sister*."

I looked down at the rug with all its colorful swirls and vase-like shapes and flowery-curved designs. There's red in there and dull greens and blacks and it feels good to run your fingertips over the short stiff hairs. On each end of the rug are frayed white tassels that look like the hairs of someone's brand-new mop and I like to think about who tied them on there and how far away from here they live. Lulu likes to touch 'em and when Mama slaps her hand away, it makes her want to touch 'em more. I can't see how Lulu peein' in the middle of her sleep has anything to do with me. But I know if it happens, Mama's gonna lash out good, scream her head off while I blot the stain with a sponge. She'll stand over me and whine worse than Lulu, walkin' back and forth until I soak it all up. 'Til she says it's gone.

Mama makes me buy the diapers at the CVS 'cause she's too embarrassed to do it. She says she used to know the manager in high school and doesn't want him to think she's the one wearing them. Whenever it's time to buy a new box she fishes for coins in her tinsel-red purse and reminds me that she was a runner-up for Ms. Danville County when she was just seventeen years old. "Way before Dinwiddie," she always says and points to a black and white picture on her bedside table. In the photograph her hair's in a bee-hive and she has a smile that shows every one of her pearly white teeth. She says her hair was blond in those days, "as blond as Bri-gitte Bardot's," who used to be a famous actress. Mama always reaches up and tugs and pats at her ratty brown wig whenever she talks of those days. I tell her she still looks beautiful because I know she needs to hear it. But she looks like someone else entirely in the picture. She's got the gray skin of a booze-hound now, loose and mushy on her skinny-bone frame. I look at her spine and her hips and her pointy elbows when I hand her a towel after her bath. I can see what she'll be after she's gone and I sometimes wonder if she's trying to leave us, trying to get away. When she's not home I lift the swirly frame off the table and try to see my Mama in the eyes of the beauty queen. But I see Lulu in those eyes more than I see Mama. I used to get crazy-mad that I don't look like them, that my eyes are poop brown, that my hair is black as tar. It says in my social studies book, page 216, that Pocahontas was a princess. It says her Daddy was an Indian chief right here in Virginia over three hundred years ago. Mama says my Daddy was a monster and that's why my hair is so coarse and my nose so long. When she's cold sober she'll touch my hair and tell me my face is "ethnic." She says when I get into high school all the smart boys will think I'm beautiful. But these lies end as soon as the party begins. She'll tell whoever's in the liv-ing room that my Daddy was a big-nosed, stingy Jew and that's why even Lulu is prettier than me. I used to wish my Mama dead when she'd say these things. Her scummy friends with their wasted grins and foggy eyes, laughin' with their hostess, laughin' at me. But when I got older I knew I wouldn't trade my brain for Lulu's for a million dollars, or even more. I watch my sister bang her fore-arm again and again on the moldy cracked tile on the bathroom floor, or watch her nibble on her thumb until her skin cracks and bleeds on her clothes.

Mama told me Lulu's Daddy was an alcoholic who'd drink holy

water if he thought it was spiked. I see a ripple in her jaw when she brings him up, and her tired eyes fill with her thoughts of him. One late night after Tino's, while sitting on the end of our bed, Mama thought I was sleeping and started to cry. "That man left me with more than I can handle" is what she said through her tears and then laid right down where she sat and fell asleep. I know Mama wants to be the person in the photograph, the one with the smile and the long ivory gloves. I know if somehow she could be that person she'd leave us all in a blink and run towards her past, far away from today. I told her I understood about buying the diapers at the CVS. But, inside, I think pretending Lulu isn't her daughter is wrong, and might be as bad as a sin. Ms. Tamms says Fragile X has nothing to do with a man who'd drink holy water. Ms. Tamms says it's Mama who's the carrier. She says it's genetic.

That first night on the oriental rug from China I couldn't sleep. I kept closing my eyes but couldn't stop thinking about Lulu and her leaky diaper and how much trouble this could be. I could hear The Tonight Show and the laughter of the audience in the living room. Uncle Lloyd laughs like a car engine tryin' to turn over in the dead of winter. I laid there wide awake, thinking about him and what he was doing in my bed, wishing he'd just go home, wherever that is. I shook Lulu's shoulder but she didn't wake up. When I shook it a little harder she said, "From China," and looked me in the eyes.

"You gotta tell me when you gotta go, Lulu. You gotta tell me when you feel it inside you, okay?"

"Okay," Lulu said, her sticky long fingers curling around themselves, her eyes half shut.

"Just tap me, Lulu. Just wake me if you feel it, alright?"

Lulu yawned and her eyes blinked closed.

I brushed a long blond strand of hair from my sister's cracked lips, and pulled the blanket up to her chin. "Just wake me."

On Friday afternoon I finished the ninth grade and it was finally time for the summer break. I picked Lulu up at Ms. Tamms' house and gave her tiny white Poodle, Kinko, one of the Hershey's Kisses I got from my homeroom party. Ms. Tamms is blind and very old with sheet-white hair and a mothball smell. But she has more patience for Lulu than anyone I know. She combs her hair and sings her songs from a music book she got at her church. Lulu's favorite is called "Scarlet Ribbons" and she tells Ms. Tamms to sing it to her before we even get in the door. Lulu asks me to sing it too, before she goes to bed each night. I tell her I can't 'cause I don't know the words and besides, I can't sing to save my life. Sometimes when Lulu doesn't know I'm listening, I'll hear her sing it, almost every word. But if I ask her to sing 'em she'll get all quiet and look at me like she's never even heard the song before. I once told Mama that Lulu knew this song because Mama says that Lulu is as "dumb as a doornail" and can't remember the day she was born.

"Come on, Lu," I said, "show Mama how you know all the words."

She just tucked her chin low and mumbled "Scarlet Ribbons" real soft, and that's all.

"You're being cruel, Lorna," Mama said, smiling. "This girl can't learn the words to no song."

"I've heard her do it, Mama. It's about this poor girl who prays to God for some scarlet ribbons for her hair. And one day they just appear from nowhere. Come on, Lu, 'Scar-let Ribbons,'" I sort of sang.

"Scar . . . ," Lulu squeaked with three fingers in her mouth, rocking back and forth on the kitchen floor. And that was all.

Irene, Ms. Tamms' daughter, is the one who put the sign in the laundromat that said "Discount Day Care For The Mentally Handicapped." She says she had a daughter with Down syndrome but she died, I'm not sure how. Even Mama says it's a blessing in disguise that Ms. Tamms and Irene exist. They only charge six bucks a day to watch Lulu Monday through Friday until I pick her up after school. But Mama's never even been to their house, so I don't think she knows what a blessing it is. They live three blocks away on Lurner Avenue, not far from the junior high and the CVS. The house is white with black shutters and flower boxes and looks like a huge doll house from the outside. It's filled with old bird houses and cuckoo clocks and I've never even been on the second floor. Irene says her mother's been a bird-watcher for most of her life. When she first said it I thought she was joking because blindness and bird-watching don't seem a real good match. But she told me that bird-watching is also bird-listening. Irene's a really sweet lady with thick round glasses on a chain that she pushes up on her nose all the time. She wears Sunday dresses almost every day with ruffles around the neck and wrists like she's on her way to church or somewhere special. She asked me to close my eyes one day on her front porch and just listen to the sounds I could hear. She put my hair behind my ears with a gentle stroke of her finger and rested her hands on my shoulders and squeezed. She whispered, "Listen, Lorna," and I did, but thought more about her kind, warm touch than the birds in the trees on Lurner Avenue.

When we get home that day Mama says she got a job at a place called "Thank God It's Friday" and I don't believe her until she says it's a restaurant and that she'll be a waitress in the bar. Uncle Lloyd claps his hands real loud when he hears this and actually stands up from the couch. He tells Mama that things are gonna change around here as soon as his government check catches up to our address. "A new life," he shouts at the ceiling and sticks out his tongue. He holds his hand up to Mama like he wants to high-five but she just flinches and stares at his raised palm. Uncle Lloyd laughs at her with his hands on his bony hips. "Haven't you ever seen a high-five, Lurleen?"

I laugh because Mama's face looks shy and she has to laugh a little too. Lulu flaps her hands like she does when she gets excited and starts jumping enough to make the TV rabbit ears droop.

"Lur*leen*," Lulu shrieks, "*Lurleen!*"

"Now you got her all revved up," Mama says to me and her smile falls from her cheeks.

I tell Lulu to calm down and she screams "Lurleen" over and over 'cause she loves to repeat and I think she knows it makes Mama nuts. Mama's jaw clenches up and she goes into her room and slams the door. Uncle Lloyd stares at Lulu while she jumps and flaps her hands. He lights one of his mentholated cigarettes as he plops back down on the sofa and pats down a few of his floating thin hairs. He exhales a stream of smoke from the corner of his mouth and keeps his eyes pinned on Lulu. She finally stops saying "Lurleen" but then starts making a sound that Mama calls the "stabbed cow." It sounds more like a lawn mower to me, one that never guarantees to turn off. I grip Lulu's forearms and try to look her in the eyes, the way Irene taught me. But she's way too excited. I think it's 'cause she saw Mama smile.

"What you all worked up about now?" Uncle Lloyd says, over the drone of Lulu's voice. He points at the TV with his chin. "I can't even hear my program over that racket. What's your problem, Lulu?"

"She's just excited."

"Now I didn't ask you, Lorna. I asked your sister."

"But she doesn't understand."

"I've heard her say things."

I rub Lulu's back with my palm wide but it doesn't seem to help. "It's okay. She's just excited."

Uncle Lloyd squints at Lulu through his next exhale and stands and walks towards her as she keeps up the moaning mower. I think he smells like he needs a bath and I'm glad he's smoking even though I hate that smell too. He has dark rings under his eyes like a barfly and hasn't shaved his face since he arrived on Tuesday. He changed his shirt a few times but he only has two and the torn, gray long-johns he wears give off a smell that's much worse than Lulu's diaper. I think it's funny that I'm taller than him even though I'm only fifteen. But I won't tell him. He puts the cigarette in his mouth and points with his head for me to move away from my sister. Lulu groans even louder when I let her arms go and reaches for me with her fingers spread stiff and her eyes wide. Uncle Lloyd grabs her forearms like I'd done but I know he's squeezing harder because Lulu glances down at her arms and winces. "Ow," she says.

"You shouldn't squeeze 'em so tight," I say, standing real close and staring at his little fingers pinching her arms.

"Girl like this needs to know she's not in charge."

"She doesn't think that."

Uncle Lloyd snaps his head towards me and my eyes go to the flaky dead skin in his scalp. "And how do you know so much about retards, Lorna. Are you one too?"

"No."

Lulu starts yelling the word "No" over and over and Uncle Lloyd gets a look in his eyes like he might get mean.

"Now, Lulu, listen good. I'm gonna help your Mama lock your ass up if you don't cut this out."

Mama swings her door open, grabs Lulu by the arm and yanks her inside her room.

"Mama, wait," I scream, but the door slams louder than my voice.

I knock hard on the door with my fist, know better than to open it without getting permission first. I can hear Mama slapping Lulu and screaming at her to shut up like she always does. Uncle Lloyd smiles a little and shakes his head as he walks back to the couch. He fixes the rabbit ears on the TV and turns the volume up even louder. There's a soap opera on and I can hear Mama screaming at Lulu during the long silent breaks in the words.

"You gotta let that girl's mother teach her how to behave, Lorna. You ain't that girl's mother."

"I'm her sister," I say, my forehead leaning on the door.

Lulu shrieks and cries inside the bedroom and Mama screams louder to "shut the hell up."

"Why doncha just come on over here, Lorna. You're gonna get your Mama even more pissed off than she is. You watch the Guidin' Light?"

I walk over to the kitchen without looking at Uncle Lloyd and stare out the tiny barred window over the sink. I can still hear Lulu inside the bedroom but I try to think of other things while I count the vanilla-colored bricks on the building next to ours.

"You got a boyfriend?" Uncle Lloyd says, and I can hear the smoke pouring from his lips.

Lulu stops crying and I turn and walk back towards the bedroom.

"Girl as pretty as you. I'll bet you got a few, huh?"

A commercial comes on the TV. It's a song about frozen dinners and Uncle Lloyd knows the words. "You like Salisbury steak?" he asks me, and my Mama's door opens. She comes out alone and walks into the kitchen. She's wearing a maroon shirt with a big, round TGIF button on the pocket and black pants.

"Lorna?"

"Yes, Mama."

"Now that you're done for the summer, I want you to watch Lulu everyday. I can't afford that Ms. Tamms lady if you're gonna be wasting time doin' nothing."

"I thought I'd get a job, Mama."

"Doin' what?" she says and laughs out loud, glancing at Uncle Lloyd.

"There's a Help Wanted sign in the ShopRight window."

Mama opens the fridge and grabs a pack of Marlboro Lights from the butter dispenser. "That ain't gonna work out this time, Honey. I'll give you some money for watchin' her. Uncle Lloyd's gonna be staying a few weeks, helpin' us out. After that, this won't matter anymore."

"What won't matter anymore?"

Mama flashes a look towards Uncle Lloyd and tugs at the bangs of her wig. His eyebrows go up but he pretends to watch the TV, pretends he didn't hear.

"Never mind that now. I need the help, you're out of school, this is how families act."

"But, Mama, what am I gonna do with her everyday? She loves goin' over to Ms. Tamms' and Irene's."

"You'll go to the park. The jungle gym. You told me she likes that, didn't you?" She tosses a white apron over her shoulder and pats my cheek.

Lulu slowly walks out of the bedroom with her chin dipped to her chest. She's eating something chocolate and has it all over her lips and face.

"Get back in there," Mama says with a pointed finger.

"No."

"Get your ass back in that room! You want me to take that Ring Ding back?"

"No."

"Then *get!*"

I grab a napkin and walk towards Lulu, take her by the hand. "We'll go right now, Mama. We'll go to the jungle gym, okay, Lulu?"

Lulu nods with her head still dipped and presses the Ring Ding against her mouth. We walk past Uncle Lloyd but I keep my eyes from him on purpose.

"I'll be home late, Lorna," Mama says. But I've already shut the door, before she can even say my name.

I sit on a bench in the park and watch Lulu stare at the other kids climbing on the jungle gym and pumping their knees on the long chained swings. She sucks on her hand and takes tiny steps towards them like she does every time we come. In a few minutes she'll arrive at the slide and lean against it with her shoulder. She'll lower her head and put her fingers near her mouth like she thinks she can't be seen. She'll glance back at me every few seconds to see if I've left her, I guess. Sometimes she'll wave back when I wave and other times she'll just watch the kids fly down the slide with their mouths wide and their sneakers in the air.

I sometimes pretend Lulu has a normal mind when I watch her in the park. I think about what she might say to me and how we would laugh together just walking down the street. Irene says that Lulu is lucky 'cause she's so pretty and that no one can tell she's got Fragile X from just looking at her face. She says that many times the people who have this syndrome have long faces and large ears, or sometimes their eyes get "lazy" or they have flat feet and heart problems. When Irene asked me if Lulu'd been to a doctor that year I told her with a smile that of course she had, she'd been to a few. But I lied and wasn't sure when the last time Lulu went to the clinic was. I think of this lie a lot. I thought of it when Irene told me that Lulu should be on medicine. Medicine that would make her stronger, make her move and climb better. I think about my lie when I see her finally get over her fears and step up the ladder, onto that long silver slide that ends in the dark wood chips. Last winter I dreamt that Lulu fell off that ladder. Her shoe-tip slipped out from under her and I saw her mouth smash the edge of the metal step. Her top lip got split wide and I saw her blood and teeth sitting there in the chips. Lulu's body was face down on the ground and when I rolled her over I woke up from that dream, my heart throbbing, fear in my throat. And when I saw her next to me on the sofa-bed sleeping like a baby, safe from that fall, I felt a relief that made my eyes fill with tears. When I tried to go back to sleep that night I brought my knees up high and made sure they touched my sister's nightgown, so I'd know where she'd be.

Mama doesn't believe in doctors, says they only get rich because they fill our heads with things, like diseases nobody gets. I told her that Lulu has Fragile X even though I know she knows. I told her that Ms. Tamms and Irene said she should see a doctor but like I said, my Mama'd rather talk about anything than "the syndrome." One night while sippin' her Beam, Mama yelled, "Survival of the fittest," and filled Betty to the rim. "If we were lions, we woulda left Lulu way behind," is what she said next. I told her that's not funny straight into her face, and she told me, "It wasn't meant to be," and to "watch my tone."

"Lorna," Lulu screams from the top of the ladder with her eyes wide, gripping the bars at her side.

"I see you," I say and stand from the bench.

She lowers her butt to the slide with her arms over her head, her hands still pinned to the rail. I can see her belly button 'cause her T-shirt is hiked up and I say, "Let go, Lulu, let go of the rail." She looks panicked for a second but then opens her hands and slides down the chute with huge eyes, pure joy. When she lands in the wood chips she laughs with her eyes squeezed shut and her fingers and legs splayed in frozen disbelief. I walk over to the end of the slide and put my hand out for her to grab.

"Did you see me, Lorna?" she asks me, and I tell her I did. She puts her hand in mine and I tug her to her feet. So many times when I look in her bright face I wonder whether she knows who she is, who she'll always be. Lulu runs back to the ladder and starts to climb again. I'll wait for her at the bottom this time. I'll be there when she comes down.

Before I put the key in the door I can already hear the TV and I know I'll see Uncle Lloyd sitting on his back with cracker crumbs on the neck of his undershirt. Lulu runs towards the set when she sees the sight of cartoons. She flops down in front with her head tilted back and I tell her once again what Irene says about sitting too close. Uncle Lloyd lifts a paperback off the floor as if to say he wasn't watching the Road Runner doin' his thing. He blocks his face with the open book then splays it on his chest while he pulls a cigarette from a shiny green package with his teeth.

"This place needs some cable, Lorna. You don't know what you're missing."

"Cable costs money."

"Well, I'll help your mother out there. It's why she called me anyhow."

I wash my hands in the kitchen sink and when I cut the water off I hear Lulu giggling at the boops and bops of the zany cartoon world she loves. I walk over to the sofa and Uncle Lloyd is kind enough to move his feet so I might sit. He pulls the green afghan over his bony knees and strikes a match for his smoke.

"My Mama called *you?*" I ask him with my eyes on the TV.

He tosses the book of matches on the floor by a box of Triscuits and I can see the smoke from his mouth pass my view.

"You thought I just showed up here unannounced," he says, and I can feel him staring right at me. "Not my style."

Lulu laughs out loud and turns to see if I saw what made her do so.

"So you're saying Mama called you for money?"

Uncle Lloyd spins on his butt and puts his feet on the floor. He steps into two corduroy slippers with torn brown tips and flicks his ash over the top of a beer can. "She said she was having some thoughts. I told her I might be able to help."

"What kinda thoughts?" I ask, and he stands to turn the volume down.

Lulu reaches for the knob as soon as he sits and turns it up so loud I leap to cut the piercing noise down. Lulu makes a face and screams "Lorna," like I just ruined her whole year. "It's fine," I tell her, "you don't need it so high."

"I want to hear," she says all upset but in seconds settles back into the rhythm of the boops and bops of the Road Runner's day.

Uncle Lloyd takes a deep breath and points his finger at the back of Lulu's head without making a sound. "Those kind of thoughts. Thoughts that might rid your mother of so many . . . *unusual* responsibilities."

I look at him when he says this and I can see behind his silly face that he's been talkin' to Mama about Lulu.

"You understanding my meaning?" he says and wipes something from the corner of his mouth with his thumb.

I turn back to the set and think about how much I hate my Mama sometimes. Lulu laughs again and I pull her back from the TV just an inch or two. "No, I don't think I do."

Uncle Lloyd stands and heads into the kitchen. When he opens the refrigerator I can see his long scar lit in the light of the door. He yanks a can of beer from the plastic six-pack holder and cracks it open before the door shuts closed. "You know what they do to little girls who get born in China," he says plopping back down in the indent he's made in the couch. "Do you?"

I glance at him for a second then face the TV.

"They got a rule over there called the 'One Child Policy.' And that's just what it is, Lorna." He dries his hands on the hips of his long-johns and pulls his legs back up on the couch. "The government in China says you get one shot at having a baby boy. Want to know why? Because *sons* in China take care of their parents when they get too old and can't take care of themselves. Not girls. See what I mean? So baby girls are *useless* in that society. Even healthy ones."

I turn to my Uncle Lloyd and watch him pull from his can of Schlitz. He dabs his sleeve to his lips and pulls the afghan back over his legs. "So . . . it don't matter if you're rich or famous or have a best friend who guards the Great Wall, see. You have a baby girl in China, the first thing you got to do is get rid of it."

"Lorna? Lorna?"

"What, Lulu?"

"I'm hungry."

"We'll eat soon."

"I'm hungry, Lorna."

"Watch the TV, we'll eat soon."

"Do you have any idea what they do to little girls in China whose parents have left them behind? Left them near river banks or by the side of the highway, Lorna? They put 'em in orphanages even though they're not officially orphans. And do you have any idea what that looks like? Do you?"

I shake my head, but I guess he wants more.

"Do you?"

"No. I said I don't."

"Well, try and picture a baby sittin' in a wicker chair with no bottom on it, sittin' in filthy clothes. Now, this baby has her legs held wide open, tied with rope. Now picture a split down the middle of her trousers so when it has to go the bathroom it just goes right there into a bucket underneath, or on the floor even."

"That's not true."

"It *is* true, I don't make things up. And it's all girls, Lorna. Hundreds of 'em just waitin' to die."

Lulu laughs again and nibbles on her hand. I pull her arm by her elbow and she puts it right back in.

"The government has a word for girls in China," Uncle Lloyd says, lifting his cigarette to his lips. 'Maggots in the rice.'"

"So what? What's that got to do with me?" I say and walk into the kitchen. "What you want for dinner, Lulu?"

"Ring Dings, please."

"Very funny, whatchu really want?"

"Ring Dings, please."

"So the point I'm trying to make here, Lorna, is that . . . the good news is that Lulu doesn't live in China."

"In China," Lulu says and turns her head to Uncle Lloyd with a grin that she drops when she sees his face. He's still a stranger to her. "Tell me when you feel it," she says softly and looks back at the TV with cautious eyes.

I grab a can of ravioli from the cabinet over the sink and reach for the can opener.

"The bad news is that your Mama's got to put this girl in a home so she can get back to her normal life. Be a normal citizen, Lorna."

I put the can opener back down on the counter. I rest it there gently so it doesn't make a sound. The boops and bops of the cartoon world still flow and I listen to the chase and try to feel what I just heard.

"Compared to the kids in China, you're sister's just gonna be moving on to Club Med. I'll tell you one thing . . . I bet they got cable there."

Before I know it I'm in the living room and I got Lulu by the hand.

"Ow," she says, staring frightened into my eyes as I stand her up and pull her towards the door.

"Where you goin'?" asks Uncle Lloyd.

I say nothing and decide I'll put Lulu's coat on when we get outdoors. I think about lifting her because she takes the stairs so slow and holds the rail with both hands. But she's heavier than she used to be so I can't. When we get outside the sun is on its way out and we walk down Lurner Avenue back towards the park and I think of banging on Ms. Tamms' door and telling her to call the police. My mind is racing and I can't figure out what I'm doing and I know Mama's gonna kill me and I wish the air was just a little warmer and that I grabbed Lulu a snack or one of those juices she likes with the straw on the side.

"Are we goin' on the slide, Lorna?"

"No."

"I'm hungry, Lorna."

"I know, I know, we'll go over to Ms. Tamms' and Irene's, okay?"

"Okay."

I figure I'll tell Ms. Tamms and Irene what they're planning on doing and how Lulu's not seen a doctor in years and how my Mama will slap her in the face to get her to stop being crazy. I tell myself I'm doing the right thing, that this will all work out as I pull my sister by her hand. I wish I brought her a Ring Ding or one of those juices or something but there wasn't any time and I wish it was just a little warmer but the day is starting to end. Lulu is always cold when I am and I can feel the chilly night air against my skin. I can feel it.

Kinko is barking inside the house when we get on the front porch. He puts his paws up on the back rest of their couch and stares at us through the living room window like he thinks he's a pit bull. I let Lulu push the bell like she always does and I close my eyes and pray that they're home. When a few seconds pass I put my nose up to the window and look past Kinko with my hands blocking the glare. Lulu runs and jumps on the porch swing. "Scarlet Ribbons," she sings, and the swing squeaks where it's bolted into the wooden beams. I can see Ms. Tamms' piano and the wooden crucifix near her kitchen cuckoo clock. I can see a gold-barred, empty bird cage and a small purple dish on the coffee table with pastel-colored candies stacked to a point. I can see song books under the piano bench and another clock near the fireplace that looks like Felix the Cat, moving his eyes and tail to the rhythm of time.

"I'm hungry, Lorna."

"I know. We'll get you some dinner real soon, okay?"

"Kinko. Kinko's barking, Lorna."

"I know."

"Kinko," Lulu says, and walks underneath me, pressing her face against the window like mine. "Hi, Kinko."

"Do you see them in there, Lu? Do you think they're home?"

"No."

"Why not?"

"They're watching the birds."

I look down at Lulu. She's blowing on the window, trying to see her breath and I realize I put her jacket on inside out. Ms. Tamms and Irene are gone for the weekend, she's right. They go bird-watching somewhere near Shenandoah once every month. I think about the day Irene told me about listening to the birds. I remember hearing a car horn and some kids playing nearby. I wanted so badly to hear what she wanted me to hear, but I couldn't. I was thinking more about her warm hands on my shoulders, and the way her finger felt against the skin behind my ear.

"Scarlet Ribbons," Lulu sings, "Scarlet ribbons. Lorna, I'm hungry."

"Sing 'Scarlet Ribbons' to me, Lu. I know you know the words."

Lulu reaches up and touches the glass like she's petting Kinko. I walk over to the porch swing and sit down with my head in my hands. I picture Ms. Tamms and Irene walking up the front steps with smiles on their faces when they see us. They tell us that there just weren't any birds up north this weekend and they decided to come home. We go inside and get a warm meal and Lulu falls asleep not long after dinner. I write down all the words to "Scarlet Ribbons" so I can know them and sing them with Lulu. I hear Kinko start to whine and bark again.

"Lorna, I'm hungry," Lulu says and walks over next to me on the swing.

I hold her by her forearms and look her in the eyes. Her nose is running and I pat my pockets for tissues. I don't have any. I run my sleeve under her nose and pull her closer to me, close enough that our heads nearly touch.

"Lulu. I want you to sing 'Scarlet Ribbons' for me. I've heard you sing that song. I've heard you do it and I want to hear you sing it right now, okay?"

"Okay," she says and turns her head to the window when Kinko starts to whine.

"Come on now," I say and turn her face back to me. "Scar-let Ribbons. Scar-let Ribbons."

I sit back on the porch swing and stare at her lowered head. Her fingers curl around themselves and her tongue comes out to lick her running nose. Her lips are a light purple and shake from the cold.

"Lulu?"

She drops into a crouch and puts her pinkie into a small hole in the porch floor. I reach out and touch her blond hair, let her soft ponytail fall through my palm. I run my fingers down the side of her face, her cheek, and all I can think to do is cry. But I don't. I stand from the porch swing instead. And then I take my sister home.

Uncle Lloyd leaves the TV off this night. I find another blanket for us to wrap ourselves in to sleep on the rug from China. It's warm but old and ratty-yellow and used to be an electric one but the cord is ripped out. It's past midnight and I know I won't see Mama until the morning. I stare at the ceiling while I wait for Lulu to sleep but she's restless, playing with the tassels from the rug and humming over and over like a soft motor. The longer we're silent the sooner she'll sleep. I turn on my side and close my eyes. Lulu reaches out and touches the back of my head, my back. She touches me softly like she thinks I might be sleeping, and I really like that she knows this much. I feel myself drift, begin to dream.

"If I live to be . . . a hundred. I will ne-ver know from where. Came those ribbons . . . lov-ely ribbons, scar-let ribbons, for my hair."

When I hear her breathing her gentle breaths, I slowly turn to see her. I pull her hand from her mouth and rest her arm at her side. I tell her in a whisper that I will love her and never leave her alone. And then I kiss her just above her ear. As close to her mind as I can get.

Claire Tristram

ICE CHEST

We laugh about it now, you and I, and I have never told you the truth. Sister of mine! Childhood is not a garden. It is a wasteland, cold, bleak, and vast, where the strong survive only by devouring the weak. And now that we are grown, and more miraculously still, now that we are what one might even call a *close* family, I can see that same murderous will to survive in my own two daughters. They compete for my attention the way a whelp crawls closer to a mother-wolf's teat by stepping on her litter-mates. It's not that they hate one another. Not at all. But they have an understanding, pure and animal, that each is an obstacle to the other's survival. Each is, for the other, hardly human at all.

You sit at my sunny kitchen table with me, two mothers together, gazing out into the yard where your one child has joined my two, and you smile over your coffee cup and say, "Isn't it lovely, the way they get along?" I look out and see my elder daughter brandishing a longish stick. From the way our children have positioned themselves on the lawn I see that my daughters have formed a temporary

Claire Tristram's work has appeared in a wide range of publications, including *Wired, Entrepreneur, Chicago Tribune Magazine, Fiction International, The Massachusetts Review,* and *The Best American Erotica 2000.*

alliance, a power base from which to taunt your son, who stands there, arms limp at his side, a troubled sense of the world's injustice beginning to settle onto his bright features. But you have only seen the good in the world. That's why you're still so gullible. It's a family joke, the way you will believe the most outrageous tales. You would do anything I told you when we were growing up.

It was an old ice chest, the kind you hardly saw anymore, even back then. Metal, blue underneath the dirt and rust, with a heavy lid and a huge metal clasp that flashed in the sun across the field where we played, drawing us to it. Someone had dumped it there overnight. I was five and you were four.

Now your son has turned his back on my two girls and is walking away, his back stiff with pride. After a brief huddle my girls follow him, walking six yards behind, with linked arms, their common enemy forging a temporary intimacy. They move out of view. I stand up to call them back.

"Oh, let them play," you say. "They're old enough to stay out of trouble."

I sit down, still wary, but I smile at you.

"Like we did," you say. "Might as well have been raised by wolves, for all anyone ever worried about us."

I wonder, not for the first time, if you can read my mind, and if you can, I pray you've forgiven me. We hear our children now, the little pagans, slam the back door and rush in, their cries echoing up the hallway to where we sit. A long, keening wail comes, possibly from my younger daughter. The alliances have shifted. Our eyes lock. You shrug. Now a door slams upstairs, and my other daughter and your son appear in the doorway, settling down in front of the television set.

It's not that I ever told you to get inside, exactly. I was too clever for that. As we stood there together in the field, mosquitoes circling our ears and grass seeds stuck to the backs of our legs, I began to tell you a story about that ice chest, with an eloquence that startled me. The magic box, I told you. It will take you anywhere, if only you get inside and close the lid. The heavy lid. Your eyes were skeptical—you were already familiar with my teasing—but your breath began to come in shorter and shorter bursts. I fanned the flames of your anticipation to a fury, and then I walked away, across the field, knowing that you wouldn't follow. I felt my legs move through the tall grass, step by step, and I left you behind, knowing that I would soon be free of you, until I was running, running free up the concrete stairs and into the house. Our mother—how I loved her!—was standing by the kitchen sink, peeling potatoes. She turned to scold me for banging the door open, took one look at my joy, and dropped her work, her face white with terror. "Where is your sister?" she cried, and she kneeled before me, eyes wild, and shook me until I gestured across the field; then she flew away from me, calling your name before her on the wind like a flag unfurling. And I knew that she would find you. She would find you with the unerring instinct of a she-wolf. She would open that ice chest and see you there, blue at the neck, but still alive, and would gather you up into her arms, weeping from the joy of it, and from that one, still grateful moment that you lay in her arms in the field, oxygenated blood rushing back into your cheeks, you would always and forever be the one that she loved most.

Stephen Guppy

MOTELS OF THE NORTHWEST: A GUIDEBOOK

1. The Avonlea Auto Court, Coquitlam B.C.

The motel is right where it should be. Even in the dark, it's no problem to find it: you come down off the exit ramp, and there it is, right beside the river. The Parkway's new, of course, and the exit ramp and cloverleaf and all that. But the basic terrain hasn't changed.

I park between a couple of beaters and have a look around for unit 11. This is perfect, I'm thinking—meeting up with my sister in a roadside motel. Carlene and I grew up in transit.

"Hey, Carly," I whisper while I rap at the door, even though I know she can't hear me. There's some scratching sounds from inside the unit, while Carlene gets the night-chain figured out. The next thing, she's opened the door.

"Carlo," she says without inflection.

"Yeah sure. How you doing?"

Stephen Guppy has published two books of poetry and a collection of short stories. His work has appeared in *Best Canadian Stories,* and one of his stories was recently short-listed for the Journey Prize for Fiction. He teaches at Malaspina University-College on Vancouver Island.

She steps back to let me into the unit. The warmth of the oil-burner hits me, and there's a whole bunch of smells I remember from a long time ago—lino and heating oil, stale cigarette smoke and Pine-Sol. Carlene and I stand there and check each other out, the both of us making adjustments. She's pretty much the same as I remember—shorter than me by half a foot, with the down-turned mouth she got from Mom and the doubting gaze I remember from our father. Her hair's that jazzy neon red the punker girls go in for. It looks a little out of step, Carlene being forty-five and all that. She's put on a pound or two, but she still looks okay. I suck in my gut and try smiling.

"You remember the smokes?" Carlene asks.

"Sure," I say, rummaging through the pockets of my coat. "Menthols, right? Craven M? King-Size?"

She nods, but has apparently lost interest. I toss the pack of cigarettes on the arborite table and follow her through the kitchenette and into the living-room-slash-bedroom.

"You been to see Mom?" I ask. "She okay?" This is all stuff I don't want to get into, subjects of purely historical interest, but I feel I should make conversation.

"This morning. We're driving down to Butchie's place tomorrow."

"Oh yeah?"

"Yeah. It's April tenth today. Wednesday. Butchie will be forty-two tomorrow."

"True fact?" I say, "Forty-two?"

"True fact," Carlene says.

* * *

Carlene and I are fraternal twins, born twenty-three minutes apart in the spring of 1951, on the same day as the first ascent of Everest. While our mother was screaming, strapped to a gurney, Edmund Hillary and his Sherpa guides were struggling through ice fog hundreds of feet above their base camp, relentlessly ascending toward the summit. As they hacked at the ice for footholds, she shrieked and rolled her eyes, all the gravity of the earth balled up inside her.

Carlene appeared first, tearing our mother's tissues with the violence of her birth. I was wheedled out with forceps, lank and jaundiced. While we winced beneath the glacial sky of the incubator's bulb, Sherpa Tensing caught his first glimpse of the apex.

"They've arrived!" the attending nurse informed the physician. "They were saying it on the radio in the lunchroom just now! Me and Betty had a smoke there and heard it."

"Well, that's cause for celebration!" the doctor replied, dropping the bloodied forceps into a kidney dish pooled with blood and placenta.

"Who's arrived?" our mother managed to say, her mind fogged from altitude sickness.

"Why the Everest party, of course, dear," the nurse replied, tucking the sheet more tightly around our mother's milk-filled breasts. "Which one of the babies do you want to see first?"

"Neither," our mother would have said, if she had been capable of forming the concept. The arrival of her children alarmed her. That such terrible plenitude could issue from her body! Sex, which she'd naively envisioned as a kind of communion, had paradoxically shattered the world into two equal pieces, each of them ruled by a mad, shrieking god. She closed her eyes and gasped for air, unable to draw sufficient breath from the attenuated atmosphere of the summit.

"Relax," the nurse told her, cupping an oxygen mask to her face. "You'll catch on to feeding them in no time." Our mother inhaled pure oxygen, the roots of her dyed-blonde hair boiling, and clung to the top of the coverlet against the buffeting of stratospheric winds.

2. Baxter: The "Shamrock"

This is from prehistoric times. Before Carlene and me were even born. Before Butchie was even thought of. Our mother, who is not yet our mother, has run away from home. Her boyfriend, who has only recently discovered that he is going to be our father, has taken her from her parents' house in his powder-blue '49 Meteor. They have driven over three hundred miles in one day. They are heading for the coast, for the Pacific. Exhausted, they have pulled in at the Shamrock Luxury Auto Court, which is right beside the Texaco station on the highway outside Baxter, Alberta. The world is just a stretch of road, a two-lane highway running west, arcing off into the foothills. Tomorrow they will cross the Rockies, the Meteor winding gradually up toward the gap between the mountains. They will almost be in heaven then, alone in icy blue.

They lie on the bed in their little room, too tired to speak or get properly undressed, our father in his undershirt and his Levis with their rolled-up cuffs, our mother in her half-slip and panties. Though this is, in a sense, their wedding night, they do not even try to make love. It is late in the summer, but the air is still warm. Outside their unit, birds come and go through the branches of the yellowing larches.

Our father is thinking of engines, machines. The Meteor has been running rough, and he wonders whether it will get them to the coast without a tune-up, for which there is neither time nor money. He could gap the plugs himself, of course, but his feeler gauge and spark plug wrench are in his parents' garage back in Lethbridge. Though he knows it will not be possible, he imagines the various steps he would take to remove the plugs, clean them, and adjust them. Envisioning this simple mechanical task makes him feel calmer and more in control than he has since he found out that our mother was pregnant.

Our mother, for her part, feels mindless and stunned. All the way out from Lethbridge, she has emptied her brain, let the highway flow through her like a creek through a culvert. Now, when she closes her eyes she can see it: stunted trees, Texacos, Smokey Bear signs, cirrus clouds frosted with sunlight. She has never been this far from home, never slept in a motel without her parents. If she allowed herself to think of this, the tiny stabs of panic that she can feel in her lungs when she breathes too quickly or too deeply would increase in duration and intensity until she began to sob or scream. To relax, she looks up at the ceiling, which is plaster and covered with whirlpools and swirls. This, she decides, is what outer space looks like. Vast swirling spirals of stars of all colours. She thinks of a Walt Disney movie. *When you wish upon a star!* If she could wish upon a star now, she decides, she would wish that she was dreaming. She would wish, most of all, that she would wake from this dream, sit up in her bed down the hall from her parents' room, get up and put on her quilted pink housecoat, go downstairs and fix herself a cup of hot Bovril. She would not, of course, be pregnant. She would not be in a dark motel room. She would not be driving west beside this boy she hardly knows.

Carlene and I are in this picture too, though we are invisible to the naked eye, like x-ray stars or viruses or the healing hand of Jesus. We are curled side by side in our mother's swollen uterus, breathing her essential fluids as if they were the atmosphere of some throbbing-red, overcast planet. The nascent stubs of our developing ears hear the tremulous *whump-whump* of her heart-beat. When our parents talk to each other, which they have done very rarely ever since they left home, we are aware that they are talking. Their voices, our mother's and father's, are an aspect of the climate, like thunder or terrible winds.

The thunder continues long after we are born. Look, that's us over there in the doorway, the girl in her blue-flowered nightgown, the boy in pajamas with a sad yellow bear. We are watching from the hall between the kitchen and the living-room. Our father explains his theories in a raspy, smoke-decayed voice. He was trapped and deluded by a woman, he asserts. This has happened to other men, historically speaking. He provides some examples: his uncle, a cousin, a friend of his from school. Our mother whines and splutters. We feel both afraid and exalted, like primitives watching an electrical storm. Our parents amaze and alarm us. Like lightning, they are beautiful but dangerous.

3. Regal Holidays

An arborite counter with a stainless-steel sink. A neon crown that winks right in the window while you sleep, as if you were creating your own constellation in your dreams. The sounds of people arguing before dawn in the adjoining unit, a man's voice and a woman's voice. Someone's car in the parking lot at sunrise, refusing to start and go anywhere at all. This is the Regal Holidays Motor Hotel in Abbotsford, British Columbia. Carlene and I are six years old, and our new little brother, Butchie, is a toddler. Imagine the three of us, three little kids. We are sitting on a patch of rug in the center of the lino, watching the launch of the Mercury spacecraft. Outer space, it seems, is black-and-white, as is Mission Control at Cape Canaveral. Our parents have bought us Plasticene, which is yellow, red, and oily blue, little pliable turds like dogshit. We are building things out of Plasticene: spaceships, in particular, are easy to make with coloured turds—you simply make a cylinder by rolling the stuff between your palms, then you narrow one end to a point between your fingers, being careful not to make it too fragile. There, now you've built a rocket. The only thing left to do is to launch it into the stratosphere, which I accomplish very easily by throwing it up at the ceiling, where it flattens out on impact and adheres to the stained white tile.

"Carlos!" our mother moans. "Can't you see I have a headache?" She is lying on the bed with a handkerchief pressed to her eyes. The handkerchief is pale blue silk, and it used to belong to her mother. If I pressed it to my face, it would smell of cologne. It is never used for anything but headaches.

I look up at my rocket ship, which is starting to peel from the ceiling. Carlene throws a wad of Plasticene that hits me in the shoulder. Butchie starts to shriek. On the TV set, a man with a suit and a crew cut is pointing at a diagram of something. It's a rocket ship, or part of one—one of the stages that dropped off before the spacecraft left the Earth's gravitation. Here too, dead parts are dropping off. Our mother, whose migraine has made her acutely aware of the curvature of space-time, can feel her lost youth vanishing like a burnt-out rocket engine. Launched toward infinity, she sprawls on the sagging Hide-a-Bed, gravitational forces tugging irresistibly at her hips and thighs and breasts. Our screams, the nasal pronouncements of the Mercury men at Command Control in Houston, have become in her ears the cosmic whoosh of pure acceleration. She is rocketing out of her former self, toward the ice of space.

4. Jupiter

In the hottest weeks of August, we move to the lake. This is old Clarence Larter's place, as Mom and Dad call it. Tall Timbers Recreation Park. A Wilderness Setting for Real Family Fun. We rent, as we always do, a cabin. Mornings, Carlene and I lie on our cots and re-read our *Archie Double Digests*. Go for walks on the Nature Trail, avoiding the slugs. My father, who rarely swims, sleeps until noon. My mother remains in the cabin all day, immersed in her summer-long migraine. On her good days, which occur sporadically, usually during rainstorms, she drives the car into the village to pick up gin and mixer. After dinner, she walks the beach, squinting at the distant flares of bonfires.

Abandoned by our parents, Carlene and I sit by the gravelly beach and eye the other children. This year, Carlene has made a new friend. She is Jessie. Her hair is red and almost as short as a boy's hair. Her face is round and bisected by two sprays of lurid red freckles that arc across her wide, curving cheekbones. Her eyes are blue and spacy. She has gaps between her teeth. She and Carlene both have hula hoops, which they spin around their hipless waists while undulating their sunburned arms like the girls in *Blue Hawaii*. We are all the same age, which is twelve.

Our father has bought us, Carlene and me, a six-transistor radio, which is plastic and Made in Japan. The girls use it sometimes, while they hula; in the evenings, though, I take it to the edge of the lake and press it as close to my ear as I can to make the voices in my head go away. The surface of the lake is grey and still and marked with the intricate curlicues of the milfoil that grows under the water. Nothing moves but the skittery mosquitoes. The water itself smells of mold, like our cabin. Our father drinks beer on the porch toward nightfall. He is taking his two weeks' vacation. He is having, our mother has told us, a hard-earned and well-deserved rest.

My favorite channel on the radio is KZOK 950 from Bellingham, Washington, the Voice of the Pacific Northwest. All day it plays the Hit Parade, but at night, when I sit by the lake by myself and turn up the volume a little at a time as the whispers inside me grow darker, it always plays old cowboy songs. The voices of the country-and-western singers are tranquilized and hollow, echoing out of some parallel dimension. They are sitting in the Church in the Wild-woods. They are riding down the Streets of Laredo. They are kneel-ing at the Old Rugged Cross. The disc jockeys also sound drugged and disconnected, their voices fading in and out as if they've been blown there and scattered by the wind. Of all the singers that KZOK plays, I like the Late Great ones best. The Late Great Johnny Horton, for example. The Late Great Hank Williams. The Late Great Patsy Cline. I imagine their airplanes falling like comets, descending into a featureless landscape as white and unmapped as Alaska, while their voices, still crooning of love and betrayal, reverberate endlessly out of the dusk.

"If you were in the bath," Jessie tells me, "and I threw that tran-sistor of yours in the water, you'd be fried up with electric shock and die."

"Shut the fuck up, freckle-face," I tell her.

"I wasn't SHUT UP, I was BROUGHT UP," she chants, "and if you don't GROW UP, I'm gonna THROW UP!"

Jessie's mother is a Seventh-Day Adventist. She sings about God while she's washing the dishes. You can hear her singing Bible songs through the fly-screen on their cabin, which is thirty or forty feet away from ours, behind some trees. Jessie also likes to sing, but her songs are not invariably religious. She sings when she's twirling her hula hoop and dancing, and she is teaching a few of her songs to Carlene.

> Jesus Christ ALMIGHTY!
> A mouse ran up my NIGHTIE!
> BIT my TIT and made me SHIT!
> Jesus Christ ALMIGHTY!

On weekdays, Jessie's mother works at the desk at the motel. She also keeps an eye on the Snack-'n'-Save store beside it, both of which are owned by Mr. Larter.

Clarence Larter is a long-boned old man with a little hook beak and icy-blue eyes that look huge through his coke-bottle glasses. His arms are incredibly thin, poking out of his short-sleeved shirts like straw from a drainpipe, and his forearms are covered with mud-coloured spots. "Lookit here," he says, holding up a miniature hand-carved totem pole, one of several he keeps on a display shelf beneath a sign that says GENUINE CANADIAN INDIAN. "You think any self-respecting Indian carved these things? They make these things over in Hong Kong. True fact."

He replaces the crudely-painted ornament on the shelf beneath the fallacious sign, shaking his head in amazement. "True fact," he repeats, as if someone had tried to contradict him. Then he shuffles off into his apartment, which is right behind the store. When he's gone, Jessie's mother takes over.

Jessie, Carlene and I spend a lot of our time in the store. We examine the boxes of candies with care, considering each before making our final decisions. There is quite a selection to choose from. Candy cigarettes. Licorice whips. Double Bubble Bubble Gum, each rubbery pink slab of gum wrapped in a cartoon with a riddle. *Why did the Little Moron throw the clock out the window? To see time fly!*

One evening in our last week at the campground, our mother tells Carlene and I to keep an eye on Butchie while she drives into town to get beer. She has, as she always does, a migraine. She is wearing dark glasses and a headscarf, like a movie star appearing in public. She wobbles on her pointed heels as she heads up the trail to the car.

Carlene and Jessie sit on the floating dock, leaning back against the upturned canoes and dangling their feet in the water. Jessie, who is already sunburned, is rubbing Coppertone into her thighs. Her arms are the colour of crabshells. Carlene, like our mother, wears dark glasses all day. Butchie and I come down to the swimming beach beside the dock, Butchie walking with that rolling, drunk-sailor's walk of his, the two of us in Dacron Bermuda shorts cut down from our father's dress slacks and Tall Timbers T-shirts with totem poles on the front. As soon as they see us, Carlene and Jessie start to chant

> GIRLS go to COLLEGE
> to get more KNOWLEDGE!
> BOYS go to JUPITER
> to get even STUPIDER!

I ignore them and just keep walking. Nothing they do can bother me, really. I have no interest in college or knowledge. To be beautifully dead is my ambition. I envision myself in a sequined shirt and Stetson, waving from the window of a private plane as I leave for the last show of my final world tour. Women, every one of them in love with me, wave sorrowfully back from the tarmac. Sad music starts up as the plane leaves the ground.

The girls' song gets to Butchie, however: looking straight up at the cloudless sky, he walks past the ramp that leads to the floating dock and hurls himself into the water. This kamikaze routine is Butchie's response to anything that confuses or upsets him. Carlene, I decide, should know this.

"You just better get him out!" I say, making my voice as deep and threatening as I can, in imitation of my father's. "You just better hope he doesn't drown!"

Butchie, in fact, is doing exactly that: drowning. The sandy bank of the lake turns to mud about ten feet out, and it also drops off sharply. He's out there, Butchie, already fifteen or twenty feet from shore, near the end of the dock on which Carlene and her friend are sitting, but not near enough for either of them to reach him. They both just sit there anyway, Carlene with a handful of Coppertone poised above her thigh, her face locked into a look of blank incomprehension, Jessie regarding Butchie's distress with evident disgust.

"Jesus, Carlene!" I say. God knows what I'm waiting for, but for some reason it still hasn't occurred to me to run into the lake. I stand there on the shore in my Tall Timbers shirt and watch as Butchie flails and snorts. His head disappears, bobs, goes down again. He surfaces and trumpets like a sperm whale.

I open my mouth to yell at my sister again, and something knocks me over. It's my father. I can hear the water churning around his legs as he powers his way out into the lake, then he's swimming with that harsh, chopping overhand I've never been able to learn.

I pick myself up, still slightly winded, and hobble toward the edge of the water. Carlene and Jessie are standing up now, Carlene screaming, "Butchie! Oh, Butchie!"

My father drags his youngest child bodily out of the lake and lays him on the sand beside the dock. Then, inexplicably, he turns toward me. I can feel my father's anger, sense his purpose in the angles and planes of his body, the mass of his shoulders and the width of his wet, hairy chest. Then he hits me, a open-handed slap, very hard, on the side of my head. I go down again, already crying.

"Can't you even look after your brother?" he says. I wish I could die now, or kill him. I lie there, my face raw and throbbing, a smear of blood or snot across my distorted, whining mouth.

"It's his fault," I hear Carlene say. "He can't even look after

Butchie." But my father has already left us, striding back up the beach to the cabin. Butchie flops at the edge of the water, like a fish that is hooked but not dead.

5. The Bluebird of Happiness

Our little brother, Butchie, is retarded. In the future, thirty years from now, there will be other words for boys like Butchie. *Disabled. Challenged. Special.* But now, in 1966, he is *Mentally Retarded.* That is not, of course, what other children call him. When he shambles across the playground or the school yard, they yell at him, chanting the names they have learned for boys like him: *idiot, imbecile, moron,* they say. *Garbage-brains, peckerhead, retardo.*

To our mother, Butchie is none of these things. To our mother, Butchie is *slow.*

"Butchie," she whispers, fingering her handkerchief, "has always been . . . *slow.*" Her voice comes apart before the last, fatal word, almost dissolving into a whimper or a sob, then she bravely regains her composure, rescued by that bland, soothing word.

Slow.

The Matron's hand hovers for a moment just above her box of Kleenex, then returns to her desk when it finally becomes apparent that our mother isn't going to break down. She nods instead, ever so sadly.

Our mother, having regained her composure, stumbles into another halting sentence.

"It's been difficult for me, of course, what with the children's father having . . . "

Matron nods frantically. Yes, yes. Of course. She understands.

Refusing to be deterred, Mom hangs above the final word like an alpinist clinging to the lip of a crevasse. *Left,* I want to scream. *Made a run for it. Fucked off like he always does. Departed.*

Carlene shifts her hips on the sticky vinyl chair, her legs in patterned mod socks with vertical stripes twisting languidly around each other like the trailing roots of some epiphytic plant. She rolls her eyes and stares toward the ceiling, as if examining her bangs for split ends. Her fingernails, painted frost-white to match her lipstick, pick at the hem of her new houndstooth mini. She is dying, her body seems to be saying, of the agony of being with our mother. She is Cinderella, pining away behind the scullery door. Rapunzel in her captive's tower. Snow White, pricked by her stepmother's pin. Her bony shoulders hunch around her despondent little breasts.

Ignoring Carlene's sighs of boredom, our mother and the Matron proceed with their elaborate mating-dance, bobbing their necks like flamingoes as they agree about the impossibility of anyone—not just our mother, but anyone, absolutely *anyone*—coping with raising a child who is *slow*.

If one didn't have others to think of . . . (significant glances at Carlene and me).

If there was any hope of his, well, developing further . . . (sympathetic nod from Matron).

If circumstances weren't quite so complex, you understand . . . (eyes averted toward our absent father, who is apparently residing on the green plaster ceiling, like God in a Renaissance fresco).

If there weren't such excellent professional care available . . . (gratified smirk from the Big M, ingratiating smile from our mother).

Etc., etc., etc.

None of this is of any importance, of course. The matter was decided weeks ago—Butchie will be dumped, disappear like our father, and the rest of us will go on without him. Soon we will return to the Bluebird of Happiness Motor Hotel, conveniently located near the Woodlands Park plaza, the Uplands Miniature Golf Links and Fun Fair for Kids of All Ages, the Community Recreation Pool, the go-kart track, etc., etc.

Leaving the institution, Carlene begins to perk up. She swings her new patent-leather handbag, which is rectangular and too small to hold anything but cigarettes and Kotex. Her hair swings in time with the handbag, and her skinny, candy-striped legs stride along purposefully beneath the flag of her tiny skirt. "In Europe, they used to gas the retarded," she says. She says this loud enough for our mother to hear her, but our mother is either too busy staring back at the upper-storey windows of the buildings to pay any attention or decides to ignore what she hears.

"True fact?" I ask.

"True fact," my sister tells me. "They gassed all sorts of people. Jews. Homosexuals. Gypsies. Old bags who hid bottles in the toilet. Anyone who wasn't blonde and perfect. I'm sure they would have done away with *you*."

Carlene and I run laughing toward the lump of our mother's blue Buick. We both suddenly need to be active and loud, to feel sunlight and air on our faces.

Far above, on one of the upper floors of the institution, our brother is acquainting himself with his new home and family. He may even be making new friends. Soon he will learn to be useful, mastering simple crafts and carrying out his chores. In time, he will take on the characteristics of his surroundings, becoming as grey and shapeless as the sprung divans and armchairs in the sun room. Weeks or months from now, the next time we see him, he will be almost indistinguishable from the lino in the halls. He is one of the shufflers now, one of the lost. His life has no more meaning to our own.

6. El Morocco

I'm two hours late for Dad's wedding. By the time I show up, they've left the JP's office and gone back to their motel. Later on, they're driving down to Whidbey Island. There's a casino there these days, on the Lummi reservation. It's *Honeymoon in Vegas*, or almost— Dad and his new wife, Esther, will be playing the slots for the rest of the weekend, then it's back to North Delta, where Esther's a receptionist at a plumbing supply firm.

"We'll be heading along pretty quick," my dad tells me. I give him my present, Crown Royal in an Antique Cars gift box, which I picked up in the duty-free shop. He sits down on the red velour couch to open it while Esther gives me a welcoming kiss on the cheek. She's tall, and smells exactly like lilies.

"I'm so happy you could join us," she tells me. She touches my arm as she says this; her hands are incredibly fine-boned and gentle.

I wasn't prepared for this Esther. Sweetness always blind-sides you, takes you by surprise. Dad seems okay too, all things considered. He's thickened out since the last time I saw him, and his hair, which he wears a little longer than he used to, is white as cigarette ash above his sunburned face.

"Just look at you two guys," Esther says. "I don't believe it! Where's my camera, Frank? I have to get a picture of you boys."

Dad and I follow her into the bedroom, one wall of which turns out to be a floor-to-ceiling mirror.

"Stand right over here, Frank. Now Carlo, you stand here."

She arranges us side-by-side, a father-and-son portrait, Dad in his powder-blue leisure suit and snazzy white loafers, me in my old leather jacket. I'm looking at the floor-to-ceiling mirror, in which I can see Esther's back.

"You still singing, Carlo?" Dad asks me. This is what he says every time I see him. He's blinking like crazy from the flash. So am I.

"Not really," I tell him. "I kind of got out of that. Performing and all."

"Frank's told me all about you and your singing," Esther chimes in. She's looking in the drawers of the bureau, opening each one and closing it again, checking to make sure they haven't left anything behind. "I think that's so exciting, to actually get up and sing for a living. I wish I had the talent for that."

"It gets to be a job," I say. I stand back against the wall so that Dad can get past me.

"We got to get moving," he says. "By rights, they could already ask us to pay another day."

Esther looks up from the closet, which she's inspecting for stray shoes and clothing. Our eyes meet and she smiles at me.

"I sure hope we remembered everything," she says.

I smile back, I can't help it.

"What is there to forget?"

7. Base Camp

The Group Home is an ordinary two-storey house, almost square, with small bedroom windows and a blue Cape Cod roof. Carlene and I help Mom out of the back seat of Carlene's Suzuki.

"This doesn't look too shabby," I say. The place where Butchie used to live depressed me. It made me think of insect life, dust mites and silverfish, termites. I'd be walking down those lino halls, Butchie shuffling along beside me like his hips had worked loose, and the only thing I could think about was insects.

"It's a nice house," my mother agrees. "A *group home*," she adds, as if she likes the way it sounds.

Mom's done okay, all things considered. Her second husband, Freddie, left her pretty well off—after Dad, she'd learned to tank up on insurance. Last year, she flew out to Kathmandu. The tour was set up by a club she belongs to, vegetarians and homeopathic medicine fans, people who are deeply into bean curd. They camped in the Himalayan meadows, hundreds of feet above sea level, when the mountain rhododendrons were in flower. She sent Carlene a snapshot, and Carlene passed it on to me. It's terrific, really something—I love it. There's Mom with this Sherpa, a professional guide; the two of them are grinning at the camera. They're both wearing knit caps of brightly-coloured wool, but Mom still has her Hollywood shades on. Behind them, there's a blur of blue, a million tiny alpine rhododendrons.

I tell Mom and Carly to go in without me while I grab a quick smoke. I could use a little Jimmy, a shot in the arm. I haven't had a whack since this morning. When I lay off, I get voices, little fiddles made of wind. The songs they play are pretty enough, though they're always kind of mournful. Old cowpokes crooning trail songs in the clouds.

"Come on in," some female person hollers out the minute I crack the front door. "Your brother's right here waiting. Aren't you, Butchie?"

I nod a few times in a neighbourly sort of fashion and wander into the living-room, wondering if I should have slipped my shoes off. The woman who called out to me gets out of her armchair and heads for the hallway. I gather she's someone who works there—a Caregiver, if that's still what they're called. My mother has installed herself on the sofa next to Carlene, who's perched on the edge of the cushion, ready to leap up at any moment and get the old girl whatever she requires—a cup of herb tea, a tuna melt, organ transplants, you name it. Next to her, of course, is Butchie.

"Hey, Butch," I kind of whisper.

My brother glances up at me, his eyes opaque as marbles. He's wearing shorts, I notice. A sweatshirt with a cartoon duck. Air Jordans.

"Well, isn't this great?" Mom asks us. "The whole darned bunch of us together in one room."

"Yeah, right," I say, "fabulous."

Carlene kind of winces, like the light hurts her eyes. I'm wondering if she's inherited Mom's migraines.

"How long's it been?" Carlene says. She looks at me like I ought to remember. "Seven years? Longer?"

"Seven years," our brother echoes. He states this with solemn conviction, as if he were citing some fact he'd researched.

"What a long time!" our mother says cheerfully. "And so much has happened!"

She turns and looks at the wall right over Butchie's head, where there's a poster of the Himalayan mountains.

"I've buried a husband!" Mom informs us. "I've been to Kathmandu! I've *lived!*"

We all sit and look at the picture. It isn't a blow-up of one of Mom's snapshots or anything like that, just an ordinary travel-bureau poster. It's beautiful, though, in its way. There's two main peaks and a couple of lesser ones; they're all blue and covered in glacial ice, except for the summits of the two taller mountains, which are brilliant as gemstones in what appears to be evening light.

"Which one of these is Everest?" I ask.

"That's it on the left," Mom says. She's finally taken off the Ray-Bans, and her pale eyes seem to focus on the mountains themselves, not the surface of the poster on the wall. "The one that looks smaller and blunter."

"You sure, Mom?" Carlene asks. "You sure it's not the other way around?"

Mom gets up and walks between the armchairs. "Of course I'm sure. That's Everest there"—she places her hand on the poster—"and that's Nuptse. I ought to know, Carlene, I've been there."

"I guess you got Butchie the poster?" I say.

My mother doesn't answer me, she's too busy staring at the picture. I remember how she'd stare across the lake at Tall Timbers, gazing through her black-out shades at somebody else's fire.

"I gave it to Butchie when I got back," she finally says. "I wanted him to know where I'd been."

"Speaking of which," she adds, as if there were some obvious connection between the two subjects, "I guess I better find the little girls' room."

She heads off down the hallway, peering into doorways as she goes. Mom's moving a little stiffly now, I notice. All those years of gin and hide-a-beds takes a toll on a person's system. The body forgets how to mend itself, the wear and tear mounts up. Mom would be what now, I wonder—sixty-nine? Seventy? A long ways off the warranty, that's for sure.

"That's a pretty nice poster, Butch," Carlene says. She fumbles in her bag for her menthols. When she's pulled out a cigarette, she sticks it in her fuchsia lips and then roots around in the bag again, foraging for matches or a lighter. I watch my brother watching her; this is the first thing that's got his attention. Something skitters to the surface of his eyes.

"You're not supposed to smoke," he says.

"What?" Carlene says. She sits there looking blankly at our brother, like she can't quite grasp the meaning of his words. I'm struck by the contrast between them, the woman with her punky tufts of chemical hair and the bald man with his toddler's eyes and sneakers. I'm thinking: *This is us, this is what we always were—this mismatched set, my family.* I'm thinking: *Nothing stays the same with us, but nothing ever changes.*

"Don't smoke!" Butchie bellows. He's losing it now, you can see that. His face has that spaced-out robot look that it gets when the small, safe sphere he occupies dissolves into the larger world beyond his understanding.

"Sure, Butch" Carlene whispers. "Whatever you want, Butch. Whatever." She puts away her cigarette, drops the Bic lighter back into her handbag. Butchie, however, is unimpressed. "You're not supposed to smoke!" he roars. "It's not allowed! She's *smoking!*"

Carlene gets up and heads down the hall. Next thing, she's back with the warden. The Caregiver, Social Worker, whatever she is, puts on her professional, understanding smile and asks my brother if he'd like to take a nap.

"Carlene's smoking cigarettes," Butchie tells her. He says this in a small, hurt voice, a three-year-old informing on his sister.

"I'm sure your sister wouldn't do that," the Caregiver says. She takes Butchie's hand and he stands automatically. He follows her down the hall, glancing suspiciously at Carlene over his shoulder. His sneakers squeak like crickets as he walks.

"Still gets a little intense, though, doesn't he?" I say.

"No shit," Carlene whispers. She shrugs, looking rattled, and sweeps her orange hair off her forehead.

Mom comes out of the washroom and wanders back into the living room. "Where's Butchie?" she asks us. Carlene and I glance at each other. Apparently, Mom's missed the whole episode.

"Jupiter," Carlene informs her.

"No shit," I say. "Jupiter, that's it." We both break out laughing. Pretty soon we're doubled over, the pair of us red-faced and out of control.

8. The Mountain Vue, Just East of Sedro Woolley

This is over thirty years ago, July of 1967. Carlene and I are fourteen years old. We are sitting on the stoop outside our unit. Our mother comes out, stepping carefully between us in her ivory high-heeled pumps, and minces across the gravel to the Buick. Then she puts on her sunglasses, which she nearly always wears, and angles the mirror to check her hair and make-up. When she's done with that, she rolls down the window.

"Don't you be late for the bus, eh?" she says. "And keep an eye on Butchie, all right?"

I wave, Carlene ignores her. Our mother's life is transparent to us; she is drawn by predictable tides. We know where she's headed, and we know when she'll be back. The time between is none of her business.

"Old hatchet-faced bitch!" Carlene whispers as our mother drives off.

I have nothing germane to add to this discussion, though I spit into the gravel to establish my complicity in the plot against our parents.

Mom's Buick bucks out of the lot.

Carlene peels the wrapper off her chunk of Double Bubble. She removes the cartoon and unfolds it carefully, like it's an important coded message or a pirate's treasure map.

"Why did the little moron put his shoes into the fridge?" Carlene asks me.

"Why do morons do anything?" I ask her. We both turn and look at our little brother. Butchie is eleven, but he still looks like a baby— his limbs are pale and flaccid, his face is as smooth as the moon. He is playing in a concrete tub of dirt which presumably once held shrubbery or flowers. He scoops the dirt out of the tub with a dessert spoon from the kitchen and adds it to the pile between his feet. He is sleepy-eyed and chubby as a seal.

"I hate him too," I tell Carlene. She nods, her face impassive.

"He's weighing us down," she whispers.

She's right, of course, the problem is Butchie. The particles of his fragmented soul, dense as atoms of plutonium, have held us in this orbit since Carlene and I were three. If he hadn't been born, we realize, our childhoods, our lives, would have been completely different. We would probably have had our own house, our own front lawn, a basketball hoop in the driveway. We might even have made friendships and kept them, instead of wincing away from strangers in the hallways of unfamiliar schools. Our father would not have changed jobs every season. Our mother would not have to hide her eyes, her gaze that seeks a vanishing point beyond the walls of the smallest motel room, behind a pair of midnight Ray-Bans that she wears like a snail wears its shell. The thunderstorms that roll across our heavens would disperse.

"Butchie," Carlene says. "Want to play a game with us?"

Our brother looks up from his mountain, his Everest of parking-lot dust, the spoon in his meaty fist glinting.

"I'm the Mummy," Carlene continues. "You're the baby, and Carlo of course is your dad. You have to do whatever we tell you."

"Pick up your breakfast spoon, Butchie," I say.

"You need a nutritious breakfast," Carlene adds.

Butchie raises the spoon with its scoop of grey dust.

"Eat it up now, that's a good baby."

Butchie hesitates, the spoon poking out of his plump little fist. There is a moment, a flicker of pure possibility, when it seems as if he will actually—voluntarily—place the spoonful of dust in his mouth. Then his moon-round face crumples and tears actually shoot from the corners of his eyes.

"No!" he cries. "I won't! You can't make me!"

"Now Butchie," Carlene says soothingly. "It's for your own good."

I kneel behind my brother, encircle his soft, pliant body with my arms, pin his arms to his sides and hold him, my chin digging into his shoulder to make sure that he can't stand up.

"Open wide!" Carlene says. She picks up the kitchen spoon and thrusts it into Butchie's mouth. He spits dust and mucus, drools saliva down his chin. Carlene prepares another scoop of gravel.

"You kids are so ungrateful," I whisper in Butchie's ear. My brother's body shakes with rage, but I hold him like a brother should, protecting him from fear and harm, from even his own unworthy thoughts. He needs to be protected, to be spoon-fed. It's our job.

"You're giving me a headache," Carlene says. "Stop making all that noise! I can't stand to be around you children, it's so stressful!"

"Eat your breakfast, Butch," I whisper. "I have to be getting to work. They'll fire me if you don't eat dust, I'll never hold a job!"

"Dust is one of the four major food groups," Carlene intones. "It is vital for maintaining existence!" She is trying to pry open Butchie's blubbering lips as she says this, but she is laughing so hard she can't control the spoon.

"True fact, Carlene?" I ask her.

"True fact," she says. She wipes her eyes and gasps for breath. The spoon glints in the gravel. Our retarded brother sobs and trembles, trapped forever in his parody of childhood.

I look up and squint into the steep summer sun at the "Vacancy" sign beside the highway. It's a white plywood triangle, cut to look like Mt. Baker, with a blue base and gleaming white apex. In the morning light, it shines as clear as heaven.

Cynthia Riede

DARWIN'S KITCHEN

On a hot Saturday in August, Roger comes over to help me defrost my ancient Frigidaire. We sit at the kitchen table, drink cold bottles of Corona with slices of lime, and watch ice melt. Zsazsa sleeps at our feet while Darwin preens, his blue-green feathers drifting down to rest on Roger's sneakers. When the ice thaws and begins to release its grip, I pry loose the bottle of Cuervo and we do shots. We watch the ice melt—the stalactites and stalagmites—and I look for signs of God in the smooth veins on the back of Roger's hands.

I look for signs in the upsurge of fizz after I shove a slice of lime into another bottle of beer.

Last week, my father told me he saw God in a tree outside of his room at the Evergreen Nursing Home. "He sits there on that high limb, with four little donkeys." I squinted into the tree, hoping to see a gray bearded man in a robe, but all I saw were leaves, and they were still because there was no breeze.

The nurses told me my father prowls around at night, searching for a phone book.

"Who does he want to call?" I asked.

Cynthia Riede's work has appeared in *The Laurel Review, Room of One's Own,* and *Wisconsin Review.*

"The Vatican," a small wiry nurse said. "He wants to talk to the Pope."

The ice surrenders the frozen peas.

"Do you believe in God?" I say.

Roger bends to pick up the battered black case that rests beside his feet. "I believe in something bigger than me," he says, snapping the case open and removing his violin. "But I do not know its name." He positions the violin beneath his chin and draws his bow across the strings. Darwin listens with his head cocked. As I chip away the last of the ice and mop the buckled linoleum, the two of them engage in a duet of sorts. As Roger plays, Darwin blinks and sings. "Oh-aaaaa." "Ooh-aah-aahh." It sounds like the fat lady at the opera muttering after the show, like an elderly schoolteacher singing the blues. When I am finished, I walk through the apartment, flick off all of the lights. We sit in the dark. It seems cooler that way. The paddles of the fan churn and whir. Light from a street lamp angles into the kitchen, and in its soft glow, Darwin sings.

Later that evening, after Roger has gone home to practice, the high, irregular rasp of his violin eventually ceases to filter through the floorboards of my apartment, and I hear a light tap on my door. Zsazsa opens an eye, but her great white mass shows no sign of budging. I open the door to find Roger in the hallway, wearing polka dot swim trunks and a Hawaiian lei. He has a towel tucked under his arm.

"Wanna?" he says.

We walk down the hill to a modern apartment complex owned by an amateur violist Roger knows, a dentist who provided financial support for Roger's quartet in its early days. "He can't play worth a shit," Roger says. "But he comes to our concerts and he sits in the front row." The gate to the pool is padlocked, so we slip under the fence, cement scratching the backs of our legs.

At the edge of the pool, we sit and dangle our feet in the water, which still holds the heat of the day. Most of the apartment windows beyond the pool are dark, but in one the colored light of a television shifts across the walls and ceiling, and in another, a woman sits on a couch and shuffles a deck of cards.

"Look," Roger says, craning his neck to gaze at the sky. "Stars!" The stars are diluted, as if a power surge has dimmed their glow, but Roger points at faint clusters and gives them names. "That's Casper," he says, indicating a knot of stars in the west. "And hovering above us, that's Orphan Annie. See her?" I squint at the mass directly overhead, try to make out curls or an insipid grin. "And over there," Roger gestures, "that fat star on the horizon—that's Bruno, Leaving."

Bruno lived with Roger for five months; he spent his nights mopping the floors of a research lab and his afternoons watching soap operas on Roger's couch before suddenly deciding to do volunteer work with a team of scientists who study frogs in the rain forest.

"When are you going to get over that guy?" I say.

"He left me with things one can never get over," Roger says. He shrugs and folds into the water. I watch as he glides along the bottom, as he weaves back and forth like a sea creature, eventually surfacing on the other side. "Come in," he stage whispers. From where I sit, his head looks like a seal bobbing in the water.

I submerge myself all at once, and there is no shock, no need to adjust to the temperature: the water is as comfortable as my own skin. I paddle over to Roger. We tread side by side, watch moths flit around lights in the parking lot.

"He sent me a post card," Roger says. "A few weeks ago. I never told you—haven't told anyone." He dips his face and blows a spray of water from beneath his mustache. "He said he's positive. On a lousy post card. Positive."

I do not know what to say. I listen to the swell of crickets in the grass beyond the fence, to the gulp of the filter vent behind us. The water feels suddenly cold.

"I tested negative a few weeks ago," Roger says. "But you never know. Sometimes it takes a while." He runs a hand through his slick hair. "A post card," he says, then he plunges beneath the water, his feet kicking up a spray that showers the sidewalk surrounding the pool. Drops of water bleed into the cement: they evaporate quickly, until all traces of them are gone.

Afterward, we walk to Betty's Kitchen. The restaurant is nestled in the midst of the city, with lighted windows full of people lifting forks and mugs of coffee, reading newspapers or smoking. It looks like something out of an Edward Hopper painting. Above it all, on a garishly painted sign next to the words BETTY'S KITCHEN is an immense likeness of Betty herself: a robust woman in a pink waitress uniform, her cheeks aglow, her white teeth flashing. She lifts a platter of pancakes high over her head, as if offering food to the heavens.

We order tall stacks of pancakes and de-caf coffee.

The restaurant is full of late night people: hospital workers and cab drivers, college students and donut makers. I see the writer who lives in 2B sitting at the counter, drinking coffee and jotting in a notebook. Roger watches a group of men in the booth opposite us, who take turns impersonating John Wayne as a gay man. Roger observes the men for a while, then sneers. "I'm over it," he says.

"Over what?"

"Sex. Over it, over it, over it. Look at me: I'm celibate now, just like—" He pauses while his eyes flick over the muscled John Wayne impersonator who has left the booth and is walking toward the bathroom with an exaggerated swagger.

"Well, almost. Phone sex. I still do that."

"Sex with a phone?"

"I call men. You know, services. They have them all over the country. I just dial, say, 1–900-HOT BUNS, and I'm all set. Hot and heavy. Clean and—this is important—healthy. It meets my needs, and there's no danger. None of that running off to the rain forest, for instance. And no messy death stuff."

"But it's so impersonal."

"Funerals are impersonal. Everyone is so polite."

I watch as Roger peels the cover off a packet of creamer. His face has a slight gray cast to it, and I know, despite all of the airy bravado, he has been losing sleep over this. It's not like him to go it alone: he always has a man in his life. "What about flesh to flesh contact?" I say as he dumps the half-and-half into his coffee. "Won't you miss that? Holding hands during a moonlit walk on the beach. Cuddling in front of a fireplace on a chilly winter afternoon."

Roger takes a sip of coffee and shudders as he sets down the mug. "You live for Hallmark moments, don't you?"

"I don't see what's wrong with holding hands. And a Hallmark card every now and then—it's not a bad thing."

"Unless it's a sympathy card. And everyone you know is dressed in black. No thank you. I see the road that leads to love and it's lined with a traffic jam of hearses. I can't imagine gazing into anyone's eyes without seeing them weighted down with nickels." He's clutching his mug as he says this, leaning toward me slightly, as if simply by diminishing the physical space between us, he can help me to comprehend his words.

"So, what?—you're going to spend life alone?"

"Alone, alone, all all alone. My choice. I don't do death well."

"What about love?"

Roger doesn't respond. Instead, he picks up the salt shaker, twirls it between his palms. The John Wayne men leave.

"Roger?"

"I just can't love someone knowing they will die."

"We all die, Roger. I could walk out there now and get hit by—"

"No, it's not the same. A car is not the same. This—this!—is like a time bomb ticking. It's like cancer you can give to the one you love most. I can't do it. Nope. I'm done."

The waitress brings our food and we spread butter over our pancakes without saying anything more. We chew in a companionable sort of silence.

Later, Roger will give me a peck on the cheek at the door to his apartment and I will walk upstairs to my own place. I will go to bed, but he will dial a toll number. He will talk to some stranger in San Francisco, or Kansas. Desire will crackle through the line, but it is nothing you can touch.

Darwin knows about spending a life alone. Parrots mate for life, but the man who owned the two of them died, and Darwin and his wife ended up in a pet shop. She had been sold by the time I came along, but I brought Darwin home and tried to ease his sadness. At first, he was pathetic, sitting in his cage, staring out through the kitchen window all afternoon at the clouds drifting by. In the evenings, I'd play Billy Holliday and he'd murmur along. The blues seemed to cheer him, and though he still occasionally sings fragments of "Stormy Weather" or "No Regrets," I like to think he's not as sad as he used to be. I like to think he finds some comfort in spending his days with me. He is a beautiful bird, with a smoky blue belly and a splash of white on his head. His eyes are ringed with peach. His tail feathers, when spread, are sunset rose. He spreads them now and one drifts to rest on Zsazsa's back. Zsazsa snorts and turns in a circle, trying to get the feather. After I cover Darwin's cage with a towel, he sings quietly to himself, like a child humming beneath his breath, until he falls asleep.

In the morning, Zsazsa is still asleep in her bed at nine, and I give her a nudge with my foot to make her stir. Zsazsa is my father's dog, but I took her in when he went into the home. She scratches all the time and farts, and sometimes she pees on the carpet. She snores in her little bed in the corner of my kitchen like there is no tomorrow: great whistling hoots and grunts that bounce off of the walls like buckshot, which Darwin has learned to imitate. The two of them sound like a gun duel from the Old West. When she wakes, she yawns, her cavernous mouth stretched wide, her pig eyes squeezed shut. She scratches and blinks up at me as if I am an alien or a burglar, then trots to her water bowl—on which my father has stenciled CAMEL—and drinks until the water is gone. Afterwards she sits at my feet and lets go a tremendous belch. I clip the leash to her collar, and she glares at me as if it is some ancient form of torture.

Most days, Zsazsa lopes around the block like any normal dog. She sniffs at bushes and phone line posts, squats every now and then in a clump of grass. But some days she gets it in her head to stop at the furthest point away from my apartment, to strain against her leash with all of her might. I have had to wrap my arms around her torso at times, have had to carry her home as if she were some sort of clumsy piece of furniture: her feet splayed before us like table legs. My father told me once she used to do the same to him. "Who knows where Zsazsa wants to be?" he said. "Who knows what she is running toward?" I think if I were to unclip her leash, perhaps she would leave me behind and keep going: trotting over the city pavements, through the green shade of suburban backyards, all the way out into the country, where she'd gather with other lazy white dogs in some farmer's field, and they would howl at things we cannot see.

Sundays, Zsazsa and I visit my father at the Evergreen Nursing Home. Lately, I've noticed he is disappearing. He grows smaller and smaller each week, and his bones rattle and shake when Zsazsa leaps up to greet him. His voice is dwindling to a flimsy shadow of words. Today, he is sitting in a large armchair, watching an old western. His eyes are huge behind thick lenses, and his hair stands in a tuft. He looks like an exotic bird. Zsazsa stands with her paws on his knees.

"They won't let me use the phone here," my father says. "They won't let me call anyone." His eyes flicker as cowboys on horseback ride at full speed through the great rolling dust of a stampede. "It's just as well," he continues. "The lines are bugged anyway." He reaches out to stroke Zsazsa's nose; she turns it toward his hand, nudges it into his palm when he stops petting. "You're a nice dog," he says. "What's your name?"

"It's Zsazsa," I say. "Zsazsa!"

"That's a ridiculous name," he says. He named her after the actress.

"She's your dog," I say.

"She's not my dog. No one has dogs here." I study him. It's hard to believe that only nine months before he lived on his own, in the house he built by hand forty years ago. Even as I watch, he seems to be shrinking, folding into himself like a crumbling jack-in-the-box.

Sometimes, I expect to get a call from the nursing home in the early morning hours. The copper voice of a nurse will tell me my father is missing. She will say he hadn't packed any clothes or personal items. She will say that the little bit of money he had is still in his bedside table drawer, and the photograph of my mother still on the dresser. "He didn't eat the ice cream we brought him the night before," she will say. It melted into an ivory puddle in the bowl. And no one will know where he is, whether on a bus station bench or drinking coffee in town with other runaway old men. Wherever he is, he is barefoot, having left behind his shoes.

"Have you seen God lately?" I say, settling on the bed and glancing out at the tree.

He looks at me as if I am crazy.

"God," I say. "You saw him last week in that tree."

"No," he says carefully. "No, I haven't seen God." He turns his head toward the door, as if hoping someone will appear, then faces me again. "Who are you?" he says.

As Zsazsa and I are leaving, a nurse stops me in the hallway. "Your father sings at night now," she says. "He sings himself to sleep."

I laugh, but she doesn't laugh with me. "That's kind of sweet, don't you think?" I say. "His singing?"

"He can't carry a tune and it bothers the others." She frowns slightly, turns and walks away, a mixture of Pine-Sol and lipstick wafting behind her.

Once, my father was a strong man who built houses. He rode me on his knee like a pony when I was a girl, and carried me after I fell from a horse years later and broke my ankle. But gradually, pieces of him began to disappear: a finger in a table saw, the tip of his ear lost to a wayward sheet of glass. His left testicle was sliced off after the doctors found cancer. But it was when the aneurysm exploded deep inside my mother's brain and she died that the biggest part of him left. He wandered around their house and cooked canned things. He forgot to pay the utility bills and sat in the dark. He let Zsazsa piss on the carpet until the rank odor seeped into the floorboards. When I finally convinced him to move to a nursing home, I crawled around on my knees in that house, ripping out the carpet with an utility knife. I shoved it into large plastic bags, while Zsazsa sat on the porch and grinned.

When Zsazsa and I arrive home, the door to Roger's apartment is cracked open, and he is sitting on a kitchen chair in his underwear, applying resin to his bow. He looks up when he hears us on the landing, and I know he has been waiting. His hair juts up in a pompadour as it always does before he combs it in the morning. "Coffee," he says, raising a glass mug at me. "Iced."

I fill a mug and drop in three ice cubes, settle on a chair across from him. Zsazsa humphs down beside my feet, worn out from the exertion of visiting my father. Roger plays a few trills on his violin, lovely notes that dance up toward the ceiling and hover there like gloss.

"A preview," he says. "You coming on Friday?"

"Play more," I say. I have been turning the news he gave me the night before over in my head. When I first woke, it haunted the peripherals of my mind, like an understudy learning lines, but as I drove home from the nursing home, it strode into center stage, demanded in a deep brassy voice: what if Roger dies? I told myself that just because Bruno is positive it doesn't mean Roger is, too. I told myself the phone sex is a good turn: no more hairy-chested men in Roger's apartment in the morning, no more risk. But looking at him now, watching as his thin arms move in rhythm to the music, as his frail chest rises and falls with each breath, I realize it wouldn't take much to blow Roger away.

He finishes a glissando, flicks his bow away from the strings with a great flourish, and laughs. "Flash trash," he says. "My big solo."

Zsazsa grunts in the sudden silence.

Roger leans forward, places a hand on my knee and says, "How's your father doing?"

"He didn't know me today," I say.

"He comes and goes, doesn't he?"

"Today he was gone. He wasn't there. It's creepy, like one of those old body snatcher movies." I imagine aliens waddling along the corridors of the Evergreen Nursing Home in the dark of night, entering my father's room and replacing his brain, turning him into a man who doesn't recognize his own dog. "It's sad, too," I say.

We raise our mugs to our lips; the ice cubes clink and pop. Outside, a haze has accumulated, and looking through Roger's living room window, I can barely see the skyscrapers in the distance.

"How about you?" I say. "How are you doing?"

He shrugs, flips through the pages of the music on the stand, and smirks. "I'm a tired old man," he says. "Up late last night having myself a good old time. Lord, my phone bill is going to be outrageous!" He positions his violin on his shoulder. "I go tomorrow to get the results of the test I had on Friday."

He raises his bow suddenly, and plays a note so sweet and clear it causes Zsazsa to lift her head, to gaze at Roger as if he is some sort of god. "Come to the concert on Friday," he says. "I've got free tickets for you." He plays a few more notes, then stops to scratch his nose. "Bring your father along. Music can be very healing, I've found. I bet he'd enjoy it."

"I'll think about it," I say, and I leave him there, surrounded by music, though some of it follows me home: it accompanies me as I say hello to Darwin, as I open the door to his cage. He scampers out, perches on top, and puffs out his chest.

I have read that birds are descendants of dinosaurs—the evidence being in the wishbone—and though there is much scientific debate around the issue, I like to believe it is true. I like to picture Darwin, ten stories high, stomping around in a jungle. He eats the tops of trees. He bathes in the river. And when he talks—the mighty words emitting from his beak like a roar—the world listens. He will live on through the ages in one form or another, the wishbone connecting everything. He will never disappear.

On Monday I call the library and tell them I won't be in. Zsazsa and I sit in the kitchen all morning, watching pigeons scratch around on the roof across the street, while Darwin entertains us. He runs through his repertoire of barnyard noises—horse whinny, rooster crow, moo—ending with a Superchicken fanfare that climbs to a high pitched 'Oui-oui!' He's singing "She'll Be Coming 'Round the Mountain" for the fifth time when Roger knocks on the door.

"Negative," he says, and the relief that washes over me is immense.

I pull the Cuervo out of the freezer, slice a lime and grab the salt shaker on the stove. We each do a shot, and then another. A giddiness expands the room, the feeling that Roger has some escaped some grave danger, for the present, anyway.

"Wouldn't it be great," I say, licking salt off my lower lip, "if we never had to worry about these kind of things? If something in us had evolved to fight off disease? You know, some kind of mega-powered immunity system?"

Roger thinks for a moment, picking at the label on the tequila bottle. "But what would we have to celebrate right now, if that were the case?" he says, raising the bottle to pour another shot. "The only reason to celebrate is if there is some danger—some possibility that things could have turned out another way, or that they have been worse, and are better now."

I think of my father, then, watching the flickering images of old cowboy movies on his portable TV, roaming the nursing home hallways at night searching for a phone and his shoes. I think of him sitting in his oversized green chair, peering out at the trees for so long he finally sees God.

"If there's no danger," Roger continues, "we may as well be dead."

I imagine my father singing at night, alone in his room, the words and the tune coming from some place far away, some place on the other side of sleep.

On Friday evening, I drive to the Evergreen Nursing Home and pick up my father on the way to Roger's concert. He is dressed for the occasion, wearing a tweed blazer and a pair of brown oxfords that the nurses must have dug out from the back of some closet. And though he thinks I am his sister Edith, who died fourteen years ago, he is aware that we are going to hear chamber music. "I do love Brahms," he says as I help him into the passenger seat. His head nods in rhythm as I buckle the seat belt over his baggy khakis, as if he is listening to some inner melody. When I settle into the driver's seat, he is humming.

We arrive at the hall early, and I guide my father to a seat at the end of an aisle. He sits studying the program, and as the house lights begin to dim, he leans over and whispers into my ear, "I am so glad to be here with you, Edith. I have missed you so."

I take his thin hand in mine and give it a squeeze. "I miss you, too," I say. As programs rustle and someone behind us coughs, I savor the warmth of his hand. I hold it until the musicians appear on the stage. Then he pulls it free in order to clap.

Whenever I hear chamber music performed live, I can't help but believe there is a god. Before the first violinist nods to the others, life exists in an ordinary way: I'm thinking about paying my Visa bill, thinking about whether I should stop for gas before or after I drop my father off. I am wondering if it will rain tomorrow. But from the moment Roger nods, and the first notes of the Brahms Piano Quintet breathe into the hall like a sigh from the universe, there is nothing else.

Sometime during the second movement, I begin to expand. My solar plexus opens inside of my chest, and my mind clears. My body and mind become light and free, as if I am being filled with helium. Even the tips of my hair seem to swell and waver in the air. I glance over at my father and see that he seems larger, too—seems, in fact, to grow even as I watch him. We will float upward, I think, if we do not grasp onto the arms of our seats. We will hover high over the attentive audience, the music keeping us afloat. If the ceiling weren't there, we would keep on going, on up through the stratosphere and into space, where we would orbit with the rocket that carries Leonardo da Vinci's sketches of the human form, a recording of Beethoven's Ninth Symphony, and a map that shows earth's position in the universe.

This is how Darwin must feel when he sings and puffs out his chest, when he pushes himself out so far it seems he will burst into nothing but a spray of feathers that will drift to the kitchen floor.

I watch Roger draw his bow back and forth across the strings, his eyes closed, his heart listening. We are all in danger of exploding in our lives. We either explode, or fade away. One or the other.

At intermission, my father looks over at me, his smile large, his hands trembling. "Beth," he says, recognizing me for the first time in two weeks. "When are you ever going to get married?"

The truth is: I'm in love with Roger.

After the concert, I drive my father back to the home. The lights of the traffic on the highway are bright, and the metallic hum of so many vehicles driving east or west sings in the night. We ride with the windows down, and the breeze that tosses our hair carries traces of damp grass, warm pavement, and exhaust. I still feel dilated—content and alive—and I can tell my father does, as well: his eyes are luminous, and he hums as his fingers tap the dashboard.

But as soon as we pull onto the grounds of the nursing home, my father begins to shrink. His muscles lose air, his hair falls into thin tufts on his head. By the time he is in his pajamas and tucked into bed, he is a frail shadow of himself: a bundle of bone and organ and skin, with whiskers on his chin and clouds in his eyes. I want to gather him up in my arms, run with him far out into some distant field, let him go and watch as he floats toward the stars, carried by the breath of violin and cello.

But instead, I leave him in his giant bed, and even as I walk down the quiet hallway—past those rooms where old men wheeze in their sleep and old women lie awake and stare out at the moon— I feel myself shrinking. I shrink as I drive through the suburbs, where lawn sprinklers hiss in the dark and men with flashlights walk dogs. I shrink as I drive into the city, past people sitting on stoops, smoking cigarettes and holding cool drinks. As I drive past the bakery—the air swelling with the scent of tomorrow's donuts— my heart deflates: its walls collapse and a soft puff of breath exhales as I coast to a stop at the light. Across the intersection, Betty towers above her restaurant, her mighty platter of pancakes hovering perpetually over head—breakfast for a god who never shows.

By the time I arrive home, I am my usual size, worrying about the rattle coming from my muffler, wondering who left plastic bags full of garbage out for the neighborhood cats to tear into. I smell the faint scent of garlic. Upstairs, I find Zsazsa waiting at the door, disappointed as always that I am not my father, but holding no grudge. We walk in the cool night air and she sniffs at overturned trash cans and kicks up gravel with her hind legs. She does her stiff-legged little dance and smiles into the night. Back home, the two of us pause outside of Roger's apartment. Through the door, I hear the rise and fall of his voice as he murmurs to someone in Cleveland, or San Francisco, or Seattle. Then Zsazsa and I turn away and continue up the stairs. After I unclip Zsazsa's leash, she trots to her tidy bed in the corner of the kitchen, turns around three times, and settles in for the night. At the Evergreen Nursing Home, my father turns onto his back and begins to snore. I turn out the lights. In the dark kitchen, Darwin begins to sing, the cadence of his song echoing back to the dawn of time.

Michelle Fogus

GRAVITY

I twist the ring around my finger and listen to them in the other room. Yeah man, I know that one . . . fucking L.T. . . . those c-rats, you remember the peaches?

This guy's name is Anderson. That's what Pete calls him, or sometimes Boots. I can't help wondering where that name came from. It was probably some dumb kid's prank: wearing size-13s on his maybe-size-8 feet, or pissing in the boots of an unpopular lieutenant. Or Boots for something more sinister, like cutting off some VC's legs at the knees.

Anderson. Another guy without a first name. It's almost always like that: Pete brings them here and they sleep in the room next to ours, eat at our table, rummage in our medicine cabinet. After a week or two, they leave, and I never even know what their real names were. Most of them I remember by their nicknames. Red, Tiny Tim, Smokey. The names they gave each other when they were just boys. I don't understand why they'd want to hang onto that: names belonging to the kids they were twenty-five years ago, when they were ass-deep in rice paddies or humping through jungle—

Michelle Fogus has recent work in *The Seattle Review* and *Sou'wester*. This is her second appearance in *Alaska Quarterly Review*.

but that's Pete talking, his words. I hear myself doing that sometimes. Kids anyway, living in a war zone. I've asked Pete about it, but he doesn't have an answer either. His own nickname, Piper, still follows him.

He says it came from all his dope-smoking, and then it stuck because the little Vietnamese kids used to tag along after him in all the friendly villes. Like the pied piper, he said. But do you think of yourself as Piper, I said. He said yeah, sometimes, because he could still hear his buddies calling him that. Piper, man, I'm dying for a beer. Piper, watch out for them gook kids—they'll cut your nuts off.

Anderson mumbles something and Pete says fuck, yeah. His Vietnam voice. The toughness, the other words, like some kind of code: SOP, perimeter. Never Vietnam, but Nam. Sometimes he even says, fucking gook. I hear that and my whole body goes cold, because that's not Pete. That's Piper talking. Piper, some guy I don't know—a kid scared out of his mind, living right here in my house, getting into bed with me at night.

Boots, everyone goes through that, man. Me and Ann . . .

I put in the earplugs because I don't want to know which story he's telling this time. Boots is sitting in there—this guy built like a fire hydrant, tattoos on both arms—hearing about something we went through. All over the country, there are men walking around, strangers, who know these things about my life. Our life. There are still things my family doesn't know, or even my closest friends, that Red and Smokey and the rest of them know. This is what Pete has chosen, for both of us.

Ears plugged, wrapped in the blue blanket (the one Mahar slept under), I read my book. Soon they'll finish in there. Anderson will go to bed, or smoke out the window, or do whatever it is he does at night. Mahar used to cry in his sleep.

When Anderson is done talking, Pete will come out into the living room, sit down next to me, and start. It happens every time there's a new one here. I don't know what it is about these men's presence that makes him want to make love. I've tried to ask him, but he says I'm imagining the connection. I'm not. Every time, it's the same: a new one comes, and for a few days Pete won't leave me alone. Then things settle down again. Maybe he's proving his manhood to them. Maybe he's even taunting them in some way: so many of these men have been alone, their wives long gone. Maybe he gets high from the feeling of helping them. Or he wants a distraction after all the war stories, or a warmth to climb inside of. I don't know what's going through his head. I'm not sure I want to know. What if it has to do with something that happened over there, some terrible thing that turned him on when he was just a kid? Watching a woman get raped by his buddies, seeing a prostitute cut or shot, something like that. Pete has never mentioned anything like that. But then, I doubt he would. His honesty with me has limits. I once heard him tell one of the guys, I don't trust anyone who wasn't over there, man, you know? Ann—well, yeah, I try to give her the benefit of the doubt.

I finish my chapter and go in to bed. In our six years together, how many times have we made love? There were some good nights, and too many nights when he was full of rage. Lately we make love less often. This is largely my choice. Once it was Pete who couldn't, wouldn't, make love. And later it was Pete who had to be pacified by it; otherwise, I never knew what might happen. Now things are different. Better. And yet, my desire for him is almost gone. Some nights I want to touch him. Most nights, though, I don't want to be touched by him. My body remembers every other time. He reaches for me and I flinch, or go rigid. I want to cover my breasts, protect them from his hands and his mouth. I roll over with my back to him.

And when a new guy comes, Pete tries everything all over again. As if our history might have disappeared. He caresses me, whispers to me, lights candles. He comes to me urgently, wishing passion might be contagious, the way fear is. He weeps. And sometimes I roll over towards him and take him in my arms, for the sake of everything except physical desire. I do love him. I just don't want him anymore.

* * *

Pete brought Mahar home two years ago, when things between us were bad. Mahar wasn't like the others. A quiet, well-educated guy who was raising his two daughters, teaching at the community college. But he cried in his sleep. There were dreams almost every night, he said. Mostly they were dreams about his girls getting raped or knifed, shot up, stepping on mines. All those nights, while he slept, his daughters died over and over again.

Mahar didn't avoid me like most of them. He came in that first night and introduced himself and asked me if I was sure it was OK for him to stay. He offered to help with dinner, with the dishes after. He sat all evening in the living room with both of us, Pete and me, and described the nightmares. He showed us pictures of the girls, Katey and Sarah.

He was with us almost two months. He used to invite me places—to see a movie with him and Pete, or go to the zoo with his kids. We talked. I told him a couple of the stories from the bad days. Not the really bad stories, but the ones with happy endings. I wanted to give him confidence. I wanted him to believe he'd be OK, because I believed he would be.

He slept under the old blue blanket all those weeks. I lay there sometimes in our room, thinking about him in there, in the single bed. Just a wall between us. I thought about him weeping in his sleep while his daughters died again. I wanted to go in and lie down next to him and put my arms around him, shush him, tell him his little girls were fine, everything was fine.

Mahar was the one who could have done anything. The one I'd have done anything for. I was in love with Mahar.

* * *

Pete and Anderson are sitting at the table, smoking and drinking coffee. Anderson nods at me when I sit down, then looks out the window. Hi, babe, Pete says, reaching over to kiss me. How was work?

Fine. A little slower. My favorite corgi came in for his rabies shot.

Ann works for a group of veterinarians, Pete says to Anderson.

Anderson nods again and tries a smile. He has long hair, pulled back in a ponytail. This is my first good look at him. I can make out the tattoos: one says Amy Jean, another Semper Fi.

Pete used to look more like Anderson when we first met—the long hair, Grateful Dead T-shirts. More of a peacenik trip than Anderson, but still in that '60s mode. I guess it was a way of repudiating the Nam look, the military hair and uniforms. To try to blend in with the kids who weren't over there. Pete told me he used to lie about it, the first few years. Nam? No, man. Wasn't there.

Now Pete has come back to some kind of middle ground. His hair just touches his shoulders, he wears Levis and plaid shirts, work boots. He blends in. Guys like Anderson, they're blending into something that hardly exists anymore—which is to say, they're not blending in. Anderson has a hippie look until you get to the tattoos, and then he starts looking more like a biker. He walks that way, too. Aggressive. A fuck-you walk, Pete calls it.

Where are you from? I ask him. Looking for some safe ground.

Montana. Anderson shrugs. He says it like he doesn't want to talk about Montana anymore.

After a little silence, Pete brings us around to the point of the visit. I was telling Boots how much the VA helped me, babe.

Yeah, I say. It did. He's a hundred percent better.

Anderson looks out the window again. He shoves back from the table and finishes his coffee in one drink.

Go for a walk? Pete says. Let's get some air.

After they go, the house is quiet. So quiet I get a kind of edgy feeling. I'm hardly ever alone here anymore. I wander through the house and wind up back in the kitchen, where Pete has laid out things for dinner. Tomatoes, basil, onion, garlic, peppers, spaghetti. He works half-time, so he does all the shopping and cooking during the week. It's one of the things we've worked out. We're trying for domestic justice.

I start chopping. The way Anderson was looking, they might be gone a while. Maybe Pete will walk him all the way out to the reservoir.

Anderson probably hasn't been to the VA yet. Which means he hasn't seen the water tower there, four stories high, surrounded by wicked looking barbed wire.

They put it up after Mahar jumped. He was the third guy in seven years. After the first guy, they put up a fence. The second guy scaled it, and then there was some discussion of barbed wire; but the budget was tight, and there was one faction arguing they didn't want the place to look like a prison. So Mahar went over the fence, too.

I used to wonder what would have happened if the barbed wire had gone up before Mahar checked in. Maybe nothing. Maybe he'd have thought about it, then given up on the idea. Looked one more time at those pictures of Sarah and Katey. I told Pete that and he said no way, Mahar wanted out. That guy had enough guns and ammo at his house to blow his brains out a hundred times in every state of the union, he said. He wouldn't have done that, I said. Mahar wasn't the type to spatter his brains around. Pete said how did I know so much about Mahar. It's not that, I said. I just don't think a jumper is the same kind of person as a shooter.

Pete knew, on some level, how it was between Mahar and me. He could feel it. He never came right out and accused me of anything; but once in a while, a certain edge would come into his voice when Mahar's name came up. I wanted to reassure him. After all, nothing happened—nothing like what he thought. But that was irrelevant, really, because I was in love with Mahar. And after he was gone, there was no way I would deny that—not even to Pete. Love is precious. You don't give it away so easily. You don't betray it.

* * *

I met Pete in an English class. He was there as a guest speaker, talking about fiction and poetry that came out of Vietnam. It was a good talk, intelligent and thoughtful. Afterwards I introduced my-self and told him I was working on a paper about Tim O'Brien's nar-rative technique in *Going After Cacciato*.

There's something there, I said, in the circularity, that has to do with war. I was hoping I could talk to you about it. Bounce a couple ideas off you, you know?

All right, Pete said. I've got some time.

We went to the cafeteria and I studied him. His ponytail, his scraggly beard, ripped T-shirt, beat-up Jesus sandals. You want to know about circularity? he said. OK. He took hold of the neck of his T-shirt and stretched it out over his shoulder so I could see his scar. You know how many times I've relived that one moment? How many times I've dreamt about it, thought about it when I un-dressed? Some guy from my unit calls me up, I haven't heard his voice in twenty years, and I tell the same damn story about the operation and the guy coming out of the trees, how I could see him lift his gun like it was all in slow motion, and I'm being shot again.

He let go of his shirt. I didn't know what to say. I said, I don't know what to say.

Look, he said. He pulled the shirt out again. It's still there, right? Every time you look, it's still there. I'm telling you and I'm seeing that guy come out of the trees.

OK, I said. Thank you. I'm sorry.

I still didn't know what to say. I felt small, and somehow angry, though I didn't know what for. I just wanted to get out. But I couldn't figure out how to do it, not after that.

Anyway, Pete said, smiling for the first time, there's the theatrics. I should confess it's not the first time I've used that one—used to do it in some of my presentations, when we were talking to delin-quents about the realities of war.

Well, I said, it's effective. I watched him, thinking he wasn't like anyone I knew. Thinking I wanted to touch him. Maybe I wanted to touch his hand, or kiss him on the forehead. Unwrap the rubber band holding his hair back.

He said, You know, I love *Going After Cacciato*. The guy's fuck-ing brilliant.

Yeah, I said. He is. I don't know much about Vietnam, but I know about writing.

Do you remember anything about the war? Pete said. I could tell he was trying to guess my age, doing the math.

So I told him what I remembered: glimpses of the war on TV and my parents sending us to bed; the POW/MIA bumper stickers; the bracelets. And the stickers my father and his friends passed out.

They were dark blue with a white peace sign and the words Footprint of an American Chicken.

Pete laughed and shifted in his chair. Our knees bumped under the table. Then I started telling him some of my ideas about repetition and variation—that this is how life feels to me, this is the truest kind of writing—and everything started. Just like that, we were in it.

* * *

They're in the other room again. Anderson hasn't come out since dinner, except to go to the bathroom. I hear Pete say, fucking gook came out of the trees in slow motion, you know . . .

Then I start hearing it, the echoes coming down from twenty-five years ago: Piper, man, watch out for them gook kids—they'll cut your nuts off.

There are a few pictures. Two or three of Pete with the Vietnamese kids. Another of him holding his rifle awkwardly across his chest. The pictures are heartbreaking because Pete was one of those boys who looked even younger than he was. Nineteen, he looked fifteen or sixteen. The way he's holding his rifle, it makes me think of a kid holding onto a girl at his first dance. Awkward, proud.

Not Pete, though. I have to remind myself: Piper. All of them just boys, posing for each other with their guns, giving each other nicknames. In one of the pictures of Pete with the little Vietnamese kids, there are two other guys hanging out in the periphery. One got a leg blown off his second week in-country. Pete saw it—or Piper did. But it was like it wasn't real, Pete said. I was watching him walk across a paddy and then there was this boom, and it really didn't seem very loud, and he went up in the air and came back down. He never made a sound. His leg was just gone. Not laying next to him or something, but completely gone. No trace. And I didn't feel anything watching it.

That kid, Piper, is still around. He's in there right now talking to Anderson. Piper, all grown up, but still Piper. Fucking gook, he says. And I know he's not really looking at Anderson; he's off somewhere, looking right through the here and now, watching that guy raise his gun again, feeling the shot rip into his arm again. Just like Mahar watched his daughters die, over and over, every time he closed his eyes.

I've seen Pete get shot so many times, it's like I was there. I dream about it. Sometimes in the dream I put my finger into the wound to staunch the blood; sometimes it stops and sometimes it spurts out around my finger, spattering us both. I dream of a guy coming out of the woods and raising his gun toward me. I dream I'm him, coming out of the woods, taking aim at Pete. Or Piper.

And once in a while I dream of Mahar. Those dreams are the worst. I wake up crying and frantic, and Pete asks me what was I was dreaming. I can't tell him. We hardly ever mention Mahar. Mahar is a newer wound, still raw, that we inflicted on each other. We need time to heal. Years and years, I think.

Anderson's voice comes out to me, gravelly. I hear my name: Ann. It makes me shudder, hearing it like that. Like he's talking about someone else who died over there.

I go into the kitchen and make some tea. Mahar stands in the doorway, watching. He smiles, but he doesn't talk. He never does. I miss that the most.

I close my eyes and touch him. I let myself say his other name, the one I keep locked up: *Michael.*

Then I feel hands on my shoulders and I startle, look up to see Pete. It comes over me again—that sense of not knowing what my body has been doing. Did I say Michael out loud? Reach out my hand?

Pete kisses my lips. I miss you, baby, he says.

I know, I tell him. I'm sorry. Then I take him in my arms; but it isn't Pete I'm holding, really. It's Michael.

* * *

I work later and later now. Sometimes I go in on weekends. The house is no longer a refuge—none of the space is mine. Our bedroom is crammed full of Pete's books about the war, his articles for the Veterans' Non-Violence Outreach Project, newspapers, letters. The other bedroom has been given over to his vets and to Pete's souvenirs. My desk is still in there, but I rarely use it. Even when no one is staying there, it feels like the room belongs to someone else.

Sometimes, when I do go in, I sit at the desk and I can feel Mahar behind me. He was never there. I mean, when he was alive, he never stood behind me like that. But I feel him there. I want to turn around and talk to him, hold him. I can't, though. It's as if he's forbidding me to. Mahar knew how it was—that I would have given him anything, everything, if he'd just asked. He wouldn't let me. Once, the one time we held hands, he took my ring between his thumb and forefinger and turned it gently around. Then he kissed my wrist and let go of me.

I go in to work, liking the deserted Sunday feel of the office.

There's a note on my desk about the annual holiday party. If I go, Pete will insist on coming, too. He hates parties, but he feels obligated to go with me. All night he'll stand near the door, anxious among so many strangers, unable to keep up any kind of small talk. And I'll have to stay close by, keeping an eye on him, trying to look like I'm not. It's always the same.

I told Mahar about it once. He understood. Not my dilemma, but Pete's. A lot of us do that, he said. I always have to be in a kind of surveillance position when I'm in a group, you know? Standing where I can see everyone, and all the entrances and exits. I have to plan my escape routes.

You? I said. You don't seem like that. You never seem anxious.

All the time, he said. It's worse when the girls are with me. I tried to take them to Disneyland once, and it was a disaster. Too many people everywhere, and sounds, and I felt like I was lost—I didn't know how to get back to the exits. They were running all over trying to get to Mickey and Goofy, checking out the rides. Made me frantic. I was chasing them down, trying to keep them together and close to me. I was shaking like crazy. Sweating. We only stayed an hour, then I had to get out of there. The girls were crying. It was awful.

I know how Mahar cried in his sleep, watching his daughters die and die and die. What kind of effort did he have to make every day, waking up from that? How did he manage to give them as normal a life as he did? I can't begin to imagine how it felt to him. He told me once he could hardly bear to watch them get on the bus every morning.

They must be teenagers now, or almost. I'd like to see them sometime. I want to talk to them about Mahar. I want to talk to someone about him. Someone else who loved him.

* * *

I walk in and Anderson is snapping beans into the sink. Pete is stir-frying marinated chicken and vegetables. Hey, I say. Smells great in here.

Boots volunteered to do the beans, Pete says. I told him that was your job, but he swears he likes doing it.

Well, great. Thanks.

Anderson nods in my direction, still never looking at me. He finishes with the beans and rinses them in the colander, puts the steamer into the pot, turns the burner on.

Pete leans over to be kissed. When he turns back to the stove, whistling a phrase from a Monk tune, I look at his narrow back and notice, for the first time in a while, the way his shoulder blades are so defined. I want to take them in my hands. Just hold onto them.

I put my arms around his waist instead and lean into him, resting my chin against his back. He turns his head a little, surprised. I kiss his neck and let him go.

* * *

We didn't sleep together the first few months. We hardly touched. Pete was living in a kind of communal house then, six men and four women. But he kept apart from the group, mostly. He lived an ascetic's life: single bed, a diet of rice and beans and vegetables, no possessions except his piles of books. He had two pairs of pants, five shirts, one beat-up pair of shoes.

I counted it all. Taking inventory, Pete called it. It's just that I don't understand, I said. Why are you living like this? Are you punishing yourself or something?

I'm trying to keep things simple, he said. Anyway, I can't afford much.

He was working intermittently then, part-time, washing dishes or painting houses, selling wood planters out of the garage. I was still in school, working during the day and taking classes at night toward my degree in American Studies. Weekends I went to Pete's or he came over and we sat and talked. He'd read almost everything; but once in a while I could find something he hadn't—Grace Paley's stories, early Updike novels. He gave me books about Vietnam. I read memoirs, poetry, novels, clinical studies, histories. Sometimes I got tired of it. I didn't know what Pete wanted from me. So, I said, am I going to understand you when I get done with this book, or the next one? Pete just told me to keep reading.

We went to poetry readings, jazz concerts. We ate out when there was money. But all that time, Pete never tried to touch me. Not even to hold my hand or just to rest next to me, our arms touching. I was afraid to touch him. The books he gave me were frightening: men who had flashbacks and locked their wives and kids in the house. I didn't know what he was telling me with those books. Was that what his life was like, somehow, out of my sight? His real life? Or was he trying to shock me, or test me? Giving me the worst-case scenarios so that his troubles would seem manageable in comparison.

One day we were at a bookstore, sitting out on the deck drinking coffee and examining our purchases. Pete had a new book of war poems, and I had Updike's *Couples* in hardcover. Pete read me something. A guy trapped in a tunnel, listening to VC voices, not knowing if they were underground with him or outside.

I reached over and took his hand. Pete, I said. Enough. I can't take anymore.

He looked disoriented. What? he said. He looked at our hands.

It's not my war, I said. I felt like crying. Then I felt angry. Then drained, too tired to say what I wanted to say. Look, Pete, I want to know about the rest of you, too. What you were like when you were a kid, what happened after you got back. I can't read one more sentence about bombs and booby traps and POWs getting tortured and water buffalo being shot and napalm.

He looked at me and bit his lip. Ann, he said, that *is* my life. Can't you understand that? Whatever happened before that, it was nothing. Just kid's stuff. And everything since is all tied up with what happened over there.

I let go of his hand and looked at the river, thinking it was time to stop this. I was in over my head. Twenty-four, seeing someone who was forty-two. Living with a war I didn't even remember.

Pete reached over and took my hand. Ann, stay with me. Please. We're doing OK. Things will get better.

I don't know, Pete.

I do, he said. Trust me. We're going to be good together.

He squeezed my hand, and I tried to believe him. I wanted to take him home and make love to him—to feel what he was saying, to hear it in his body and hear the answer in my own.

Pete did come home with me that day. He lay next to me and held my hand all night, so tightly that I didn't sleep. I told him I loved him. He squeezed. I told him I was scared, and that I didn't think I could wait for him anymore. I told him it wouldn't work. He told me to be patient, that he was trying, that everything would come in time. And in the end I said OK.

* * *

We moved in together. Everything was OK except for the sex. We lay in bed together, every night, with our failure between us. He tried to bridge the space with his voice. I'm sorry, there's too much in the way right now, it'll happen.

Months passed and I didn't tell anyone, not my sisters, not my friends. It would have been too much of a betrayal. Sometimes I stayed up until I knew he was asleep. Other nights I went to bed with him but insisted on a certain distance—don't touch me there, not that way, I told him—and some nights we'd try again. I'd ask him, is it me? Tell me. I'll do whatever it is.

No, Pete said. It isn't that. It isn't you. I swear, baby.

How many nights did we get so close? Nights of passion and urgency, me straddling him, rocking my body over his. And then I would try to sink my body down onto his, or Pete would try to thrust his body into mine, and he'd go soft again and we'd fall back onto our own sides.

It was after another night like that that Pete took my hand and rubbed my fingers and said he wanted to marry me. I don't want to lose you, he said. I'm so afraid of that.

I can't, I said.

I was thinking of leaving him. It wasn't a new thought. But sometimes I wouldn't think it for weeks at a time, sure of loving him, and believing that was enough of a reason to stay. Then I'd think it again: I have to leave.

It wasn't only the sex. Pete was bringing vets to the house by then, and it was a part of his life he tried to keep separate. He stayed in the spare bedroom with them for hours with the door closed. When they came out for dinner, we usually ate in silence, or else stuck to small talk: where are you from, have you ever read this book, do you like Indian food.

I thought it was the other guys. They were going through something, and they didn't want to deal with me. They didn't trust me. A woman, and too young to even remember the war. That's how Pete explained it: they only trust other guys who were there. Don't take it personally, Ann.

But it was Pete, too. He's always been different with them than with me, and I think it was too hard for him to find a middle ground. He couldn't say gook to me without provoking an argument, and he couldn't talk to guys like Red and Smokey the way he talked to me—they weren't ready to hear about how much the VC suffered, too; they weren't ready to think about the war in some other context besides the one they lived twenty years ago. I've tried to imagine what would happen if Pete had told Red early on, You know, buddy, those guys were just like us—scared shitless, a bunch of kids fighting a war they couldn't even figure out. To Red, they were still fucking gooks. He had an American flag tattooed on his bicep.

So there we all were, Pete in the middle, trying to communicate with the guys and with me, speaking two different languages. And I was tired of being shut out of everything. Hiding in corners in my own house, keeping quiet. Trying not to hear Pete when he was talking to those guys. Trying not to think about Piper living inside his skin somewhere.

I thought about leaving so many times. And then Pete said, marry me. I can't, I said. For a couple of months, I said that: I'm sorry, Pete; I'm so sorry. I can't.

Then I said, yes, I will.

* * *

Some things should go unrecorded. What good does it do to remember Mahar, for instance? He's gone.

I was the one who was supposed to save Pete. He never said that, and I never thought it in so many words, but it was there. Pete was still fighting his memories, and trying to deal with the scars all the other vets bore when they came into our house looking for some kind of help. Pete was trying to save them, and I was trying to save him.

I was part of his proof that he'd gotten himself together: the wife, the house, the steady job, the counseling. Pete thought if he had all that, he had to be OK. They all thought that. Guys like Red came in and saw Pete's life and it seemed to them that he had it all. Red was living in his car, his wife and kid long gone. Smokey lived with his mother, except when she threw him out; then he moved into the Y for a few weeks until she relented. I think that's one of the reasons Pete likes having the guys around. They look up to him, see him as someone who's dug himself out of that deep, dark hole. Pete can see it in their eyes: this self he wants to believe in, looking back at him.

* * *

It was a few months after our marriage that we first fucked, as Pete referred to it. I'd expected to be elated if we ever accomplished it; but all I felt was violated. It happened one night after Pete got back from a weekend retreat with some other vets. He walked in the door, pulled me to the bed, and lay down on me with an insistence and a fury that I have never seen in him. Neither of us was even fully undressed when he pushed into me, grunting and saying something I couldn't make out between clenched teeth. It took me by surprise. And it hurt. Afterwards, he rolled off me. Well, there, we did it, he said, as if he were angry at me—as if I'd made him do something he didn't want to do. He walked out of the room and turned on the TV. I lay there listening to the six o'clock news. I was sore, but I didn't feel much else. There was a numbness. Then I was furious. Fuck you, I yelled. You goddamn son of a bitch.

After that, our attempts were always a gamble. Sometimes we

made love and it felt as if all the bad times were behind us. Sometimes Pete attacked me, like the first time; then I screamed at him and cursed him, and he was angry with me again as if I'd forced him into it, and we slept apart for a while.

Then Pete came into the bedroom one night and pushed me onto the bed, and something in me snapped. I kicked him and punched him until he left me alone. He moved out for several weeks, went back to seeing his counselor, only came by when I said he could. I told him I wanted a divorce.

Two weeks later, he was back, and there was no more talk of divorce. There wasn't much talk at all, in fact. Pete was staying out a lot, doing talks and working on conferences. When he did come home, I often went out. I spend a lot of evenings in the office, reading.

That's where things were when Mahar showed up. Things were bad for him, too: his ex-wife's parents had refused to return his daughters after a weekend visit, and they were going to court to try to get custody. Then—and it wasn't until later that Mahar told me the truth about this—he'd set his house on fire. It wasn't destroyed, but there was enough smoke and water damage that it wouldn't be livable again for a while.

Pete had already told me what he knew, about the kids being taken away and the fire—though he didn't know Mahar had set it. But the truth is, I didn't immediately feel much compassion. I was thinking about all the other guys who'd passed through, and I figured Mahar was another case of someone whose life was out of control. I'd steeled myself to it by then.

So I opened the door to Mahar that night expecting more of the same. Another Red, another Smokey. Hi, I said. Come on in. Pete's expecting you.

He held out his hand. I'm Michael, he said.

It's one of the moments I can get lost in: holding the door, stepping back, feeling his coat brush against me as he stepped inside. My body knew. My skin registered even that slight, indirect touch, prickling all along my arms; I think I leaned just a little bit towards him. Or anyway, that's how I remember it. A feeling of being pulled towards him physically. A sense of gravity, bodies exerting their influence on each another.

That night I lay in bed and never slept. Michael Mahar was one wall away, lying under the blue blanket. I could have walked the short distance to his room and climbed in next to him so easily. And what would have happened then?

It was his own house that Michael burned down. I could have understood it more easily if it had been his ex-wife's; but then, I think I would have loved him less.

Now I try to understand how it must have been with him. I try to understand why he turned all of his pain against himself. Pete is different: his anger and his loss drive him to hurt me. I know that he hates himself for it. I hate myself, at times, for absorbing it—for believing that, in this way, I can help him.

I think sometimes that Pete has a stronger survival instinct than Michael must have had. Pete will do anything to save himself. Maybe I'm more like Michael that way: it's easier for me to accept a certain amount of pain, even if it destroys me.

It's this way with animals, too. There are those who survive because they are stronger, because they are predators—and it isn't wrong; it has nothing to do with morality. It's simply the nature of things. There are other animals who are weak, who are prey.

Mahar's burning his house down was like the rabbit who chews its own leg off to escape the trap. It was all he could do to save himself. But finally, it wasn't enough.

In spite of everything, so much of what we know and are is centered in our bodies. When Mahar walked through our door that first time and brushed against me, my whole body moved in response. A body at rest, pulled by a body in motion. The simplest thing. His skin didn't touch mine: but even so, I felt it as if it had. I felt the warmth of him, the pulsing of his blood and the involuntary flexing and contracting of his muscles as he breathed.

When Pete forced himself against me, my body understood that, too. I felt his fury and his helplessness in the way his fingers gripped my wrists, the weight of his bones pressing me down into the mattress. My own body, under attack, first fought him. My muscles bunched and pushed against him, my breath came in harsh gasps. I bit him. But finally I gave up. The fight was over, I had lost, and everything shut down, waiting for it to end, in whatever way it might end.

When we make love now, my body is still shut off. There is no longer any need to fight, but there is no pleasure, either. This body moves, acting and reacting; and so does Pete's. At other times, when we are touching each another but not making love, there is a tenderness that makes me want to cry—not with joy, but from a deep sadness, because I don't think we'll ever learn how to translate that tenderness into lovemaking, the way it used to be with other lovers: men whom I didn't love as much as I love Pete, but who were capable of doing this thing that he can't do.

* * *

Smoke drifts out from under the door, and I hear Anderson talking in a low voice. It scares me for a minute, because I know that Pete's gone; but then I realize that he must be on the phone. I wonder who he's talking to. Maybe he has a girlfriend somewhere. Maybe kids. The truth is, I don't want to know. I want Anderson's life to touch mine as briefly and as lightly as possible. I hope that, once he walks out our door, that will be the end of it.

Some of them keep in touch. There are post cards and letters, a few cards at Christmas. Every once in a while, one of them calls or shows up at the door.

Jesus Christ, Anderson says, his voice louder now. Quit fucking with me.

I can feel it starting, and I try to block it out.

Anderson is yelling now. Fucking bitch, don't tell me what to do.

I leave by the back door, easing it shut behind me, locking it with my key.

* * *

There is something else my body knows—a secret. I am carrying Pete's child. But this child won't survive its own birth.

Until things changed between us, I insisted on birth control. The first three years of our marriage. And then, slowly, I began to want a baby. Pete and I talked about it and we said we would try. But two more years passed without a pregnancy, and I had started to believe that this was an impossible thing for us.

Pete is out, showing Anderson the VA facilities where he'll go when he finally leaves our house. He's agreed to it, Pete says. A six-week stay, then later, two more six-week programs.

Mahar sits in the chair in the living room, smiling at me. It's a sorrowful smile—not like the one he used to have when he was alive. He is apologetic. He knows how he's hurt me, how he's hurt his daughters, and everyone else who loved him. I try to tell him that I understand, almost; but still he comes to me with that sad smile.

I tell him about this child. It won't live, I tell him. I can feel it. This baby will destroy himself before his time, and there's nothing I can do about it.

Mahar listens. I know he's thinking about that fire, the desperation that drove him to set a match to the house where he lived. He's thinking about his climb, very early on a Sunday morning, up the ladder to the top of the water tower. He's also thinking about me. I can feel that. He worries about how I will survive another loss.

It's OK, I tell him. I'm so sad. But it's OK.

* * *

I say goodbye to Anderson from the couch and wish him luck. I leave it to Pete to see him to the door. They are both subdued, and Pete makes a comment about the weather; then they're at the door, and then Anderson is gone.

Pete goes into the spare room and I hear him opening one of the desk drawers. Someday I'll go in there and see what exactly he keeps—souvenirs, documents telling the government's version, medals, whatever he has in those drawers. Someday I'll ask him to sit down with me and tell me about all of it. Every last thing that he remembers. I won't say a word: I will listen, just listen, with all my heart.

But for now, I am too tired.

Mahar sits next to me and he looks at me, his expression serious. Ann, he says.

It shocks me, hearing Mahar saying my name. He's been silent all this time, every time he's come back to me. I thought he'd never speak to me again. Michael, I say. I whisper it.

I couldn't stay with you anymore, he says. I wanted to. I couldn't.

I nod. The tears are too close to let me say anything. My husband is in the next room, alone with his war.

Michael doesn't say anything else, but I know what he's come for. This is about what I will or will not do for love. This is about my war.

* * *

I was nineteen, Mahar said, and stupid. Stupid about the world. A kind of luxury you have at that age.

He lit a cigarette and pushed his empty plate away. We were in a café in Amherst, and Mahar was telling me his first war story. Pete had done that once, too. I was remembering that and thinking about Mahar's hand, the one he wasn't smoking with, lying on the table so close to me, toying with a pack of matches.

I mean, he said, I was stupid about the war, especially. No one I knew had gone over yet except this one guy from my high school. The attitude in town seemed to be that he was doing something important and courageous, even glamorous. This was in '67, and things hadn't really exploded yet. The town was small, too, and full of patriots. So anyway, when I got drafted, I didn't think much about it. At least, I don't remember thinking about it. I remember being scared, but not too scared, and excited. But mostly I was just passive. I was a good kid. Did what I was told. So I got my notice, and I packed and got on the bus when they told me to. It never occurred to me to go to Canada. Literally, Ann—it just didn't occur to me.

Mahar shook his head slowly, remembering the kid he'd been. I watched him. He wasn't extraordinary-looking at all—medium height, dark blond hair. No one you'd notice in a crowd. But everything about him moved me. From the minute he walked through our door, I wanted to feel the weight of his body, the sensation of being touched by him. Who can explain it? Attraction is a matter of the body and the heart first, and then the mind, and it comes over you like any sudden hunger, or need for warmth.

Desire must have been bred into us. I understand that it pulls us toward our biological imperative. We follow it, come together, reproduce ourselves out of its warm moist cave. But why this desire for another, even when we're already partnered—already satisfying the imperative of our genes to find a mate? Why, when Pete was at home waiting for me, did my body tell me, Love this man?

Mahar looked at me. I got off the bus at boot camp, he said, and something in me clicked. Like an instinct. There was a recruiting center a few yards away that had a big plate-glass window. I could see a guy inside, doing paperwork at a desk. I don't know what happened. But I felt this horrible fear and anger like nothing I'd ever felt in my life, and I started running straight towards the building. I dove through the window.

Mahar extended his arms out in front of him like a diver, dipping towards me across the table. Just like that, he said. He ground out his cigarette and lit another one.

What happened?

Nothing. He laughed a little. They dusted me off and hauled me to the infirmary, where they stitched me up. Then they showed me to the barracks.

I almost touched him then, too. (It was a sensation of being pulled.) The gravity of planets is documented—their pull on one another, the way they orbit other bodies. But we are not supposed to be subject to that force. I'm here to say: we are.

* * *

What's this, Pete asks, holding up the box from my home pregnancy test.

Nothing. False alarm, I say.

He stands in the dooorway, staring at the empty container. Then he drops the box into the trash. Are you OK? he says. I smile and nod at him. Yeah, I say. Just checking, you know. I was a couple days late.

Do you want a baby? he says.

No, I say. A baby now would be . . . I stop myself, thinking about the words. Too hard, I tell him.

But after he goes back into his study, I let myself cry. I am trying to be honest. I do not want a baby: not with my husband. I want Mahar's baby. But of course that's impossible. The child I want is the child of a different marriage, a different life—a child who will have to be born and raised in an imaginary space inside of me, where Pete is a barely remembered man who once spoke in an English class, and Mahar is the one whose ring I wear, whose body I hold at night in my arms, consoling and losing myself in.

I am so afraid. My body has never betrayed me before. I could feel the pregnancy so exactly: the thin cramping, the swelling in my breasts. I saw my nipples darken. My abdomen was round and full of fluid. I put my hand against my belly and I swear I could feel that fragile, sickly life.

All of that came to me through my fingertips, and I didn't doubt it. I was sure of what the test would show. After that, I would carry my secret, I would talk to my son silently—comfort him, explain to him why he couldn't join his mother and father out in this desperate place. I would love him as best I could for as long as he stayed with me. And then I would let go of him.

What else has my body lied about? Mahar walked through our door and barely touched me, not even flesh against flesh, and I was flush with desire. Another sort of pregnancy: full with wanting, my nipples pushing out in anticipation of his mouth. Weren't my arms empty? Didn't I want so much to cradle him that I bunched my blankets against my body at night and fell asleep to that small comfort? Or even reached out to Pete, his body a surrogate.

My body needed Michael. Pete's touch was terrible to me: when he took my breasts in his hands, I flinched. When his mouth closed on my nipple, I held my breath and felt his teeth grazing me. I closed my eyes against the picture of that next moment, when he would lose himself, forget what we were trying to be to each other, and bite into me. I felt that harsh, hot pain as if it were real. Ghost or not, my nipples burned. My legs clamped together without my willing it. I was dry. My body would not open for him.

And then Mahar came, and his touch was so soft and unassuming. My body, which had been wrapped so tightly for so long against the threat of violence, began to unfold and reach towards him. Desire came like a thousand-year flood, pouring over the walls and carrying me out of the sad, dark town that Pete and I had made for ourselves. It washed me downstream to a new, green place. Michael was waiting on the bank. I stretched my hand out to him to be saved, and he took it and pulled me in. But then he held my hand and turned the ring around my finger, and I should have taken the ring and swallowed it and told him everything. But I didn't. I let go of him.

I wanted him to save me. But he was the one who needed saving, and I let go. He drowned himself in the sharp winter air.

* * *

Pete stands in the foyer, just inside the front door, holding a glass of orange juice. He sips from it automatically, every few seconds. His eyes look out over the rim—scouting the area, securing the perimeter. Standard operating procedure.

I put two pieces of quiche on plates, and then load Pete's with marinated artichoke hearts and broccoli and baby carrots. I take the plate to him and he says thank you, his eyes barely glancing off me and then off the plate before he returns to his surveying. Are you OK? I say, and he nods. How long are we staying? he asks. Not long, I say. I promise.

I mingle for a while and take a walk with a few other people out through the back part of the property to admire the koi pond and the handmade driftwood benches. Then I go back to the foyer and take Pete's empty plate and cup from him. I put them in the kitchen and say our thank-yous. When we finally are on the porch and I pull the door closed behind us, Pete lets out a long breath—as if he hasn't exhaled all evening. I want to take hold of his arm and squeeze it to let him know that everything is all right. And I want to turn away from him and walk off in another direction, never looking back, until I'm in another country.

* * *

I can't sleep. I roll over and watch Pete, my toes touching his under the covers. In the next room, under the blue blanket Mahar used, a man called D. T. is sleeping, or not. He was in Pete's company, although they don't remember each other. Piper, huh? he said at dinner. Then he shook his head. No, sorry, man. I don't remember.

But when Pete told him the story of how he was shot, D. T. nodded gravely. Yeah, I remember that one. Guy that got killed? He was a buddy of a guy I was tight with.

I reach over and trace the scar with my finger. He is shot and shot and shot. That bullet will never stop slamming into the bone, shattering half of it. At least Mahar's little girls have stopped being raped and bayoneted night after night. But now Mahar is jumping and jumping from that cold tower. His hands are icy from gripping the ladder. He doesn't really jump: he simply leans forward and lets go.

Mahar walks through the door and takes my hand and turns the ring around my finger. He pulls the blue blanket up over his shoulders in the next room, and I strain to hear him through the wall. We let go of each other's hands. We do this and do this; there is no way now to go back and refuse the moment—to hold on, to pull him back from the edge. He leans forward and lets go.

Pete sighs in his sleep and rubs his foot against mine, his hand reaching out for me, dumbly, instinctively. I flinch at his touch. But I don't move away. I smooth my finger over the ragged edges of his scar, as if I could rub it away, although of course I know I can't.

I take his hand in mine and lay it on my breast. He moans a little, and then his hand relaxes against me. I don't move. I practice breathing deeply, evenly. Maybe soon I'll sleep. If Mahar comes again and jumps from the tower, I hope this hand, my husband's hand, will hold me here, at the bottom of the ladder. So many times I've wished I had climbed that tall, cold ladder with Michael. Held his hand and jumped with him.

Tonight I will stay below while he climbs. I will watch him and let this love reach up to him, keeping his hands warm in the freezing air, so he will not lose his grip. I will spread my arms wide, and dream of catching him.

Stephen Graham Jones

ADULTERY: A FAILING SESTINA

in the absence of grace

Dad brings the angel home from the horse trap. He lets her sit up front, and tells her that the window on her side won't roll down, so don't try it. And she isn't so much pretty as she is fragile. He leaves her in the cab of the truck through dinner, and the dome light which hasn't worked for years extends a halogen filament like a finger across some vacuum, pointing at her as we pretend to eat.

"Another one," Mom says.

Dad nods, looks at her through the window as if for the first time. Chews his grilled cheese and tells us the story of her capture, how he found her dehydrated at the salt lick, nearly transparent. All he had to do was bind her wrists together with baling wire, then lead her to the truck. But still, when she heard the engine idling, it took all of his 220 pounds to keep her on the ground.

"This is getting out of hand," Mom says.

"I did leave the radio on for her," Dad says back.

"And her . . . the wire?"

Stephen Graham Jones has recent work in *Black Warrior Review, Cutbank, Georgetown Review, Phoebe,* and *For Winter Nights: Native American Stories.*

"It doesn't hurt them."

"Of course it doesn't."

"Like I said."

"And she believed that about the window?"

"She's an angel."

"What station, then?"

"Church," Dad tells her, laughing when he says it, and Mom throws back her bourbon in anger.

"That's not what she came for," she says. "You don't know anything, do you?"

"She's different," Dad says back, winking at us, "special," but he said that about the last one too.

After dinner and dishes and shows the dome light is still a faint reminder in the yard. Dad returns to it again and again, stands at the window, his back to the table, the living room, mumbling about the goddamn battery he's not going to let her run down.

Through the bottom of her glass Mom watches him fill the front door for a moment, then walk away.

"Go to bed," she tells us, her voice flat and hard, and we pretend to do that, too.

In the living room the television set blackens, and Mom sits on her end of the couch and doesn't pull the heavy amber drapes which would mute Dad's leaf springs and cab bushings, the dry, awkward sounds of his desire. The dome light is a sheen in his back as he leans over the angel, straining.

He returns breathing hard, with the rearview mirror in hand. It slides across the kitchen counter, nestles against the cutting board.

"Superglue?" he asks Mom.

"It won't work."

"It has before."

"Well then there you are," she says, and his footsteps slouch to the television set, his chin lowers to his chest, and he's asleep for the night. His labored breathing fills the house, and his skin in the glow of the late-night nature shows is pale blue, the color of heaven.

"Go to bed," Mom says to us again, and her hands plunder needle-nose pliers from the pocket of Dad's discarded jacket. The kind with the wire-cutters built into them. She flexes them like a jaw, an inarticulate mouth, and then fills the door herself for a moment in passing.

As she crosses the driveway, moving from the light of alternating current to direct, her layers of nightgown make it hard to tell where she begins and where she doesn't. She gets in the driverside of Dad's truck and the dome light flickers, unsure, the angel rising from the floorboard. One of them nearly transparent, one of them too much there.

The angel offers her wrists because angels by nature are trusting, and Mom bites the wire with the pliers, again and again, and won't begin apologizing for hours yet.

interlude with hyenas

The thing about hyenas is they want to exist at the fringe of the savanna. Ask a talking hyena why all the night footage, the spotlights, the furtive, reflected eyes, and she'll slip off into the darkness without answering. It's not all about shame, though, as the British narrator speculates, mister tongue-in-cheek, his restrained chuckle spooling out over the hushed and expectant grassland, the concave darkness, volplaning down over the hyena, her retreat already footage: long, mismatched forelimbs collect the ground before her in an almost simian manner, pulling enough distance between her and the question that she can locate her own dead by scent, hunch over the carcass, lower her nose into the rough coat. The meat underneath will be dark, bitter, familiar. This is the answer: she doesn't eat her own out of anything so mean as hunger, but a compelling need to leave no evidence for the crepuscular light of morning to reveal. A syllogism: 1) material existence entails displacing mass; 2) displacing mass entails consumption of matter foreign to you; 3) to consume unforeign matter is to deny material existence. The African corollary: through cannibalism, the hyena as a species is accepting an immaterial existence at the night-edge of the savanna—*seeking* such an existence.

But it's not all about logic, either.

Ask a talking hyena why all the night footage, the spotlights, the furtive, reflected eyes, and she'll slip off into the darkness only to wait just past the headlights, grinning with need, her painted black lips curling in to no easy reduction point.

the legend of the moth man

Dad brings the candy home from the convenience store and fills our mouths with it. Dinner is ruined. Dinner is always ruined. He's already made three runs to the convenience store since work—one for cigarettes, one for baking soda, and the last to fill the tank back up with gas. Our teeth hurt from sugar. He's still got a candy bracelet on his wrist from the gas run, the elastic between the powdery hearts straining.

"That all you have to show?" Mom asks.

Dad smiles at her, a question almost, but then follows her eyes down to his wrist, swallows as if just seeing the bracelet himself. Dinner passes in fits and starts, Dad chewing, chewing, studying the candy hearts. Two swallows later he looks back up and tells us the story of it, how the new cashier at the convenience store has been on-shift for forty-two hours now, is giving the bracelets away just so she won't have to stock them. This draws a smile on Mom's face.

"What else might she be giving away?"

"She has a whole box of them."

"Poor dear."

"Are you wanting one—?"

"Because if I do," Mom says for him, "you can go back . . . "

"It's just down the street."

"Convenient, right?"

"I'm saying I don't mind."

"Of course you don't."

"I did get the baking soda, didn't I?"

"The baking soda, yes. What would we do?"

"Not play twenty questions at dinner, maybe."

"Here's one. Why don't you just bring her home?"

"The cashier?" Dad asks, winking for us. "It's just candy, Mom, geez," but the bracelet when he tosses it over is heavy enough to slide off the table. We feign digestion, and Dad does the opposite, claims *in*digestion, the sudden need for antacid.

He reaches for his coat and Mom's already cleaning up. "One more for the road," she says to herself.

"The children *are* listening, y'know," Dad says back.

"Is that what it takes? Then they're going with you this time."

And we do, seatbelts and all. To the convenience store. The cashier leans far over the counter in anticipation and there on her finger is a candy wedding ring, her mouth red from it. And she isn't so much pretty as she is pale from working nights. Almost fluorescent. We stand in front of the magazines while they talk on napkins, and instead of antacids Dad buys a kit to glue a rearview mirror on.

"Guess what it is," he says to Mom.

"You don't want me to."

"It's for the car. Always be prepared, y'know."

"My Boy Scout."

They stand in the hall, facing each other. Mom already has the vacuum cleaner assembled. She directs us upstairs and we don't need to be told twice. Below us the house gets severely clean. Dad counters mops and spray bottles with late-night TV, and the animals, when they die, die at full volume. Just as the bleach and ammonia reach our room, our nostrils, two separate doors close—the utility (Mom) and the front (Dad). He doesn't turn the headlights on as he backs out.

It only takes him thirty minutes.

By the time he coasts back in, his skin stained pale like the cashier's, we're already packed, or still packed from four nights ago.

"The clothes are running," Mom says as we pass him in the yard, file into the car, leave him standing under the buglight, token milk in hand. We drive around and around the loop. Mom looks at us once in the rearview mirror, says she's sorry, and soon enough the spin cycle is over and we're at the convenience store pumps with her one more time, pumping gas she isn't going to pay for, and she's staring across the asphalt at the front of the store, the cashier, one of them almost asleep, the other unblinking.

interlude with hyenas, part 2

The other thing about hyenas is that when they have to kill for themselves, they select the weakest from the herd. And they can detect the subtlest of infirmities in a passing glance, infirmities even the lioness is blind to, as if such an advantage would take the art out of all the footage devoted to her—the impossibly patient stalk through tall grass, the trademark pounce, the prey suffocating beneath her, the hyena there at the edge of the kill, the outer limit of the spotlight, yawning in anticipation, already in lurk mode. Miss counterpoint for the narrator, his opportunist of the savanna, her radically sloped back speaking to him of generations of skulking away, of lingering, of *mal*-lingering, an inexact usage, he confesses, the cocksure smile audible, but a revealing one nevertheless, an *accurate* one. To malinger in the proper sense is to avoid duty, work, etc., from the French *malingre*, itself a combination of the L. *malus*—bad, evil—and the N. ME *lenger*, used chiefly in relation to immaterial things: to have a hunger or craving; to move about in a secret manner; to hang about a place beyond the proper time; to remain furtively or unobserved in one spot, waiting. In savanna terms, to be a hyena.

But there's more to it than etymology.

The thing about hyenas is that when the lioness chases them off her kill, she does so not with the inexpressive facial features you'd expect her to use outside her own pride, but with the bared teeth and guttural vocalizations typical of intra-specific strife. Features which suggest it's personal. That the hyena is laughing as she runs goes without saying; that she's leading the lioness deeper into the night doesn't.

dr. thomson and his lucretta

Dad brings the painting home from the hospital, leans it casually on the hearth, studies it over salad. Twice he draws our attention to it by almost commenting, his fork raised in thought, but each time withdraws. And it is well-executed, give her that: a night-study of fecal matter in short grass, days of it, rendered in white so as to evoke the counterintuitive reversals involved with photographic negatives. The effect is one of incompleteness, of continuation. At the table, Mom already has her back to it.

"So are we officially her patron now?" she asks.

"Tax write-off," Dad says, winking to us, but then when we're too old for his humor, too young yet to pity him, he launches into the painting, how it's from her *Latrine* series—$Ca_3(PO_4)_2Al \cdot 5\ Ca(OH)_2$, the chemical composition of digested bone. The spoor is the spoor of nocturnal scavengers, is the obverse of the long night they inhabit; the painter is Mom's old art student, in the hospital now with an ulna that cracked too easily for her fifty-one years.

"Scavengers?" Mom asks, her voice incredulous.

"For obvious reasons," Dad says, "she's interested in bones."

"Of course she is."

"It'll be worth something, someday . . . "

" . . . to someone."

"She was admitted, M—. I was on call. There's nothing I can do about that."

"I should ring her up, I suppose."

"Yes. She'd like that."

"After all these years."

"That was a long time ago."

"Yes. It was."

"She talks about you, y'know."

"Yes. I noticed you were late."

"It's a good painting," Dad says, studying it again.

Mom smiles, for us, together at the table once more, and says that as far as feces goes, but then trails off into the obvious. We stab the salad in unison, with resolve, avoiding eye contact. It could be fifteen years ago, and for a few moments it is—it really is—but Dad's beeper pulls us violently forward.

"She has your pager number," Mom says. It's not a question.

Dad excuses himself, opts for the phone in the kitchen over the remote behind him.

In his absence Mom studies the painting with narrow eyes. Like the rest, it's a finger painting. In the lower corner, too, instead of a signature, is the imprint of an arm band from the hospital, an ID, a name rolled in backwards. Mom laughs.

Dad returns with a medical journal in hand, one of the ones he subscribes to in order to keep up with "popular" medicine. On the cover is an over-the-shoulder shot of a recently retired gentleman, the road opening up before his RV. Looming in the rearview mirror, though, are a host of maladies—arthritis, osteoporosis, Parkinson's, etc.

"So is she better now?" Mom asks.

Dad holds up the magazine in disgust. "She thinks her bones are becoming *lighter*, for Chrissake."

"She's a fragile woman."

"M—."

"She needs special attention, I mean. I understand."

"Well, you know her," Dad says.

"Yes," Mom says, "I do."

Not long afterwards they fall into their apologetic routine about having to go to bed, and, in the silence they leave, all the television has to offer in the way of distraction is the Serengeti. We mute it without forethought, can just make out Dad fumbling the straps of Mom's nightgown off her shoulder.

"Who am I?" Mom asks in the darkness of their bedroom.

The bed springs are motionless, suspended. "I'm home," Dad says, "isn't that enough? M—?"

Mom pulls him into her, her forearm surely pressing against the back of his head, and when the beeper screams on the dining room table we simply turn our heads on it, wait for it to cease.

Hours later Mom descends, thinking we're asleep, and pads into her studio, emerges minutes later with the pint can of halogen white paint from the top shelf, the one with lead deposits in it. The one we were never supposed to touch. Mom is humming to herself as she passes, oblivious of us, the fecal matter on her hearth. She turns the television off out of habit, stands in its afterglow, and then becomes the shape of our mother silhouetted against the dining room window, placing two things next to the beeper for Dad to take to work, as gifts from a former teacher: the paint with the lead in it, and her own calcium supplement pills. Because of the latter, the former won't be questioned.

We feign sleep and feign it well.

all the beautiful sinners

In the morning the smell from the horse trap drives us from our beds, and we make our way through the front door, across the drive, to Dad's truck, his angel, her wrists turned inside out from Mom removing the baling wire again and again. And she's not so much dead as she is beautiful, draped across the bench seat, her eyes still open. Trusting. We don't talk about her, though; we don't talk about anything. In the long hours before lunch we'll hang Dad's floormats on the line to dry, we'll bring Mom water to drink, but now, before they wake, before they can remember, we take the angel to the barn, remove her bones—already dry, brittle—and with the refashioned meat grinder with the battery-driven mortar and pestle with the apparatus

with desire

we reduce her bones to chalk, and to the chalk we add salt, weak glue, geometry: in this manner it slowly becomes another cube, a lick to be placed in the bed of Dad's truck for delivery, and the horses in the trap, when they apply their tongues, will apply their tongues with care, because they need it too.

Dickson Musslewhite

HANNAH: *BROUGHT TO YOU BY THE MAKERS OF ONE-CALORIE TAB*

Our lives came to a screeching halt whenever we were hurt or hungry. And we expected the world to stop along with it. I remember Hannah sitting on a park bench at Hermann Park, bawling in the shade of an oak, pounding her fist, chasing away the picnickers and ducks by screaming, "I AM HUNGRY!"

When she was not hungry, people said she looked like my mother. She had my mother's brown eyes, the thick mouth, the high, elegant cheek bones. But the clarity, the flashes of severity (or fragility) that made my mother beautiful were softened in Hannah. The thin and proud neck, the arteries and striations which let you know what my mother was thinking, were virtually missing. Imagine a dispossessed, fat, uninspired, literal kid, sitting in a sand box rubbing chocolate into her Easter dress. Plump, big-boned, athletic. Shy, a finger in her mouth. Hannah.

When the two were side by side, or sometimes, when Hannah

Dickson Musslewhite is a Donald Barthelme fellow and a recent graduate of the University of Houston. This is his first publication.

laughed, you could glimpse the beauty every now and then, but for the most part those looks were lost in all of the fat and squeamishness.

Here's my mother—loose brown hair, owl sunglasses (tortoise shell frames), a thick leather belt with a brass buckle and jeans—busting into the house with her purse flying off her shoulder, yelling for us to fetch the groceries:
"I got a new soda for us to try. It only has *one calorie*."
She held up the clear, dimpled bottle with the brown liquid.
"Says right here—*One-calorie Tab.*"
She would pay us four dollars a pound.

Here she is later, on the end of Hannah's lawn chair, handing us each a Tab. "You don't want to let yourselves get sloppy," she says. She is braiding Hannah's hair, peeling the split ends as she goes along. She sighs and takes a foot out of one of her sandals.
"I want to get a permanent," Hannah says. "I want curly hair. I want a permanent."
"You can save your weight money if you want. I'm certainly not going to endorse you screwing up this beautiful hair," my mother says. She rubs her foot, stops and studies it for a while. "I used to have pretty feet. We used to go to the beach every summer right after we got married and the tops of my feet would get tan and look so clean."
The light's broken by the pool's surface shadows, which waver on her face, her T-shirt and jeans making it seem as though she's moving. The night's grown fat and thick and wet and all of the things it does in the early summer when the temperatures swerve all over the place almost as if the season hasn't developed its resolve.
"I was proud of my feet," she says.
We sip our Tabs.
"Now they're fat."
Hannah and I each take a sip.
"And white."
Hannah and I each take a sip of our *One-calorie Tabs*.

Calorie. What a dry, white, shriveled-up word. *Calorie:* The amount of heat required to raise the temperature of 1 kilogram of water one degree Centigrade. Before *calorie*, not-eating was riddled with terror. Before *calorie*, a good meal was a mindless swim through a thousand sensations. A thing unhinged. From the great chain of textbooks, swim meets, ball games, Sunday school, etc. It was compassed entirely. By the pan-fried, sweet purple onions. The fetid mushrooms. The hoofy smell of liver working its way through the back of your nasal cavity. For instance. A good meal was fluid, uncentered, unterrorized, a relative meaning changing with each new combination. It was . . . *a volatile interaction between opposites, whose end result is surprise* (Molly O'Neil, *New York Times Magazine* food critic).

That summer, surprise went out the window. *Calorie* gave our pain a purpose. It gave my mother a language for her terror.

There were the 10 calories burned per minute while we were cycling, the 9 per minute while we were jogging. There were the 8 per minute on the 22-minute walk to the store and the 11 per minute on the 33-minute walk back from the store, with 10+ pounds of groceries.

I remember a lot of grapefruit, dry salad and cottage cheese. Gone were the days when we would pretty much sit in the air-conditioning, watching television, grazing on whatever was in the pantry or the refrigerator, and looking through the fogged windows at the fat spring lawns withering in the heat along with the rest of the ruined world. Gone, the cold change from the tin in the cooler of the HappyFreeze van.

That summer, the taste of everything that went into my mouth was ledgered against the calorie. A 92-pound ten-year-old trying to trim to 85, I was allotted 2,000 a day. Hannah, 125 and shooting for 118, was allotted 1,800.

We found calories everywhere: in our Cheerios and celery, in the burger, the ketchup, the lettuce, the tomato, the onions we ate.

By June, the whole world was redefined:

> chicken pot pie: 460,
> Cream of Wheat (no sugar, no milk): 100,
> the Eucharist: 11,
> French Toast breakfast (3 pieces, with 4 tablespoons of maple syrup): 710,
> a hamburger (1 large patty, 2 slices of commercial white bread, 4
>   tablespoons of ketchup, iceberg lettuce and a slice of tomato): 480,
> and so on,
> and so on.

This is the summer that a Pasadena roustabout wandered into the polar bear exhibit at the Houston Zoo. He was "devoured piecemeal. Parts were found below the waterfall, covered with a light layer of gravel." They killed all but one of the bears.

Salt pills and rubber jogging suits were the order of the day. We'd wake up at 9:00. We'd run/walk 1.3 miles around the neighborhood. After a cold shower, we'd sit down to half a Ruby Red, salted to draw out the sweetness, and some dry wheat toast, too wheaty for someone weaned on bleached white Baird's.

We developed a four-, five-, six-quart-a-day Tab habit. It tasted like antifreeze. But it was a hot summer and we were hot and thirsty. And we had no more Dr. Pepper. And water was too prosaic for taste buds weaned on the spectacle of pink aerosol icing and red KoolAid. And there was a faint-plum-sugar-something-just-on-the-edge-of-the-vast-expanse-of-anti-freeze. And on a hot day, we'd crack ice out of the aluminum trays, watch while the Tab fizzled maniacally, and after the first sip or two, after we'd made peace with the taste, set about hunting the sweetness down.

We were like rats or ants. Wherever there was sugar, we'd find it. Hannah became an expert at bleeding the last remnants of icing from Betty Crocker's aerosol cans. She would take an ice pick to the top of the can, stab it into the nozzle. The icing, usually pink or light blue, would ooze out along the ice pick's stem.

She stabbed me once for hogging the icing. I was laboring over a can of pink icing, trying to bleed it. I was taking too long. She snatched the pick and the can from me and when I snatched the can back she plunged the pick into my knee, above the knee actually, about a quarter inch, all that a fourteen-year-old could muster.

We went to Church for that one. We needed a little spiritual fortification for our undertaking. We were told to pray for a little discipline. We were told to consider the life of Christ. *He spent forty days in the desert. Forty days without a thing to eat.* And I was considering the life of Christ when we walked up to the altar and knelt at the railing to receive the Eucharist, as the minister walked along the mahogany railing and blessed the little lambs coming into the fold. I grabbed a cracker from his brass tray and let it rest in the middle of my tongue. It was sweet and salty and buttery and my stomach growled. I washed it down with the blood of Christ, trying to look past the grape sweetness and at the forty days He spent in the desert. I was trying to think of Him with my eyes closed when I heard the Minister grunt as Hannah reached up and grabbed every last little cracker off that plate and, with her hungry little fist all balled up, shoved the 80+ bits of the flesh of Christ (880+ calories) into her anxious mouth.

Don't let your mother starve you, Mrs. Taub would say. *Don't let her punish you because she's losing her Cotton Bowl Queen looks.*

She's waiting for a Tab to settle in her dimpled glass. We're upstream, in the kitchen of the Taubs' Frank Lloyd Wright rip-off which disappeared in the old growth along the bayou. The kitchen is in the back, flying out into a sycamore, which is shedding a fine-haired husk from its seeds. The three of us, Taub, myself and his mother, are sitting around the Formica-topped island in the kitchen and I can see Mrs. Taub through the copper pots hanging, unused, from the cast-iron rack.

I've made the mistake of revealing my special knowledge that Tab tastes better with lime.

"Sounds like something one of my girlfriends would say," she says. She takes a long, pointed drag of her cigarette and lets the smoke out slowly. She threads a smirk around her Kool Menthol. She knows what's what. She wears pigtails.

Taub makes a face.

"Don't be rude," she says.

From the porch, through the kitchen window, she calls to me: "Don't mind him. He doesn't understand what it's like to have to worry about his weight."

Taub wears a puka-shell necklace. He is one of those kids with his mattress on the floor. His mother makes house with a guy who has twenty-eight pairs of yellow shoes in his closet. The year before, a cow had washed up on the bank of the bayou opposite his house. Taub laughs. He has one of those cool, effortless, older-kid laughs.

"Warren?" Mrs. Taub shouts from the porch.

"Yes ma'am," I say.

She mimics me gently. *Yes ma'am,* she says. "Don't say that," she says. "You make me feel so old."

"Yes ma'am," I say.

"Honey," she begins. "My Tab needs some gin. You wouldn't mind freshening me up." The ice clinks as she shakes her glass. "It's in the hall."

"He's not your nigger," Taub says.

"Since when does a Taub say *nigger*?" She is looking out over the railing of the deck into the thick green canopy, not at us. "You've taken remarkably well to this culture. You've turned out to be a real

Southern goyim. All that lovely Southern charm and everything."
She's up from the redwood deck chair and back in to the kitchen.
"You make a mother real proud," she says.

My mother was worried about another Arab oil embargo. She
was worried about the state of affairs in Cambodia. Ever since the
Exorcist, she was worried about the movie rating system. Every
Monday, Wednesday and Friday morning she manned the phone
lines for the Depelchin Women's Center.

Spousal abuse, gas lines and *calories*—her terror had a couple of
names.

She left at eight forty-five. We had to be out of the house with
her. She wouldn't leave until she saw us trot a ways down the street
in our grey rubber suits. She wouldn't return until noon. This meant
that we didn't have to do the 1.3 miles around the block.

On Mondays: *8 oz. fruit salad, 1 slice dry wheat toast, 4 oz. orange
juice (Breakfast); 1/2 cup steamed rice, 1/2 cup black beans, 12 oz. Tab
(Lunch); 2 cups of salad, 6 oz. meat, 12 oz. Tab (Dinner).* We ran to the
Hendersons', to the North side wall, and hid in the shade of one of
their azaleas for about a half hour. The Hendersons were childless.
They both worked. Their azaleas were the coolest, safest place on
the block.

On Wednesdays: *1/2 grapefruit, 1 slice dry wheat toast, 4 oz. orange
juice (Breakfast); 1/2 cup steamed vegetable, 1/2 cup beans, 12 oz. Tab
(Lunch); 2 cups of salad, 6 oz. meat, 12 oz. Tab (Dinner).*

And Fridays: *1/2 cup unsweetened oatmeal, 1/4 cup blueberries, 4 oz.
orange juice (Breakfast); 1/2 cup vegetarian chili, 12 oz. Tab (Lunch); 8 oz.
baked redfish, 1/4 cup brown rice, 1/2 cup broccoli, 12 oz. Tab (Dinner).*
We'd run the 1/4 mile down Hunterwood Lane to Taub's house,
because Taub's mother studied tai chi those mornings and Carl, the
boyfriend with yellow shoes, was, as always, away on business.

We'd help ourselves to the Nutterbutters, Pushups, Crunches,
Oreos and Eskimo Pies and one of the two of us would run up to
Carl's closet and grab a stack of *Penthouses* from the bottom sock
drawer. We liked to read the *Forums* out loud. . . . *and I brought the
caged seagull into the beach house. I stripped . . .* Hannah liked to rate
the models, to critique their bodies: *You can see they airbrushed her
tits. Only cows have tits that big. Only things with four legs. No human
has tits that big.* Occasionally, we played in the lot between the Taubs'

and the Hendersons'. It had been clear cut, the ditches for the piping had been dug, but construction had been stalled since March. We liked to sit with some Oreos and *Penthouses* in the plumbing ditches of the unfinished house, where it was cool.

Driving past the stripped lot, my mother'd say: "Put another notch on Caryl Henderson's belt." From the driver's seat, there was my Dad: "You don't know that." "How do you know what I know?" she'd ask. "I thought you were going to be friends with her," he'd say. "You know something I don't?" she'd ask. "I know you both love tennis," he'd say. He might turn on the radio, tune it absent-mindedly and then start humming a tune he didn't know.

"Look at all of these houses," she might say, sweeping her arm across the stretch of two-story antebellums thrown in with the Frank Lloyd Wright jobs, all of them tucked in here and there among the little stands of left-over woods. "One big rain and they'll all wash away."

He'd wait until he had pulled into the garage, so that he could have the last word. "You don't know that," he'd say.

Every Friday: *3 oz. serving of meat, 5 oz. stewed cabbage, 12 oz. Tab and 4 oz. fruit for dessert*. Hannah and I waited in the laundry room before dinner. My mother was coming down with the chart, the last twenty pages of my Big Chief spelling tablet. We were being *weighed*, and waiting in the laundry room, still heavy and hot from the day's washing, salivating over the thought of our 2-ounce salisbury steak, no gravy, and stewed cabbage dressed in vinegar was something we all dreaded.

If he was around, there was my dad from the table: "Can't this wait, Irene?"

And she: "You know it can't. I can't get a clean read after dinner."

"I don't think it'll matter with these servings."

. . . if you don't want to help. Fine . . .

"I want to help. I will help. Listen to your mother," he shouted at us.

My mother reached out and pulled Hannah's finger from her mouth. "You're going to ruin your teeth," she said.

"They're mine."

"I've got a thousand dollars in 'em says they're not."

"You never made a thousand in your life."

"Get on the scale," my mother said.

Hannah did as she was told and then they were both looking at the gauge spinning wildly. When it stopped, Hannah said, "Four dollars." She was saving for a permanent. She planned to have curly hair by the end of the summer.

"Says 122," my mother said.

"A light 122," Hannah said.

My mother looked up from the scale. Some wet clothes were thumping in the dryer. "Do you think I do this for pleasure?" she wanted to know. She clenched her jaw, bringing out all of the severity in her face.

Again, from the hall, my father: "Irene."

She said to me, "It's your turn."

He stood at the end of the hall, his napkin in his shirt front, his hands hanging by his side.

"Warren," she said.

I pulled my head back into the laundry room and just as I was about to get on the scale, the dryer stopped and the buzzer went off.

"There's the dryer," she said. She had the Big Chief in her hand, was writing something importantly in it. "Another load of your laundry."

Trying not to completely derail the prospects for dinner, "Sweetheart, give me a break. We go out to eat three nights a week. You learned how to scuba dive last year. We've got a pool in the backyard. A garden. We've seen Switzerland, Scotland, Rio de Janeiro. We've taken the kids to the Grand Canyon."

She dropped the Big Chief on the ground, threw the pencil down and, walking out, shut the door to the laundry room. Through the door, Hannah and I heard her say: "Caryl Henderson? Caryl Henderson?"

"Don't be ridiculous," he said.

"She's mousy."

"You're making this up."

"I hate the way she whispers everything. Like the world's a kindergarten and she's the teacher."

He walked the length of the hall and tried to hug her.

"Don't," she said.

"Why?"

"What did I major in?"

"History," he said.

She pushed him away. "You haven't even said anything about my birthday."

"I've got three weeks." He was falling towards her. She pushed him away, again. "I was going to take care of that as soon as I got back from Scotland," he said.

"What'd I write my thesis on?"

"The Moldboard plow."

"You only know that because I was talking about it the other night. Because Caryl Henderson was whispering on and on about DNA."

"The French had to use a steel plow because their soil was so heavy. You wrote that the plow necessitated co-ops, the first step towards democracy, the French Revolution . . . " Then he was kissing her again. Again she pulled back.

"I want these kids to be able to go to the beach. I want Hannah to be able to walk down the beach and not hide herself in one of your T-shirts," she said. She was wiping her lips with the back of her hand.

We could see his hand reach around to her leg and clasp as he pulled her to him. It rose as they moved into the kiss, long, wet, full of crushed squeals and little groans, *smacky*, Hannah would say. The short, pleated tennis skirt lifted up, revealing her tennis panties, and then he danced her down the hall, holding the embrace and the kiss until he was just about ready to turn the corner and pulled himself loose with a little sigh as if he had taken a deep breath and was reaching for air. "Amen," he said. "Don't say that," she said. "Caryl Henderson would say something like that." And then she was laughing. And after the laughter died Hannah turned to me. She dragged me over to the scale and picked up the clipboard. "It's your turn," she said.

Dawn along the bayou was always late. It was a stark contrast to the tidy, aromatic Hunterwood mornings. The air in the old-growth corridor was thick with seed husks, dragonflies and mosquitoes and the smell of raw sewage. The light down there was different. Unlike the bleached light rising off of the concrete grid of Hunterwood, it was green and heavy. There were no trimmed oval shadows. By the cow, the sky was a narrow blue strip snaking through the dense canopy. It was like a river. And, caught in the high limb of a willow, someone's lost shorts were wedged like a red stone.

The cow had washed up high on a bank below the Westside Tennis Club, where the bayou was a nicotine red because of the run-off from the clay courts. The cow was caught against the base of a cypress, looking deflated in its loose hide. The muscles along the jaw were dried, going grey, looking like lead poured along the bone.

Taub, in his yellow shoes, is poking a stick between the short and the loin. He says: "So much cow." He gives it a whack and there's a blossoming of dead cow. From the round, it's bleeding maggots. We're still. It's quiet, a dragonfly and the slow reddish-brown trickle of the Racquet Club run-off lets us know as much.

Her small plump feet planted firmly in a pair of moist and splattered yellow shoes, Hannah's sitting on a stump on a sand bar, which is littered with the broken concrete the road construction had left behind: fragmented chunks of cement with rebar running through them, pieces of broken road, some of them with the curbs already poured. She's looking at a *Penthouse,* prattling on about how fake everything is, when Taub's had enough. "You're just jealous," he says.

Hannah walks over to the sandy edge of the bayou and as though she could see herself in the red water, she primps her hair. "What do you think of curls?" she asks.

Neither of us says a word. Taub gives some milkweeds a whack.

"Curls will look good," she says on her way back to the log. Hannah takes an Oreo out of the package melting on a chunk of concrete. She cracks it open and, with her two big front teeth, scrapes the cream off. She smashes the two cookies back together. She wipes the white filling from under her teeth and then sucks on her finger. "These are hot," she says.

"They're good that way," Taub says. Tanned, no shirt, half his face lit up by the sun, the other half spotted by the shadows of sycamore leaves, he's more or less talking to the tomato he's carried in one of his yellow shoes. "It's got such smooth skin," he says. He kisses it. He licks the tomato with his tongue, sticking his tongue into the top where the stem had been.

Hannah looks up from an Oreo and notices me watching. "That's not how you do it," she says. "Here." She walks over to Taub, who grips the stick tightly and plants the end firmly into the sand. She forces his mouth open by leaning into it. And then she comes up for air. "Go ahead," she says, pushing him to me. "Give it a try."

"No," I say.

"Just once," he says. He moves towards me, into the deep shadows under an elm, puts his hand around my neck, pulls me to him until I can smell the chocolate on his breath. I taste the chocolate in his mouth.

"Amen," he says.

"What'd you say?" Hannah wants to know.

He walks over to the cow, tees off on the underjaw. Again there's the foul plume. "Amen."

"Where'd you hear that?" she asks.

Taub tosses her the tomato. "Kiss the tomato," he says. He

swings the stick like a bat and knocks the wind out of the air. Hannah misses the tomato. It sticks in the soft, wet sand. We're frozen, regarding the tomato in the wet sand with the rest of the afternoon way way above us. Hannah speaks as if she's talking through water: "I want to know something," she says. "How come your mother calls herself Mrs. Taub?"

"She married a man named Taub."

"He's dead. So she's not married."

The tomato in her hand, made clumsy by the yellow shoes, Hannah picks her way through the broken concrete and climbs the short bank up to us and the cow. She stuffs the tomato in the unhinged jaw.

"How'd he die?" I ask.

"Told you. Vietnam."

"Was not," Hannah says. She's squatting, looking at the mouth of the cow. She shades her eyes when she looks at Taub. "He'd be too old."

"He was a Captain in the Air Force. He was shot down and taken prisoner and died in a POW camp in Hanoi."

"He killed himself," she says. "With antidepressants."

Taub tees off on the tomato, filling the air with a fine, seeded red mist of tomato and cow, covering Hannah's shirt front. "Jesuuuus," Hannah says, picking the little yellow seeds off of her grey rubber top. There's the trickle of the clay court run-off. A horsefly or something. "Fucking orphan," she says.

"I'm getting hot in this suit," I say.

Taub looks at Hannah.

"That was your old man's El Dorado on the gravel this morning," he says.

"I'm hot," I say.

"What're you talking about?" she wants to know.

"Did you see the drive this morning. There were two dry spots on the gravel drive. My mother only has one car."

Concentrating as if she were still pulling threads, Hannah is picking seeds off her rubber suit. "My dad's in Scotland," she says.

"Wrong door, Eileen. Who else was my mom cooking pancakes for this morning?"

"He left last night," she says.

"He left this morning. He had pancakes, talked about the Astros losing to the Reds, talked about the Astros needing Morgan back and then left . . . " He pokes the cow and moos. " . . . on the 9:15."

The air is thick and cluttered, the light heavy and green—like water. He makes a fish face, puckers his lips. His hands pushing him through the thick green air, he swims over to Hannah. "How's about a kiss?" he says.

For the record, Hannah was as fond of Taub as she was of anyone. I'm sure of it. Only she could understand the true Taub: Taub beyond the ponytail, Taub beyond the bed on the floor, Taub beyond the stick in the rib of the dead, secret cow. And she cherished her secret understanding of Taub's true nature because Taub, the unknown Taub, was proof that the worth of the world was hidden behind false exteriors, that a new Hannah would emerge from the grim march of counted calories—hollow-cheeked, coveted, loved, adored, the religion of every adult male within a five-mile radius.

After we got home that afternoon and showered, Hannah took the sixteen dollars she had earned from four lost pounds and walked to the store, spent $14.95 on a pair of pantyhose, two Betty Crocker chocolate cake mix boxes, a can of aerosol red icing, pastel sprinkles, two tubs of chocolate icing and those little blue and pink candles. It was a three-mile walk one way, since part of the idyll of the suburbs was that our daily lives wouldn't be demeaned or corrupted by something as coarse as grocery shopping.

The next morning we got up early and put on our rubbers, our tennis shoes and jogged the 1.3 miles around the block. We ran it, Hannah never leaving my side, pushing me along with her ridicule. And when that was done, we came home to a breakfast of grapefruit, dry toast, fruit salad. With my mother at the Depelchin, Hannah set about making a two-layer cake, icing in between, a thick layer on top and in red, bovine, adolescent letters *Happy Birthday Irene.*

She couldn't contain herself when my mother got home. She couldn't even wait until my mother had put away the groceries. The cake was a little chocolate layered square arranged neatly on a blue plate. The candles were arranged in neat rows. "There's sixteen of them," Hannah said proudly.

"That's stupid," I said. "She's a lot older than that."

"You're stupid. It's cause she doesn't look it," Hannah said as she carried the cake into the kitchen, the candle light fluttering as she walked.

My mother had a can of peaches in her hand. She looked back from the cabinet. "That's sweet, honey." She put the peaches in the cabinet. "But it's not my birthday."

"But it's going to be."

"Not until January." She was looking at Hannah. "And I can't afford to eat that much cake on just any ole day. I can't afford that kind of extravagance." She walked over to the cake and took it from Hannah, squinted and then blew out the candles. "Know what I wished for?"

We didn't.

"I saw Mrs. Taub today," she said.

"This has low-cal icing on it," Hannah said, licking the side of the cake. "I don't know how good it's going to be."

"I saw Taub's mother at the store. She called me over to the courtesy booth where she was buying cigarettes. She yelled it across the store in front of everyone."

Hannah was up in a cabinet, pulling down plates. "Why don't we cut the cake?"

"She took a great deal of pleasure in letting me and anyone else who was interested . . . or not interested . . . know what I'd raised."

Hannah was pulling the candles from the cake. I was picking them off the plate and licking them.

"What I want to know is where you learned it was okay to hit another human being in the head with a rock."

"Cement," I said.

"I didn't have a choice," Hannah said.

"I don't know where you got that."

Hannah picked the uncut cake off the counter and walked into the den. And my mother was right behind her. "You don't know how much you've embarrassed me. Not to mention your father," she said.

"Who cares about my father?" Hannah said. She sat in the chair staring at the idle television, the cake between her legs.

"From what I understand, the rock had metal in it. What would you've done if the metal'd hit the boy in the eye?" It had been a piece of concrete broken off the unfinished streets above and thrown by the road crew down into the bayou. And Hannah had used the protruding rebar to swing it at Taub.

"It wasn't his eye I was aiming for."

"Ten generations of scratching out a civilization in the wilderness come to this." She was pacing. "Do you know your great-grandmother put three boys through college with a forty-acre corn farm? What do you think she'd have to say to that?"

As if to answer, Hannah shoved two fingers into the cake and scooped it up and out, sending a small shower of sprinkles down the white shirt she'd washed and pressed herself. There was a strand of chocolate threatening to slide down the backside of her arm and she put her mouth around it first. She sucked on her fingers, her eyes hard and narrow.

"You disgust me," my mother said.

"You made me," Hannah said. She had another scoop, this time letting out a little groan.

"I demand to know where you learned you could hit someone with a rock."

Hannah plunged two fingers through the heart of the *Irene*, leaving the *I* and the *e* intact and her face smeared with red and brown icing.

"I will not abide you willfully destroying your natural looks. I'm not going to sit here while you make a mockery of the rules," my mother said. She stormed over to Hannah, saying, "Give me that. Give me that this instant." Hannah, clutching at the cake, with a smile and some icing in the corner of her mouth, staring, her lids pulled back so that you could see the whites above her irises, said nothing. My mother reached for the cake, had the blue plate in her hand, had lifted it off of the chair, when Hannah bit her. It was a fairly deep bite in the fleshy part of the underhand just below the thumb.

She screamed. And her scream was the same wet-lunged screech that had groped its way out of Hannah and slithered in the fetid rust-colored water of the bayou. At that moment, she hated Hannah. And she didn't hate Hannah. She dropped the cake. She tried to steady her hand long enough to look at it. There was a little quarter of flesh, the size of a young girl's mouth. About an ounce. Let's say it was an ounce. And at an ounce it was no more than 45, maybe 50, 55 calories tops.

Janice Robertson

KNOW YOUR TARGET AND WHAT IS BEYOND IT

When I was twelve, my dad took me to Quality Farm and Fleet and I looked through a glass case at jackknives. I wanted a jackknife because my dad had one. I knew that my dad would buy me a jackknife if I stood staring at the case long enough because whenever I showed an interest in "boy" things he was thrilled and pulled money out of his rarely opened billfold.

This time he approached me, put his hand on my shoulder, and said, "Whatcher lookin' at, Janer?"

I shrugged with my head still lowered and blinked at the nearest hilted bayonet, then the plug bayonet, the commando knife with sheepskin sheath. Knowing that these were out of the question, I pointed to a Bushmaster 2¼" stainless steel blade which had a wooden handle with brass trim.

"Now what would you use one of those for?" he asked me.

I had seen him use his knife to slice pears, trim line on the boat, and open stubborn boxes at Christmas.

Janice Robertson has recently served as an editor of *Third Coast*. This is her first publication.

"For things," I replied.

He understood the practical uses a twelve-year-old girl would have for a Bushmaster 2¼", things for which any ordinary pair of household scissors would suffice. He summoned a clerk over to unlock the case. The knife sat heavy as a stone in my hands the whole ride home.

When we returned home I went upstairs to the room I shared with my sister, Lora, and sat on my bed. The room was distinctly divided: on one wall was plastered Michael Jackson posters; on the other, mine, hung cowboy posters. Real cowboys from the Wide World of Sports rodeo circuit, not fake cowboys from film stills.

The knife slipped a couple of times in my unpracticed hands. I pried the blade out with my fingernails and held it up to an imaginary light. It gleamed and smelled like my marble collection. With the tip of the knife I worked out the dirt under my fingernails like I'd seen my dad do sometimes. I closed up the knife, then opened it again. Closed then opened. It was tough to open, not as smooth as I'd seen my dad's come apart so I smeared some hand lotion from my sister's night stand into the joint of the knife. This actually worked.

From downstairs I could hear my sister making a snack, the snap of the old refrigerator door handle and the jar lids rattling on the counter. Every night before bed she would make herself an egg frittata with colby cheese, mayonnaise, and Dijon mustard, a Dijon flavored with champagne. She called this a "cheese chow" and the recipe made it into our seventh grade cook book.

I held onto the tip of the knife blade, the handle pointing downward, and practiced trying to isolate the motion to only wrist action, throwing the knife across our bedroom in the direction of Lora's posters. The first few tries it bounced off the paneling then I jumped off my bed as I saw the blade sink with a whump into Michael Jackson—pre-op, circa *Thriller,* the poster itself three feet in length, Michael's eyes closed, mouth open in a "Hoo-hoo!" and on his toes in black patent leather shoes, his bootay captured in mid-writhe, the glowing blocks of light beneath his feet—a still from the "Billie Jean" video. Lora treasured this poster, had ironed out the creases of it with a luke-warm iron after she had carefully removed the staples which held it in place to the center of *Right On!* magazine. Now a knife slit through The Gloved-One's shoulder. When I tiptoed to the other side of the room to pull the blade out (from downstairs, she always knew when I was on her side of the room because the floor boards creaked), I hesitated as I remembered that you should never pluck a knife out of a person's flesh because the withdrawal of the blade may cause more damage to the tissue than the entry. I examined the wound, pressed my forehead and fingertips to the poster and wall to get as close as possible. About an inch of the blade had gone through the poster and the paneling behind. The hand lotion had made the joint of the blade loose, either that or all of my fiddling had loosened the knife's single screw so it bent in half, creating a 90 degree angle to the wall. I watched the handle slowly sink in toward the wall. Now the handle weighed down the blade, threatening to dislodge it from Michael's shoulder and send the whole knife itself thudding to the floor. Swiftly, I excised the knife with both hands.

The poster hung rather slackly from the wall, making the slit more prominent than it would've been had it lain flat upside the wall. Whenever I opened the door to our room the breeze would ruffle the poster like it was a sail in dismal humidity and my sister would say to me, "Open the door more careful next time, idiot," then flip the page of her Laura Ingalls Wilder book with malice.

I picked off the four tacks which held the poster to the wall and repositioned them so the poster practically clung to the wall like plastic wrap. I had to make new pin holes in each corner of the poster but the plastic hem of the push pins covered those. I pushed at the opening of the slit with my index fingertip then examined the poster from all sides of the room using light—overhead, lamps alone, night light alone—varying from dim to bright. It wasn't that noticeable. I approached the poster again and ran my thumb along the length of the slit. Nearly seamless, as if I had mended it, fused it with spit. I did this, licked my thumb, then pressed the glossy paper. When I withdrew my thumb tiny wet lumps appeared around the seam of the break. I had pressed the poster into sand particles or something trapped in the lacquer of the paneling so on the poster now stood what looked like the beginnings of a raised, Braille message: "Other" or "Diet," the bas relief symbols on drink cup lids from McDonald's. In the center of these tiny spots the black of Michael's suit had bleached to white from the pressure. I removed the top two tacks and eased down the top half of the poster to uncover what was trapped in the paneling grain. Shot pellets from when I dismantled a 20-gauge shotgun shell the previous Christmas. To annoy my sister I had super-glued them to her side of the room. I had forgotten that I'd smeared glue and shot pellets over most of her wall. Instead of turning me in to Mom, she put up the three-foot-high Michael, a punishment which she knew would irritate me more than anything our mother could conjure.

The gun my dad bought me the day after I received a 96 out of 100 score on my gun safety test was a Remington 20-gauge smoothbore shotgun, single barrel, suitable for water fowl, woodcock, and pheasant. In my Christmas stocking had been, along with Storybook Lifesavers and candied raspberries, a box of 2¾" 20-gauge Game Load plastic shells. I remember I had opened this box, extracted one of the shells, and pried open the crimping. Out poured the tablespoon of pellets, the wad, and the charge, the coal-like remnants of which stained the pale yellow carpet in my bedroom for a month. I kept the primer of that shell in the jewelry box my grandparents had given me; it was the only ornamentation I had. A primer is a tiny metal nubbin which, when the trigger is pulled, the hammer strikes to ignite the powder which in turn shoots the wad and pellets out of the plastic shell. I already knew the order of a shell's contents when I received my first box of Game Load because for many years my dad had packed his own shells. He warned me that if the charge and the pellets somehow got reversed, the gun would implode. I packed countless shells for him and his gun never imploded. He scared me into being mindful when packing shells by using the word "implode"; I never reversed the charge and the pellets.

My Remington did not have any engravings on the forearm or stock but the breechblock bore the inscription "Remington" and I swaggered inwardly over that label as some twelve-year-old girls swaggered over the Calvin Klein label on their designer jeans. I couldn't wait to go along with my dad to his hunting friend's farm for target practice. I had been out to Bud Stressman's farm many times but only to watch. My interest in Stressman's farm was another indication to my dad that I belonged with him. Now, I should clarify that my parents were never divorced but they inhabited two very different worlds. The first time all four of us went out to Stressman's farm, my mom and my sister would not get out of the car.

"They live in poverty," my mother had said. "You can tell from the mismatched siding."

But her eyes followed Stressman's two daughters, Joy and Lynn, as they ran around the yard. Joy and Lynn were not clean. The fact that I got out of the car that day put me in my dad's favor but I never said hello to any of the Stressmans. Not on that visit or any other. I never played with Joy or Lynn, one and two years younger than me, because my mother told me not to, and also because they thought I was a boy and instinctively kept their distance. I got out of the car that day because it was routine for me to side with my dad but I was disdainful of what looked to be only a junkyard.

Usually when I was out at Stressman's farm I fed their caged rabbit, Bunsy, Timothy grass strand by strand through the holes in the chicken wire, secretly hoping I would make it sick and see a rabbit throw up, something which I'd never seen, could not even imagine. I had seen Stressman's dog, Dixie, throw up from eating Timothy grass, her stomach flat to the earth, limbs sprawled, the green-smeared tongue lolling out of her mouth, then the vomit.

Now as my dad unloaded my gun from the back of his truck for my maiden practice shoot, Dixie trotted over to him, her whelp left behind in the kennel to the side of Stressman's house. They were five days old and Dixie's teats swelled beneath her, rode against the sand as she walked. The teats, two rows of them, were as irregular in size and shape as a set of hand-blown glass bulbs, their tips gritty. My dad scratched behind her ear. Dixie followed us behind the house. She had heard Stressman earlier remove a duck from its cage and his deft hands slap string over the wings and feet. This was to be my target. My gun was cracked in half to show that it wasn't loaded. As I walked I carried it in the crook of my arm. *Never load a gun until you are ready to shoot it: Question #19.*

We stopped, looking at a bank of pine trees. Stressman stood behind me, to the left. Dixie settled, alert, at his left side, ready to bring back the duck when I shot it. My dad stood directly behind me. He spoke in his low voice, "Just take two deep breaths. Tell Bud 'Pull' when you're ready for him to throw the duck in the air." I drew one shell out of my coat pocket and put it in the barrel's receiver, remembering to aim the primer toward the hammer. I snapped the gun shut and drew it to my right shoulder, felt the rubber butt plate fit snugly into my shoulder. I looked down the ventilated rib of the barrel through the front sight: pine trees with thunderheads off of Lake Michigan rolling over their tops, except all that I smelled was asparagus. Stressman farmed asparagus and his field lay between us and the stretch of pine. I clicked the safety to "off" then quickly back to "on." I lowered the gun.

It's not that I didn't want to kill the duck. It quacked in Stressman's hands; it had been through this before, shot at, missed, perhaps one pellet stuck in its breast, yet still retrieved by Dixie's soft mouth. Dixie never chewed, even on the live ones. I thought that day, though, what trauma it must be for the duck to have a dog's saliva matting its feathers no matter how little it felt teeth gripping its gullet. The duck's eyes wobbled. But I was used to this. Out in canoes on Bar Lake I had thrown countless ducks, bound at the wings and feet, for my dad's own Labrador. One had even laid an egg in my hand. The shell was translucent, not quite firm, and after turning it over in my palm a few times I discarded it into the water like it was a plastic cup.

I was afraid to shoot the gun. I was afraid of the kick a shotgun produces when fired; I'd seen my dad's 250-pound body stumble backward from the kick. And I'd seen liver-yellow bruises on his shoulder from an afternoon of target practice.

The second time I raised the gun to my shoulder and took two deep breaths, I heard one of Stressman's daughters, who had gathered behind Dixie, say, "What is taking him so long?" Neither Stressman nor my dad answered. Neither had said a word for a good five minutes. It wasn't until I had the barrel pointed skyward again, blinking rapidly through the sight at the pines, holding my breath so that the gun shook in my arms that my dad said, "We're going home." Without looking behind, I lowered the gun, cracked it in half then tipped it up to extract the shell. *If a gun fails to fire, keep it pointed in a safe direction then unload carefully, avoiding exposure to breech: Question #57.* By the time I had the courage to turn around, Dixie was back to her whelp in the kennel, Stressman had unbound and recaged the duck, and my dad was sitting in his truck, his windshield wipers clearing away the first drops of rain.

I used my mom's furniture blemish marker to cover the white spots on the Michael Jackson poster. The only problem was that the marker was brown instead of black and waxy instead of glossy like the magazine paper. I tacked the upper half of it back in place and got into bed to read my nightly chapter of Trixie Belden: *Mystery in Arizona* or *The Mystery of the Haunted Mansion*.

When my sister finished her snack and came upstairs, she said, "You'd better not keep that light on much longer, gay wad." She pulled the covers over her head and fell asleep without noticing the poster.

But the next afternoon when I returned home from basketball tryouts and climbed the stairs to my bedroom, I heard scraping noises. As I entered the bedroom, my mother and sister glared at me, outfitted in yellow rubber gloves and sweat pants. They both turned back to chiseling the glue and shot pellets from the paneling. The poster lay folded in half on Lora's bed, the brown raised spots face up, the slit gaping. I gathered a clean pair of jeans and a flannel shirt then went to the bathroom to change my clothes.

Around that time, Lora appeared on a local television morning program demonstrating her recipe for bread pudding which also made it into our seventh grade cook book. I watched her on the television break eggs with just one hand and calmly guide the wrist of the addled host to show her how to properly whisk cream into eggs to make a frothy paste for the bread.

One of the questions I missed on my gun safety exam asked about proximity of spectators to the shooter. A spectator should never stand parallel to the shooter's trigger but always behind it. I answered that spectators may stand alongside, parallel to the trigger, but not further up the stock or barrel. Wrong. Still, I wished my sister could've been beside me on Stressman's farm that day, one of her hands stuffed inside the pocket of her red and black leather *Thriller* jacket, the other offering a finger on top of mine to help me finally squeeze off that trigger. Or maybe she could've walked with me back to Dad in his truck and sat on the hump in the middle of his cab between us to cushion his silence on the drive home.

Pedro Ponce

THE REVELATION MUSEUM

In the Revelation Museum, we will lie on wooden pallets and look up through rented binoculars at pictures of the future. You will marvel at the Millennial Tapestry, at the embroidered dragon shown nesting in the remains of the earth. You will part your lips and arch your back at things that are yet to be. Through my smudged plastic eyepiece, I will see the shower-damp strands tucked behind your ear, the slice of tanned skin exposed by your shifting hips, the train ticket peering from the pocket of your handbag.

In the future, movies will consist entirely of previews. There will be all the sweep of a promising beginning with none of the sad sobriety that comes from ending, the soft drink traces that sour the tongue, the slow shuffle toward the exits, the manufactured daylight that rouses the audience home.

We will wander through familiar exhibits: The City of Tomorrow. Fashions of the Future. In the Hall of Prophets, you will say that I don't have to.

Pedro Ponce's work has appeared in *Ploughshares* and *Gargoyle*.

Don't have to what?

Follow me. Out. Just leave me at the gate.

We will stand before the wax figure of a bearded man wearing purple robes. I will stare at the astrolabe he wields behind thick protective glass, ignore the glass-mirrored image of your profile turned toward me. I will remain mute and standing as grade school tour groups overtake us, as you unlace your fingers from mine and walk away.

Psychic stalkers will terrorize America. They will elude authorities and confound the courts. The lovelorn, lacking paranormal foresight, will employ them illicitly for surveillance work, consoled in the knowledge that the objects of their longing are always predictably within reach.

The hall that houses the Giant Clock will grow vacant in the waning afternoon. Solitary visitors will linger along the minute track and contemplate their warped reflections in the steep brass bezel. From the terrace of the Cafe Nostradamus, we will watch as tourists gather at the center of the clock face. Some will look through the transparent semicircle beneath their feet and, ignoring posted warnings, take pictures of the exposed wheels and springs. Others will look up at the hour and minute hands as they make their slow progress above the thinning crowd.

I will raise an old argument: What does a consultant do, anyway, and why must they do whatever they do in such a distant city?

You will smile. As you fold and unfold an empty sugar packet, you will explain about markets, projections, polls. You will mention your larger apartment and the inexpensive airfare there and back.

I will not be listening. I will be looking down at the hands of the Giant Clock. They will stretch in a nearly straight line over the crowd below. The shadows they cast will grow broad in the dimming daylight, dark wings veiling the faces of the young and old.

In my best dreams, you won't be naked. You will be leaning close against me, your breath teasing the crook of my neck. I will feel my hand in the easy grip of your fingers, your body cleaved to mine in an unbroken stillness.

As we stand before the Posterity Capsule, I will see you check your watch. You will see me see you, then you will look down to read the exhibit placard. It will invite us to contribute to the cap-

sule's contents, which will be buried on Museum property and exca-
vated after five thousand years. On seeing the crammed bottom half
of the open capsule, you will ask, What more do they need?

Grabbing the ticket from your handbag, I will say that no time
capsule is complete without a souvenir of ancient transportation
systems. You will try and fail to look serious as you ask for the ticket
back. I will have only meant to dangle it over the capsule's edge,
but I will find myself digging deep beneath layers of letters, snapshots, and pocket New Testaments, until I am pressing the ticket
flat against the cool metal bottom.

Your shouts will attract Museum security and the irritation of
passers-by. One of the officers will ask if there is a problem. I will
withdraw my arm without answering.

I will wait until I know you are seated before going out to the
platform. Straggling passengers will rush toward the last open cars,
their luggage swinging heavily from hands and shoulders. I will
think I see you in one of the train's tinted windows, think I recognize
your profile sipping water from a bottle. I will watch the window
closely until the train begins to pull out, until I can't tell which one
of us is really moving.

In the neighborhood grocer's, I will handle packaged meat and
lettuce heads, cereal boxes and dented cans. I will return my basket,
unfilled, to one of the narrow check-out aisles. The familiar smell of
cheap newsprint will stop me and for the rest of the night, I will
find distraction in the weekly news of the world:

> Medical Experts Confirm:
> **Too Much Sex May Be Bad For You!**
> Second Noah's Ark Set to Launch!
> **... Will You Be Onboard?**
> Resurrect the Dead in Ten Easy Steps:
> **Georgia Minister Shows How!**

September will bring rain spots to the windowsill, strange hairs
lingering in unturned sheets, the corpse of a moth clinging to a bed
of dust.

We will trade the day's events by phone. I will ignore the awkward pauses that break up our conversation, the way your voice
grows more distant the longer we talk. You will send me kisses before hanging up, but through the static of a bad connection they
will grate my ears like the drone of an alarm clock.

In the Revelation Museum, I will stand alone between howling infants and dozing travelers to view the wonders of the Virtual Community. Two adjacent displays—one marked "Los Angeles," the other "New York"—will portray simultaneous social functions. In Los Angeles, mannequins in shorts and shirtsleeves will share drinks on a sunlit patio. In New York, revelers will hunch avidly over a board game. Over the border between displays, two figures will face each other wearing thickly visored helmets. Holding empty champagne glasses, they will raise a toast across a simulated continent.

There will be consultants in every home. They will use market research and demographics to determine dinner menus, argument outcomes, schedules for intercourse. They will survey neighbors on the curbing of noise pollution and the upkeep of lawns. They will quiz near and distant relatives for topics to avoid during holiday visits. If numbers fall below a predetermined level, they will have the power to dissolve partnerships, bolstered by pie charts, graphs, and quarterly reports.

She will be close enough. She will be attractive enough. She will be willing enough. She will sleep through my sleeplessness, curling indifferently around the space I leave behind in bed. I will not return until daylight glazes the tops of trees and the chill of morning sends me shivering back for the nearest warmth.

I will attend too many weddings, too often unaccompanied. I will be trapped in too many conversations about the bride's beauty, the groom's charm. In hotel reception halls, I will drain watery cocktails as couples descend to the dance floor. Bob Marley will sing to the solitary and spoken for: *Everything is gonna be alright*. Later, nursing the beginnings of a hangover, I will think: *But nothing is gonna be great*.

Government officials will be elected by beauty pageant. Celebrity judges will consider candidates based on interviews, special talents, and appearances in evening wear. To preserve national morale, the swimsuit competition will be eliminated.

Romantic attachments will be determined by popular vote. The attractive and eligible will debate each other and make their cases on daytime television. Those candidates who cannot afford a viable campaign will be sent home with door prizes and encouraged to swell the diminishing ranks of the clergy.

You will meet him through a friend. You will meet him by accident. He will be merging businesses, writing the great American novel, fighting for the people. He will be teaching the poor children of the world how to fight for the people, how to write the great American novel, how to merge their own businesses. His appearance will promise you beautiful Teutonic babies. His fucking will be an epic that begins without the need for muses. He will lurk behind the pauses when we speak, the receiver cold in your hands, your voice betraying nothing.

You will not age well. In the golden years of your marriage, your husband will wake up next to your sagging body, your crusted mouth, the stench of your incontinence. He will shut his eyes, turn away, and think the thoughts of an aging Romeo, longing for the dagger that could have stabbed you both into everlasting love.

I will forget you easily. Only my hands will remember. They will seek you at the periphery of daily routine. They will feel your wrist in the handle of a brief case, your mouth in the tug of a wet dish-cloth, the rise and fall of your breathing in the cold smoothness of new bedding.

It will be discovered that the world is the delusion of a street-corner psychopath. His unmedicated hallucinations will be exposed as the source of all reality. An international debate will ensue: Should treatment be risked at the expense of the world as we know it? After months of discussion, doctors will hazard a moderate dose of Librium. This will free the masses from junk mail, the common cold, and jury duty. The public's favor will last until a dose of Compazine does away with cable television. There will be riots, protests, all too late. Curiosity will get the better of the scientific community as treatment continues. Xanax will take out the environment. Risperdal will dismantle the economic infrastructure. Men of the cloth will globally decry the waste of life and resources until Thorazine takes care of them and their churches. The earth will grow flat and barren until an overdose of Stelazine eliminates the scientific community. Released from medical scrutiny, the patient will preside over what remains of the populace, haunted by those delusions too stubborn for treatment: progress, coherence, posterity, destiny.

Foresight is a fiction. We are merely predictable. The future is visible to any open eye. It waits in the empty luggage at the foot of the bed, in the moth that crawls on the windowsill, in the tick of a second hand in the blue light of morning, in the slope of your bare shoulders sighing with sleep.

I will not follow you out. I will leave you at the gate. I will make my way out of the station and wait by the deserted taxi rank. Across the broad boulevard, the marble angel that guards the Revelation Museum will put its lips to a gold trumpet. I will listen for the noise of movement behind me, knowing that you are already lost, even before the track lights begin to blink, even before your train creeps out under the void of a new moon.

Margaret Broucek

BEAUTY PARLOR CENSUS

I am just old and sleep less and less for thinking about my grave
marker and how it should read. My biggest fear is falling before I
get it decided, and I don't know whether this falling is more or less
stoppable than my old things I worried about, that my husband'd
drink again like during his bad spell, my baby eat a too-large object,
my house flame up in a drought. For the falling, I stay in bed, but I
hardly can sleep anymore for that marker. I guess it was the census
form reminded me of it this time.

Don't get old. Or if you do get old, don't let your son live in the
house. Live alone or live in an old-folks home. Some have salons
right attached on. That's what I recommend. I have just come from
the smoking beautician in too far-off Marysville, where I wrote a
letter to the Census Bureau about my facts. All us girls at the salon
had just got our forms, and most brought them in for complaining
visuals. We all decided, then and there, that if they make a judgment
about who you are, they should let you tell what YOU want to tell.

Margaret Broucek's work has appeared in *TriQuarterly* and *Sudden Fiction (Continued)*,
and she has received a "Distinguished Stories of the Year" citation from *The Best
American Short Stories*.

Well, truth is, I started it and it came to me to do this under the dryer, because if you want to know, those forms don't ask the right questions and they don't give a blank page or any space at all. So I'll send this letter with the form:

Dear Government,

My son Stuart is filling out the form and I want to say some things for myself. I am the Widow Masterson and have not gone to college like my son who went to the University in Kansas City and he tells me he put down that I am blind which I am not in any way blind.

My people come from Georgia and not here where there are only hillbillies and such. This house is also worth more than what he writes you. Double it.

My Great Granddaddy owned half the island of Trinidad at one time I am told, and my father had a stable in Savannah which turned a dollar.

Stuart is not married and won't be anytime soon.

Sincerely,
Mrs. McGiver Forrest Masterson

My friends Flossie and Lela took up dryers next to me and wrote some letters too, and I'm going to give these to my son to correct for reading. Lela wrote:

To whoever is concern:

In the first place this address is wrong, it should read 4233 Culls Hill Rd., Shell Knob Missouri please correct. Now to explain this Census form.

I am a widow. Lela Lamston born May 25th 1917. I live alone in a old 65 model double wide 2-B-R mobile home sits on 3/4 acre of land. Its not much value to anyone els but I own it I have paid for it and I expect to die in it. I own nothing els but I am tryin to make it on my own. [She is.] I'm using a magnifying glass to read and I cannot fill out this form. I hope this will give you the information that you ar seeking. I'm almost 73 years old. I live alone and nobody els lives or stayes here. Thank you.

Used to be I lived on a reglar big farm and house til Mr. Lamston died and May's husband [her son-in-law] moved me in here by the lake. Thank you.

That's good. Flossie wrote:

Dear Sir,

Our names are Mr. Willie E. Snocker, Mrs. Flossie Snocker, we are man & wife.

Mr. Willie E. Snocker, age [here she left a blank]. Date of

birth [another blank, she will ask him to fill in, I guess]. Mrs. Flossie Snocker age 69. Born 1920—date September 25.

We are White.

We have lived in & on Fairdealing Missouri Rt. 1 all our lives we are just the 2 of us now.

We had 3 children one is dead the other two live other places. Not much to tell we have all ways lived a very quite life just keep to our selves.

Thats about the end of it there is not any thing els to say
I never got to go to school much when I was growing up
There is no more I can tell you
Thats it—

Yours truley,
Flossie Snocker

I don't think we sound too bright. But facts are girls didn't cross over beyond grammar school back when we was children.

I always told the late Mr. Masterson, God rest him, our children would go to college, including girls. Before we got married I said that. We didn't have any girl children, but my son Stuart did go over to Kansas City and he passed all his tests. And now he's forty-three and living with me. He is not in charge of anything, 'cept maybe me, in his imagination. When I go the beauty salon, he drives me and he doles out the money for it, my money, like I'm not a grown woman. And I don't think he gives me enough for a good do. Last time that smoking beautician gave me a do fit for a clown. And no beautician should smoke in a salon with the chemicals there.

I like being under the dryer best—the hum and heat and insulation.

We, at the beauty salon, didn't like the information they ask for on the census form. We don't think it hardly touches on what's important to know. We want to add to it. For instance, under "How many children," we'd put two columns—Living and Now Dead.

"What," we would like to ask, "did you think your life would be like at this time and how close are ya?"

I stare right at my beautician and say they should ask, "Do you smoke? And why?"

Lela is referring to Flossie when she says, "Please answer yes or no, do you talk back to the television?"

Belle wants to ask, "Have you ever bit anyone?" And we are all derailed for a few minutes.

Then, instead of just "How much money do you have?" we want

to know "How much money do you have hidden in the house?" Different question entirely.

Irma says, "Include the yard."

"Why did you marry your husband/wife?"

"Was or is anybody upset about it?"

"If you never married, have you looked at the truth about yourself? Do you get the problem?"

"Do you drink spirits out in the yard or car?"

"What do you think God wants you to do?"

"What smells good to you—like the best smell?"

"What's the nicest thing you ever did?"

I want to ask, "Have you ever heard of lung cancer from second-hand smoke for God's sake?"

Belle'd like to be able to check a box to say yes, she wants to be informed of where her husband is living at this time, which the government will know when they get all the forms back.

"Do you struggle with impure thoughts, and who wins?"

I want to ask something, but everyone poo-poos it. I want to ask, "What would you put on your marker if you were to go today? Would you put, 'Here rests . . . ' or 'Here lies . . . ' first off.

Would you rather have your relations to your kin on there or some saying you always said? Like 'Don't get old' or 'There isn't any more pie'?"

The days are ticking for me, I know. Living forever is not an option unless you think you continue in other people, like you live on in your children.

Like I would live through my son.

Oh, no.

Anyway, now he's picked me up and I'm back home here. See this sweet cat? This is Lover. Is this Lover?! No this isn't Lover! This is Lover's baby. No name. And she is forever throwing herself at your feet. Could trip and kill myself over Lover's baby. I worry all the time over that.

Some say cats'll smother you when your time comes, lay over your mouth while you sleep. I don't sleep. But I might just pretend to some time.

Well, I guess you should go on. Stuart'll be wanting dinner now, and afterward I'll ask him to correct these letters to the government, make 'em sound good.

Virginia Hartman

TANGIBLE ASSETS

This is how the argument goes: I do what I think is best, and my mother sighs, rolls her eyes, taps her fingers. We get along fine.

We live in different places: my mother and father in Tucson, and I in Seattle. I live in Seattle because it's everything Tucson is not: wet, green, and full of surprise.

This is my job: I find people who make art. You can't find these people just anywhere. They don't advertise, and they're often amused at my interest. They're just doing what they do. Some of them are woodworkers. Others construct things out of match sticks. Others, out of junk. Some make sculptures out of farm implements, lawn furniture, toys, buttons. Outsider art, they call it. I bring it Inside.

This is my mother's job: Raise me. Keep raising me, even though I am raised. Help my father be lazy. Excuse his laziness. Cook. Clean. (Empty wastebaskets on Tuesdays, vacuum on Wednesdays, mop on Thursdays.) Sew.

Virginia Hartman's work has appeared in *The Hudson Review* and *Iowa Woman*. She is the editor, with Barbara Esstman, of *A More Perfect Union: Poems and Stories About the Modern Wedding* (St. Martin's, 1999).

As she sees it, my job is just a hobby. Something to do until I get married. A married woman's business is the family. She thinks I'll go into her business. The family business.

Your father isn't lazy, she says, and she is right. Not by nature. Only by conditioning. He used to work. He got recognition. Money. He worked nights sometimes. He worried about what his supervisor thought. He prospered, provided. Now he relaxes. Drinks milk with dinner. Honey, can you refill my glass, he says. He does not know how to operate the washer.

My mother will never retire.

I phone my mother, tell her I'm getting married. She doesn't say It's about time. I'm excited, she says. A girl should be married, she says. She thinks I am going into the family business.

She likes my choice pretty well. Robert. He's the right religion. He makes art. Insider art. He's well-established. I tell her about the piece he's working on. Indirect Touch, it's called. Dollar bills pasted randomly to a canvas. People touch money, I explain, then pass on their touch. She hopes he'll get a job soon.

She wants to make my dress. A proper wedding dress, she says. I want something unconventional, I say. There is a silence.

I drop my cat off at a friend's house. I leave rainy Seattle and come to sunny Tucson. My mother has picked out the fabric for my dress. I pick out different fabric. I make doodles on the pattern. I re-design.

She looks at me like I am an odd child. I act like I don't mind. I pour out all the buttons from her button box. She cuts the fabric.

This is my mother's button box: a tin that used to hold sugar cookies. A round metal box with pictures of blue windmills and photos of the blond cookies. There is a tight-fitting lid. When I was little she had to open it for me. Now I spread a pillowcase out on the floor, as she used to do. I dump all the buttons on the pillowcase, and begin to touch, to sort. Not for purpose, but for pleasure, for remembrance, for contact. The buttons shine: colors and textures and sizes and shapes.

* * *

My mother tried once to teach me to sew. I resisted. Great bunches of thread were wasted, run under the machine needle too many times, purple tangles under the puckered fabric. If I couldn't sew, she said, what would become of me? I was twelve.

Some of my artists sew. They make quilts. It is art, partly because I say it is. I like their choice of colors, patterns, weights of fabrics. I put the quilts in the museum. I supervise while someone else hangs them. My taste is trusted. I am getting away with something. The artist is getting away with something. People come and look and nod their heads. They look close up, they stand back. They move on to the next object.

I spread the buttons out on the pillowcase with my hand. They are smooth. They make a light rattle under my palm. I know where each of these buttons is from. My mother's butter-colored housecoat from 1966. My father's white shirts, now rags. My aunt's pink cashmere cardigan. If Robert saw these buttons he would want them. He would hot-glue-gun them to a sculpture. He would encase them in Plexiglas. He would burn them, melt them, alter them. He is not unkind, only unschooled. Doesn't know the value of a button.

My mother stops the Brrr Brrr of the machine. Time to try it on, she says. It is the dress I want. More or less. I try it on many times. She doesn't like the lace on the bodice. I dipped it in tea in the middle of the night. On purpose. Expensive lace, and you stained it with tea, she said. Yes, I said.

My grandmother did it for her dress. You boil the water, then steep the tea, then dip in the lace. Nothing else gives such good color. Ivory, not white.

* * *

She doesn't like the length. Three-quarter length, not floor. I want my high-button shoes to show. I got them in a thrift store. I'm an old-fashioned girl, I say. She pins it the way I want, sighs deeply, leaves too much fabric in the hem. You don't want to look like that, she says. Like what, I say. Let me lengthen it, she says, you'll see how much nicer it is. Tomorrow, I say.

At night I cut the extra material from the hem.

It was an accident, I say.

She doesn't go to bed early anymore. Instead, she stays up late sewing. The wedding's approaching and she's afraid she won't finish. This is what she says. Really she is guarding the dress.

Robert comes to town. We go camping in the desert. Robert sketches me, standing in the dryness. I look out over a red cliff. On his pad, I am a series of lines. The cliff is a series of lines. I don't look like myself. The cliff doesn't look like itself. It is a good sketch.

My mother thinks camping is not the same as spending the night together. When we come back, she puts us in separate rooms.

The dress is almost finished. My mother is tired from staying up late. After she has fallen asleep, I pick out buttons from the button box. I am careful not to make a noise. I choose the best whites. All the different whites. This is what they look like: satin-covered buttons, mother of pearl, vegetable ivory, bone, see-through white plastic, big shiny coat buttons, patterned, wooden, wood-look, gold-rimmed, translucent, four-eyed, two-eyed, no-eyed, flecked with brown, flecked with pink, rainbow sheen, clamshell, square. So many different shades of white. I sew them around the neckline, around the three-quarters hem. Around the pointy princess sleeves.

So what, I used to say. Sew buttons, she'd reply.

There is a tiny light inside the horseshoe-shaped sewing machine. I sew buttons by the light of the machine. I am careful with the delicate lace; I take my stitches on the silk underneath. I pull my needle in and out like an expert. Like a quilter. Like an artist. Like my mother. I try to imagine what goes through my mother's mind. There are a few rules a girl should follow, she might say. Modesty. Chastity. Industry. Deference. I like the way the buttons look.

I once met a man called the Button King. I invited him to Seattle, along with his art. He'd covered his car, his guitar, his coffin, his clothes, his mailbox, his shoes, with buttons. My mother would say, what did he do that for? Only to please himself, I'd say. I take a stitch and pull the needle toward my ear. The Button King would like this dress.

In the morning I am finished. My mother comes into the sewing room. She raises her eyebrows, looks at the dress. What have you done, she says. I've sewn buttons, I say. She looks toward me, then back to the dress. She fingers the sleeves, pulls at the hem. It's too much, she says. It's just enough, I say.

In the middle of the night I hear a noise. I get up, go to the sewing room. The door is open a crack. I peek in. My mother is sewing something to the dress, below the buttons that trim the neckline. Next to her is a mass of white fabric. It is her wedding dress. I know it from playing dress-up when I was small. She reaches over with her scissors, snips a tiny covered button from her dress. She knots a thread and sews her button beneath the ones I have sewn on mine. Neckline only. I watch her for a minute. Then I go back to bed.

* * *

This is what the dress looks like when I walk down the aisle: Drop waist that points downward. Lace top, silk underdress. Three-quarter length, old-fashioned shoes showing. Buttons around the neckline for trim. Hers and mine. I took off the buttons around the hem, around the sleeves. My mother was right. Less was more. I look real nice.

Robert looks good too. White linen suit. Like the ice-cream man.

In the receiving line, when everyone has been received, my mother turns me toward her. She touches a mother-of-pearl button at my collarbone. Well, it's you, she says, it's definitely you.

For a honeymoon, Robert and I go camping in the rain forest. It is wet and warm.

Deference. Industry. Modesty. Chastity. I didn't go into the family business exactly. I love my husband because he is good, he is virtuous, he is mad with insight, he is a mixed blessing. He loves me, though not for my housekeeping. In domestic affairs, I sometimes defer to my father's example: Robert, could you refill my glass?

In my job, industriousness does not seem to apply. My confidence is taken for expertise. I stay late, but only to walk through the silent galleries. I touch the quilts and other works of art that bear the sign "Please Do Not Touch." If my mother comes to visit, I will guide her through the museum after hours. I will let her touch.

As for modesty, Robert and I have no need of it. We sleep and wake naked; we walk about the house enjoying the sight of each other without clothes. This is something my mother would not want to know.

But she does know her buttons. I saw it myself the night before the wedding. It was late. I couldn't sleep. I sneaked into the sewing room, tried on the dress, looked in the mirror, and knew at once. Neckline only. I unzipped myself, got out the small scissors, sat down. The buttons from the sleeves and from the hem, I snipped off. I pushed them into a mound on the sewing machine table, then scooped them up. I held them for a minute, feeling their weight. Then I pocketed them, quick.

I keep them in a silk pouch with smooth black drawstrings. I sleep with them tucked just under the mattress beneath my pillow, where I can reach them. At night, when Robert is asleep, and the breath comes out in soft regularity over the curve of his lip, I make a well in my pillow and pull the pouch from beneath the mattress. I spill the buttons out onto the pillowcase and touch them. The contents of the pouch are like teeth brought by a magic fairy, like stones made smooth in a creekbed, like soft and precious coins I will never spend. Robert doesn't know I have them. My mother thinks they are lost in the tinned sea of buttons she may someday use. But they are separate. They are borrowed, but they are mine.

The cat jumps on the bed, sniffs the buttons, moves to the place in the bed that my body has warmed.

This is what I know: A calico cat in a warm spot on the bed. Robert breathing in and out, dreaming a new shape for his vision. A handful of milk-white buttons making a gentle sound as I ease them back into a soft silk pouch. And my mother, twelve-hundred miles away, sitting in a room dark except for a horseshoe-shaped light. She pierces fabric with a needle, takes a stitch, pulls it toward her, and tugs.

Heidi Schulz

DRESSES: A LOVE STORY

Dresses are like ghosts, the souls of vanished women who roam the earth on the backs of their living sisters. Or else, they are like visions, conjurings of women yet to be. If indeed they were ghosts or visions, it would explain the uncanniness of certain dresses, the feeling of instant recognition and adoration they arouse, or the reverse, loathing. And it would explain why they seem, even on the hanger, animate and full of personality, and why a very vibrant dress appears to be riding the wearer, using her to get around and express itself.

Like most of my contemporaries, I don't wear dresses very often. I wear pants and T-shirts and sweaters, most of the time. Only in summer do dresses seem as comfortable and practical as the boys' clothes I usually prefer, and even then I am more likely to opt for shorts and a tee. Nevertheless, dresses pervade my imagination, where they receive the same sensuous, reverent attention as do my other obsessions: food, books and language, my husband, my children, sex.

My daughter's doll now wears a dress I once wore, the first of many my grandmother made for me. Needless to say, it is tiny and

---

Heidi Schulz has recent work in the *Birmingham Poetry Review*.

pink, a tiny pink confection cut from a shimmery synthetic, with short puffed sleeves and buttons down the back, trimmed with lace and ribbon rosebuds. To a little girl, irresistible. When my daughter was two, I came upon the heartbreaking sight of her trying to put on this dress, which was cut to fit a newborn. Having no real sense of her own size (she would try to get into her doll house, too), she could not be persuaded with words that the dress was too small, so I had to let her force her plump arms through the unelasticized sleeve openings and then witness her outrage as she realized the circumference wouldn't move past her elbows and she was stuck in the dress, flailing her foreshortened limbs like a livid allosaur. No amount of soothing or distracting would console her; she wept and shrieked to the point of exhaustion. I know just how she felt. Naturally I have no memory of wearing this dress, but I do remember putting it on my doll and regarding her with great ambivalence—on the one hand (how beautiful she looked!), I felt intense admiration and aesthetic pleasure, and on the other hand, sheer envy, even disgust, that she should wear the dress when I could not. To this day, I continue to have a version of this reaction whenever I see a woman who is not me in a beautiful dress. On occasion it is how I feel when I see a really exquisite, prohibitively expensive dress in a shop: I love it and I hate it, as you love and hate what you desire and cannot possess. Desire and Possession are the twin goddesses who rule my relationship to dresses.

I like pictures of dresses, but I like best to see them in person, in shops, where they are allowed to be the provocative ghosts that they are. A dress filled out with a dress form, standing alone in a shop window is freest to communicate its essence. Many times I have come upon this sight and said out loud, "How beautiful!" For there is something about the dress shaped like a woman but headless, armless, isolated and pressing toward the glass as if longing for the world, slightly elevated above the passerby in the street, like an ascendant dream.

When you fall in love with the dress in the shop window, it is truly like falling in love. The instant of desire gives way to imagined possession as you sketch yourself into the dress—your head, your arms—just as you would sketch yourself into the life of the beloved—into his head, into his arms. It is difficult to know which is more urgent, the wish to possess or to be possessed. Rarely do I think, "How lovely I would look in that dress," but rather, "How lovely that dress would look on me," as if I wanted to be consumed by its radiance, effaced until the dress and I were a unified expression of ardor.

The dress that still reigns among the dresses I have owned is a vintage black velvet, the first dress I ever chose for myself that felt like a twin, like a long-sought double. I wore it for dress-up all through college (most memorably during my semester in Paris) and then I was no longer thin enough to wear it. The velvet is incredibly fluid and drapey and fragile in the places the dress is fitted; if you look closely you can see where it will eventually tear, or has torn and was mended. The sleeves are short and puffed, each gathered into a little knot, like a bud. Constructed in two parts, the bodice is softly shirred over the bust then tightly fitted to the ribcage and the waist. There are three tiny buttons in back that secure the dress at the neckline, then there is an unclosable opening to the point where the dress becomes tight, and then a zippered closure the rest of the way to the tailbone. The bodice gives way to a skirt that skims the hips and gradually picks up fullness so that it falls in ripples around the ankles. The legs, walking, agitate the skirt like hands in water.

This dress, along with one other, I have saved as souvenirs of a time in my life defined by sensuality, exploration, passionate learning. The other dress is one I designed and my grandmother cut and sewed, a summer dress as light as air, with very thin straps holding up a small, close-fitting bodice and a softly gathered skirt that ends in a scalloped hem, which my grandmother hand embroidered. I can still see her working on this dress, especially the handwork, which was her passion and gift. She had learned her trade in a time of great scarcity and never lost the habit of treating the cheapest materials to her sumptuous embellishments. But *I* bought the fabric for this dress, and it was very expensive, an almost sheer Italian cotton floral, printed with beautiful detail and dimensionality in shades of purple on black.

I think of those two dresses, the velvet and the cotton, as my winter and summer souls from that era in my life. In my memory I picture them as the dress in the shop window appears, ablaze with their own identities, my body and face only faintly penciled in. They have come to evoke not my vanished young physical self, but still vivid thoughts, feelings, and experiences, a whole way of being that is past though living, incorporated into my present life.

In the way those two dresses marked the rise of my powers as a woman, which I think of as a gendered sensuality strongly linked to the intellect, the waxing and waning of my interest in dresses has consistently followed the expansion and contraction of those powers. There have been phases in my life when I was almost completely alienated from my own sensuality, or intellect, or both: on the one end of the spectrum, graduate school, and on the other, pregnancy and new motherhood. Then, after my second child passed his first birthday, I felt a new sense of self emerge, tempered by the heat of my experiences with the extremes of mind and body. For this self, the intellectual and the sensual are more than just connected, they are fused.

There are dresses for this self, such beautiful dresses made from mutual adoration between mind and body. While many exist in my imagination, sometimes I see dresses like that in the world. They are evocations of my spiritual sisters whom I recognize and love immediately. Some of them are simple day dresses, some are elaborate evening gowns, but all of them could clothe and, more, somehow express a woman fat or thin, dancing or reading, holding a child or a lover or her own solitude, well groomed or completely undone. Dresses are usually specific as to occasion and use; there are work dresses, play dresses, sun dresses, prom dresses, and so on. Certain dresses, however, while maintaining this specificity, get at something deeper, an idea of beauty and the possibility of self-expression that imbues them with a life of their own. Of so many dresses you can say, "That will do just fine." But of certain rarer dresses you think, "If I could relive my whole life in this dress, how different it would be." The former serves an already well-defined role and style. But the latter, if you let it, would bring some wild, inhibited part of the soul to the surface where it would remake you in its image. Sometimes it is a great relief to find that kind of dress, if it ushers out a part of you that felt unjustly caged, and at other times it is an agony, if it stirs what you've determined to stifle and deaden.

I have always been suspicious of my mother's perennial advice to me: buy a new dress, put on a nice skirt, make yourself lovely. It is part of her generational baggage, I tell myself, this insistence on making yourself attractive to men, even, or perhaps especially, after marriage. The alternative reason, to make myself attractive *for myself* makes even less sense to me. I have always known better, believing in the beauty of intelligence and accomplishment and personality. Yet even as I have rejected my mother's suggestions, I have carried on this interrupted but tenacious love affair with dresses. So many times, I have become obsessed with a dress and gone out of my way to visit and revisit it—look at it, touch it, decide once again it could serve no purpose in my life—until the day it vanishes; someone else has taken it home. Then I regret my guilty ambivalence. Meanwhile, the dresses I own too often seem like an unfortunate compromise between my idea of what is wearable and my idea of what is breathtaking.

But recently I've started to get it, the wherefore of this passion and its vindication. My dress obsession springs from a deep-rooted appreciation of the feminine. Of all articles of clothing—discounting lingerie, which is too exclusively sexual—the dress is the most expressive of femininity as a construct, as an idea or aesthetic. Dresses, I think, are the only garment that can stand in metonymically for the feminine. (The often-used "skirt" is disturbingly truncated.) That is why men, even men who don't wear dresses, can be as passionate about dresses as women. I think of Proust describing the intricacies of Odette's many gowns, with a stamina and ardor that nearly exhausts my own lust for such detail. And I think of the male owner of a dress shop in my town whose love for his dresses clearly exceeds his affection for his customers; in fact I believe he harbors a bit of the resentment my daughter and I have felt toward our dolls. "*Your* dresses are so beautiful," I tell him, not as a compliment to his eye, but as an affirmation of his sense of possession. Dresses are a means to adore the feminine, which is perhaps more enthralling to those of us who do not enjoy sensuous relationships with real women, in other words, heterosexual women and gay men.

A little at a time, I have learned about my lifelong relationship to dresses by indulging my desire for them, yielding to the temptation of owning certain dresses after having fallen for many. I learned that sometimes trying on the dress will cure you of desire, either because it does not look as beautiful on your body as it looked on the hanger or because, as beautiful as it is, it is not right. If it is right, you don't necessarily need to have it: this, too, is instructive. Some relationships are meant to stay in the imagination. But sometimes, just occasionally (perhaps there is a special party coming up, or perhaps it is your birthday) it is okay to buy the dress. You may hardly ever wear it, but having yielded to an acute desire can teach you a lot, as I have learned that my desire was not to make myself more attractive to men (though that's part of it), nor to make myself attractive for myself (though that, too, is part of it). My romance with dresses is a romance with the feminine and with the feminine parts of myself. The few dresses I have bought that are to me just wildly gorgeous, have allowed me to create a romance with that woman within me who is a fusion of intellect and sensuality. This is a form of erotic fantasy that has nothing to do with acts and partners; it is the self possessing a romantically imagined self, both desiring and desired in a state of sexual completeness, like a flower.

Cinderella is so much more about the dress than the prince. I learned that from my daughter, who is never interested in the story beyond the point at which the dress is conjured in a whorl of shimmery, magical ecstasy. To her, that moment is the story's climax and Cinderella's ultimate triumph. All the rest puzzles her: the ball, the prince, the race against the clock, the search for Cinderella, and even the revenge against the stepmother and her daughters. These aspects of the narrative involve concepts and relationships beyond her four-year-old mental grasp. But desire for the dress and possession of the dress she understands completely. All the bitterness and grief my daughter feels on Cinderella's behalf is tied to the cruel thwarting of her desire to wear a beautiful dress, which in turn is tied to the cruel thwarting of her desire for her mother. Seeing the tale through her eyes, but with an adult dimension, *Cinderella* seems to me the story of the birth of an erotic self, culminating in the appearance of the dress on her body. Persecution, confinement, and the absence of her mother sharpen Cinderella's longing for a female other, and sweeten its attainment. This other—an ally who can usher her to a better place—is found within herself, externalized by the dress, and liberated into a space where her erotic dreams can intersect with reality. It is not really that the prince finds Cinderella, but that she summons him in her state of enchanted reverie, and then draws him into her harsh reality, which can then be transformed.

As a little girl, my favorite book was *The Hundred Dresses* by Eleanor Estes. It is the story of Wanda Petronski, motherless like Cinderella, raised by a poor immigrant father. Wanda, again like Cinderella, has one dress, faded and mended and always clean, which she wears to school every day. One morning, a group of her schoolmates gather to admire one girl's brand new red dress. Wanda joins them and shyly interjects that she has a hundred dresses at home, all different, all lined up in her closet. Two of the girls—Peggy, glamorous and popular, and Maddie, her best friend, who is poor like Wanda—begin to tease Wanda, interrogating her about the hundred dresses that she claims to own but never wears. Every day after that, they wait for her on the walk to school and tease her all over again: "Tell us how many dresses you have, Wanda," to which she always replies, "A hundred, all different, all lined up in my closet."

Then, on the day of an art contest, Peggy and Maddie come into their classroom and discover its walls covered with pictures of Wanda's hundred dresses, exquisitely done. But Wanda is not there that day, and the teacher reads a note to the class, sent by her father, who explains that he has moved his family to the city, where he hopes no one will make fun of his daughter again. Maddie, whose conscience has bothered her about the teasing, is torn apart by her grief and remorse at having hurt Wanda so badly. She and Peggy write to Wanda who writes back and bequeaths two particular pictures to Maddie and Peggy. Alone in her room with this gift, Maddie discovers that Wanda has sketched Maddie's own head and body into the dress in the picture. Wanda, even as she was persecuted by Maddie, created this beautiful dress just for her.

There is so much in this story that spoke and still speaks to my imagination. The tale of Wanda's bullying was acutely painful to my school-girl self, as was my empathy with Maddie, who, despite her better instincts, was not courageous enough to stand up to the meaner Peggy. But I am still haunted by Wanda herself, as much as I am by any great character in adult literature, her attempt to convey her inner life with a few timid words, which are turned against her, and then her triumph of expression in her art. That this drama should revolve around dresses seems entirely apt to me. With the dresses that paper the classroom, Wanda projects the gorgeous fragments of her self-created self onto the walls for all to see, who had seen only an awkward girl in a faded blue dress. We learn about her desires and her powers in this moment, how profusely and intricately she has reenvisioned herself through the creation of dresses she will never wear, but which she possesses as surely as she possesses her own imagination. Finally, that Wanda should do for Maddie what she could not do for herself, conveys the depth and richness of her gift in the midst of her impoverishment. Wanda and Cinderella are heroines of reverie. And that quality of dresses, that they can seem like materializations of imagined female selves—visions or ghosts—is what gives these two heroines voice and power.

We are so often like the iris in winter, an image of ourselves in bloom stored deep within us. I go through my days. I dress for the purpose and the season. Meanwhile, in my secret heart, the mood is wintry or summery, and I am always wearing a dress: it is velvet, or it is cotton.

Marcy Dermansky

HAT SHOP GIRLS

The other girls in the hat shop didn't like Betty. She wore lipstick. The owner of the hat shop, Boris, didn't pay hat shop girls. At the end of the week, we were given coupons for food, allowed to pick out a hat, and that was it. You might see us wearing the same dress day after day, but we always wore a different hat. My favorite was a red bowler, a man's hat, which I never dared wear outside my tiny bedroom. My three brothers wanted it too much to take that kind of a risk. They'd poke me with various sharp objects: the serrated edge of the bread knife, the rusted TV antenna, jagged strips of soda pop cans. Life would have been easier for me, but I wouldn't give them that hat. Betty didn't wear hats. Boris paid Betty in lottery tickets. She won things.

I started working in the hat shop when I was ten. My mother and my grandmother and my great-grandmother made lace for Boris's hat shop and other hat shops, hat shops all over Devushka. Nobody makes lace anymore. My oldest brother Nikolai blamed the end of lace making on Modernism. He cited changes in literature and art, blaming the circumstances of my sad sorry life on machines

Marcy Dermansky's recent work has appeared in *McSweeney's, New Orleans Review,* and *The Barcelona Review.*

and the war, the development of artificial fibers. Nikolai was a porter for the railroads. Books, especially literary criticism, weren't allowed at the train station, but his uniform included a red felt cap and that pacified him plenty. Nikolai would protect me from my brothers, but only after I'd handed over all of my food coupons and cooked the family dinner.

Ten was the age for learning how to make lace in our family. I'm almost a woman now, according to Nikolai, old enough in years, but have the skinny body of a girl. My mother's mother pulled her out of school when she was ten, and my mother assumed the same was right for me. Their lace was famous all over Devushka. Boris still talked about my mother's intricate cross-stitch she did with snow white poodle hair. When the lace market came crashing down, my mother sold the dogs. She was a licensed poodle breeder. Poodles made loyal pets, and she trimmed their fur for a soft, warm lace trim, a style that was always popular during the bitter winter months. My brothers wept when she decided to sell the last poodle, Lilianna. Nikolai threw a potted plant against the wall; he smeared the scattered dirt along his cheeks and he pounded his fists against his bony chest until my mother sold me to the hat shop and kept the dog. A week later Liliana swallowed a deadly dose of rat poison and my poor mother jumped in front of the six o'clock train.

Boris claimed to have a heart. He sent me back to my brothers. I worked in the hat shop during the day, and at night trudged home through the heavy banks of snow to work for my hateful brothers. They paid Boris thirty tribbles a week; I cooked for them, cleaned for them, did their laundry. They slept all day long on the hard mattress, huddled under blankets, reading, all of them, gaunt cheeks and pent-up anger, waiting for me to come home. I made Kraft macaroni and cheese each night, imported cheap from the Americas, and I didn't care how much they complained. I didn't stop even when our bowel movements turned orange. I liked mac and cheese fine. Mushy and warm. My comfort at the end of the day.

You see, life was hard in Devushka. The sky was non-stop gray. The stone buildings were heavy and gray. The water of the great lakes, lapping at the edge of the city, were murky and gray. The hair on poor people's heads: wiry and gray. Only the very wealthy could afford the cloth for a colorful outfit. Hats were the rage, a burst of color in the dull landscape. Most people couldn't even afford hats. And then there was Betty, bubble gum pink lipstick and cherry red lipstick and mocha brown lipstick on those full, pouty lips. How could I hate Betty? How could I not love Betty? Her hair was jet black and shiny. Her cheeks burned hot red. I'd never seen another woman like Betty. I understood why Boris chose her above all the other hat shop girls.

This story starts when Betty fainted in the hat shop. The ten years I spent working for Boris, lonely and afraid and deprived of basic food nutrients and affection, are not interesting. Ten years of Boris calling me imp, scrawny chicken, skin and bones, my brothers calling me brat and kiddo and sisterslave. I'd forgotten my name. I'd forgotten my face.

And then Betty fainted. I was handing her wigs as she dressed the store mannequins when she collapsed, slicing my shins with the sharp edge of her peach-colored glass slippers.

"Out," Boris yelled. "Get her out of here."

Boris didn't like to be kind to Betty in front of the other girls. The hat shop girls already loathed and despised Betty because of the lottery tickets. Kindness would incite them to madness. One girl had slipped arsenic in Betty's pea soup when she came to work wearing a blue satin sash around her dress.

"Imp," Boris yelled, pushed me to the ground. "Go."

I slid my arm around Betty's waist, kissed the fabric of her dress, inhaled her perfume, and then helped her to her feet and down to the basement of the hat shop. I hadn't been back to the basement of the hat shop since my mother's death when my brothers decided to rent me. As we walked down the steep, winding steps, the wood creaking beneath our feet, I began to shiver and my legs began to shake. The ends of my hair tingled with the kind of electricity produced by sharp pangs of fear and we leaned against each other, collapsing side by side on Betty's cot. The walls were made of yellowing bricks and sealed tight with heavy mortar. Three missing bricks in the wall made a window, the wall so thick that no light from the outside could pass through. Icicles hung from the ceiling. A gust of wind came through the room and an icicle dropped onto the thin cover on Betty's cot between our legs.

"Feel my forehead," Betty said. "Feel it."

Betty was burning with fever.

"You're sick," I said sadly. Suddenly, I understood the brilliance of her cheeks. "You're ill, terribly ill."

Betty shrugged her shoulders. "It'll pass," she said. "Or I'll die. Are you okay? Would you like some caviar?"

I hugged myself tight with my arms, shaking my head. No. I didn't remember much about the room, except the noises at night, furry bats banging blindly against walls. Betty had a brand new

General Electric refrigerator in the corner of the room. Inside it, there was a tall stack of Godiva chocolate bars, two lobsters, and a bottle of cherry nectar. "The lottery has been kind to me," she said.

Betty scooped spoonfuls of pink fish eggs onto a thick piece of bread and handed it to me.

"Nah," I said, looking at the strange food.

The day I cooked my brothers their first box of macaroni and cheese, I kissed the mysterious bar code on the back of the box and made a bargain for my future happiness. Any chance I had in this world depended on eating that warm comforting mac and cheese and waiting. My mother had taught me deprivation but good. I couldn't try the caviar, couldn't gorge myself on chocolate. I wanted to cry and I was going to cry. Boris didn't give food coupons to crying hat shop girls. I never cried. I didn't cry when my mother died; I was so mad about her choosing the dog. I never cried. Tears welled out of my eyes and poured down my face, but I didn't make a sound.

Betty hugged me, her embrace so hard and sudden that I fell onto the floor, banging my head on a tin water bucket at the foot of the bed.

"Oh no," said Betty.

I saw hats. Red hats, blue hats, an emerald green fedora.

"Oh no," said Betty.

She sat down on the floor, putting my head in her lap. I think I moaned. She mopped up the blood with a silk robe that hung over the bed. "I'm so sorry," Betty said, pressing the robe against the top of my head to stop the bleeding. She kissed my forehead. "Do you know you're the first hat shop girl Boris sent down here who hasn't gobbled the whole jar? You smile at me in the hat shop. You like me. I've noticed you. You. We're going to take care of each other."

Three-cornered hats circle round my head, swooping down fast and then soaring high.

I woke to the sounds of the bats.

"Mama," I whimpered. "Mama, I want to go home."

Betty was packing. In the flickering light of a small votive candle, I saw her wrapping jewelry into gray linens and placing the bundles into a gleaming silver trunk. The mattress I lay on was wet and sticky. Icicles wrapped round my blood-crusted hair.

Betty rushed to my side when she saw that I was awake.

"I thought I killed you," she said. She kissed me on my lips, and I sneezed. Betty reached under the bed, pulling out a heavy mink coat, which she draped round my shoulders.

212

"Baby," she said. "We're going to drink some cherry juice, eat the lobsters, and then we're leaving."

"Leaving?" I said. The fur coat was so soft. I rubbed my chin against my shoulder, felt my eyes closing again, until another bat crashed into Betty's refrigerator and then hit the floor. "Can we leave?"

Betty smiled. She leaned so close she was almost kissing me again. She didn't actually say something out loud, but her lips moved. "I have an entire book of lottery tickets," she mouthed.

I nodded. In Devushka, there was no such thing as a losing lottery ticket. Only the wealthy could afford them. The wealthy ran the lottery, they picked the prizes, and they distributed the tickets amongst themselves. I'd heard rumors of the ultimate grand drawing in the hat shop. I knew that many of the hat shop girls were having sex with Boris just to get a lottery ticket. They were stupid, all of them. Boris gave lottery tickets only to Betty. "I found a razor in the mattress," Betty said, steadily emptying her closet, folding colorful clothes. "Another hat shop girl was in here. They do that. Try to kill me. Search for lottery tickets. Steal my make-up. You almost lost a finger."

Around my pinkie, Betty had tied a strip of scratchy gray cloth. It was steeped in blood, a gorgeous red. I hadn't noticed any pain from my hand because of my aching head.

"Such a beautiful color," I said. I was mesmerized by the sheet. I didn't know there was so much red in me, signs of life as bright and exciting as Betty's lips.

"We have to go," Betty said. "Now. Before the light comes up. So drink." Betty held the jar of cherry nectar to my lips and I swallowed, the flowing juice pouring down my throat and spilling down my lips, dripping down my chin. I belonged to Betty, and though I would not understand this until much later, the next day, until the end of this story, Betty belonged to me.

Betty wasn't good at running away.

We stood in the middle of the alley behind the hat shop, completely and entirely defeated by her trunk. It was too much for one person to carry alone, and with my injured hand, throbbing from the weight of it, we were only able to manage a few feeble steps.

"Yes. I got attached to my things," Betty said. "These are the kind of things most girls in Devushka never dream of having. Precious objects. It would take me months in a brothel to buy one of those sweaters." The sweaters Betty spoke of were made of chenille and accentuated her ample bosom.

Betty extracted two cigarettes from her bra and handed one to me. I'd bought cigarettes with my food coupons but I always made sure to give these to Nikolai to guarantee his kindness.

"For me?" I said to Betty.

Betty shook her head. "Idiot," she said.

And then it started to snow, snowflakes swirling, falling hard and furious in our faces, coating our skin. The snow doused the flame of Betty's matches before she could light our cigarettes. I stared at my cigarette with longing and then I started to cry again, the second time after a ten-year drought, tears streaming from my eyes, freezing onto my cheeks. Betty either did not notice or ignored my state of distress.

"All right. Fuck my things. We are going to die if we don't move fast. We'll freeze in the snow, and Boris will find us frozen and he'll laugh. Find himself another hat shop girl. He'll buy her black hair dye. Oh, will he laugh. So we leave the trunk. Come, Baby."

Betty put the wet cigarettes back in her bra, hooked her arm around my shoulder, and we were walking, unencumbered by possessions or a past I still can't remember; we were free, cleansed by the fresh, gray snow. I looked back over my shoulder, saying a silent good-bye to Betty's shiny silver trunk, to her lipsticks and chocolate bars and silk scarves, to the lobsters I would never eat, and the cherry juice that dripped down my face that I would never, ever get to swallow.

I was staring at her trunk, Betty pulling my arm, when there, at the end of the alley, illuminated by his red felt beret, I saw my brother Nikolai. He was on the way to work at the train station.

"You!" Nikolai yelled. He strode across the alley, pulling a luggage rack at his side. He shook me. "We didn't eat last night, little sister. If you're smart you won't go home at all. They broke into your room and stole your hats, all of them, Sergei's got the bowler."

"Oh," I said. My bowler hat. Red and beautiful.

"She's not going home," Betty said.

"Where did you get that coat?" Nikolai tugged at a sleeve of the mink. "You're too skinny for a lover, kiddo."

Betty calmly handed Nikolai a cigarette. He still hadn't noticed her. Or the trunk. Or that our thin shoes were getting wetter and wetter as we stood there getting yelled at. It took Nikolai longer to drink in reality than most people. He was as nutrient-deprived as I. He never talked to women. He was plain scared of them. He dropped his precious cigarette in the snow. And then it was gone, covered by the heavy snowfall.

"You work at the train station?" Betty said.

Nikolai nodded.

"And that device," Betty pointed to the piece of equipment at his side. "Has wheels? For transporting luggage?"

Nikolai stood dumb, his arms hanging limply by his sides.

"Is he stupid or what?" Betty said.

She put another cigarette directly into Nikolai's lips, and this time he lit it with the Zippo lighter he always kept in his front pocket, part of his uniform. Porters often had to light cigarettes for rich patrons in inclement weather that was frequent in cold, gray Devushka.

"Better," Betty said.

Two more cigarettes came out of her bra. Soon we were all smoking.

Nikolai loaded Betty's trunk onto his luggage rack, and then we were moving again, trudging through the snow, to the train station. My heart beat fast as I imagined the train that Nikolai would put us on. Nikolai had told me once about the coach cars, the hot coffee that got served to travelers in first class.

"I'll lose my job," Nikolai whispered to me, but he walked on, pushing the creaking luggage cart, heavy with Betty's silver trunk, wiping the snow from his face and sneaking sidewise glances at Betty. "Boris will whip you when you get back. He might kill you. Is she an heiress? A movie star? Where are you going?"

Betty reached back into her bra.

"I'm a hat shop girl," she said. "Just like your sister. You need to be quiet and move quickly and help us get out of Devushka. We'll need two tickets and a private berth."

I nodded my head fervently while I coughed. Betty laughed at me, patted my head with affection. She was going to get us coffee.

She flashed a single lottery ticket in front of Nikolai's face, and then slid this ticket beneath his red beret.

"Huh?" Nikolai said.

"There are more," Betty said. "When we get to the train station I'll give you another."

"No," I said, but it came out as another cough, a mangled note. It felt so good, this coughing. I was hacking out all that was dead in me. Stupid brother. Who protected me only when it suited his purposes. Who let Sergei steal my bowler hat. "No. Never. Nikolai is my brother and he'll help us for free. You will. And I'll see to it that you are poisoned if you don't. You better believe I will."

"Huh?" Nikolai said.

Betty grinned. Her cheeks had turned purple. We walked quickly, quickly. The cart lost a wheel, but we didn't lose speed. Nikolai moved us forward, spiriting us to our freedom. Poison was easy to purchase in Devushka, cheaper than food and sold on every corner. Ever since the Modernist era took hold, there were no restaurants in Devushka. The chefs of Devushka, in protest of their long hours and low wages, poisoned a Friday special of goulash and thousands of citizens died. Those that survived were blinded.

"Come on, brat," he said. "Aren't I helping? Maybe I'll come with you. You never know when you'll need a man around." Nikolai stopped at the corner and lifted the rickety cart from the sidewalk to the street. We were getting close. I could see the thick smoke coming from the trains in the station, a dense black cloud floating menacingly overhead.

How did I get there, to the train station that I'd only seen once before when my mother took me with her to sell the poodles. I'd never stood up to any of my brothers before. My hands were warm, covered by Betty's woolen mittens, and sunk deep into fur-lined pockets of Betty's mink. I loved her fur coat. I could taste sweet cherry juice in my mouth, beneath the smoky taste of wet cigarette. All this good fortune because of Betty fainting. Because I refused to eat caviar. Because my brother appeared like magic in the alley. I smiled at Nikolai. My big brother. He'd gotten us to the train station. There was no reason not to love him. I loved Boris because he gave me Betty. Wherever we went, Nikolai could come and carry our bags.

Betty didn't feel the same way.

"Harumph," she said. "I'd rather give you lottery tickets before I let you come with us." I took my mittened hand from the mink pocket and squeezed Betty's arm. "I'd rather die than take a man with me. I will not have one more sad, pathetic man in love with me. I will die. I'm already dead."

"Huh?" Nikolai said.

Suddenly it was impossible to hear anything. The wound in my head began to tingle, the wet bandage on my hand began to bleed anew, and the ground beneath my feet shook, the thick coat of gray snow shimmering. I put my hands over my ears. We had made it to the crumbling curb in front of the train station. In the grand alabaster archway, a one-armed man banged on an immense brass gong. He wore a velvet jester's hat—the kind we sold at the hat shop—that was red and yellow and blue with bells at the ends of each flopping crown. That had been part of my job, gluing loose bells from the factory back onto the jester's hats. They never stayed on long.

"This is highly unusual," Nikolai said.

He straightened his hat as we walked into the station, lagging behind us as porters are instructed to do.

Single file, we walked past the jester into the train station. The four-foot-high, gold-plated fireplace at the far end of the lobby was filled with trash. Citizens sat on the tiled floor in clustered circles, hands over small newspaper fires. The station smelt of singed hair. After every beat of the brass gong, pieces of plaster fell from the ceiling.

Betty removed a small compact from her bra and applied a fresh coat of cherry red lipstick to her full, delicious lips. Her hands, however, were shaking, and she applied lipstick to the tip of her nose and the bottom of her chin. A large chip of plaster bounced off her silver trunk, denting the shining surface.

"Oh no," I said. "No."

Always there was loss. I lived in a world filled with loss. I was sure to lose my hearing from the brass gong before the sun rose. Wasn't I beaming with happiness moments ago? You couldn't trust anything to stay good for long. I wasn't surprised to see Boris across the black and white tiled floor sitting at a table by the juice stand drinking a large orange juice. The juice looked so good, so orange. With every sip, his head turned to the left, to the right, back to the left. As if he was looking for someone. A new girl. I'd heard rumors that he caught some of his hat shop girls here in the train station. He would buy them orange juice, offer them some food coupons and a place to sleep.

"It must be the lottery," Nikolai said. "Sipsy always bangs the gong whenever there's a big winner, a color TV or a can of oysters, but it's never like this. This must be a big one. Really big. Look." Nikolai pointed. The floor popped open from the center of the room, and a dozen soldiers emerged, rifles pointed high, wearing tall gray hats purchased at Boris's hat shop. They marched directly into the new Starbucks. Soldiers drank coffee for free in Devushka. Their heavy warm hats were free too. So many times my fingers bled as I stitched thermal stuffing beneath the gray felt. "There's the mayor," Nikolai said. "There's Devushka's network camera man."

These men also went into the Starbucks. "SOUND PROOF" read the sign on the Starbucks stained-glass windows. I'd read in the newspapers that they piped in music, played CDs smuggled from the Americas. It was deafening inside the train station. My ears had already adjusted to the vibrations of the gong and was honed in on other sounds: the clanging hiss of steam engines, citizens moaning as their newspaper fires burned out, beggars singing old Bette Midler songs, an electronic voice calling out the train schedule—delayed, canceled, sold out, the words hanging in the air.

Betty bit her lips. She had lipstick on her teeth and her nose and chin. She kissed Nikolai on the neck. I could see him tremble. She left an imprint of her red mouth on his neck. I reached my mittened fingers out to touch the spot. "Go. Get us some tickets. Hurry."

There were no tickets to get. The train conductor had just said so, but Nikolai ran to take his place in the long, winding line. I watched as Boris ordered another juice, this one pink, pink grapefruit juice. I licked my lips. I shivered. Whatever happened next, I knew that it was bad for us to be in the same room as Boris. He was looking for us. He was looking for Betty.

Betty shook me with her shaking hands. "I've won it," she whispered. She kissed my ear, and, just like Nikolai, I trembled. Warm. "It's me. I have the winning ticket. Thirty-two million tribbles."

Boris, I thought. The acid in the juice would turn him mean. Meaner. He was already mean. He bought me from my mother for only 60 tribbles, the amount you'd pay for a used toaster. We should have been running. There was Boris, drinking delicious juice, looking for us. But for the last ten years, I'd eaten nothing but Kraft macaroni and cheese. I was missing essential vitamins, proteins, fibers, everything. The teeth in the back of my mouth were loose and my reflexes were slow. *Boris,* I thought.

Betty beamed at me.

"We won," she said.

"How do you know?" I said.

"Let's get out of sight." Betty took my hand and began dragging me to the bathroom, the bathroom that was directly past the juice stand. "Do you see the banner hanging from the ceiling. It's my number. Mine. I have them all memorized. Boris will wish I was dead when he finds out."

"Betty," I said as she dragged me through the station. My eyes traveled fast across the room for help. Nikolai was still on line to buy tickets, arguing with the flute player standing behind him. "Betty."

"Hurry," Betty said. We'd left the dented silver trunk in the doorway. Betty was almost skipping across the floor. "We'll get a better one. We'll fill it with all the colors tribbles can buy."

"Betty," I said. We were getting close to the fresh juice stand, so close that I could see the pulp caught in Boris's teeth.

"Boris," I said. But nothing came out. "There's Boris."

"Huh?" Betty said.

"You hussy," Boris screamed. "I want that ticket. I want that ticket. I want it." He knocked over his table and leapt over the railing that separated the juice stand from the main floor of the station. He tripped over a one-legged blind woman selling pencils and kept running. Betty ran, too, a firm hold on my arm so that I was flying across the station, trailing behind like a ragged paper kite. Into the women's bathroom we went, flying into a stall and locking the door.

"Up," Betty said. "On the toilet."

We both stood on the toilet, Betty locking the door, and Boris slammed into the bathroom right behind us. "Hussy." Bang Bang. "Bitch." Bang pound. "Whore." Bang kick. "You're the most expensive hat shop girl ever." Kick bang. "You weren't worth it. I'll get that ticket."

I didn't know what to do. Betty was tracing her lips with that cherry red lipstick, counting tribbles feverishly. I pounded back on the bathroom stall. "Monster." Pound bang. Pain shot through me. I'd forgotten about the sliced finger. I could feel blood oozing out of the bandage, soaking the mitten. But I could feel myself waking up, and I was angry, angry like I'd never been before. "Child abuser." Hit bang. "Slave owner." I pounded the door with my good hand. "Rapist." Betty watched me with wide eyes. "Ugly, worthless urchin."

Boris yelled back, kicking the door repeatedly, I could see the hinges bend inward. I kicked the door back, falling off the toilet.

"Evil monster. Evil monster. Evil monster."

When the door flew off the frame, knocking Betty's lipstick out of her hands, I pounced before Boris had a chance. My head landed squarely in his stomach, and he tumbled backwards on to the bathroom floor, and I was biting and punching with all the strength I had. Boris wouldn't get close to Betty ever again. He couldn't detach me from his belly. He couldn't stand up.

"I want that lottery ticket," he cried to Betty as she ran out of the bathroom. "I want that ticket. It's mine. Who is this girl? Ow. Come back here. Damn it. Ow. Betty. Get her off me. Betty."

I didn't even see Betty go. All I could see was the gray weave of Boris's overcoat. Tears streamed down my face making it only slightly harder to bite Boris. I'd bitten the buttons off his coat, my teeth were through his sweater, hitting skin. I didn't feel his punches. Betty was gone. All I would have left of her would be that one lipstick that had rolled to the corner of the bathroom floor. I let go with my injured hand to reach for the lipstick and Boris threw me against the mirrors above the sinks. I could hear the glass shatter. I lay stretched across three cracked porcelain sinks when a dozen police officers in the gray hats and the one-legged blind woman rushed into the bathroom.

"That's him," the blind woman cried. "I can smell the orange juice."

"That's him." Betty came crashing into the bathroom behind them. "He tried to rob me. I have the winning lottery ticket. It's here in my bosom."

The police officers surrounding Boris turned to inspect Betty's bosom, but one officer managed to cuff him, and then Nikolai burst into the bathroom as well.

"No porters in the women's bathroom," a police officer said. He took a set of cuffs from his pocket and cuffed Nikolai. Another officer took out a rope and tied a knot around Nikolai's leg, attaching him to Boris.

"But, I got tickets," Nikolai said quietly. "For us." He looked at Betty. "You, me, and her, my sister, the girl in the sink."

No one, not even Nikolai, remembered my name.

"Come here, baby," Betty said. In front of the police officers and the one-legged blind woman and Nikolai and Boris, Betty lifted me up from the sink. Her black hair shone. Her cheeks blazed pink. "You saved my life. We won the lottery. Nothing is ever going to be the same."

Betty picked me up. She removed the shards of glass from my hair, and carried me past the crowd through the bathroom. After we passed through the door and into the train station, Sipsy the gong player resumed his inscrutable beat. Devushka's camera man snapped our picture. The mayor rushed to our side, leading us to a plush, purple velvet couch.

"Congratulations," he said, holding out a bouquet of pink and purple tulips and two steaming hot yellow mugs.

"Coffee," I said before I passed out.

Betty cradled me in her arms like an infant.

Michael Hyde

HER HOLLYWOOD

The girl was Mary Alice Bunt and they found her by the river. My brother Wade and I thought we'd see the print her body made but rain came and the river jumped its banks before we could find the spot. It's a good thing the search party found her when they did. She's liable to have been washed away and lost because everything came rushing in that brown flood: flat tires, TV antennas, a doll carriage like one I used to push.

The dead girl before she was dead lived in Tobo. In wagon train days there used to be a Tobo Hotel. That's how the place got its name. It was a layover for travelers, some place for them to steal a breather, get a drink, maybe spend the night. But the hotel's gone now and it's nothing but cheap trailers—one lived-in box after the other—lined up along Tobo Road.

Mary Alice Bunt was pretty. I know this for two reasons. Reason number one is because her picture was front-page in both morning and evening *Dispatches*. Next day they put her picture in the obituary section, too, except smaller. Reason number two I know Mary Alice Bunt was pretty is because Mom said so. Wade and I'd just come home from school and there Mom was bawling her eyes out.

Michael Hyde has recent work in *Ontario Review* and *CrossConnect*.

Her make-up wasn't smeared so I figured she hadn't been crying long. "Always the pretty ones that die," she was saying over and over and didn't have to say anything else because I know she was thinking I was safe as could be. Plain Jane she liked to call me, teasing me to get me shouting my lungs that my name was Connie not stupid Jane. She got a big kick out of it and laughed like it was the joke of the century. Even when she'd let me sit down beside her at the vanity she'd start comparing our faces, hers with mine, and she'd always throw in "You can thank your father for that nose." The way she said it I knew I didn't need to be thanking anybody.

When Mom was crying over Mary Alice, Wade and I tried to give her a hug because that's what I thought she was expecting but she pushed us out of the way and started walking around the kitchen—her head bent a little bit to the side—moving like a statue would move if it could. I don't need to tell you that Mom was an actress at the community theater. She taught me and Wade from the very start about *drama* which she said translated into English as meaning "larger than life." Thanks to her, Wade and I were drama experts. We'd have to be, the way she changed moods like clothing. We all remember Mom's Mary Alice act as one of her final performances because ten days later she left us for Hollywood. It's strange how those two things happened, boom-boom, one right after the other, that girl dying and my mother going away.

I didn't know Mary Alice Bunt but she was a junior at my school, two grades above me and in the same grade as my brother Wade. Wade didn't know her either but that was because Wade didn't know anybody. He wasn't smart about people or in general but I still loved him in the way you have to love dogs that can only stare at you when you've thrown a stick for them to fetch. At school the kids called Wade *LD*. He was in the special class for kids with *Learning Disabilities*. There were only three other LDs at our school. Wade and them had class in one room painted bright yellow over the cinderblocks. "Hey LD," kids said when they saw Wade in the hall. "Hey, LD, what's 1 + 1?" Wade was older than me but I always thought of him as my little brother. Like Mom said once: Wade's head's just not what it's supposed to be. He'll never be like other kids, no matter how hard he studies or practices or tries.

When she was alive I never would've cared who Mary Alice Bunt was. Or anyone like her. And since Wade wasn't smart about people and since I didn't care about them, he and I were always together. I'd find him each lunch period standing at the front of the cafeteria, straining his neck 180 degrees until he'd see me. The kids at school made fun of us both because we were together so much. Somebody saw me dragging him by the hand one time home from school, so after that everybody called us boyfriend and girlfriend and sometimes made kissy noises so loud the teachers could hear. The teachers didn't do anything and I stopped expecting they would.

Except for the kids bugging, I didn't mind Wade. He needed somebody and I was the only somebody left. When Mom left for her Hollywood, Dad turned into a ghost and sat all the time in front of the tube, watching talk shows and how-to programs on the public channel. He stopped brushing his hair. It stuck together and shot in all directions, it was so oily. He let his beard grow out too and would sit rubbing his hand across his face, making that sandpaper sound I can't take for a minute. He only moved for the bathroom. He'd make it to bed at night sometimes but usually he stretched out on the couch and cloaked himself with that ratty black afghan. He was like an invalid, he loved Mom that much.

I tried not to notice but our house was falling apart, creaking and complaining anytime you'd move. The barn got a big hole in the roof and let in rain. Wade and I had to take care of the cows but we stopped shoveling their shit every single day. One heifer would stare at us and bawl when she couldn't find a warm place. I used to take pride that we didn't live in one of those cheap Tobo trailers but after Mom ran off that pride shriveled up to nothing.

That's when I got the idea to look for where Mary Alice Bunt died. Finding it wasn't easy. First Wade and I tried piecing together pictures from the news and the papers. We spent whole afternoons zigzagging from our farm to Tobo and the Tunnel Bridge further downstream. It was exhausting even though our river was more like a creek. You only needed twelve steps to get from one bank to the other.

When mine and Wade's searching didn't work we tried talking to Tobo kids. The ones I asked acted like they never heard of Mary Alice. Her living seemed as forgettable as the plastic milk jug some were kicking around because they didn't have a ball. A part of Mary Alice—a memory, I mean—had to be somewhere. After all she'd lived her life there, under those stupid pink and yellow and green pool-party lights hung from the trailers that tried to fool you into thinking Tobo was a happy place.

Mary Alice's little brother was the one finally that showed us the way. We didn't know it was him at first so he was a lucky find, sitting in the street, pushing a toy submarine across gravel. He was eight or nine and dusted white from the shale. Wade said to him, "Do you know where they found that dead girl?" and I looked at

Wade queer for saying it that way but that's when the boy nodded and told us he was the dead girl's brother.

"Can you show us where they found her?" I asked.

He led us down to the river like we were visiting tourists who'd never been before. I watched the thick band of dirt around his neck when he ducked under briars and jumped over the black logs in our way. Wade had trouble keeping up because he was tall and sort of large and said a couple times that he was gonna go back. "Shut up, Wade," I said. And he did.

The boy took us to a place where the river snaked hard around a bend. Three gray trees leaned at the water, their roots and the bank had been worn away so. You could tell there'd been the flood even though the high water was gone. A lawnchair with all the stringing busted out sat up straight in the shallows. In other spots fallen branches made it look like somebody'd been trying to build a bonfire the way the branches had stacked themselves. The boy ran for the chair and kicked it over into the water.

"There's where," he said. He pointed with his submarine at a small green island halfway across the river. He was proud to be showing us.

Wade ran ahead too and bent over the lump of land. He was wearing his cut-offs and creek-shoes and at its deepest, the water came up to Wade's knees. "I think this is where her head was. I can see her skull-print," he said.

I followed him, looked to where he meant, but he was seeing what he wanted to see, trying to impress me. His face was wrinkled and stupid with excitement. I wanted him to go away. Suddenly all I could think about was that: how I wanted to be alone. In this place where Mary Alice Bunt had spent the last seconds of her life I wanted to be by myself. The small green island probably not much bigger than Mary Alice had been was somehow mine.

"No, that's not it," I said. "The boy's lying."

This was all it took for Wade to shove Mary Alice's brother. "I'll teach you for lying," Wade said. He snatched the submarine and zoomed it through the air high above the squealing boy's head.

"Give it back to him," I said. Wade looked at me ashamed. Finally he gave the toy back then yelled after Mary Alice's brother, who ran off toward Tobo.

I looked at the green island, the size of a coffin, and imagined Mary Alice there face down like the newspaper mentioned. I imagined her underwear yanked to her ankles, her shirt pulled up over her head, her goodies—as my mother called them—showing. I wanted to be alone with her. What was it like, living and dying in your pretty body? I wanted to ask.

The next day after school I told Wade I was going for a walk without him. "Why, Connie? Why?" he asked.

I told him I was sick of him hanging around all the time. I told him I needed space and that I didn't want to be his girlfriend anymore.

He was about to turn on the waterworks so I walked off quick enough so I didn't have to see. I heard him following, so I ran. "Go away! Leave me alone!"

In Tobo four kids were playing maypole with snapped clothesline and the pole it was tied to. They ducked in and out of one another's way until they tangled and ended up arguing over whose fault it'd been. I could hear the sound of the river humming just under their angry voices.

Across the street two boys my age were rolling tires around a car they'd set up on blocks. They had their shirts off so I could see the tattoos on their arms. They watched me, stopped what they were doing and watched me. I stared them straight in the eyes.

The one boy's face looked like you were supposed to see it from one side. The other half was all messed up and pushed together like it'd been smashed by a brick. His mouth had space where teeth were supposed to be and when he smiled a black nothing spread between his lips.

The other boy's face was wide open like a book and red with freckles that matched his hair. His right arm was bigger than his left. "Woo-hoo," he whistled. I just stared at him, thinking how easily he could've been the one that'd killed Mary Alice, thinking *you are the one you are the one you are the one* until the boys and their car were no longer in sight. Until I'd walked so far they disappeared along with their litterbox trailers.

I got to the spot where the river turned. The chair Mary Alice's brother kicked over was still on its side. Small crayfish scooted when my shadow came near. The only difference was that one of the three leaning trees had finally given up and fallen. Its branches speared down into the water a few feet from Mary Alice's island.

The water was cold and I could feel mud and pebbles squishing inside my creek-shoes. The water swallowed me to my knees but I didn't care. Mary Alice's island was in front of me, so bright and green and with a single strand of blue chicory that looked more a silk flower than real poking up for the sun. I lay down like the island was a bed I hadn't slept in before. I could feel it resist me, me resisting it until I stopped caring about mud and dirt and resistance dropped away.

Putting together the lost life of a pretty girl, I started with her killer. Was he fat? Thin? Bald? Tall? All the men I'd ever seen flashed in my head. It was like choosing the right color to paint a room. Lighter or darker? Brown? Black? Or red? Red, yes it would be red, and I thought of the boy fixing the car. Not the boy with the smashed face. The pretty girl's murderer would not be so ugly. He could be plain but not so ugly as to be scary and not so scary as to make the last moments of her life unbearable.

So I thought of the red-haired boy. He was easy to make in my mind. I had him standing over me: his face dripping red gums dripping red freckles dripping. He was hurrying to undo his pants with his thin arm. He pushed me down. He told me he was going to kill me and that I might as well enjoy it. I might as well enjoy it while it lasted and ride the rest of my life out in a limousine. His hands were on me pressing together my breasts, his fingers fumbling. I was there on the point of something when he turned me over and pressed my face into the green-grass island, into the fish silt and the smell of the river and I couldn't breathe anymore. Inside my head I was screaming: "You're dead, Connie. Now you're dead."

My hands were where his hands had been and for a second my heart stopped. It wasn't a complete stop but more like my heart couldn't decide whether or not to keep on beating, like somebody waving her arms to keep balanced on a circus wire.

After that first time at the river I'd been murdered many times. And never the same murderer twice.

There was a big man covered with thick hair across his chest and down his back. Dark eyebrows lowered like feathers over his eyes.

There was a man with a hump.

A man with twisted teeth.

A man who whistled the entire time it happened.

They'd all tell me what they were going to do before they did it. They weren't horrible men as people might imagine. They were just men.

When I couldn't get to the river I'd stretch out on my bed, turning my head into the pillow and breathing it in like it was Mary Alice's island. Once Wade walked in on me when I was being murdered. It was raining. The river was so far away in the colored party lights of Tobo. I was on my bed and waiting to die. Mr. Farris, second-period algebra, had forced me onto my stomach right away. He held me by the hair. I knew with one flip of his wrist he could push my face into the mud and make me breathe the river into my lungs. He made me repeat again and again that I loved him, that I'd never leave him, that I'd follow him anywhere. I kept thinking of his hand clutching my hair, his gold watch wrapping his wrist just below that hand, the gold watch I had to notice every time he bent over my desk smelling good or wrote on the board. I heard that watch tick-ticking in my ears. "You're dead, Connie," I started to say when he finally pushed my head into the mud.

That's when Wade walked in. I'm sure I looked strange to him, my nightgown pulled over my head, my legs swim-kicking at the bedroom air.

"Help me," I said to him, before the river found its way to my throat, before it drowned my voice.

He pulled my arms, slid the pillow from under my face, but he was too late. I told him so. "I'm dead," I said. "You let me die."

"What are you talking about, Connie? What?" His breathing was hard. He was staring at my breasts.

For a crazy second I started memorizing Wade's face. His fat nose. His marble-blue eyes. His open mouth that could change from pain to pleasure in a second. He'd never yet been one of my murderers. I felt him taking shape in my mind. But the more I looked at him the more impossible he seemed and I said "No." Wade couldn't be a murderer no matter how hard I imagined.

Then came word from Mother. The postcard she sent was plain white and said "GENERIC POSTCARD" on the front and on the back along with our address she'd scratched a message in big letters. She was reading for several things, she said. Quite a few "independent films," she said. "Acting is hard life," she said. She signed the card *Francine Barlowe*. Meaning her the actress. Not Francine Pratt my mother.

I got a sheet of paper and pen to write her and tell her all the things that'd happened. Like how Dad was going out nights. Or how Wade's teacher sent home that note saying he wasn't progressing like he should. Then I remembered Mom hadn't told us where she was going exactly; Hollywood was all. I looked on the postcard, thinking she'd squeezed her new address into a corner. The only thing I found was the postmark—Norristown, PA not Hollywood, CA—smudged over the stamp of an orange-bellied bluebird.

I shoved that postcard way back in the kitchen junk-drawer—

behind the Scotch tape and screwdrivers and worn-out batteries—
so no one would ever have to know about it but me.

* * *

One day, on our way home from school Wade and I were walking
along the road, kicking up gravel. We walked to school every day
just so we wouldn't have to ride the bus with those Tobo kids. I was
listening to him tell about how he'd been the only one left at dodge-
ball during gym and no matter who threw the ball he'd been quick
enough to dodge it. The game couldn't start over until he was got,
so this guy came running at him—into the circle where he wasn't
allowed!—and blasted the ball into Wade's face. Wade got a bloody
nose, had to go to the nurse, but the game kept on going. "No harm
done," was what Wade's gym teacher said.

I was staring at Wade's bandaged nose and thinking how it could
mean *No harm done* when Arnold Berry drove up beside us and
honked. Wade jumped in his skin but I'd seen Arnold coming. It
was hard to miss his dark green Thunderbird skulking along the
empty road.

"You want a ride?" he said wagging his hand out the window
to get our attention. He was a senior at our school, the kind of person like me and Wade you passed in the hall for four years but
wouldn't take good notice to. The funny thing was I'd noticed him.
He'd killed me before. I don't remember how he did it but I know
I was staring into his pimply face and feeling his wild sideburns
scratching at my skin. He had nice green eyes. Which is the main
reason I chose him. His eyes made him a standout to me when he
was a nobody to everybody else.

"So you want a ride?" he said again. Wade, all of a sudden deaf
and dumb, just stared at him. Wade was afraid of older kids, especially seniors who drove their own cars. When I looked at Wade he
was shaking his head at me. I knew he was saying "No no no no"
inside but I told Arnold "Yes."

Wade climbed into the backseat where two giant speakers spit
out loud music. I looked at him in the side-mirror, could see him
covering his ears, so I decided not to look anymore.

"You like Bon Jovi?" Arnold said to me.

"Sure," I said though I couldn't tell a Bon Jovi from a Whitesnake,
a Whitesnake from a Poison. I started to bob my head too like I was
into it.

Arnold drove with one hand on the steering wheel, the other
hand behind my shoulder, his arm propped along the back of the

front seat. I kept waiting for him to grab me but he didn't. I guess because Wade was in the back.

Arnold didn't say anything the entire ride home. I figured out he smoked from all the cellophane wrappers on the floor. They crunched every time I'd move my foot. The pine air-freshener hanging from the rearview had faded. The car windshield was filthy except for two half-circles where the wipers had washed clean. Arnold chewed at something and kept leaning out the window to spit. He would've been the worst boyfriend but as a murderer he was fine.

When he dropped Wade and me off at our lane I stalled a few minutes by the car door. Arnold just kept chewing whatever it was that was in his mouth and looked straight ahead at the road.

"You want something?" he said finally. He turned his head like he was watching the words form inside me.

"I want you for a date," I told him, "but you have to ask me first."

Arnold's eyebrows raised up a bit but lowered then like he was enjoying the taste of what I'd said. I could see Wade fidgeting at the side of the road. Finally Arnold nodded. "Okay. How 'bout Saturday?" he answered me, his voice thick.

"One o'clock," was all I said back, as if it were the most natural thing in the world.

When Arnold drove away I knew that I'd be going somewhere I'd never gone before. No going back. Wade asked me to explain it to him but I couldn't. He'd never understand.

On Saturday Arnold came only fifteen minutes late. I could tell he'd tried to doll himself up. His straggly hair was greased back and he was wearing a shirt I was sure his mother'd pressed for him. "Sorry I'm late," he said.

"No biggee," I told him and got into the car. I'd spent all morning getting ready. I wanted everything to be perfect: the short skirt, my underwear.

My father didn't even argue when I told him I was going out. Before Mom left he would've pitched a fit if he knew his twelve-year-old daughter was going on a date with a senior. But not this version of my father. He didn't even get up from his couch to wave good-bye. He just raised a glass of pop to his mouth, held an ice cube between his lips, then spit it back into the glass.

Wade followed me out to the car. I know he was wanting to go along or not wanting me to go at all but I said "Bye" and that was that. When Arnold drove me away I could see Wade trying to hide himself behind the maple tree in our front yard.

Arnold and I went mini-golfing. He was clumsy and not so good at aiming the ball. I played even worse than he did because I didn't want him to feel bad, like he was any less a man. I watched his ropy hands draw the putter back. The ball went bouncing out of bounds. Arnold got frustrated and whacked the ball so hard it almost hit a woman's face. Seeing this I knew he'd be perfect.

We didn't have much to talk about so over ice cream when I told him I wanted to give him my goodies, he looked shocked. "You're crazy," he said at first.

"No, I'm serious." After that he looked at me and smiled like it was what he'd been wanting all along.

I took him down to the river. To my favorite spot I told him. I didn't tell him why. I sat on Mary Alice's island, the grass pushing up under my skirt. I could tell Arnold was thinking that I only wanted kissing. He was sticking his fat tongue into my mouth and grabbing my breasts but he didn't try any of my clothes so I told him to. He started mumbling about not having a rubber.

"I don't care," I said.

That was all he needed. He dropped his pants and I could see the dark stains on his white underwear. This made me think he hadn't planned to get this far, that maybe he'd respected me. But that wasn't what I wanted. I wanted to be Mary Alice. I wanted his rough hands to touch me, to take me from me.

Soon he was rocking back and forth on top of me and it wasn't at all as I'd imagined. He was like a fish floundering and flapping his arms like he didn't have any control. The sharp pain was there as I'd expected but he kept saying love things like "Oh Connie oh Connie."

I said to him what I knew he wanted to hear: "I'll never leave you. You're so beautiful I could never leave you."

His breathing got heavy and he whimpered. Then he altogether stopped. I felt wide and dirty and new and that's when I said it to him. "Kill me." Calm and serious. "I don't care how," though I wanted him to push my head into the island. But really who could tell killers *how* to kill?

"Ha-ha," he laughed.

I repeated myself and he stopped laughing. "You're one crazy girl," he said. He started to put on his clothes that were wet in places from the river.

"You have to," I said again. I didn't move from where his body had left me. I'm sure my print was pressed into the island.

"Are we gonna go?" he asked zipping his blue jeans.

I didn't move and looked at him thinking *you are the one you are the one you are the one.*

"Listen. I can't do it again if that's what you want."

"I want you to kill me."

"Come on. Get up." When I didn't he shook his head, slinging his shirt over his shoulder. "See ya," he said.

"You can't go." I grabbed him by the arm.

He jerked away. I dug in my fingernails, dragging them along his skin, leaving red scratches from his elbow to wrist. He looked at his arm, then at me, and shoved the side of my head. I fell so that my hands and chin pressed into the silt.

All I could do was lie there, my breath hard and caught in my chest like a trapped bird. I thought Arnold was getting ready, wringing his hands, preparing his strength but then I heard walking, his feet shuffling across water and rock. He was leaving. My body expanded but didn't relax.

A car engine started, revving so loud it beat its way into my mother's voice who was saying over and again—chanting almost— that always the pretty ones got killed. I tried to picture her over-hanging a balcony, under hot Hollywood sun, reading for a director she might sleep with to become an updated Juliet. "Romeo, Romeo," she would say dragging out the O's like she did. I wanted to see her writing to me and Dad and Wade from a yellow hotel room where someone important was in her bathroom taking a shower. But she was somewhere else, somewhere in Norristown, living in a trailer maybe, reading for no one but herself.

I rolled over to face the horrible sky as the sound of Arnold's car became smaller and smaller along Tobo Road. "Murderer," I said. Like it was a proper name.

Quintan Ana Wikswo

LOVE'S BABY SOFT

The child resembles a wild beast, which, naturally fierce and
accustomed to live in the woods, has been brought up, as it were,
in a prison and in servitude, and having by accident got its lib-
erty, not being accustomed to search for its food, and not knowing where to conceal itself, easily becomes the prey of the first
who seeks to incarcerate it again.

—Machiavelli

I will spend the summer in my Aunt Sarah's bedroom where she
died when she was my age. My toes snag on her long shag carpeting
nightly as I make my way to her bed; there is a long dark stain
between the bed and the dresser which initially frightened me—my
grandmother, Sarah's mother, says Sarah broke a bottle of perfume
there and shows me the shattered glass she's kept, tied up in a cloth
in the drawer. Photographs of Sarah line the pink walls. She has
yellow hair like I do, and a wide spooky smile that shuts her eyes
closed from the camera. We are different in that she is faded, and
slightly fatter, and her clothes are too tight.

My mother has deposited me here in the summer for safekeep-
ing: I am too young to be left to my own devices during holiday
and besides, my mother says, my grandmother is still lonely for her

---

Quintan Ana Wikswo has work in *Denver Quarterly, Urchin,* and *Stay Awake.* She is
an editor of *Fourteen Hills.*

youngest daughter who died when she was young. My mother says I will not be the right age—Sarah's age—for long and so she very generously shares me, cleaves her cool, crisp city chic from me and forsakes me down in the country where there is no one for miles but my grandmother. My mother drops me off in her red convertible with its creamy leather interior that must be protected from me by a layer of towel—its chrome and glass surfaces are hard and clean like my mother. When we arrive at the house she remains in the car, just waves one hand at her mother and with the other hand grasps my arm to propel me forward.

My grandmother lives in the house by herself—it looks like a church with its high-pitched roof and arched windows set deep into the peeling white exterior. It seems impossible that my mother became who she is in this house whose rootcellar smell of barnyard and funeral parlor can be detected from the front yard. Insects arc and stir. The grass in front of the road has given up, overcome by low clumping patches of dandelion, jimson weed, chicory and sourgrass, pockmarked with the deep brown circles of dog holes. A nearly unidentifiable assortment of corroding metals cower within—shapes vaguely reminiscent of tricycle wheels, shovel heads, motors, broken cooking pots, links of loose chain—all doing their best to return to their natural state of ore.

As unlikely as the house itself could have ever contained my mother, it seems similarly impossible that this woman ever gave birth to her. My grandmother stands in the yard solidly. Her mouth splits her jowls into four sections of a face lacking eyebrows but replete with flesh of all kinds. Large dry lips, a bulb of nose, earlobes stretched out by the weight of enormous earrings. Her blue cotton housedress has tiny red and white flowers whose colors have faded to pink and grey over the mounds of shoulder, breast and hip. The fabric covering them has frayed. Suddenly her feet carry her across the ground as though they are a roadcrew preparing a surface for asphalt and cement, an impression magnified by the velocity of her embrace.

I have seen no pictures of my mother as an infant but it's likely that she emerged from this woman's womb disdainful, in sharp high-heeled shoes, manicured in crimson and perfectly coiffed, bearing a tiny pair of sterling silver scissors with which to cut herself free of the cord. Right now the only thing linking my mother and her mother to the same family is their shared tight jawline expressive of disapproval and impatience. My mother passes me off to my grandmother and suddenly I feel like a prisoner at the border, a baton in a relay race. Which of them will take off faster? My mother's tense bejeweled fingers are replaced heavily on my arm by my grandmother's puffy ones and after a brief gin and tonic kiss from my mother, the yard is engulfed in a cloud of carbon monoxide and she and her car have disappeared. My mother is gone and the summer has begun.

* * *

My grandmother shows me the bedroom that will be mine for the summer. On our way through the house she talks to me, her deep, accented voice matches the house's contents, slow and heavy with evidence of disuse. She has filled the house with flowers. Some fresh, some wilted or nearly dead hang over the edges of their vases by their stalks. She has cooked more food than could ever cumulatively have been eaten by all the residents of this place, much less a little girl and an old woman. Plates of food on the windowsills. Candies and nuts lie in glass bowls on every table. All of them my favorite dishes. She says they were my Aunt Sarah's favorites too. As we pass through the house she breaks off a piece of this, takes a handful of that and tells me to eat it. *You're too thin,* she says, *dangerous thin, sinful thin,* and fills my pockets with food when I indicate that my mouth is stuffed.

My grandmother tells me that I am to stay in my Aunt Sarah's bedroom, the one where she died when she was my age. She tells me that everything I will be using still belongs to my Aunt Sarah, the Dead Aunt, *the little girl who blossomed but to die,* she says. My mother was nearly fifteen years older than Sarah, left the house upon her death without saying a word. My grandmother is smiling at me with her mouth while she examines my body with her eyes. *Skin and bones,* she says to me again, *no meat on you at all.* I wander around the room. It has become the repository for Sarah's belongings, for everything she might have owned or touched while she was alive. Some of her possessions are like my own, like the things I left in my bedroom in the city, but they make mine look like cheap replicas of ancient artifacts, like the shiny reproductions sold in gift shops at historical sites. Her dolls have mottled skins; some of her books have familiar titles: Caddie Woodlawn, *Black Beauty, Little Women, Heidi,* the Bobbsey Twins. In her hairbrushes are long yellow strands. Next to a pair of patent leather shoes lies a pair of crumpled white lace socks. My own shoes snag on her long shag carpeting as I make my way to her bed; the long dark stain between bed and nightstand somehow frightens me—I am expecting a blood stain and here it is. But my grandmother says *bend down,* and the misery in her voice makes me lean down just a little. I can smell it, the stale odor of Sarah's cologne. *I put a little there each day,* my grandmother says, indicating the carpeting, *just a few drops where she spilled it the day she died, to remind me of her.* And taking my wrist she rubs on it some liquid from the bottle, draws the neck of the bottle across my throat. *Don't that smell good,* she asks. I look at myself in the mirror and my blond hair looks greenish, my skin mottled with dusky blotches of mildew. My grandmother says, *don't it make you look real different.*

* * *

In this house I have been rocked and coddled and fed with cakes and dumplings and grits, bacon and ham and ice cream. I eat and lie in the bath all day to stem the sweating. My full belly pushes out the front of my nightgown and in the moist heat it adheres to my body immediately. After my bath, my hair is wet and drips down my face and neck and I wipe it away with the back of my hand before my grandmother can, rubbing it off on my bare legs. She comes in here at bedtime to put me to sleep. I'm unaccustomed to having an adult in my bed. At home in the city my routines of tooth brushing and grooming, of climbing pyjamaed under the covers are not public acts and furthermore if I wasn't to do them no one would know the difference. It is possible that my mother doesn't even know where my room is: sometimes when I've woken from a bad dream I've thought of her, imagined her circling the apartment for hours in her satin househoes, slipping a little in her increasing haste, calling my name with urgency, opening closet door after closet door in hopes that one, when opened, would reveal my bedroom. Here, however, my grandmother comes in to my room every night, comes in here at bedtime to put me to sleep.

At bedtime my grandmother looks like a giant faded ragdoll with her waxen grey hair in tight curls she's pinned to her scalp and pressed underneath a blue hairnet. Her breasts fold heavily over the belt of her bathrobe like two fleshy buckles. Although I am too big for this, she slips her thick hands into my armpits and lifts me into the bed where Sarah wore a shallow fold down into the mattress, down the middle. I fit perfectly. No matter in what position I fall asleep I end up lying in this furrow, pressed slightly down and in, my legs together, my arms at my side, staring, no matter which way I turn, at the photographs which could be mirrors on the wall.

When I am lying down my grandmother sits beside me, leaning over me, her breasts falling to the side now so that they are hanging over me: they pull away from her in unison and sway down towards me. She lifts up my nightgown and says she can tell I'm getting fatter, and pats me proudly before covering my body with the flannel sheet. I know she means that every night I look more like Sarah, and I wait for her to say it although she never does. Instead she asks me if I've seen her. *Really seen Sarah, not just in those old photographs.* Have I seen her sitting at her vanity, brushing her yellow hair? *She might be taking a dislike to you being here, you know,* my grandmother says. *She might be angry at you.* I imagine my mother in the city right now, lying on her bed in a negligeé, drinking her third Campari, undressed but on her mouth still wearing the same shade of lipstick that rims the filters of her cigarettes. Ashing her cigarette in a crystal dish, then taking another sip of her drink, the ice cubes clinking red against the glass.

She might be angry at me, for keeping you in here. My grandmother believes in her daughter's existence and suddenly her heavy face displays fear. *They come in through your mouth, you know,* she says, *ghosts. They come in through your mouth and fill you up with themselves while you're dreaming. They come in through your mouth,* she repeats, licks her finger and with it parts my lips, pushing her finger inside my mouth, back along the inner sides of my lips, runs her fingertips slowly along the valley between my cheek and gums. I press my tongue up to the top of my mouth. *Until one day you see yourself in a mirror and it isn't you there at all,* she says. Her finger is swollen on the end where the flesh rises over her nail: on it I can taste the salt and meat from supper; her rough cuticle and nail scrapes slightly at my mouth and slides against the nubs of my teeth. My tongue feels larger than necessary. She looks at me and says, *someone's in the mirror who's not you any more.*

She says I have to keep something in my mouth while I sleep. *So she don't come in,* she says, and takes a pack of chewing gum from the pocket of her bathrobe. Her lips begin to move in preparation: she unwraps the chewing gum and piece by piece chews them up slowly, her mouth slightly open. Then she parts her lips and between them emerges a wad of chewing gum. She pulls her index finger out of my mouth and takes the gum from hers, rolling it into a round pink ball between her thumb and forefinger. She pushes it past my resistant lips and presses it up against my back teeth. She does this six times, wedging more and more of the viscous sweetness into my mouth, not waiting for me to swallow, my sticky spit running down her fingers and collecting around the band of her wedding ring and then in the folds of fat around her wrist. When she is satisfied she wipes her hands on her robe and kisses my lips goodnight, resting the entire weight of her head on them for a moment. She says we will do this every night: she says it will keep the ghosts from coming inside me.

* * *

At night when I'm in bed I can hear the ripping sound of dog claws tearing up the weed roots outside, the thick wet snufflings of nose and muzzle in the loose dirt as they search through the soil, the snort as they clear their noses of muddy mucus before resuming the digging. Sarah is buried in the church cemetery—I know this, my grandmother has taken me every Sunday to lay flowers and candy on her grave. But at night in the catacombs of this house it seems possible that she buried her outside, out in the yard, where my grandmother could watch her from the window. The dogs' activity only convinces me further that they too know she's nearby, that they too can smell her and are driven mad by the tantalizing closeness of her body.

I dream at night that my body has expanded. In the dream my grandmother brings me clean laundry and when I put them on, my city clothes, the shirts won't button over my chest which suddenly possesses breasts; the pants won't close around my hips. The clothes have shrunk, I cry out in my dream, but when I look down, my entire body is covered with long strands of yellow hair. Yellow hair pours out my mouth, grows between my hips. My grandmother watches me struggle with the garments. My mother hovers, clutching her pair of scissors. *You're growing*, they say to me, *you're growing up*. Did Sarah get breasts? They aren't sure, they take out a photograph to look. Through the glass Sarah reaches out her hand to me and draws me into the picture, offers me her body. *Go ahead*, she says, Sarah's lips are full like my mother's, her sister's. Aunt Sarah offers *take my breasts. Would you like my lips?* She offers me artifacts of herself here where the collections of things long dead are already vast and overflowing. *Come here*, she says, and begins to brush my hair but my mouth is full of it, a continuous flow, her yellow hair pours in long golden streams from my lips, it tastes like sugar but I can't breathe. I gasp for air and above me Sarah laughs and drinks perfume.

When I wake I slip out of bed and go over to the stain on the carpet. I get down on my hands and knees over the stain and inhale through my nose; I bury my nose and chin into the strands of the shag carpeting and sniff: dank bittersweet mold and vinegar and finally the faint odor of perfume that mixes with the fruity scent rising up from the gum in my mouth. I squat over the stain and pee, again, a few drops each night, a small narrow stream into the carpeting.

Karen Offitzer

AS EASY AS ALL THAT

.

It came late for me, the realization that one's place in the world is not reversible; that where you are and how you come to live is not easy to change once you pass a certain age. That particular age, of course, is difficult to assess; nevertheless, the very fact that at some age, for all of us, we can not take back our decisions is what led me, on a warm but windy September day in Southern California, in a place I had chosen to live but was loath to embrace, to finally admit that what I had now was mine to keep.

I had grown up in a different climate; not just the changing seasons of western New Jersey, but one filled with an eastern, Jewish, middle-class morality: higher education followed by career, marriage, children. Here, in the warmth of my new husband's Southern California life, I was among a different breed: neither my husband nor most of his friends had finished (or even attended) college, the jobs they held were working-class: postal workers, tile setters, build-

---

Karen Offitzer's recent work has appeared in *Phoebe: A Journal of Literary Arts, Sunset Arts, Ararat,* and *Artist and Influence.* She is the author of three non-fiction books and teaches at Loyola Marymount University and National University in Los Angeles.

ers of other people's homes. What brought me to California initially was a whim, a desire to take advantage of what I believed was an opportunity to grab life with gusto: I had been asked to leave an ungraciously humid New York August for six weeks to run a small company in San Diego while the owner—a former boss for a related New York company—fired and then would attempt to hire a new director. My jobs at the time were part-time and exchangeable—a library assistant at the Museum of Natural History, a cashier at Shakespeare and Co. Bookstore; my only reluctance was in missing the birthday, five weeks from the date of departure, of a recently-ex-boyfriend whom I was convinced I would one day marry. The former boss offered to fly me and my dog to San Diego, put us up in a hotel, pay us a large weekly sum, and get me home again in six weeks. A few phone calls, a promise to family that of course I'd be back in time for a cousin's Connecticut wedding, and I was off on what I had begun to think of as my newest adventure.

It seems to me now that it was not as easy as all that, that in the moment I got off the phone after the offer to leave sweltering New York for California I had, possibly out loud, said of course I can't do this, of course I can't quit my jobs on a moment's notice and leave New York. And for what? To go to a city where I knew no one, and one in which I couldn't possibly get around: I didn't know how to drive. My family was here, I was in a writing group, I knew the take-out menus for all the nearby restaurants. In the same moment, and perhaps it's exactly that moment I need to return to, I told myself this is precisely the kind of life I wanted to live: unburdened, spontaneous, free. I had just turned 30, had just begun writing again, had just finished the first semester of a graduate program at City College, and had just experienced a summer of heartbreak. I know I made frantic calls that evening, among the first to my ex-boyfriend, who, I found out the next evening during our farewell dinner, had already been seeing someone for several weeks and was, he said, happy that I was finally moving on. Another call to the married, soon-to-have-his-novel-published man, 22 years my senior, with whom I had just weeks before begun a romantic interlude unlike anything I had ever imagined for myself—plane trips to exotic locales, dinners on the beach, oyster feasts with wine and more wine. We had just returned from what neither of us imagined was our last trip together; on the return from a southern town, where we had wined and dined and swum naked in a seemingly haunted lake, we cuddled in the Detroit airport lounge while waiting to switch to the second leg of our flights (he, to his home in the Hamptons; I, to New York). It was here that I told him of the ex-boyfriend I knew I would marry and he told me about the wife he would leave (but didn't, and still hasn't, to the best of my knowledge). And my not being able to reach him that night through the "code" we had concocted—two short rings, exactly 3 minutes apart—made my leaving New York seem all the more thrilling and misguided.

But then it was over, the deciding, and I was on a plane to Los Angeles. The compromise for bringing my dog was that I would fly direct to LA and drive, with another friend of the former boss, now a stand-up comedian performing in San Diego and LA, to my temporary digs in a hotel on the edge of Balboa Park.

Those six weeks stretched, as unplanned interludes in our lives often do, into months: after a few weeks I joined a writing workshop at a college and met the man who would later become my husband; I flew back home as often as my office manager's schedule would allow (she being the only able bodied person I knew, other than my new boyfriend, who would walk and feed my dog in my absence); I agreed to stay a month, then two, then longer, as the former boss bribed me, first with a mountain bike, then with trips to LA and New York, then, finally, with money. It was seven months later, in March, after I had sublet my rent-controlled, Upper West Side studio apartment twice (both times without my landlord's approval) and after, on a trip back east, I had overheard an always cranky prior dog-walking companion who lived two brownstones over remark that California was to heaven what New York was to hell, that I realized I had to give up one or the other.

I'd like to say, for my husband's sake, that the choice was an easy one: I was in love, had a well-paying job, a one-bedroom apartment, money in the bank, and was learning how to drive. But then there were the smells of Columbus Avenue on that crisp, sunny day in March (or maybe it was raining): the wet garbage and burnt coffee and fresh croissants from the corner deli; the way the black, wrought-iron gate wound its way up the brownstone stairs to the heavy, black doors I had often struggled to push open when clean laundry or food from Fairway or arms full of bargain books from the Strand made reaching the handle impossible. How can you give up the sense of neighborhood that develops when the well-dressed business executive across the street and the burly fireman-dog-walker on the corner and the not-so-sweet-smelling drunk who lives, when he's not sober enough to make it up to his hole in the wall on the fifth floor, in my hallway, all nod in approval when you rush your new puppy down three flights of stairs during the first attempts at housebreaking and he poops, obediently, on the sidewalk? These are the things that made the decision more difficult than any I had made before.

It was finally a matter of choosing a person over a place; at least this is what I said, in the end, to those who asked, and it is what I believed, for a while, when I packed up what I could ship on the plane and boxed the rest to store at my brother's house in the country. But the truth of the matter is this: I didn't believe for a moment that this decision, nor any I was making during this odd time in my life, was in any way final; I was, you see, convinced that these decisions—to go to California in the first place, to put off graduate school, to fall in love—were decisions that, if wrong, could be righted just as easily as selling off my meager belongings—a roll-top desk, an old piano, a set of 1960 encyclopedias—turned out to be.

A few months after I let my New York apartment go, the earth shook in my spacious one-bedroom apartment in San Diego's Hill-crest District and the dog barked, once, oddly, and I ran to the window to see if a large truck had rammed into our building. There was nothing, of course, and a phone call from the man I would eventually marry told me I had survived my first earthquake. The people I would normally call when things like this happen—my mother, my brothers, my best friend—all lived in a time zone three hours away, in a city everyone kept referring to as the East Coast, and on the East Coast all the people I knew were already sleeping. I had not yet made any close friends out here, probably for the same reason I had not yet hung any pictures on the wall. So I called no one, at least not until the next morning, and by then the thrill or the fear or the realization of what could have happened had worn off.

More time passed. I visited New York for another cousin's wedding, I changed the address on my Macy's card to California, I thought, seriously, about finishing graduate school somewhere else. My boyfriend and I discussed moving in together; the dog picked up fleas and worse: he tangled with a skunk outside my apartment and had to be bathed, repeatedly, with tomato juice, which the local Sav-on Drugstore sold me, in quantity, at a reduced price. I remember thinking this was a nice thing for them to do, but then I did smell like skunk when I went in, and they probably just wanted to rush me out. But still, in New York, it would have been tough to find so much tomato juice at such great prices, or so I said to my boyfriend, who nodded in agreement.

We moved in together, to a house in a suburb of San Diego, and just when I thought it was time to return to New York again, another earthquake happened. This time the television said it wasn't an earthquake, and the radio said it wasn't tests done by the nearby naval base, and the dog, now four, puked in our newly dug vegetable garden. I went outside, where the dog was, and talked to him in the voice I think one is supposed to use when someone is scared, or sick: soft, reassuring, calm. "Here boy," I called, and he came over, a spot of yellowish foam dripping from the corner of his snout. "You're a mess," I said, and he wagged his tail, a reminder to me that he doesn't understand a word I'm saying, never will, but that it doesn't matter. And I thought about how in this place I've tentatively come to call home, when the dog pukes in the vegetable garden I can simply brush dirt over it and give it some water and then, later, eat the tomatoes and cucumbers and green peppers (which I thought were chili peppers, since that's what the little packet had said when I planted the seeds, but weren't) and that it's okay if I don't find out exactly what shook the house because, after all, it's still standing. And, as everyone who lived nearby told me, it's really nothing if nothing gets broke.

We moved further north, me, my boyfriend-turned-husband, and our dog, this time to a place everyone called "the Valley," and, still, the thought of investing more than a weekend's time in fixing up the house seemed wasteful; after all, it was still only temporary. I took jobs teaching college English; my husband began working in the film industry. Our jobs lasted finite periods of time: a ten-week semester; a six-week shoot—we made plans only as far as the end of the next job. Our rented house began accumulating things such as my high school yearbooks, a summer camp photo album, a fuzzy stuffed bear named Breezly; items I had left behind, at my brother's place in New York. On one trip back I came home with a small, metallic cat for which I could now attach no significance. I placed it in a box labeled "stuff."

When I became pregnant we moved again, to a bigger house, still in the Valley. A few weeks after moving, the bed jolted at night, and this time my husband of two years was home. When I asked him if it was an earthquake he said yes; the cement blocks surrounding our driveway were already noticeably altered from the "big one" in Northridge, not far from where we now lived. I looked quickly at the dog, now six, who was asleep at the foot of the bed, and who stayed that way, even though the boom was louder than before, and rattled the windows even harder, and this time made me feel like puking in our new rose garden. I thought about who I might call, and what I might say, and what I was doing living and preparing for a baby in a place where a boom would lead me to such thoughts, and I noticed that I, again, had not hung any pictures on the wall. It was a small thing, I knew, but it was something I could not justify not doing any more. And it was at this moment, here in the bedroom of our rented house in a suburb of Los Angeles where I had planted roses in the garden, that I realized that this way of life, at least, if not entirely permanent, was one that was going to be a part of me for a very long time.

As I began banging a nail into the wall above a low book shelf, the perfect spot, I thought, for the antique-framed photograph of my favorite grandmother, who had herself begun life over several times, the dog lifted one ear in response to my banging and I noticed that his tail was wagging, and I tried to imagine what thoughts or emotions were triggering his pleasure. Perhaps it was the warm smell of roses filling the spaces between each bang; perhaps the sound of snoring from my almost-back-to-sleep husband. Whatever it was, I took this as a sign that, at least for the moment, while there was no going back, what we had, now, was definitely worth keeping. And I finished hanging my grandmother's picture on the wall, while the dog went back to sleeping on the bed.

Harry Albert Haines

ETHIOPS

The bedroom drapes don't fit together at the top and I lie on my back looking at a slender, pie-shaped slice of blue parking lot light on the ceiling at two-something, thinking of my high sperm count and all the other things that hang over and under my life. The second date, we have sex, and, bingo, she's pregnant. We get married. Fine, I'm sure. Come to think of it, not as sure as I was ten years ago. She's beside me now, breath coming and going. The faint light outlines the curve of her hip. I rise on one elbow then lie back and flip through the mental remorse file—should have bought American instead of Lexus. Get a hell of a Buick for 25K. We have four thousand in a CD, 39K in condo equity. Condo payments are thirty-eight hundred then there's the Lexus, club dues, Zelko's braces—two pair a year at four K each—health insurance, life insurance, the 401K, dental, clothes, travel, a third of everything for taxes. I'm making over a hundred-fifty thou and we're living on the edge.

In six years, I'm fifty. I close my eyes and lie still, aware of Jordan's body next to me. I inhale and pull into my nose, mouth and

Harry Albert Haines is a retired Arkansas journalist whose work has appeared in many journals, including *The Georgia Review, Missouri Review,* and *Gettysburg Review.*

lungs her cologne. Her hair wanders out over the white pillow. I touch it, fold a strand around my index finger, let go and sleep until five when I get up, make coffee, get the paper and check the comics, sports and front page before going to the classifieds, where a late-model, used Buick is advertised for twenty-one. Most of the warranty's left. I pour more coffee and take a multi-purpose vitamin. I do the bathroom thing, dress and leave while Jordan sleeps.

"Four-letter word for exotic bird." Jordan's lying on the couch, back against the armrest, legs extended, doing the crossword. There is a wonderful, full quality—women call it body—to her dark hair. My own is wispy blond. Jordan will look great when she's fifty. At fifty, I'll look fifty.

"Erotic bird? How about woodpecker, or titmouse, or . . . "

"Exotic." She doesn't laugh. Forty-one, five-six and one-twenty-two. Her hair under most light looks black, but actually it is a rich, deep brown that loops down in relaxed curls. Her eyes are big and dark, her brows heavy and natural, and her waist must be about twenty-seven. Mine's thirty-four and counting.

"How about myna?" She puts pencil to puzzle but doesn't comment. "Hello? Did I help solve the Great *Times* Puzzlement?" I feel like a desperate talk show host, trying to score conversational points.

"Thanks."

She wears a white cotton robe printed with small blue tongues of flame. It falls open a bit and I see a little thigh. Beside her on the floor is *Light in August*. She's re-reading Faulkner.

I know not why, but our marriage is brittle. I need to earn more. She doesn't seem aware of the money problem. She takes tennis lessons at fifty per. It's difficult to reconcile this and then there's what's going on and not going on at my office—New Millennium Concepts.

Over a year ago, I took aboard Foster, thirty-one and a Vanderbilt M.B.A. His white scalp shines through thin black hair. He's in charge of sales. Hard working, loyal, keeps great records. An organizational man, who's screwing our good-looking receptionist, a stereotypical office type with long, straight blonde hair and a tiny overbite which makes her face interesting. From time to time she raises a suspicion of intelligence. The problem is Foster. This good man, this smart man is sales manager, but couldn't sell pussy on a troop train. A detail man, he's out of his element in sales. I brought him here from Nashville. Paid moving at three K. He should be fired. I'll talk with him. Again.

Zelko is twelve. He was born with orthopedic and neural problems, a physiological train wreck. He inherited Jordan's toughness, thank God. He wears steel braces on each leg, uses a walker and attends public school. He's bright and somehow optimistic, which reminds me to be optimistic, which is harder to do. I try not to think of him, because he easily could occupy all my thoughts and all my energy, all day, every day. People who dwell in tragedy become heavy drinkers and lose their minds.

I pour a Scotch and think about the drinking thing. Jordan sips Diet Coke. Her robe falls away from legs on which lingers the solar seasoning of our beach trip. She still can wear bikinis. I sit strategically across from her so I get a better take on her legs. I drop my pen—as in Immanola Junior High—and, retrieving it, look up all the way to her white panties. She doesn't notice. I clink the ice in my glass. Her cologne is ambiguous. I'm always looking for messages. It's how I make my living. Advertising. I'm a messenger.

"An embryonic cell from which another develops." When she frowns, her brows gather above the bridge of her nose. When she moves her head, light slides off her hair like bright water. "Ten letters." She adjusts her little demi-specs. "Sometimes when I start to think about something, when I try hard, I can't think of any words. Like fowls. At a party I might be able to talk about parakeets and penguins, Baltimore orioles and mallards. But I get here alone and try to think . . . "

Alone?

". . . . and I can't come up with the name of a bird."

"Did myna work?"

"How about seven letters for advancing?"

"Did myna work?"

"I thanked you for that. Advancing. Advancing."

My glass is empty and I'm retreating, retreating to the kitchen.

Zelko has a TV in his room. We assuage our guilt by giving him anything he wants. Second date. On the couch in her apartment. Had we waited a day or two; had we done it in a bed rather than on the couch; had we not smoked grass; had we not been drinking wine; if the moon had been full, or not full, Zelko would have been different because we would have altered that particular element of randomness. We carry this guilt unspoken. We think of it. What would have happened? Never can tell. You did what you did and this is what you got. Might have gotten a pink-cheeked blue-eyed girl.

If.

If.

It's all random. We do what all parents do: blame ourselves.

"I love that little boy with his dark eyes and curls and white neck," she says as we discuss letting him get the TV. I don't want to get into this Who-loves-him-most thing and say, "If you think it's okay, get him one." This is called caving in.

Zelko has a new video game: images of men rip each other's heads off, tear out their hearts. I talk about this with him. "I appreciate that you're thinking of my welfare, Pops, but I'm okay on this."

Pops.

He can't play football, or anything like that. When he's home, he's mainly in his room, propped on a day bed/couch that sits along one wall and fronts the TV. It has a rust-colored slip cover decorated with tan X's and flowers. The pillow has a depressed, darkened spot in its upper middle where his head stays year after year. A computer sits in one corner.

He's a beautiful guy and I wonder about girls which are in the future of all teenagers. I have no idea what will happen to his sunny psyche when his difference becomes so obvious. Will some girl date him? Will she be anything like an attractive girl? A girl someone else wants?

When the three of us go to a restaurant, I let Jordan enter first and watch the male heads turn, watch the men's eyes slip while they pretend not to look. Then they see Zelko scrabbling along on his walker and their eyes go back to their plates, to their partners and what they do says a lot about me and all of us. No one wants to think sex in the presence of the object's crippled child.

I don't approve of Foster screwing the receptionist, but on the other hand it's none of my business as long as it doesn't affect my business, which means it will be affecting theirs. I have no hard evidence, but it's like living with someone who's having an affair—you know. How could you not know? The bits of intelligence—working late, whispered conversations at the vending machine, the phone that rings once. A spouse always, I suppose, knows about the partner's affair although he doesn't want to acknowledge it, doesn't want to certify the chicanery and hopes for the best. The body sends out early warnings and the spouse picks up on this. Like dogs smelling fear, or randiness.

There's Jordan and the tennis pro, a young, blond, slender South African with curly white hair on his lean, tan legs. She spends an hour or two a week with him, but I'm getting no messages. She talks to him on the phone in my presence. "I can't make our three o'clock. How about Friday?" Could this mean anything? Indeed. Anything.

When Jordan crosses her legs this evening, I'm treated to a heart-quickening flash of white nylon; an alkie allowed to sniff a damp cork.

"Black iron oxide," she says. "Seven letters."

We haven't made love since April 22. And that was the first time in seven months, at which time there were tears on her face. The sexual encounter before that was the first in nine months and was tainted by my insistence and lots of wine. We're now at two years, since we fell into each other's arms with joy and passion. A drinking buddy says she asked her West Texas grandmother, "How much of marriage is good sex?" The old lady, who was eighty-seven, said, "Ninety percent, if you don't have it. Ten if you do." I've read that since. Someone stole the old lady's lines.

I've gone from a deodorant to an antiperspirant. I had my dentist check me out for bad breath. Found a small cavity. Sixty bucks.

"Amy," I say to my secretary. She looks up with bright, brown eyes. "Ever noticed, well, body odor?" And think I'd sooner ask her to take off her clothes than to ask her about my body odor.

"Jesus, Mr. Oxford," she says, sniffing her armpit. "If I've offended . . . "

"Not you. Me. Do I smell, for God's sake?"

She moves to me, leans in and sniffs. "Yummy. What's the cologne?"

"Tuscany." Whoa. "But thanks."

"Any time." She sniffs again, closes her eyes then leaves me watching her yummy bottom swing as she walks away. An hour later that adjective—adverb?—ricochets within my head. Yummy. Never noticed the titillating aspect of yummy before. An interior light changes from red to yellow.

This evening's view of Jordan's legs is promising and means new fuel for my masturbatory fantasies. Taking what I can get, I scan her leg up to where her derrière begins its marvelous curve. With her slightest move—she's working on the *Times* puzzle—I again see her panties. I sip my Scotch. She's deep into the crossword. I'm not certain if she's entirely unaware of these displays she makes of her body. "Want to talk?" I ask, looking away to my right where there's a small white piano on which stands a framed photo of Zelko, grinning and holding up a modest fish. A crappie. He's in his room, deep into his computer. God knows what he's finding. A chat partner. He'd be charming. Some old lady in South Africa. Seventy-two. Telling him, "I'd like to shower with you then jump right into bed and . . . "

"About what?"

"Jorrr-duhn, darlin', we never do it." I look back from Zelko's photo to the top of her head.

"Do what?" Not looking up, frowning though. "Oh, that. Not true."

"I'm your husband. You can tell me. We should converse about this." The Scotch tastes like NyQuil, but I drink it down.

She lays aside the puzzle and opens the Faulkner, absently pushing her hair away from one eye. "Let's not fight." I go to the kitchen and pour from the Chivas. All us drunks blame our drinking on someone else. I'm not a drunk, but I drink too damned much. The next day, the dull post-alcoholic edge keeps me from my best thinking. I don't make automobiles, or power mowers. My commodities are ideas. I need to quit drinking and toughen up.

Amy, my secretary, is twenty-six and recently divorced. She's five-four with short, straight black hair. Her construction features intriguing hemispheres. She's a beagle to Jordan's Weimaraner. I have this vision, it's post-coital and we're in a motel room and she's slipping her red dress over her head, it falls down over her body like water. She tosses her head back. Smiles at me and winks.

To other mammals, sex is no more important than a good meal, or a night's sleep, according to a veterinarian I once met up with while jogging. He said no species thinks about sex any more than it thinks about a bowel movement or its hunt for meat; said that man is the only animal who wants sex when his mate is not rutting. Says man is the only animal who thinks of mating while doing other things, like shaving, eating and jogging. I think he's wrong and have read that bonobo chimps perpetually are at it. They masturbate, too. A relief, to know. Why the hell is that?

Two-forty-two A.M. and her bottom is toward me. Hand on her thigh, I gather up folds of her gown, drawing it up four, five, six, seven inches. "Jordan?" I'm whispering. Stiff as a stone, she lies facing the digital clock.

"I can't believe you'd awaken me at this hour. You don't want to, uh," she pauses, sleepily searching for the word, "talk?"

"No." I remove my hand. Indigestible breath tightens my chest. I kiss her neck through her long hair, roll over and wonder if Amy wears white panties. From her side, Jordan whispers, "I love Zelko." Puzzled, I reply I do, too. What the hell is this about?

When he was born, Zelko lay on his back, legs no larger than pencils, splayed out toward the sides of the bed. I had never seen a child lie like this, not in photos, or in friends' homes, not on TV.

Jordan and I had committed a pediatric accident. "You can't tell," the OB said in a voice weakened by doubt, "he may come around."

Such is the blessed capacity of the human heart to hope that three years later we're standing in the darkness by Zelko's bed and Jordan says, "The OB said he'd be okay some day. Didn't he?" No, he didn't, but I don't say anything, just stand looking at his knees pointing outward. The OB had been pointedly, meaningfully vague. I don't remind her. It would lead to an argument.

Ten-thirty-one P.M. and we've just turned out the light. Apropos of nothing she says, "I love Zelko as only a woman who brought his little body into this world could." There. What the hell do I say to this? There is no response I haven't made dozens of times. As a man, I didn't bring his little body into the world. Am I supposed to apologize for my lack of female reproductive organs? The condo is getting heavy with the smell of our marital malaise. In the dark, I look up at the blue light pie slice on the ceiling and think about Foster screwing the receptionist. Where do they meet? How often? The thought of Amy's thick thighs adds another straw to my guilt burden. I don't like the sort of thing that Foster's got going. And this brings me to ask myself if I'm considering the same damned thing.

"Oh," Jordan says from the darkness on her side.

"Yeah?" I raise up on an elbow.

"The seven-letter word for black oxide is ethiops."

Even first thing in the morning, when we sit at the black and chrome kitchen table, her skin looks good, even luminous. The only window is on the north and although the room is white, it doesn't explode. I say, "Ever thought of getting help?"

"With what?"

"The sex thing." I fold over the sports. She reaches for the main news section. "I'll go with you." Marmalade slides from my knife as I bring it over an English muffin. "There's a guy named Cassius. I hear he's good."

"From whom do you hear this?"

From Amy, but to hell with that. "One of the clients. Tom Conine with the drugstore chain."

"You're not serious?" When I don't answer, she says, "I didn't think so. I'm not going to discuss my sex life with a stranger."

Sex life?

Come evening, I approach the living room with a drink. As a kid I fantasized about Farrah Fawcett. I was in love with her. I got over it. Fantasies wear thin and I've been fantasizing about Jordan for two years. There's healing in hopelessness and the libidinal steam loses its pressure. Takes years, but my meter's been running a long time.

"Nine letters. Begins with *D*. Slatternly woman. What about men?"

"Don't follow."

"Why is it always slatternly women, not men?"

"So, how's single life?" I ask, not because I want to know. It's 5:32. The office is empty. Amy puts pens in her desk drawer, tears off the top page of her desk calendar and fires it into the wastebasket, lets go a big breath and says, "Okay, I guess." Like me with Foster, I think Amy dimly perceives my situation. Maybe someday they'll find it's olfactory; ancient scents coded in our DNA that leak from the skin and tip off people. Standing, as she hunches over her desk, I am treated to the secrets of the single woman's handbag—little pieces of paper (receipts?), lipsticks, keys, two upscale-looking business cards which inspire quick jealousy, a checkbook, a pill bottle that's not The Pill which comes in circular things as The Pill of Days. Single life—AIDS, condoms, bars, health clubs, aerobic classes, spandex, "Hey, how you?" and serious drinks, girls with round, firm happy butts, waking up on Sunday morning in a new bedroom, feeling fulfilled, but only in some superficial way that is unimportant, but only after it's been attained.

"Single life," she says, "isn't a rose garden, but neither was marriage." She leans, putting her upper arm in contact with mine. Circuits are energized. For some time, we stand touching, enjoying the contact of another human being, one we know and trust. Out the window a yellow school bus rolls down Union.

"Don't try to be a swordsman. You got nothing to prove. I see this. Guy gets crossways with the old lady and puts moves on the first thing that's got a pulse. Mama hires an eye and gets photos. Husband loses big time because his ass is destined for litigious hell. Relax, while we see where this is going."

"Relax? Oh, sure."

"Yeah." Rubens has dense black hair. His white shirt is monogrammed on the breast pocket in Columbia blue. He can send a fax and make enough to have one shirt personalized—eighteen dollars.

From his drawer, he takes a small, brown pill bottle and washes a green cap down with a Dr. Pepper that looks as if it's been on his desk for days. "They come in here saying they want a divorce and the next think you know they don't want one. I try to keep them out of bars and beds. I tell them not to fondle their secretaries. I don't charge for these explanatory-exploratory visits. I'm telling you to cool it."

"Cool what? I got nothing going."

He shuffles papers, a signal that this exploratory session is over. Custody is on my mind. I want it without knowing if I can take care of the kid and run the company and date girls, all high on my list. Rubens says I can forget custody and hope for "reasonable visitation."

Jordan and I haven't discussed divorce. I don't want it, but I've been hanging on and my fingernails are weakening. There's an unhealthy aura around this situation and I want to cleanse myself of it though I know it means practically losing Zelko. In my more honest moments, I admit, if only to myself, that, at least for a while, being able to operate as a single man would put a lot of excitement back into my life. Feeling sorry for myself. Looking for an excuse to bed a toothsome employee. Amy is interesting and interested. It's exhilarating and terrifying to realize I want her and she wants me. I think.

I'm certain.

Jordan and I have been talking about sending Zelko to a camp for kids who made bad draws from the gene pool, or who took a corner too fast on their Harleys. Challenged, they call it. This place works on the self-esteem thing. There's physical activity, even for Zelko who, they say, will be swimming and riding. He's eager to go, which heartens me. Also heartening is the fact that in looking at the details, in talking, discussing this, Jordan and I are like a marital team again. Sort of.

She wears her tongue-of-flames robe. "But five weeks?"

"He'll see all these handicapped kids and get pep talks on getting by, on succeeding, learning something physical. Maybe he'll . . ." My God. I get a mental picture of Zelko weaving a basket, an attack of unreason that roils my stomach.

"Wild goat. Four letters."

"Ibex."

She prints the word into the little squares.

"So," I continue, "he's going, then?"

"I guess." She's into the crossword, but adds, "I don't know." We use job and hobbies to hide from the gritty reality that we have a crippled son. "There'll be other kids on crutches," she says looking into the crossword.

"There'll be kids in wheelchairs. Blind. Deaf." I don't know what the hell I'm talking about but this is a chance Zelko desperately needs and I don't know the blind and deaf won't be there. I ask if she'd like a Scotch and she says yes. Hopefully, I stride to the kitchen as she fishes camp applications from a drawer. The form is long and involved and includes requests for medical history which, I'm surprised to find, Jordan has. She crosses her legs and the robe falls away, causing a silent groan to rise from my body's center. I put a hand on her shoulder. She doesn't shrug it off, but works on, filling in the application. I like holding her shoulder, but after a few minutes feel like the groveling fool I am. I take my Scotch to the bedroom and watch the Braves lose to the miserable Pirates.

We take the Volvo wagon, packing Zelko's stuff plus enough of our own for a weekend in Asheville, the nearest city to the camp. We move from Interstate 40 to two-lane blacktop, to—climbing now— gravel and then a trail through the woods. "Camp Inspiration" is written in wooden letters—natural bark finish—above the entrance on a rustic wooden arch. The letters are made of bent willow and the *I* dangles from a single, off-center nail.

Dr. Atkinson, a Duke Ph.D., is camp director. He wears a plastic pith helmet and has draped a large, white handkerchief over his shoulders. From time to time, he takes this off to fan himself. He has a small pot belly, his skin is white and he wears heavy, steel-rimmed glasses. We ask about medical facilities. "Fifteen minutes, in Asheville," he reassures us with a smallish lie, but a lie nevertheless because Asheville is half an hour. I hope Jordan doesn't catch this, but she's so caught up in the emotion of letting her son live on his own—not factually true, of course—that she doesn't notice.

We carry Zelko's stuff to Cabin Eight, a reminder that he can't carry it himself as thousands of kids are doing in thousands of camps this very minute. Cabin Eight is a small, square, brownstained frame structure. From a half-way point, the cabin is screened. Overhanging shutters doubtless are dropped in the off season. The roof is tin. A young man approaches in a motorized wheelchair. His hair is short and lies close to his head. He wears trendy, small lens specs and looks to be about twenty. "You must be Zilko!"

"Zelko," Jordan and I correct in chorus.

"I'm Lance." He puts an open palm up in front of his smile. For an awkward moment, we maneuver around the wheelchair and shake hands. I can't recall seeing Zelko ever shake hands with anyone before. Lance calls himself a "graduate" of the camp and says he's a junior at Duke. Jordan, encouraged by this, smiles cautiously.

"Want some cookies?" Our son's counselor motions toward the dining hall and we fall in behind him as his chair whines and crunches up a rock path. I take a chocolate chip, though my mouth is dry and my stomach is tight. Jordan has black coffee. The cookie tastes medicinal and I covertly drop it into a napkin. Jordan's big eyes reflect the anxiety I try to conceal. I lightly take her arm and lead her to one end of the table. We hear Lance ask, "So you're from Memphis?"

There is a gathering darkness in Jordan's face. "Look at him," I say. "He's adapting. This Lance is his kind of person." I want her to know the good things I see. There is a roar as a huge fan mounted in a gable begins to revolve.

"We can't leave him. I can think of something. My sister's coming next week. We pack him and go. Right now." She makes a move, I take her arm and together we look about the rustic, old dining hall with its screened walls and concrete floor, wooden tables and benches. Mentally, I fumble for an argument. This thing has taken on an importance that surprises me. "We'll not spoil his first chance to be independent. College is drawing near. This is basic training."

"I'm not sure." We're whispering at the end of the table. Other parents slowly move past and nibble at cookies. I look over their shoulders and up at the fan. In the kitchen a big black man in white hat, shirt and pants sits on a table swinging his legs.

"We simply must," I say and she sags into me, nods and brings a small handkerchief to one eye. Her body stiffens, her back straightens. She lifts her chin and we move back where Zelko and Lance are having a lively conversation about megabytes. She tries to return my grin, nods, and I can see—and admire—her quietly being brave. "Good girl," I think. We decide against a tearful goodbye, pat Zelko on the shoulder, shake again with Lance and head the Volvo out the gate, sharing a feeling of guilty relief.

We have planned this, have reservations in an old Asheville resort hotel, a place where F. Scott Fitzgerald and Zelda once lived. It's been renovated and our room is huge and comfortable, old but having all the decadence of luxury. From a suitcase, I take a bottle of Mouton Rothschild '76 for this is a celebration in the way Easter is a celebration; a commemoration of triumph over tragedy. I stand at the window and look down on a perfectly green fairway lined with rigid pines. In the gloaming, retired men in white make their way toward the eighteenth green, getting off golf carts to walk as if their feet hurt, one foot going down carefully in front of the other.

I leave Jordan with a new *Times* puzzle and, full wine glass in hand, enter the bathroom. I set the glass on the wide tub edge before stepping into a violent hot shower. Behind the curtain I put both hands on the wall and let the water batter my back. More money?

More sales. It's time to act. The game plan: I give Foster a sales objective and ninety days and he can screw whomever. But he produces one new account, or sayonara. Standing under the water fusillade, I sip wine and feel Roman. Moving along: I invite Amy to lunch and, if things go well, a day or two later, I ask her for a drink after work. I'm feeling pretty damned good and haven't had but a half glass of wine. Life reflects the order we bring to it.

I sit on tub's edge, drying, and cloak myself in the hotel's luxuriant white, terry cloth robe, turn out the light and enter the bedroom feeling like a Caesar as my bare feet luxuriate in the deep carpet's soft massage. The sun has disappeared behind the woods backing the eighteenth fairway and the room, like the golf course, is in an early, azure nightfall. Jordan sits in bed, back against the headboard, sheet drawn to her armpits, leaving exposed toothsome upper breast rounds. "Hurry," she says.

Maya Sonenberg

SHADOW PLAY

I'm dreaming when I first hear the phone ring, looking through
the windows of a doll cottage and watching the rooms grow to human size. I stop in the doorway between living room and kitchen
and look down at the bare linoleum. "Someone was murdered here,"
I think and see a stain spread at my feet like red lace. It's one of
those dreams that should be terrifying but isn't, one of those dreams
that make your friends shiver when you tell it to them even though
you say you woke up smiling. In the dream Barry is gone, but I'm
not scared, I'm not even lonely; instead, I start planning what I'll
use to fill all the empty rooms since I have no furniture. I think of
swing sets and tea tables, chaise longues, pots and pots of pink
geraniums, and they appear magically, arranged just as I'd like.
Then all the walls disappear, leaving forest and blue sky. Still the
phone keeps ringing, the persistent ring of Kim's husband. He calls
late at night now that he's taken off for Indonesia and my sister is
staying with us. Dashing Paul and beautiful Kim. If he wants to talk
to Kim, he'll never let up, so I push the quilts aside and ignore

---

Maya Sonenberg's collection, *Cartographies,* received the Drue Heinz Literature Prize.
Her work has appeared in *Santa Monica Review, Gargoyle, American Short Fiction,* and
Princeton Arts Review. She teaches at the University of Washington.

Barry's grumbling. He came home at ten like he has every night for at least a month, kissed me on the forehead, and dropped his brief case on the kitchen table. "I'm going right to sleep," he said and headed toward the bedroom before I could say anything.

Now I see the outdoor light is still on, left burning for Kim's return, and the light in the hall too. Even so I stumble into things— a chair, a pair of wet boots. And the rain's still coming down hard, the same as when I went to bed. In the living room, I pick the receiver out of the dark.

"Kim?" he asks. "What took you so long? The whole house is probably up by now."

"No, it's Anna." I've never heard him like this before, almost angry. "Is that you, Paul?"

"Yes." He hesitates, gathers breath. "Is Kim there?"

I stand by the phone shivering, trying to remember where my sister was going. She was wearing the heels she usually carries in a bag when she goes to work and a red dress she borrowed without asking just like she's always borrowed things. I buy clothes and she goes out in them before I even have a chance to wear them once. She left the closet open too, blouses slipping off the hangers. Maybe she didn't say where she was going. "I'm not sure," I say and cover the receiver, pretending to go look for her even though I feel silly. I don't know why I'm doing it. Her car keys jingled, swinging from her fingers as she went out the door into the rain. Then the screen door slapped shut, and I sat for two hours in the dark waiting for Barry to come home. Now I'm cold, tired, the whole house seems damp. I'm afraid the rain will wash it down the hillside. Or the bay will rise and swallow it—all this rain. Suddenly I'm mad at everybody.

"Anna, Anna," Paul is saying when I put my ear back to the phone. "Don't wake her. Please don't wake her," he says.

"I guess she's not in yet," I say.

"She's not? Isn't it sort of late?" He sounds upset. Who can blame him? "I just wanted to see how she was," he says. "Has she gotten my messages?"

In the light from the hall, I can see the last dark dozen roses he sent on the mantle, still in the plastic vase the florist brought them in. "She got all the flowers and letters," I say. I remember Kim and Barry were in the kitchen when the flowers came to the front door. As I bent to smell them, I could hear the two of them arguing over some small point, who should do the dishes or put the laundry in the dryer. The odor was heavy and sweet, palpable as a hand in my throat. I stopped, burying my face deeper and deeper in the flowers.

"I sent you something too," Paul says. "Did you get it? It's the last puppet in the set."

"Yes, we got him yesterday. He's wonderful. It's Rama, isn't it?" I've hung the shadow puppets flat against the living room wall, a frieze of brightly painted, cut-out figures, the perforated leather against the white like filigree. The prince, his wife Sita, and the other heroes, clowns, and giants from the Ramayana march in single file around the room.

"Yes, yes, it's Rama," Paul answers. "Kim always liked him the best. She thought he was really hot."

I hear him laughing a little, uncomfortably, trying to joke. In some far off distant past, I can remember Kim looking at some guy and saying, "You wouldn't think it, but what a stud!" Back when she used to talk to me about such things. I could tell Paul that Kim went out on a date but I don't really know for sure. And besides, it would only hurt him, not her. I think of all his sweetness, his letters and presents and phone calls. "I'm not sure when Kim'll be in," I say. "I think she might be at Mom's. Or maybe she said she was going out with Greta—her friend from high school? Should I tell her to call you?" I shift my weight from foot to foot.

"Well, I just wanted to see how she was—she's all right, isn't she?"

His voice sounds hollow, achy, and I worry about him again. "Of course. She's fine. She's been catching up with old friends, keeping herself busy."

"She's not too lonely?"

"I'm sure she misses you," I say. I don't think it's true, but it seems like the right thing to say. Light sweeps through the hall door, a bright triangle reaching almost to the sofa. The rest of the living room is black. I wind the phone cord around my fingers, tighter and tighter.

"I guess it's just as well she didn't come this time. She really wanted to come the first time, but she didn't end up liking it much," he says.

"Well, I had a great time," I say. Paul was researching the country's new immunization program for his public health degree, and Kim had gone with him. Her letters sounded cheerful, but once I was there I could see she was miserable no matter where we went, no matter what we did. In one village, we found a nurse giving shots to babies, and Paul and I went up to talk to her. The village was at the crown of a hill. All around, the rice fields dropped away in terraces, an unimaginable, saturated green that made the red earth at our feet sing in contrast. Each house had a carved lintel, fantastical signs and symbols, I thought, protecting the inhabitants. While the children waited for their shots, Paul did tricks for them, pulling coins and birds and candy from behind their ears. The older kids came up to us, eager to talk and tell us jokes, and when I turned around, I was surprised to see Kim just pacing in the shade, slapping her thigh with her hat. Even there, where it was so beautiful, she seemed disgruntled. "I still don't understand why she was so unhappy," I say.

"You didn't have to live here with me," Paul laughs.

"I guess I didn't. But you didn't seem so bad to me." I remember that at one temple, the carvings seemed to be alive with monkeys hurling boulders into the sea, dancers tilting their heads and spreading their fingers, gods sporting the wings of eagles or the heads of elephants. In the middle of it all, Sita turned her voluptuous body to receive a messenger, bending her odd double-jointed elbows. Paul nuzzled Kim's neck and said, "She looks like you, just like you," but she pushed him away.

"Kim's not causing you any trouble, is she? She can be such a pain sometimes."

"Don't be silly, Paul."

"I'm just sorry I can't be there."

"Stop worrying. We go through this every time you call. You know everything'll be OK."

"OK," he says.

"This is costing you a fortune, Paul."

"I know, I know," he says, but he insists on staying on the phone. Is he waiting for Kim to walk through the door?

"I should go," I say, but I keep hearing him breathing and behind him, silence. He must be calling from some friend's fancy hotel room. I can see his forehead pressed against the air-conditioned window, the dark hair, the shoulders bent. I can see him looking down on Jakarta, but I can't tell what he's thinking. I remember the kiss he gave me when I handed him his going away present—an umbrella decorated with frogs and lizards—and the way he backed toward the plane so he could keep us in sight as long as possible while Kim was already looking in her purse for the car keys. All these things I can infuse with meaning now, and life here rushes away from me at an incredible speed. Suddenly I need to keep talking to him. "It's raining cats and dogs here, but it's not cold any more," I blurt out. "We're all getting tired of being wet all the time. Except Barry—he just ignores it, he's so busy working. He settled that case he's been working on since September. No trial, so I think he was disappointed. He wouldn't say—he never does. But you know, he's always disappointed if he doesn't win the hard way."

"That's Barry," Paul says and laughs.

I laugh with him, but I get mad at Barry all over again. Just thinking about his calm, measured voice makes me mad. If I told Paul how I almost stole a little boy from a stroller in the supermarket, he'd laugh but he'd understand. If I told him the child looked like he came right from my gene pool, like he should be mine, Paul would know exactly what I meant. He wouldn't say, "Anna, you know that's illegal. If you want kids, just say so. You know I'm not against it," like Barry did when I came home that day. Then he rubbed my shoulders for a second, but his touch made me squirm. I hear the rain again outside, heavier now, hitting the carport roof with great force, and I think of Paul dashing in from the car. I think of him shaking the water from his hair, rain like silver beads in the porch light. After five years of drought, the rain just keeps coming. The hills up and down the Peninsula will be green through March and April, then by July everything will turn brown again if we don't all drown first. I could just leave, I think. I could just get on a plane and see Paul. "I miss you, sweetie," I say very softly.

"What's that?"

"Nothing," I say and clear my throat. "We all wish you were home."

"Soon," he says. "I have to go now. Give Kim a big kiss for me."

When I hang up, the room seems very quiet, very dark. I'm shaking but it's not because I'm cold. I make it over to the couch and curl up in its corner, tuck my nightgown around my legs. I'm shaking because I'm thinking about my baby sister's husband, this sudden longing for him—or not so sudden longing. It didn't really catch me by surprise. Sometimes it's a question of when you acknowledge these things. Why do I keep that photo of Paul in my wallet anyway? In it, he's standing in front of a gray stone temple, step after step topped by bell-shaped stupas. His face has faded to an indistinct spot, but whenever I look at it, I remember how handsome he is. Next to him, Kim stands with her arms folded, her eyes, nose and mouth shaded by a wide-brimmed hat. I know she's scowling. That day at Borobudur was breathless, silent, and the stones shimmered as I walked by them, fanning myself with a tourist brochure. On the walls, reliefs told the story of Buddha's life and insects hummed it too, in the fields and off in the distant trees. When I heard Paul and Kim arguing around the corner, I jumped, then stared and stared at the scene of Prince Siddhartha's enlightenment, half afraid they'd hear my sandals on the terrace if I moved, half listening to their fight, my heart pounding. At the airport, waiting for my flight home, Kim told me she'd never been so lonely. "I just want to have a real conversation with someone in English," she said. "Someone other than Paul. He's never around and all he talks about is which villages have TB and which ones don't or which temple to go look at next. And I have these stupid fantasies about drinking water straight from the tap. I'm sick of all this exotic stuff."

I didn't know what to say because all I could think was how silly she was being, living some place where every day was as magical as this and wanting to leave. When she put her head on my shoulder, I hoped she was going to ask if she could use my plane ticket, if she could go back to the States, take care of the house and Barry and my job and leave me in Jakarta, but she only sighed. I looked over her bent head at Paul and smiled. He seemed oblivious, practicing card tricks, getting the whole deck to leap up into the air and vanish. Then he met my eyes, smiled, shrugged. I felt my face blaze, wondering if he could tell what I was thinking.

Now, outside, a car drives through the rain. Its headlights swing across the walls, then disappear. Back in Indonesia, I could go to another shadow play with Paul, sit in the dark and watch the shadows the puppets make—sharp and dark when the puppeteer sets the figures flush against the screen, diffuse when he moves them further away. The figures swoop and fight as the dalang chants the legend of Rama—how he was exiled to the forest for fourteen years before he could become king, how he was tricked by a demon in the shape of a golden deer and his beautiful wife Sita was stolen from him, how with the help of the white monkey Hanuman he was finally able to rescue Sita but couldn't believe she had remained faithful all those years. She threw herself on a pyre and emerged unscathed, a sign of her purity. The dalang lowers his voice and growls for the demons, lilts when Sita speaks. The shadows grow until they swirl around our knees, up around our chests. I feel Paul sitting very close to me, whispering translations in my ear. As he talks, he waves his hands and I capture one and hold it very firmly between my knees until it stops struggling. I can feel his thumb on the inside of my knee, the weight of his arm. The closeness makes me dizzy. I shiver and remember I'm in my own living room, Paul miles and miles and miles away.

I hear Kim's car pull up, the silence when the engine dies, and the door being closed softly. I think how I should creep back to bed. I don't want her to find me here, waiting up for explanations the way our mother did, but I run into her in the hall.

"Anna," she says. "You're up."

"Paul called. I was just going back to bed."

"You weren't waiting up, were you?"

"He really misses you," I say and she looks exasperated. Then we both giggle when we hear Barry groan and smack the bed with his palm.

"Anna?" he says.

"Out here. I'm just talking to Kim." We hear him turn over, then she pulls me into the living room, turns on a light.

"I don't want you keeping track of me," she says. "This whole thing is *my* business."

"Don't you want to be there?" I say. "I mean, you're married to Paul, not to us."

"You don't know what you're talking about, Anna. You're blowing everything out of proportion. I'm here. He's there. That's all. We work it out when he gets back. OK? I went over there once with him and I hated it, remember?"

She starts taking off her coat, her shoes, and I remember how one day we went out stupidly at noon, and in the steaming Jakarta heat, Paul told story after story as we walked—how the government, deciding the streets were too crowded, had ordered half the city's rickshaws tossed into the harbor and never paid the owners. "That figures," Kim said grimly, but Paul and I laughed until we followed her gaze and saw a man bathing in the dirty water at the bottom of the sewage canal we were walking by. When we left for the countryside, escaping the petrochemical plants and diesel exhaust and dust, Kim seemed to breathe easier but only until the village kids swarmed up to her and all their small hands reached out to pinch her white arms. "Candy," they demanded. "Gula gula. Give me money." I only saw that they were laughing, teasing, and I found their demands weirdly amusing given the exotic beauty around them—the same way I responded to finding Madonna T-shirts for sale in all the stores—but Kim had a darker vision. "It's disgusting," she said, once her antagonism had scared all the children away. "It's so depressing it makes me cry," she said, but she couldn't explain what she meant.

She looks very tired now, and I realize how late it is, too late to be arguing. And it's true, when Paul comes back, she'll move out of our house, back in with him. They'll work it out or they won't. In any case, Paul won't throw her over because she stayed out late while he was away. "I guess you're right," I say.

"We're just different people, Anna," she says and hugs me before leaving the room.

The rain has softened to a delicate drumming, the whirr of wings in leaves. I sit and think how I'll go back to bed, keep my distance, lie there and listen to Barry breathing. I won't touch him. I won't wake him up. I won't touch him, not tonight anyway. Years ago, Kim snuck up on us one afternoon as we napped in the backyard. She took a picture, a shot angled down on twisted clothes, a tangle of arms and legs, seamless, my head on Barry's chest and my hair spread out over the grass like a flag. Kim's giggling woke us or maybe it was the sudden cool of her shadow falling across our faces. On our first anniversary, she gave us the photo in an inlaid wooden frame she made herself. Sometimes I look at it and at the photo next to it, taken at Kim's wedding. In it, Paul looks lovingly down at my sister, and she seems to be smiling up at him. But, I wonder, maybe they were looking off at distant things even then.

In Indonesia they still tell stories from the Ramayana all the time: turn off the main street in Jogjakarta at night, Paul says, and you'll find a wayang, people seated on both sides of the screen from dusk to dawn watching the puppets, listening to the gongs of the gamelan, napping and waking again. People have been telling these same stories for a thousand years. That appeals to me—all that tradition to rely on—but I know that here you'd be crazy to think for an instant of throwing yourself on a pyre like Sita did. No magic could save you, it would prove nothing but your own foolishness, and there's nothing to prove here anyway except by living. I know that, here, things change slowly. No dramatic gestures. Here, we talk and talk and end up believing that in a few days we'll see things differently; we'll be happy again. Or the argument continues until it peters out on its own, and we're left drained, standing on opposite sides of the room, and finally we look at each other, shrug, and agree everything's over, love a thing of the past.

I know all this, but still, when I turn out the light, I'm blinded by the filigreed silhouettes of the shadow puppets. Silver against black like photo negatives. They stretch their long, jointed arms and twist their heads on skinny necks, their hair like the airy curl of ferns. They dance and kick, swipe at each other, make love passionately, soar up the walls; I grasp at the fading image of their sharp noses, their shining eyes, and the parabolas of their smiles.

Hannah Tinti

ANIMAL CRACKERS

It's time to wash the elephant. Joseph has dragged out the hoses and I'm trying to prod Marysue out the door to the place we do it. Hup, I say, and poke her with a broom. I need to be careful—there is a part of me that steps into traffic: she eased her weight onto the last keeper's foot and the bones were crushed to pieces. I imagine my ex-wife lifting that giant ear and whispering, *step there*. It's a warm day and I'm sweating in my coveralls.

When I first started here the staff treated me to a beer and showed me their scars. They said it would happen sooner or later. They said watch out. Everyone who works with animals has a mark somewhere.

Joseph says big animals are like big problems. He should know, he's had his share—eighteen years old when the Army shipped him to Cambodia. He came back OK, he says, only to get his arm chomped off by a Senegalese tiger in a traveling circus. He's got a little stump coming from the end of his elbow which bends up and down. Like me, Joseph used to have a wife who isn't in the picture anymore. She left him for a man with two arms but no legs who'd

---

Hannah Tinti's recent work has appeared in *Story, StoryQuarterly, and Sonora Review*. She is a member of The Writers' Room, an urban writing colony in New York City.

also been in Cambodia. Joseph says it was his fault. He doesn't blame the tiger.

Sandy is an attractive woman if you look at her from the left. When she turns you can see the puckered skin and the crooked white line across her cheek into her chin where a gorilla took a bite out. The scar just touches the corner of her mouth, so that when she smiles the skin stretches and it looks like something's still holding onto her.

She studied biology and zoology in college and when she graduated she got hired by one of her professors as a research assistant and headed into the African jungle. She was thinking she had the touch and it made her do things she shouldn't, like get too close to a newborn gorilla and have the mother come charging out of the bushes and bury her teeth into Sandy's face until the team they were traveling with shot her down. Sandy woke up in a hospital to doctors clicking their tongues as they sewed her skin back together over the bone.

We went out on a date once. I took her to dinner and a movie and we got a drink afterwards. She told me her old boyfriend used to make her keep her head turned when they made love so he wouldn't have to look at it. It made me feel strange to hear this, the way people can tell you secrets about themselves too soon and it makes you feel responsible. I took her home after that and drove away as soon as I could.

Joseph scrubs Marysue's legs and tells me about his friend Al he met in the service (not the one who rolled off into the sunset with his wife). I listen to him describe the jungle and turn my hose on the ground to make some mud. Marysue likes to roll in it. It cools her down and keeps the bugs off. I look at her through the spray, see a spectrum of color and imagine her roaming through the forests of Cambodia, pushing her way through the tropical greens.

Al was stationed near Phnom Penh and had a pet cockatoo he'd bought off the street for a buck. It would sit on his shoulder and squawk, yellow feathers rippling, but mostly it just looked around and moved its feet back and forth. Al taught it to shit on command. He'd make it go on his friends as a joke or people he didn't like, for a different kind of joke.

One day they were at a bar with the cockatoo flying around and it suddenly landed on Al's shoulder and let loose some of its sparkling white fruit. It had never done this before—Joseph laughed— but Al just sat and stared at it spackling down the camouflage green of his army jacket. He said, I'm going to get it, and he did—somebody had booby-trapped his bike and it blew when he turned the ignition. Joseph said he saw the cockatoo flying around after that, looking for its master and finally Joseph got so mad he knocked it out of a tree and broke its neck. He still had both his arms then.

I watch Joseph to see how he's feeling, but he doesn't seem angry anymore. He rubs a sponge across Marysue's feet and says that manatees have the same kind of rounded nails on their flippers. He says they're the closest thing elephants have to a relative. Marysue picks up mud with her trunk and throws it across her back like sea salts. I take a long-handled brush and rub it in. She looks at me with her mouth open and I think she is saying thanks.

I've seen pictures of elephants swimming. It looks like they're flying. The light filters through the water around their bodies, silhouetting them against the blue. Their feet hover above the ocean floor, suddenly free of all that weight. They can go for miles, their trunks held high. Somehow they know they're not going to sink.

One evening after we split a bottle of schnapps, our pants rolled up and our feet in the sea lion pool Mike tells me this story about how he went diving after dark off the coast of Mexico with a few of his buddies. He said jumping into the ocean at night is like stepping down into a graveyard, falling through the earth, bumping into coffins and bodies and feeling all of the lost bits and pieces of souls that have seeped into the soil come looking for you. He said he'd never do it again.

They'd brought underwater lights to look at things. They attached glow sticks to their tanks, each a different color so they'd know one another—green, yellow, purple. They left someone in the boat to pick them up. They held onto their masks and regulators and fell in backwards.

They went down about eighty feet and let the current take them. Bugs swarmed their lights and Mike said he could feel little things wiggling against him as they got caught in the stream of water running through his wet suit. He saw giant lobsters, jellyfish, skates, a shark which turned away from the light reflecting off its skin, and other creatures, strange things he didn't know the names for and that he only caught glimpses of—dark scaly movements that made him afraid.

Mike reached his air limit and went up to thirty feet for a safety spot to keep from getting the bends. He was glad it was over. He watched the green glow from his friend's light stick move closer and felt relief as they bent their flippers back and forth together in the water and watched for their buddy. They could see the purple color of him in the distance.

He didn't come any closer. They got nervous and went after him but he wasn't there—it was only his tanks settled on the ocean floor, the glow stick swaying like a weathervane in the direction of a bad wind. They went back to the boat but he wasn't there either and by then they were out of reserve. They radioed for help. Mike used a snorkel and his flashlight to keep looking but he stayed close to the boat. He sensed something there—a collective spirit of darkness that would reach out and get him if it could. They never found the body.

Mike threw the empty schnapps bottle into the pool. We were both quiet for a while. I had my fingers wrapped around the railing and I thought about all the little kids who would be pressing their faces against the glass tomorrow. We had some more quiet between us and then he waded in to fish it out.

You hear animal stories everyday. How a bee stung Little Johnny and he went into cardiac arrest. How a snake bit Cousin Tom and it shriveled up his toe. How a pack of dogs chased Aunt Shirley down the street until she climbed through an open car window, rolled it shut behind her and watched the animals circling, pawing the doors, their wet noses leaving streaks on the chrome. They all mean something.

Joseph scrapes away at the bottom of Marysue's foot. He touches her below the knee and she lifts her leg automatically, as if his fingers are telling her something important. I know not to make any sudden movements now. She feels nervous and eyes me as if I might attack, because this is when another animal would come, when she is not ready to protect herself. Her pupils dilate and seem too small for such a large body. She keeps her trunk on Joseph's back, feeling around, making sure of what is happening to her.

Joseph says that in the wild when elephants feel threatened, they put the young and the weak in the middle and form a circle around them. I wonder if Marysue has family somewhere. If they tried to save her from being tagged and shipped. I picture her searching for a tail to hold onto while the others paw the ground and get ready to charge.

Ann runs the ticket booth. Her cat Stinky comes to work with her everyday. Ann keeps a small basket by her feet where he sleeps. Stinky doesn't have any fur. His skin hangs down between his legs like an old man wearing a diaper. Ann says Stinky saved her life.

She tells me about one night in September when she woke up to a blazing light in her room. Her bed was vibrating and she thought it was an earthquake until she felt her body rise and start to move towards the window. The sash flew up and the screen was ripped off. Ann says what came next was like the sting you get before frostbite, followed by a numbness which crept from her fingers and toes and moved through her thighs, her shoulders and on towards her heart. She tried to scream but her throat was swollen tight.

Stinky jumped onto the windowsill and started hissing. He had fur then, Ann says, orange and yellow swirled together and it stood on end, prickling against the beam like needlepoints. Stinky bared his teeth and Ann says his eyes reflected the light so intensely it looked like lasers shooting out of him and suddenly everything went dark and Ann dropped to the ground, hitting the back of her head on the bedside table. She clutched the rag rug on the floor around her and crawled underneath the mattress, where she lay stunned until morning. When daylight came and she laid her hands on enough courage to come out, she found the window still open, shreds of the screen in the bushes outside and Stinky, bald and quivering, under a pile of dirty clothes in the closet.

When she isn't collecting tickets Ann travels around the country going to abductee conventions with her cat, holding onto his hairless body as truth. She will not go anywhere without him. I watch Stinky through the glass as he sleeps and I think about devotion. I know Ann worries what will happen when he dies and I wonder if she curses his sagging skin, because when the light comes back into her room she'll know as she's being pulled through the window that this time she is being taken away because there is no one who loves her enough to stop it.

I pick up a bunch of alfalfa and hold it in the air. Marysue reaches with her trunk and takes it out of my hand. As soon as the food is in she's back to see if I have any more. Her trunk searches my palm as if she is reading my lifeline.

Joseph says that elephants can recognize dead relatives by feeling their bones. They spend hours turning over the remains, stroking the curves of the skull. Sometimes, they will take pieces away with them and carry them for miles before letting them go. Marysue stops nosing my hand and I feel a short sense of relief.

Ike is the owner. I like him fine, as do most of the other people who work here. He's got a story too and he told it when he hired me and I was looking for a way to end something. I answered an ad that asked for experience with animals. In the interview I told Ike that I could communicate with dogs. He had a miniature dachshund asleep at his heels and I said, watch this, and started making groans in the back of my throat. The dog wouldn't even raise his head to look at me. Ike said, you need the job that bad or are you just plain crazy? I said I needed the job and he said, okay then.

Ike's part Eskimo. He grew up near the Bering Sea in Unalakleet, Alaska. A lot of the men would work on the oil rigs and be gone for months at a time. This gave the village an abandoned feeling, even with all the women and children around, but it also gave Ike a lot of freedom. He liked to hang with boys who were older. They would go out for long hikes in the snow, freezing their asses off and coming home with frostbite. The Iditarod sled dog race came through each year, and when this happened the kids would go crazy, building ramshackle sleds and hitching up their dogs, who more often than not knocked them over and skipped, dragging pieces of sheet metal behind them for the rest of the day.

To get around this problem, Ike's friend George decided to strap his little brother onto the sled first before tying it to the family dog, a young husky with a habit of running away. The dog took off, dragging George's little brother screaming into the distance and the two boys had to track them down. They'd gone a mile out and were about to bridge a hill when they found a little blue hat, the kind that ties under your chin. Ike picked it up and they went over the top and there was a polar bear ripping the guts out of George's little brother. He'd already torn apart the dog—the snow was covered with blood—the sled overturned, the rope hanging loosely from the husky's neck. George started screaming and the bear turned to look, its muzzle wet with red, and that was it—Ike ran.

He got about ten feet away when George passed him. George was older and his legs were flying fast. Ike got this feeling down the back of his neck between his shoulder blades and he knew the bear was coming and it was almost as if he could see the arm reach out and knock him over. Ike's feet fell out from underneath him. He landed on his face, his lips stinging in the snow. He didn't move. He felt the lumbering body of the bear crunching next to him through the powder and he lost it, he pissed all over himself.

Ike heard the nose. It started at his feet and snorted between his legs. It snuffed and panted over his body and sounded like a playmate getting ready to tell a secret as it moved closer to his ear. He felt the warmth of the bear's breath and closed his eyes. There was snow on his wrists between his mittens and his jacket and he thought about the skin there, how it got red and itched by the fire while his mom cooked oatmeal on the stove and talked about her dead father and the way he would take a pair of spoons out of the drawer and play them between his fingers, rattling them against his knee until he got a rhythm together and he could sing. The nose was at his crotch again. He listened to the bear walk away.

He stayed there in the snow for a long time. When he raised his head it was dusk. In the distance he saw a snowmobile coming but he couldn't bring himself to move. Ike tells me sometimes you have these experiences, and you spend the rest of your life thinking about them. Try to shut it out and it comes back stronger, a nagging unease, an unanswerable question, and you have to go through it all over again.

Marysue likes it when I pet her tongue. It is a large and frightening muscle and as I rub my hand across it I try not to think about her swallowing my arm. I use my left, thinking abstractly that I would not miss it as much as my right. I use the hose and start a final rinse down her side. The coarse black hairs growing out from between the wrinkles in her skin hang dripping with the weight of the water. I think of these hairs later that night when I am home safe and sound and stepping out of a hot shower, having washed all the animal smells off from the day. I run the towel underneath my arms, across my chest and down each of my legs. When I reach my toes I dry thoroughly between them and think about my ex-wife again. *Step there.*

I met her in a bar in Las Vegas. She was in for a convention, a gathering of nurses who'd worked in mobile hospitals during Vietnam. I was pouring drinks. She told me a story about how she saved a guy's life in a restaurant with a steak knife and a ball point pen, performing a tracheotomy between courses. I watched her throat as she drank her martini, the way the glands clutched and moved along her neck. It was instinctive, she said, and I leaned across the bar and kissed her.

Our daughter's name is Leigh Ann. She was born with Down syndrome, and, even though she didn't say it, I could tell by the way she sniffed that my wife suspected my Midwestern genes. When she left me she took Leigh Ann to her parents in New Mexico where I would drive every weekend, spending awkward hours on their front porch with my baby in my lap. I put up in a motel nearby and Monday morning I'd drive back to Las Vegas, the desert reaching out around me in every direction as if I were the center of something great. It used to make me feel like screaming and sometimes I did, the windows down and the air rushing into my mouth.

She called the bar to let me know she was moving in with her boyfriend and taking Leigh Ann with her. I had a law school student, who worked with me paying loans with tips, get on the phone and tell her she had to let me know where they were going. She gave him an address which turned out to be bogus and I got on the highway to her parents' house. They said they couldn't tell me where she was. She said you hit her, they said.

The year after we were married we had an apartment in Carson City. It was on the third floor, a railroad, one long hallway with a window at the end that opened onto a fire escape. On warm summer nights after I got off work I would jump from the street to catch hold of the iron railing, pull myself up and climb to our place. I thought it was romantic.

One night I got to the bar and they'd scheduled two of us by mistake. Maggie, a girl from the Philippines who was into astronomy, was already pouring. She told me that Mars was supposed to be out that night and how to look for it. She told me it had a radius of 2,090 miles and that it took 687 days to go around the sun. Once I got home I stood outside our building and found it, a tiny red flickering light in the sky. It made me wonder how many other stars and planets were out there just beyond that I couldn't see, and how that didn't make them any less real.

I climbed the fire escape and found the window locked and the lights out in our apartment. I started banging on the frame and just when I thought I was going to have to go back down I saw the door at the end of the apartment open, and the light from the hall showed a man leaving.

My wife came to the window in a bathrobe. Her smile was weak as she turned the lock. She opened the sash and said, aren't you going to come in, and I reached out and touched her cheek and then slammed her head into the windowsill, and that is the first time I hurt her that night. I pushed her back into the room and she fell on the floor and knocked over a table and a lamp and that was the second time I hurt her. The third time was when I grabbed her by the hair and dragged her down the hallway to the kitchen. The fourth happened when I kicked her. The fifth, sixth, seventh, eighth, and ninth came as I slapped her, my palm itching. I thought of a knife but I took the blender sitting on the counter instead and I threw it, and that was the last time I hurt her. It knocked her out. Her nose was broken and there was blood seeping into the terrycloth. I leaned against the wall to catch my breath. Leigh Ann was crying in the bedroom.

I sat down at our kitchen table—the table where we ate English muffins and spread jelly—looked at my trembling fingers and realized that I was happy. Later, after the bruises were gone and she left me, I sat in the same place and touched my skin, my muscles aching as if my body had been pulled into pieces and hastily patched back together, but in that moment I knew that I had touched something raw and wonderful that resonated in my bones, and it wasn't until I heard the cries of my daughter that I came back to that apartment, that room, and that life which was before me and I told myself, you have a child, you have to take care.

I've heard stories about elephants that go crazy. I look at Marysue and wonder if she's got it in her. I take the broom I use to guide her back to her cage and poke it hard under her ribs. She lets out a puff and then a groan and I know it hurt. She turns and gives me a look with her eye. I rub my hand up and down her back leg to make up and she lets loose a pile of shit, her tail lifting slightly to one side.

Joseph starts picking up the hoses with his arm, coiling them around his shoulder and holding them in place with the stump he has left. He says I think too much. He says, why don't you work somewhere else. Then he looks sorry and says he's not trying to get rid of me. I wonder then if he knows, but he goes home the same time as usual and leaves me to do the final clean-up. I muck out the stall and spread down fresh hay for the night.

When I'm done I take off my shoes, lay down on the floor of Marysue's cage, touch her under the knee like Joseph and put my head under her foot. She lets the bottom rest on my ear, the cement chilling my cheek, the smell like the damp fertility of dirt under rocks. She shifts her weight and my head rolls gently back and forth. I can hear her breathing. It echoes off of the walls and sounds piped in, a recording of an elephant still living in the wild. I close my eyes, imagine banyan trees and feel a heaviness lift.

Dana Lise Shavin

THE FATHER, THE SON, AND THE HORSE'S GHOST

The rain is coming. I know it as surely as I know this horse will get well, although as we make our way around the yard in circles she looks anything but. She is fighting me to lie down, pawing the ground, making huge gashes in the grass. She wants to lie down so she can roll, because her belly hurts and rolling will make it better. I have always heard that if a colicking horse rolls it will tangle its own intestines and die. You have to keep them moving until the pain goes away. Sometimes this means walking them for hours, sometimes for an entire day or night.

The vet has been out twice already. He sedated the horse so that he could run a tube that is a half inch wide up through her nose and down her throat into her stomach. He swam, forearm first, into her anal canal as she stood quietly with half-lidded eyes and I squirmed and clenched my teeth and pressed my buttocks tightly together. If the horse gets worse over the course of the next few hours then he will come back and hang an enormous IV from the

---

Dana Lise Shavin's work has appeared in *Willow Review, Talking River Review, Kinesis, Palo Alto Review,* and *Sulphur River Literary Review.*

rafter in her stall, super-glue the tube in her nose, and pump her full of liquid. It will cost two hundred dollars and there is no guarantee that she will be well by morning. Alternatively, we can walk her in circles for many hours. This approach will cost us nothing except for one night's sleep and it will probably get her well just as quickly or slowly, depending on whether you are the horse, the walker, or the vet going home to bed.

We choose to pay in sleep and I make the first installment, walking a wide circular path just outside the pasture gate. The bats zig-zag overhead, swooping night food out of the air. The house is lighted up from the kitchen on one end to the sun room on the other. It gives me hope. My boyfriend is sleeping, fully dressed, on the bed. At 2 a.m. it will be his turn again, and I can go in and sleep for two hours with my barn shoes on and scarf knotted around my neck, lights burning to give him hope. I think I must fall asleep for the shortest moment then, because I feel a tug at the rope; I turn to see the horse handing me something like a plain white envelope in her mouth. Then I am awake again, and I realize she is going down, this is her message to me, *I'm dying.*

Get up! No! Walk now! I yell at her, yank on the rope, and she pulls herself back up with a loud groan and a flat lifeless stare. She stumbles a few steps, walks heavily beside me. The wind is picking up and the world darkens from already dark. I can smell the dampening night air though it will not rain for several more hours. It announces itself. It says *not yet, but soon.* We narrow the circle. I watch the house. *How long can I walk?*

* * *

We watch too much television. This wasn't the case a few years ago, when we both had professional jobs and prided ourselves on having intellectual pursuits. But too much time spent helping others, tending to their psychic aches and wrong decisions, and now we watch every night, good and bad shows alike, it doesn't matter, although we like it better if it is funny in an offbeat, dry-witted way. Sometimes I flip it off and say *let's talk instead,* and he says *great, let's do,* and then we don't, we sit there in some kind of dreamy dimension, staring at each other and thinking that we're talking, till one of us says *say it out loud,* and then we can't remember what we were thinking.

Earlier this evening we sat staring at each other in just this way until the phone rang and his mother's voice punctured our pretend conversation. I watched the images move on the screen while they talked, not listening to them exactly but not watching TV either, just absently processing bits of worrisome slough, sifting through the dust from my day, the dry, brittle half-thoughts and unresolved hours. What broke through was hearing him ask when his father will get out of the hospital, and then I snapped to attention and tried to figure out by his face what had happened. On the screen was a car chase and at the end both cars sat amidst the debris of a plate glass window, smoking and heaving like after-sex.

"How long has this been going on?" he asks his mother. He watches my face while she answers. All I can hear is a faint rasping sound from her end.

"Are you all right?" he asks. People are fleeing from the cars. I don't know who's the bad guy and who's the good guy. I don't know if his mother is OK, and I don't know what is wrong with his father and in thirty minutes we will wander outside to find our horse on her side and the rain moving in.

* * *

"Your father's been 'into other women,'" was the way his mother put it, though she didn't mean it crudely, which was how it sounded to me. And while it wasn't his intention it answered a lot of questions for me, namely it said that the reason we had sex so infrequently was because his father was having it for all of us, sucking the sexual energy from the air and choking it all down for himself, never mind that he was married, a "real" Christian, a deacon, God-fearing, sixty-one. He took a new partner whenever he felt the urge, and he felt the urge often, for by the time he was caught he couldn't remember how many there had been, where he'd met them, their names, their faces, or whether it had been worth it.

But it worried him. It worried him enough that he spoke to no one about it, not even God. It worried him enough that he had to do more, fighting off the guilty feelings by focusing on the conquest. Towards the end, in his hurry, he became indiscriminate, even cruising the streets of the tiny town where he and his wife lived, leaning out the window of his long pale yellow Cadillac, asking for dates at the red light. It worried him because he knew that it was wrong, that were his wife to find out she might leave, and it worried him because God was watching and even knowing that, he could not stop. He worried about getting someone pregnant. He worried about AIDS. He worried about his salvation, the afterlife, his insatiable appetite, his next encounter, and about Jesus himself, about how he had survived temptation and whether there had been physical consequences. The only thing he didn't worry about was whether he might bed a woman with herpes and pass this along like a surprise gift to his wife of thirty-five years.

* * *

Your sister has it and she's in her forties but she's not the herpes type now, he's saying. She got it from a Greyhound bus, not from the bus exactly but from a man on it to whom she offered gratuitous sex because it seemed like a freaky, seventies-ish thing to do. Three miscarriages later and one baby born through the active fire of a flareup and I suppose she has to think perhaps it wasn't worth it. For all the glory she gets in the re-telling, she suffers the every other month or so sitting-in-the-tub, worse-than-an-episiotomy kind of pain, the kind that doesn't bear with it memories of your first-born so much as reminders of being twenty-two and desperate for a story.

We talk about her because it is easier than talking about him. We are wondering what kind of woman in her fifth or sixth decade has herpes and he is pointing out that herpes can happen young, before you know better, or even when you know better but don't pay attention. He is assuming that herpes happened young to his father's partner, who we are hoping is close to his father's age, but this is not the case. She is almost young enough to be our daughter.

Oh, God. I don't want to think about what *I* have worn in the mornings at his parents' house, coming out of the shower and through the living room on my way to the bedroom to get dressed. I don't want to think about the year I believed skimpy shorts would make my thighs look more shapely, or the year I went braless, or the year of the lost underwear. I was like a six-year-old, delighting in the feel of nearly nothing on my skin but the springtime breeze, and now I wonder. *Was he looking?*

Of course he wonders the same thing but we don't speak it out loud. *This changes everything,* he says.

Like what?

Like everything, he says. *Like he isn't who I thought he was all this time. I picture him in that brown velvet chair reading his Bible when really he's out cruising the streets, picking up girls too young for me! What was he thinking? Where was this going to end?*

I think he was hoping that a call would find his father in the overstuffed chair in front of the heating vent, sweating and complaining that it was too hot, watching gospel TV and waiting for his wife to make him lunch. This was how it should have been on a late Sunday afternoon in West Tennessee in January the year we were thirty-seven and sex-starved. Instead he called the hospital where his father had been admitted the day before and asked for the psychiatric unit.

They're coming after me now, his father said, voice shaky from several days not eating.

Who?

The people who are mad. Enemies. We'll lose the farm, you know. There isn't enough money to pay the taxes. I owe $30,000 and they found out. Now everyone will know.

Know what?

How I cheated on my taxes.

What does Mom say?

I've hurt your mother terribly. Tomorrow is the last day.

Last day for what?

I'll be in prison the rest of my life.

His mother laughs. Says she's tried to talk to him, he's consumed with guilt, can't sleep, can't sit still, worried about how much the insurance will pay on the hospital bill, when they will arrest him for tax fraud, what will happen to the farm. She doesn't know where he got the number 30,000 but she's pretty sure they don't owe it. She has removed all the guns from the house, doctor's orders, bullets too.

Why does she laugh, I ask.

She's trying to keep a sense of humor about it.

That seems strange. Isn't she angry about all the affairs? Has she thought about leaving him?

She hasn't thought about leaving. She will wash his hair in the sink like she's always done, make his meals, warm his already hot coffee in the microwave, iron his clothes, take care of the house. They will live much like before only now they will both suffer the fire between their legs, and worse. From this day forward he will be faithful. When he has sex again it will be in the overstuffed chair by the vent in the living room, a dream from which he will wake sweating, complaining of the unbearable heat. He will mumble that his enemies are coming. He will cry because he is going to prison. He will worry about losing the farm.

Did you tell the psychiatrist he's still worried about the farm?

No, I didn't see any reason.

Did you tell him he's not sleeping at night?

Silence.

Mom, you have to tell the psychiatrist what's going on or he can't help him. How long since he's slept?

A few hours here and there. Really, honey, he's doing much better.

We think about this and an hour later my boyfriend calls back. His mother is in the bathroom. His father answers.

Dad, says my boyfriend. *How are you feeling?*

But there is only weeping on the other end.

* * *

A good Christian believes that God is watching. He believes that God is just, and that those who do right are rewarded, and those who do wrong are punished. When my boyfriend arrived home later that week in the winter of 1999 what he found was that God was a little drunk on Her power.

Dad?

His father sat slumped, unhearing, at the kitchen table. Seated with him and having lunch that afternoon were his sister, brother-in-law, and wife, and they were talking about the girls' high school basketball team, a favorite subject of his father's, but he wasn't listening. They didn't seem to notice.

Dad?

My boyfriend put his hand on his father's back, which made him jump, his head snap back. His eyes were yellowed with fatigue and too much sorrow, his face speckled with beard growth he hadn't bothered to shave off. He squinted.

Are you here to take me to prison? he asked.

No, Dad, I'm just here for a visit. It's me, Daryl. Are you OK?

Did you see them?

See who?

His mother laughed. *He still thinks they're coming to get the farm. You can't tell him anything.* Her face was bright and her hair recently colored and carefully styled.

His father stood, staggered to the wall, laid his arm across it, his head in the crook of his elbow. He straightened up, fell heavily into the overstuffed chair, groaned, stood up. He laid his arm across the back of the sofa and peered out the window.

Lock the door, he said.

On Sundays they go to church the way they always used to. After four months he started to drive again, but only when his wife was with him. He wouldn't return to work, even though the co-op kept his job open for him. And since he didn't drive alone he no longer had breakfast with his friends at the dairy bar. His wife quit her job and sold the beauty shop, just like she said she would if he didn't get better, and now they sit together for the better part of every day, in the living room where he sleeps, when he sleeps, in the overstuffed chair by the vent and complains that it is too hot. At night he paces the floor and although it is after tax time, he still fears that they are coming, the prison guards to arrest him, the enemies he's made over the course of a lifetime, the women he's had sex with whose names he can't remember, his mother, dead but ashamed nevertheless, and worst of all God, with night vision, who can't make sure his thoughts are pure and builds a fire in anticipation.

There are no more visits to the psychiatrist, and the medication, which had helped some with the paranoia, hasn't been refilled. At night he paces the floor and wonders where it all went wrong, why God threw him mercilessly on the bed of temptation over and over again. His wife has moved into the spare bedroom and this is where she will stay, nicely coifed and trying to keep a sense of humor.

* * *

We will walk the horse until seven the following morning, until the sun is up again, the drizzle has started, the bats have gone to bed. We will have rejoiced when, at five, she plucked a bite of grass from the ground, and again at six-thirty, when she grazed steadily for several minutes without trying to lie down. We will have argued, briefly, about what made her sick, and we will have talked about his sex and his father and God's will, in circles, from every section of the yard. Of his mother we will have said little.

At seven-thirty I will go in the house and get in bed, setting the alarm for an hour later so I can get up and go to work. At eight-thirty I am at the kitchen window watching a white flash gallop up through the pasture, the ghost of a horse that lived, that makes the creek coyotes start to howl and wakes the neighborhood dogs one by one like dominoes.

Ryan Blacketter

THE BEST KIND OF JOKE

The wrinkled green blouse clings tight to her big old self, and the bushy orange hair slants flat on one side, where she slept on it all afternoon. What she likes to do at the table is rub lotion on her hands. The long fingers twist in a yellow slippery mess. I taste the soapy smell everywhere, even in the buttery garlic bread, even in my glass of orange pop. When the lotion bottle sputters Dad quits chewing and swerves his eyes to the window, and so do I. Our eyes catch in the reflection against the dark back yard. Trying not to say anything is how his face looks. "Pretty soon"—he stops but I hope he'll keep going—"pretty soon and I'm singing nursery rhymes. Eating peanut shells."

I can never think one up on my own, so I steal one of his old ones, from the time he was looking for a job. I say, "Pretty soon and I'm riding donkeys in my bunny suit."

Nobody's laughing, especially not us.

We used to be four but Winny makes us five—screwy, uneven, her chair wedged between Mom's chair and Dad's. Her boxes and

Ryan Blacketter has won an Oregon Haystack Award and recently attended Sewanee as a Tennessee Williams Scholar. "The Best Kind of Joke" is his first published work. He teaches ESL in Atlanta.

clothes were dumped in my room and I was scooted down the hall to my little brother's room. At night her hard coughs and curses slip under our door and we get up on our elbows, necks bent in sleepiness, wishing for her to quiet down. It is her fifth day here.

Football's coming at us from the living room—grunts, cheers, whistles. Me and Dad's most favorite sport. When football's on we keep it on, always, and nobody ever touches our channel.

Matt, who's sort of chubby, motors a tiny car around his plate changing gears with his throat. "How come Gramma's so fat," he wants to know, "if she never eats?"

I say, "How long'll she be here?"

"Not fat," Mom says. "Big. Big-boned."

I talk into the pepper shaker. "Testing. Hello?"

Mom says, "Shh."

"Testing. How long'll she be here?"

Dad lifts another pile of spaghetti with the big wood forks, the saucy strands jiggling in the air, speckling red dots on the plastic yellow tablecloth. He's a great big man in a shirt with cowboy pockets and nice new square-toe boots and stiff new denims same ones as mine that we got together at Penney's. He is so big, I have to almost look up at him even from across the table.

"I'm not fat," Matt says. "Big."

I say, "Pretty soon and I'm eating butterflies."

Winny sets the lotion bottle beside her chair, keeps rubbing. "I used to beat up little boys."

"When she was a girl, of course," Mom says. "A few fights with mean boys. But you're exaggerating, Mother."

"How long'll she *be* here?"

Mom says, *"Tom."* I don't care. Winny's ugly, everything—her wrinkled blouse, her lotion smell, her coughing and her cursing. Everything is her and Mom's fault. Dad sure doesn't want any of this.

"This bunny suit is getting warm," Dad says.

"Me too." I tug at my Levi shirt red with sparkly silver threads, airing it out. A smile about sneaks in my frown, only my frown is bigger, stronger.

With her elbows on the table Mom rubs at her eyes in slow circles, sighing out quiet nostril noises like tiny planes going down.

After a careful look at his plate Dad goes to the kitchen for a box of tissue, because Winny's cough is wet things moving deep in her chest, like shaking a glass jar full of mud and gravel. He sets the box beside her plate, sinks to his chair, licks at a corner of his mustache. "You okay there, Winny?"

Winny pats her chest in quick little thuds with the mouth of her fist. "I didn't ask him for anything," she tells Mom. "I didn't ask him for tissue and I didn't ask him to take me from my home."

Mom says, "That was my decision, Mother."

"Your decision. An old woman gets a cough and suddenly decisions are beyond her powers. 'Let's take her from her home. Why not? The quality of her life is not important.'" Then she turns her eyes on Dad. "Why are you looking at me. I'm not speaking to you. I'm speaking to my daughter."

He punches his arms through his bomber jacket sleeves and stands before the game, hands on hips. The Cowboys are down, no chance of winning, so he slaps off the TV with the back of his fingers, and the big guys busting each other up and falling on their heads shrink to a white dot and are gone.

Winny's bottle farts out a string of wet lotion. I chew with my mouth closed. Mom straightens the napkin in her lap like a picture on the wall.

"Pretty soon and I'm chasing cats. Talking backwards." He still doesn't want a laugh, I can tell by his face, which isn't hard, just settled, flat. "I'm out for a drive. You boys coming or staying?"

"Coming!"

"Coming!"

* * *

We hop in the truck for a bag of ice-cream bars at Fleener's Market. In the rich neighborhood, in the south hills, where the view of town is great, he cuts the engine and coasts to a stop on a stretch of road where no houses block our view. The lights down on Center flicker how lights do from a long ways off. A smell I think you can almost smell in the warm air is leaves about to go red and orange. It's falltime but the weather isn't saying so. "Take off the straitjackets, boys. Get comfortable." Dad twists open a beer and snaps the bottle cap whirring through the darkness and I hold my breath until it tinkles far away on the road. He says it's okay if we eat two apiece. I suck my last ice-cream stick till it tastes only of wood. He likes to keep his arm around our shoulders, Matt in the middle. Matt gets to keep his hand at rest on his leg. I'm too old for that, almost ten is too old for that. What I like to do, if he asks me, is finger a cigarette from his shirt pocket, reach it to his mouth, and light it with the dash lighter. That's what I do. I like his smell of beer and aftershave and Big Red gum and cigarettes. All of them together make one smell, his smell.

I say, "They're weird."

"Who is. Who's weird."

"Winny and her."

"Your mother is not weird, buddy."

Matt scans the bar across the glowing square of radio numbers, a garble of words and music, till Dad takes over and lets it stop on news. Down in Boise they are seeing a decline in robberies and bar violence which means the end-of-summer exit of visiting motorcycle enthusiasts. Boise's where they took Winny from. I picture her swinging chairs in a bar fight, busting heads. Her motorcycle waits out front. That's just the kind of lady she probably used to be.

Dad, who's a corrections officer at North Idaho Correctional, says, "Enthusiasts. What happened to criminal? What happened to that word?" He says it out the side window to the crooked little moon. I hope nighttime is when God pours a bucket of stars over black construction paper, but my stomach knows it's not the truth.

"Dad, how long will she be here?" This time I say it to really know.

"Winny's fat," Matt says. "I'm big."

He jets out smoke in a long hard sigh which clouds the window before air pulls it out in streams. Then he flicks his cigarette spinning to the pavement, where it's a red fingertip in the dark. As if we are driving, he grips the wheel, steering slow, leaning with the curves. "Tomorrow will be a new day for the men in this family. Let's try and be good, this is hard on your mother. You boys are my front guard."

* * *

Leaves are heaped wet over gutters and the road is dry except at the edges where it's damp. After a day at St. Stephen's School me and Matt are walking up Prospect sniffing the chilly air for it to burn in your nose like cough drops. On the right a hill slips down through a floor of fog, to where the Snake runs. You can't see much in the fog, not the Snake, not even two blocks ahead. I check yards to see if they are raked good enough, making sure the leaf bags wait in rows for the men to shoulder them up to the flatbed. Nobody does as good a job as me. After I rake I like to run around my yard and snatch right out of the air leaves that fly off the tree, crush them in my hand, screech through my teeth. I am a soldier and leaves are the enemy. And it is true I will die if one touches the ground. In the fall I keep the yard free of leaves and in the summer mowed and watered. Through the screen door I called for him to come check on my job and showed him how the tire lines in the grass were straight, no wild swerves like the first time, no strips where the blade missed, and see how I put the cut grass in a twist-tied bag? He said what an excellent job. I couldn't stop grinning. The smell of cut grass, the smack of the ball in our gloves, the squint of our eyes in the sun.

The hugeness of him.

The trees will get more bare soon and I worry about when the very cold will come and all my chores will be indoors.

Mom is in the window sipping tea behind the cardboard skeletons. Matt tears on up the walk, his backpack jerking side to side, to check and see what else, like if she got the pumpkins.

In a corner of the living room I stand over the big flat vent-heater, sort of like the sidewalk grate downtown I saw a man sleeping on one morning before school. The pants of my school uniform flap and ripple as warm air twists around my legs. The fireplace I like more but it just got cold and Dad needs to buy a cord yet.

Home early from work he slumps low in his chair, one leg crossed over the other, his arms in a knot over his corduroy sports jacket. From upstairs Winny is blasting her game show at us, bells and whistles going off and a thousand people shouting Ha ha ha and then giving a mighty applause.

On his TV a cowboy in a poncho rides alone in the desert. The man and horse sway together in a kind of strut. Dad turns up the volume against Winny's bells and whistles but there's nothing to hear, only sand chattering in the wind. He gives his loud scratchy sigh like the water heater in the basement.

I think how for this past month we've been trying to be new men, how I want to go back to the kind of men we used to be, cowboys swaggering through the day, saying whatever you want. I'm tired of not ever saying anything. I go stand beside his recliner and fiddle with the arm cuffs. My head looks for a joke he has said before. Does he want to join me in a plate of postage stamps? His eyes wander from the TV to my stomach, then up my shirt to my eyes. When I've had plenty of time to wish I said or did something different, a slow grin shifts the skin on his face, cheeks puckering, wrinkles around his eyes creasing into folds. Then a laugh bursts out of him. It is ten laughs at once—deep, loud, stiffening my neck and shoulders. He tries not to laugh but he can't help it, he can't stop it. He recrosses his legs, uncrosses them, taps his square-toe boots on the floor.

Finally, he stops it. He pulls me down to sit beside him in the chair, and rests his arm on my shoulders, whispering, "I don't know, buddy, but pretty soon and I'm on the roof doing somersaults in your mother's nightgown."

At first I make myself laugh, then it comes naturally, gets louder.

Tears fill up my eyes. The TV is a box of colors. He smoothes back my hair and kisses my forehead. "Shh. Your mother's in the kitchen. Why not go see if she needs some help, buddy."

* * *

I'm at the table thinking up a list of jokes, mostly doodling crooked-hat witches in the margin. Mom's doing dishes. Against the fridge Matt bounces his rubber ball with twisting wires inside. He keeps missing the ball and it keeps smacking the cupboard by her head. "Stop it, stop that bouncing." How quiet her voice is makes you want to say okay to what she tells you. Usually she wants us to do some of her chores, aside from our own, so she can sit with Winny. But she's doing her own chores today. She told us not to touch anything that isn't our chores.

With the dishes piled up to drip dry she slips into her long purple coat and lifts the VW Bug keys off the hook by the garage door. Matt wants to go too. He wants to ride on the flat wood pushcart at Waremart Wholesale, grabbing cereal boxes and things off shelves as he glides through the aisles. I want to stay with Dad. Yesterday after church when they ran errands at the mall, me and Dad bent over the truck engine together in the garage, both of us happy to be mad at things we couldn't figure out. He said what was where and guided my hand with his hand. Sometimes he said damn it and shook his head and smoked, and it was okay for me to say, "Damn it." When he brought me for a ride I saw how to tilt your head, how to squint, bite your top lip, nodding a little. How to read the engine's ticks and pops you at first didn't understand.

But I can't be with him like that today. Mom says I have to go up and sit with Winny, keep her company. They had a scare this morning but Winny's okay. They took her to the doctor for her bad breathing but she's okay now. Mom and Dad are very tired. Would I do that special favor for them?

"Pretty soon and I'm out in the dog house. Sharpening my teeth on Sam's leg bone." That is the best kind of joke, and my first real one—the joke you make up on the spot, the one that just comes to you, without even thinking. I thought it up all by myself. I wish Dad heard it.

"Stop it. Please just stop it."

"I didn't say anything."

"Want me to get your father?"

"I didn't do anything."

The look she puts on me makes my stomach twist like wringing out a shirt. She heads for the bathroom. I hear her crying inside.

When I am the one who makes her sad—that's when I love her so much. I say to myself how bad I am and how I will be good from now on. But my stomach knows that's not the truth. It always forgets, it always stops caring, and I say to my stomach, From now on, from now on.

I knock on the bathroom door. I am going to say I am sorry and I will be good, a new man, like how Dad said. "Hey Mom, come look at Sam," is all I end up saying. My voice says she's just washing her hands in there or putting away towels. "He's chasing himself in circles at his tail and keeps banging his head on the clothesline pole."

* * *

All my things are out of here—motorbike posters, beanbag chair, comic books, goldfish. Plus my Little Suitcase Player Dad bought me with the Funny Cowboy Songs I played till I knew them like the Our Father. Now it's Winny's powders and lotions that clutter my dresser and desk, and the smell catches in my throat. She lays on my bed in a yellow dress with fat white polka-dots, her vaselined lips flashing in the TV light. The almost-finished day throws some dirty light on her. All my homework plus a TV show with Dad was what I did before I came up here.

I swing the door, one hand, other hand. "Mom said for me to come up."

Winny lifts her head off the pillow to look at me. She drops her feet to the floor, still laying down, then with both hands pushes the rest of herself up. She turns off the TV which sits on a metal cart with wheels. Against the wall on the bed is a flowery canvas bag too full of clothes for it to zip up. I say, "Where you going?"

"I never like the smell of this town. Potlatch burning paper all day, pumping out great clouds of sewer stench."

"Lewiston's the best town in Idaho."

With a fingernail she scrapes at each corner of her mouth, rubs her thumb and finger together, and wipes her hand on the bedspread. She laughs in a sniff. "Sit down."

I lick the taste of candy corn from my lips before I sit next to her. She starts talking but I'm not hearing. Downstairs is the funny sound of Dad laughing—Mom is gone, and Winny is quiet. He might have found another bad show, which is a good show for him to find, because he likes to say things about how stupid it is, things that make you laugh. I want to go down and lay on the couch with the rainbow shawl that smells like sleep, to be with him while he sits in his chair, to laugh with his laugh.

I'm squinting over Winny's talking, to hear what he is doing, what he is saying, but I start listening to her when it's the first time she came to visit, Thanksgiving, when I was three and Matt was one and in the front room sat my father with his football game. "Dinnertime he ate like a starving man, then went back to the TV. The game was so loud the rest of us enjoyed nothing of our meal. After all that hard work in the kitchen." Winny taps her palm with a finger. "I'd like to know what exactly that man does around this house besides poor-mouth into his beer and watch the game while your mother does it all."

I think, a lot, he does a lot. When Mom had to go be a phone lady at the hospital he did laundry and dishes and ironing. And now that she has to stay home, he does the security guard job weekends. I want to say so, but I'm not sure if all that counts. I think it does, I think it counts, but I'm not sure, because she knows, she knows all he does. I look the other way, at the door. I won't talk to her again. She says mean things about Dad when everything is all her fault.

A fast hard rain makes a frying pan noise in the driveway. It got dark without me even seeing, and the streetlight fills up the room with a blue glow. On the sliding closet doors raindrop shadows sink to the carpet as water drips down the window. "A boy who lived across the street from me when I was a girl," Winny says. "Every Halloween he had two pumpkins on his porch, and instead of grimaces, they had smiles." When she locks her fingers in mine, I feel the slippery cold lotion, see the deep wells between her knuckles, the bones rising and the skin tightening. "Imagine it. A smiling pumpkin for Halloween. So one year I climb his porch and squash the pumpkins. Put my shoe right through them."

"Did you? Why?"

"What about you? Would you do it?"

"No."

For a joke she gasps with a hand over her mouth, which makes her cough on both hands. When she's done, she says, "I worry for your soul, Tommy. You won't even squash a pumpkin on Halloween. What's the matter with you, boy."

"Yes I would."

"You're just saying so now."

"I might. It would have to depend. But I might."

The window rattles when Mom's car pulls up in the drive. Dad's boots thump the thin Chinese carpet and then the wood floor, the front door opens, and he yells for her to park in the garage, not in the driveway. She'll get soaked in this rain. The garage door squeaks as he rolls it up for her.

"I should go do the groceries," I say. "Want to come help?"

"I'll be down for dinner."

"Sure you don't want to?"

"Ah, yes, Tommy, I am."

"I don't know—just thought you might like to help out once in a while. It would show Dad you care, at least." On my way out I think of one more thing. "They won't let you go back. I heard them fighting. My mom says you have to stay."

Winny scoots back against some pillows where the wall corners, like to get as far away as she can. She pulls a scarf from her bag and wraps it around her hand, and holds that hand to her mouth, blinking at me.

I run downstairs half thinking I am dragging behind a bad feeling in my stomach from what I said to her. But all my stomach feels right now is satisfied. I remind Dad about Monday Night Football.

"You're telling the Headless Horseman it's Halloween, buddy." The hard rain got him when he was opening the garage door, and water drips from his wet bangs shaped like tiny moon slivers on his forehead. He grins and wipes his hair back with the pillow part of his hand. The opening music to the football game is a house-crashing thunder. I put away the groceries with quick breaths out a tight tingly chest, because tonight is me and him yelling for our team, and tonight, I know it, our team will win.

* * *

After church Matt and I sit on the porch watching snow fall in perfectly straight lines. Past houses across the street you can see wide joints of the Snake—flat, silver, misty in the cold. When Dad gets back he lifts a bag of salt from the truck bed and drops it at the steps. "Time to hang up the bunny suits and turn off the lights, boys."

I say, "Cut a hole in my head and put a candle in me because I'm a pumpkin."

The way he smiles just on one side of his face means I need a new joke. "That turkey's ready for the blade." He swings the world around and holds me up by the ankles on the porch. I scream and laugh at the upside-down yard. We are back to the kind of men we used to be.

I shovel snow from the walk and driveway, and Matt is my helper who tosses handfuls of salt from the bag. Winny might fall when we bring her to the car in the morning, to drive her across town where people can care for her breathing day and night.

Dad comes out with three leftover turkey sandwiches—the turkey Winny not only said no to help cooking but said no to eating. We are huddled in the yard around our snowman, quiet with fast chewing, snow collecting on our hats and shoulders. Mom sips tea behind the cardboard turkeys and Pilgrims. The fireplace flames bend their shapes and colors in the window.

I say, "Dig a hole for my head because I'm a ponderosa pine."

My new joke knocks a laugh out of him. "Yes, pinus upside-downus. Most rare."

"What?"

"Shit." The salt bag lays bent and wrinkled in the snow. "I meant for you to do that in the morning. Still snowing, buddy."

When I see how the salt on the walk and driveway is already covered up, all the stupid things in me crawl to the bottom. "Oh."

"Well, don't worry. Gramma won't slip. If needed, you can give her a piggy back to the car. Now go put on your union suits and one extra sweater."

Upstairs I wiggle my sandwich-baggy feet into my red cowboy boots with scuffed toes, better than rubber ones to wear if you're going sledding with your dad, and Matt buttons his union suit and then tugs up his snow overalls. Mom and Winny are in running a bath. *Not* and *going* slip loose from the noise of water rushing in pipes. "Yes, going," Matt says, like an echo giving back the wrong words. Me and Matt are walking down the hall when Winny busts out the bathroom all wet in her robe, trots toward us in what for her is a hurry, arms out like playing airplane, slapping the wall pictures crooked, one or two falling to the floor. And we are running back the other way. Mom flashes past our room saying Mother, Mother.

With my scarf over my nose and my candy cane stocking hat pulled down low, I stand at the living room window. Up past the chimneys and TV antennas the sky is white, one kind of white all over, so the snowflakes aren't really there till they streak past a house. I think how it's hard to keep thinking up new jokes. You only get one funny one for every ten, and they get old so fast. There's one joke I've been keeping for a good time to say. I say it now. "Pretty soon and I'm riding bunnies in my donkey suit because the roof is too slippery for somersaults and the pumpkins are rotten and all the butterflies are dead in the snow."

Dad swings the door open and moves his arm in a circle like a crosswalk monitor saying Okay. "What're you waiting for—Santa?"

Matt says, "Let's go!"

Rose Moss

THE PATH OF LIGHTNING

The stories keep catching in each other like necklaces in a drawer and tangle in my mind though there's no connection except the scarf in each. It's not the same scarf, though they were probably both bright and cheap and shiny. Eric would have bought something like that. He's French and tight with money though generous in other ways. He was a child during the war, and those times of chaos and hunger mark him still, like granite that rises to the surface in New England fields.

The other was the scarf Vera chose, probably also something like rayon. Vera's a young working journalist after all, in a poor country, and the scarf was not something she would usually wear. She wanted it to distract the guards at the hospital lounging in camouflage and cradling machine guns. They must not notice the small camera she would smuggle into the ward under her hair which is full, curling, glossy and black. When she wears it loose, as she did that day, it is easy to dream how it would fan over a pillow or fall over her breasts.

Rose Moss is the author of three novels: *The Terrorist, Shouting at the Crocodile* and *The Family Reunion*, which was short-listed for a National Book Award. Her stories have been cited in *The Best American Short Stories;* one won a Quill Prize and one a PEN short fiction award.

She tied the scarf at her neck with a knot and its red floating points filled the guards with fantasy when they looked at her. They wanted sex and more. Especially the young recruit outside the patient's door. Vera promises perfection and peace, like what I found with Eric when we brought all the rhythms of the world together and knew that nothing else could be as good as this. Because the new recruit is young he imagines sex and, like a saint's nimbus of light around the longing, a whole day on the beach, on the sand, among rockpools, in the shelter of a shallow cave. In the long evening, the moon shines . . . That he will take her home to his village where his uncle has a farm in the foothills, where there is a meadow at the curve where the riverbank becomes steep. It bends into a copse and makes a quiet place where he used to hide as a child and no one could find him. He will bring a blanket . . . By the time Vera comes out of the patient's room he has burrowed so deep into longings, he can hardly see anything in front of his eyes.

Although Vera does not know exactly what fills his heart, she knows that wearing the scarf will gain her admission to the patient and the story. She intends no ill and feels dismay when she hears that after her footage appears on TV the recruit is summoned for punishment, shouted at, hit, and locked up in a cell hardly big enough for the coir mattress and stinking bucket.

But he is a farm boy accustomed to harsh conditions. In his solitary cell, he saves crumbs from the thick slice of bread they bring three times a day, and puts them on the sill between the bars, and, sure enough, a sparrow comes to the sill and accepts his crumbs and looks at him with a bright eye. The bird is accustomed to wooing from lonely prisoners. Curiously enough, this time of forced isolation and spare rations becomes a time of meditation. The recruit resolves to get out of the army as soon as he can, go back to the country and work on his uncle's farm. I don't know whether, after all, he does leave the army, as he hopes in prison, or whether, released to the daily routine of work and camaraderie, he forgets that this is what he really wants. Many of us have dreams and give them up. Perhaps he was sent into the mountains to fight guerrillas and did not come back.

There is much I don't know. I imagine how a soldier dreams, guessing that our human longings are not different, though I know very well that the miracle in love seems that the longing of each requites the other uniquely. Eric and I felt made for each other and that we had known each other forever, in other lifetimes and other places. Though neither of us believed we live any life but this, with each other we glimpsed something else, immortality and destiny.

So perhaps what soldiers dream is not the same throughout the world and I do not really know what Vera's soldier longed for.

When Eric talked about his years as a soldier, a duty for every young man in France, he did not tell me about longing for women or home. He talked about science. Physics filled his imagination. He signed the letters he wrote me with the loop that in mathematics signifies infinity. He described everything between us in physics. The world rotated on our positive and negative poles. Our meeting and our love were inevitable though unpredictable, like the course of specific particles in quantum mechanics. In physics, contraries like these coexist as though they can be reconciled and we sustained ourselves for years in paradox and excitement as we snatched days and weeks together on both sides of the Atlantic. I believed our storms would smooth out one day into steadiness as simple as a blue sky.

I could not understand the physics Eric invoked, though that was the true language of his heart. Physics describing chaos, turbulence, explosions, lightning, wrecks—war rendered into science. When he was my lover, studying storms on the sun and Jupiter, images of passion and power flooded our longing, and flowed like the Gulf Stream through the fierce Atlantic between us. When he called from Paris, icebergs and whales, currents and shipping lanes, the world's ardors and mysteries filled our voices. I believed him when he said all his work breathed with our love. Like the turbulence he studied, that love drew into whirlpools and thrashed through the world like winds. It still leaves a roiling wake in my inward sea where now two scarves float on the surface, flotsam after a wreck.

Since dreams are so particular, I confess that I don't really know what Vera's recruit dreamed when he allowed her into the ward where she interviewed the woman who had been tortured and focused the camera to show the burn marks on her fingers and soles.

There are many things I don't know or can't say. After all, people died for what they said. Or what was said about them.

Last week, Vera and José, her anchorman, came to our offices here in Boston looking for help and showed us the footage they aired on TV, and some that was cut. The video they played on their news program didn't show the burns on breasts or genitals. People in their country are prudish about sex, and she did not want to offend that way. It was bad enough that she was showing evidence of torture. Of course it's not only prudery that forbade showing all the scars. The owner of the station and the lawyers knew public reasons for forbidding such sights. Reasons of state security. They did not want to give the authorities too much cause for outrage.

Though, of course, they also knew that for some, like their Minister of Justice, which is to say, the Minister of Prisons, torture is aphrodisiac too. He forgets the purpose of his curiosity and becomes engrossed in play. He savors cruelty until it becomes tenderness. Tenderness? Hunters speak of the bond they feel with the buck in the crosshairs. I do not know how to predict the contraries people reconcile.

In the end, the Department admitted that the woman Vera had interviewed had done nothing deserving torture. A typo got her name confused with that of the other woman. Mistakes like that happen every day.

It was really the other woman who was guilty, they said. The one who got in touch with Vera and José to call attention to certain documents marked Classified and Top Secret. No government can allow such things. Even if it is not a matter of state security. Even if it is personal corruption, money siphoned into private accounts, a bit of bribery and kickback, you can't embarrass men in power who hold the lives of others in their hands. It is so obvious that power corrupts I sometimes believe people condone it, though perhaps they don't. Perhaps they feel they can't change anything, that they have to accept and keep quiet. What can they do?

In countries like Vera's, even people who don't condone, don't know what to do about what they know. They feel badly, especially when they hear from a handsome TV anchorman like José.

When Vera told the story on TV, viewers could see the beauty spot over her left eyebrow, near the temple. Then they saw on TV and read on the front pages of newspapers about the woman who arranged to meet Vera and give her the papers. That woman's body was found on a median strip on a main highway. Some people say she was the one who was really guilty or, if not guilty, that she asked for it.

Alive, the dead woman was tall and beautiful and had deep red hair. Maybe that gave her confidence to do something so brave. They say she was pregnant too. Some viewers felt really bad, part of it pity, part of it fear for what could happen when there is no uproar about the mistake confessed on TV, part of it anger. Others asked, 'How can a woman be so irresponsible? A pregnant woman has no right to mess with confidential papers and TV journalists.'

Anyhow, she's dead, that woman with silky red hair, and even if people feel bad about it, what can they do? The TV program shows her father talking about her. He also has that brilliant hair, and after a few sentences, though it is unmanly, he can't help it, and his voice breaks. Anyone can see from his face that he has lived through many other troubles in silence and courage. What can anyone do? No one can reach through the glass to wipe the tears from his face—they'd only get blood on their own hands. Even his neighbors and family know that it is better not to get carried away. They believe it is God, not us, who wipes the tears from every eye, and God acts only after many catastrophes.

But when they see the footage Vera took, some feel heavy-hearted, knowing that they can't escape splashes of blood. Every-thing would fall apart without the army and police, and no one wants that. If they must live in the city where they were born they must keep quiet. Even if they are sorrowful, there is nothing they can do. If Vera came to speak to them, wearing her scarf, they would know nothing. They would look straight into her eyes like people who look at a camera for a photograph on a license.

Soldiers stand guard outside the hospital ward where one woman moves her hands to show dark burns and the other focuses the cam-era to record the fingers moving like young birds learning to fly. Wearing that bright scarf, Vera said she was the patient's cousin. She flirted with a recruit a few minutes ago, and the points of her scarf were like a butterfly. With his hand on the hip gun ready to hand, he stands at the door remembering that meadow by a river where the grass grows tall and you can look up at blue sky and imagine that you are alone in the world, or alone with Vera in a place where no one will see you, where you are king and she is willing, she opens her lips and pulls open the knot of the scarf round her neck, and her fingers slip the buttons of her blouse through the stitching made for it to open.

We have explanations for our silences in this country. Working with the Committee, I know what we condone. We say it is not our business. It is not our charter. We don't have time. We should not criticize the internal affairs of other countries. We should not believe only one side of the story. We don't know enough. Though it is im-possible to know enough. Our country has become the center of the world, and everyone wants our attention, our sympathy, our money and our power. They could tell us twelve times more than we could understand. What would we know when we know?

When Vera's boss, José, the handsome young anchorman, showed us the video of the woman killed, he said, "I carry her on my con-science." The pain passes from one to another like lightning along branches no one can predict exactly.

I remembered Eric and how it felt as though he had to tell me that story about the experiment in Japan. He did not say he was carrying it on his conscience, but when I put the pieces together I saw that he had been waiting for the semester to end, to fly to his lab on the Swiss border and deal with things there, and to come to me. He never said these things directly, but it was like other times when he was lying in bed reflecting, looking at the ceiling, absent-mindedly caressing my arm, speaking from memories he did not share with anyone else. He would tell about incidents like the first time he tasted of chocolate, a G.I.'s gift, and the time he saw an Allied and a German plane in a dogfight. He was thrilled. He was a child. But now . . .

The year before he went to Japan, Eric was so stirred with interest in fractals that he talked about them in one of those reflective moments in bed after we made love. He would lie there, eyes open, sometimes twisting the hairs of an eyebrow, not seeming to see anything, contemplating matters present to his mind's eye. In that reflective state he talked about an equation to describe the pattern that remains similar through the whole coast of Britain, from inlets and peninsulas to nooks and crannies where land and water make love forever.

Afterwards we went out walking in the dawn. The low moon was fading and he wanted to shout joy to the whole neighborhood. Yelling like that could only make trouble in an American suburb, but he did not seem to care. I scolded until he kissed me to keep me quiet and we went into my house where we would not scandalize my neighbors if we made love like starved teenagers. Another time, at Walden Pond, the water quick with blue dragonflies, he started to sing that he loved me. Loud and carrying over the water. I hushed him. After all, I was the one who would remain. He would go off to France and, if he remembered that exuberance at all, would recall only its pleasure.

Perhaps I condense into one moment the excitement of that whole time when he was burning with passion for me and for fractal mathematics. The next time we were together, when he broke his journey to Japan with one day with colleagues and two nights with me, he was suddenly struck by hunger the second night. We went to the kitchen and I made scrambled eggs, and while I was stirring them he told me about a study of cars on highways that showed that traffic never flows in an even stream. Even on roads without obstacles, cars bunch together in a pattern. The University of Paris at that time was full of people who wanted to use fractal theory to study sociology.

When he came back from that trip to Japan he was full of wonder over what he had seen—temples, gardens—and stories about how he startled the Japanese men he passed when he went jogging in the early morning or evening. Perhaps the Japanese jog now, but at that time, it seemed bizarre *gaijin* behavior. It was several nights before Eric talked about the experiment, and I knew immediately that, though he affected an indifferent tone, it troubled him. One evening while they were all at a table in the restaurant near the university where they used to eat, his group was speculating about fractal patterns in human behavior. They thought the course of a rumor might show patterns, something like the course of lightning with unpredictable repetitions, branches and bends. They designed an experiment to test their hypothesis.

They didn't think of it as experimentation on human subjects. If he had thought of it that way, Eric would not have done it. He has always refused work "on the other side of the fence," as he describes classified research.

It was one of those things you can't predict, like that typo the Minister confessed on TV.

That illusion of innocence came to the surface when José talked about the owner of the TV station he worked for. The owner was punished for the story José had told. His citizenship was revoked, his station was closed and his property was confiscated. He had not just permitted the show that used Vera's footage. He had promoted it with a series of advertisements, you know the kind of thing, promises of scandalous revelations, teaser questions, What has the Department of X got to hide? Why does the Department want to keep this story from you? and so forth.

José showed no sympathy when he showed us footage of the owner of the TV station sitting in an armchair with his hands on his thighs telling what he had suffered before he escaped to another country. Perhaps it is hard for a young journalist caught in the tangle of justice to feel for the sufferings of a millionaire, although the owner is not a millionaire any more. Perhaps it is too much to expect sympathy if the journalist is young and handsome and runs up stairs two at a time without losing breath and the owner is fat and accustomed to having people around who do what he says, and is used to doing what you must do in a country like that to get a license, and a permit to build on this site and another permit to put up an antenna, and so forth, until you have fed everyone at the table of the Leader. Now the station owner does not even have a country. The Minister kicked him out and told him to go and make trouble somewhere else. His exile is not on José's conscience. Instead of sympathizing, José said, "I wonder what he was up to, hiring us and giving us that current affairs program. We are all young. My colleagues are brave. What did he think would happen?" Here too, the line is not straight but jagged like lightning.

What did Eric's group think would happen? The question did not arise. They just wanted to see the course of a rumor. It seemed innocent enough to their western eyes, and they were theoreticians, proud to be doing research without considering its practical outcomes, and so Eric bought a scarf and gave it to a waitress in the restaurant where everyone could see that he was giving her the gift.

Eric told me a young man in the lab gave the scarf but I am sure he was the one. They would have chosen him. He seemed an impetuous and genial fellow, and eccentric enough to give a pretty scarf to a waitress he liked. He sometimes yelled with joy when he arrived at a new insight, you could hear him braying in the park in Osaka. God knows what the Japanese thought of this crazy *gaijin*. He would not have done it in France. Neither yelling nor the experiment.

She was a young girl from the country, come to Osaka to live with her uncle's family, earn some money by waitressing and learn English part time. She wanted to come to America. Her relatives in Seattle might sponsor a trip. She might marry an American and live in a big house like people on TV and have sons who would grow big and healthy and free. They would run down the beach into the sea shouting and laughing, not afraid to splash each other. Sometimes she looked at the group of scientists who talked loudly and moved with fearless gestures and sometimes wrote equations on their arms. They seemed alive in an air transparent to her eyes but opaque to her understanding, like carp breathing in water. What would it be like to live in their countries? Free and fearless like a crane stretching wings wide for flight? She had a friend who married an American and went to Los Angeles. In her New Year's greeting the friend wrote that she had learned to drive and sometimes went to movies and restaurants by herself and had more clothes than she could wear in a week . . . What else did she dream, this unassuming young waitress? No one will ever know now.

She committed suicide when her reputation was ruined. The rumor explained the gift as evidence that she was having an affair with the *gaijin*.

I don't know what that showed about the fractal pattern of rumor. Perhaps that it can strike like lightning out of a blue sky. Like torture after a typo.

The journalists who worked for José have scattered, some into exile, some to other jobs. José says, "I don't know where they are. One came to New York and tried to get work, but the only job he can find is as a waiter." Coming from a poor country, José's reporter feels demeaned. He does not guess that in New York, serving in a restaurant may be work shared with children of millionaires and successful lawyers. He feels that his life has been smashed and he has fallen into a depression. "He is also on my conscience," says José.

José's not really to blame, just as I'm not really to blame for the waitress in Osaka, though perhaps Eric's exuberance in love had something to do with that experiment. I worked out that Eric wanted me to say something that would condone. No, more. He wanted me to forgive him on her behalf. It didn't make sense, but who else could he turn to except someone who loved him? He didn't believe in God. But he never told the story straight.

When I worked it out, I knew there would never be calm water between us, we would never rest on the same shore. I was his wildness, and now I knew where his wildness had struck. It singed me too.

We get so many stories in our office. If not for that detail about Vera smuggling the camera into the hospital room with her distracting scarf and hair, I would hardly have noticed her story. Working for human rights is mostly routine like any other job, especially what I do, administrative support. Our boss wants us to know about the cases we're working on, so every week we have a presentation. That's how I heard Vera's story. We'll report it in the newsletter, call to ask the Ambassador for comment, prepare a press kit, brief the State Department, organize a seminar. These tasks, so predictable, have become emblems of peace to me. No one threatens to arrest me, no one kicks in the door or herds me into a dark cell. After all we hear, I feel this remarkable and precious.

For myself, I expect to die slowly, not like that woman who has been spared the humiliations of old age. But I expect that for me too, when death comes, it will be as though I have been struck by lightning.

Marie Sheppard Williams

THE BOOK OF SAINTS AND MARTYRS

This is a story that I have been trying to come to for more than half a century; since, in fact, I was the child I write about. The strongest image I have in my mind when I think about writing it really has nothing to do with the story. I don't think it does. But maybe it does. Since it forces its way in, like an uninvited guest, it must, in all courtesy, be accommodated, surely?

This is it: once I was on a bus in Minneapolis, Minnesota, where I have lived most of my life. A woman was carrying a little child, a baby. The child was barefoot. Suddenly the woman rang the bell to get off, and as she stood up the baby was turned toward me for a second in such a way that all I saw were the tiny soles of its feet. I was pierced with a shaft of such joy and such tenderness, fondness, that tears come to my eyes now, remembering.

Marie Sheppard Williams is a frequent contributor to *Alaska Quarterly Review*. She has received a Bush Artist Fellowship, two Pushcart Prizes, and a Wolf Pen Fellowship sponsored by the Kentucky Foundation for Women. Coffee House Press published a collection of her stories entitled *The Worldwide Church of the Handicapped*.

And then, immediately, like part of the same memory, I think of Paulie.

* * *

Who is Paulie? You want to know? Hey. Of course you do. You want to know everything, don't you?

Like Uncle Albert, you want to know God's thoughts. You would never have left that apple alone in Paradise, would you? No good saying: she tempted me, Eve did; Eve ate first.

You would have eaten it too. I *know* you; as I know my second self.

Paradise was never enough for us, fragile voyageurs: *More!* has always been our cry.

Give me another donut. Give me a piece of cake. Give me the next bend of the river. *Give me that apple, goddammit. Give it to me now.*

* * *

I have only one clear memory of Paulie.

I was two years old and he must have been six. I have the impression that it was his First Communion day: that doesn't quite fit, six seems awfully young for it, but maybe he was precocious at that too.

Certainly he had a white suit on. And why would he wear a white suit except for his First Communion? These were depression times in the U.S.A., about 1933 or 1934, some of the deepest years of the Great Depression; people bought nothing frivolous, surely there would be no occasion grand enough to call for the purchase of a white suit except a First Communion? or a wedding? or a funeral?

And I had on a little white dress and white shoes with straps: called, I think, Mary Janes. This would not have been quite so unusual: for one thing, my father had a *job*, not universal in those days, not even altogether common, and so we had an income. For another thing, I was the first child of a favorite daughter; yes, honestly; many hands sewed and crocheted for me, many fingers tucked and tatted. For me.

And I did feel my importance. Oh, my, yes.

You think I cannot remember this, but I can. Many children, maybe all of them, remember far more than they ever tell the grownups.

We were dancing in a circle, playing a child's game, Ring-Around-a-Rosy, popular then, maybe still. Well. Surely still.

I believe we might have been in a room in Aunt Anna's house, the house by the river. Aunt Anna was Paulie's mother and my god-mother. I think the room may have been a dining room, or an alcove off a dining room; in any case there had to have been space enough for our circle.

* * *

One day last summer I was at a get-together of some of the women in the family: at my cousin Dolly's apartment, Dolly is old now and has had to give up her house in Robbinsdale: her sister Tildy was there, and Dolly's daughter Serene, whom I hardly recognized, she has got so gray, and Diana, Tildy's daughter-in-law, whom I don't recall ever having met before that day. Myrna, my cousin Billy's widow. Her daughter Alix. Etc., etc.

A whole room full of women.

We have met like this now and then ever since I can remember. It used to be my aunts and my mother and us, their daughters; but now all that older generation is gone and my generation is hanging on by its teeth.

We've filled our ranks with Serene's generation: Alix, Diana.

My own daughter will have nothing to do with these get-togethers.

Your family is totally weird, she says.

My family: hear that? Not hers.

Suddenly, connected to nothing, Tildy said: to me: Joan, do you remember when we were kids, all of us dancing in a circle around the table in Grandma's kitchen?

Why, the room seemed to tilt for a second.

Grandma's kitchen? Is that where it was, then? and around the table? it surely could have been.

Hey, Tildy, I said—I felt like I was taking a terrible chance, going way out on a limb here—would Paulie have been there?

Paulie? said Tildy. He could have been. Sure. He would have been—what?—five?

Six, I said.

Maybe six, she said. And you were just little.

Two years old, I said.

No, I think you were bigger than that, Joan. I remember your head poking up over the top of the table.

She said.

And your shoulders. You had on a white dress.

Going on three, anyway.

Okay, going on three. That'll work. . . .

It would have been just before he died, she said. If he was there.

He was there. I said.

I remember the wake, she said. My goodness, he looked so bad. His face was bitten by fish. The undertaker tried to fix it, but it looked strange.

Strange. . . .

Malone's Funeral Home, she said.

We always used Malone's.

By this time everybody was listening. My word, said Myrna, did they have an open casket? Why on earth would they do that?

I remember, I said. Aunt Anna insisted on it. Aunt Anna was half crazy with grief.

No half about it, said Tildy. Anna was crazy.

I can't believe you remember it. She said. To me. You were so little.

I remember. I said.

*   *   *

I remember darkness: a dark day. Winter? Maybe. Well: it must have been winter. I figured this out years later.

I have spent my life on this quest.

I remember glass behind glass; and light sparkling off glass; and dark wood. A corner cupboard, they used to have them, do they still? triangular in shape, fitted into a corner, and shelved for treasures, fronted with glass. And locked.

There would have been me and Paulie; Paulie's brothers, younger than he, Billy and Cyril, named for saints, and having "Joseph", all of them, as second names: Paul Joseph, William Joseph, Cyril Joseph: because their mother, my Aunt Anna, my godmother, was, as they said then, "devoted to Saint Joseph." Yes, indeed. Joseph the Carpenter was her man; not my Uncle Luke, who was a barber.

There would have been in our circle also my three girl cousins, a little older than the rest of us: Catherine's daughters: Loretta Anne, Dorothy Catherine, and Mathilda Antoinette: Lollie, Dolly, and Tildy.

Probably there was no one else; my own brothers had—by my reckoning—not been born yet: the one next to me in age, Arden Jr., was, if I have figured this out right, in my mother's womb just at that time. So: seven of us: cousins. Circling and dancing and holding hands; chanting and singing and falling down in a heap of arms and legs:

Ring around a rosy . . .

A pocket full of posies . . .

Ashes, ashes . . .

We all fall down.

Paulie was across the circle from me. His white suit caught my eye and held it. The suit seemed almost to glow in the dark day. I looked down at my dress: white also. Why, I said to myself, that one over there is Paulie, and *this one is me.*

Suddenly I wore joy like a second dress. I felt haloed, clothed in light. To know that there was an "I"; to know that there was at the same time a "Paulie," an Other; was such an illumination that it must have been like the first time Helen Keller attached a word to a thing: *water:* and suddenly all the world became accessible to her: to me. That feels presumptuous, to dare to say that; to link myself with Helen: and yet, why not? Surely we are all linked? Surely all illumination comes from the same light?

I looked across the circle at Paulie, and I fell in love, for the first time, and fatally: forever.

* * *

I do remember, I said: to Tildy, at the gathering at Dolly's apartment.

You were so little, she said.

Yes: I was: so little.

* * *

There is another memory of Paulie—I am just now putting this bit into my picture, I have lived my whole life insisting that I had only the one memory, but I see now that there is another. I never counted this other memory as amounting to much, but now I think I was wrong: I think it does count.

We had a game, my three boy cousins and I, that we played on Sundays sometimes when we were all together. This game was strictly forbidden by the grownups—or at least certainly would have been forbidden if they had had any notion of what we were up to.

This is how it went: we played our regular games—marbles, hopscotch, Captain-May-I?—out on the sidewalk: and we kept an eye out for cars although it wasn't like today when a steady stream of cars flows down any street.

Paulie invented the game. Paulie was always our leader. One day he saw a car coming and he suddenly began to scream at the car. (At the car; truly; not at the driver.)

Stop! he shouted.

Waving his arms.

Stop!

He ran along beside the car, screaming at it and waving his arms:

like a toreador taunting a bull. Hey! You! Car! Come and get me! Hey! Stop!

The driver turned a stunned face toward us, but he did not stop.

Now, obviously this game had no point. And since it had no point, it became increasingly important to embroider it and surround it.

The next time we played the game, a car came along and my cousin Cyril turned his backside to it and farted at it.

Oh my God, was this rich, or what? We rolled on the sidewalk in spasms of laughter.

Well, of course Paulie had to top that. Of course he did. Another car came along, maybe ten minutes later. At the last second, Paulie darted into the path of the car and the car hit him. Not hard—cars did not go as fast in those days as they do now, nor were they the juggernauts that they are today. But hard enough to knock him down.

The driver stopped. We all stopped. For heaven's sake. So this is what the grownups were on about. So this is what they meant when they said: Stay Out Of The Street.

Well, the driver stood Paulie up and dusted him off. And he kept saying: to us: He ran right out in front of me! The kid ran right out in front of me!

Paulie stared at him. He stared around at all of us. He looked like someone who had seen another country.

Take him home, you kids. Tell his folks that it wasn't my fault. . . .
Said the driver.

So we took him home, just down the street, to his own house. Aunt Anna's house, Uncle Luke's house.

Walked in with him.

Paulie got hit by a car, Cyril said.

Nobody heard him.

Paulie got hit by a car, Cyril said, louder.

That time, Uncle Luke heard.

What's that? he said. What's that about Paulie? He held his hand up to shush the other grownups. Then we could all see how important our news was: that Uncle Luke, shy and quiet, would shush the grownups for it.

Shh. He said to them. Shh. Something has happened to Paulie.

And into the quiet: *Paulie?* said Aunt Anna. *What happened?*

Paulie didn't speak. He just kept looking into a far distance that only he could see.

Paulie got hit by a car, Cyril said. We all chimed in: Car. Hit. Driver. Fault.

Well, of course you know that all hell broke loose. Aunt Anna cried and yelled, and our grandmother felt Paulie all over and counted his arms and legs and pronounced him whole, not a bruise on him, not a bone broken, a miracle. . . .

Thank you, Saint Joseph!

That was Aunt Anna; at last it seemed that her devotion had paid off.

Did we tell you to stay out of the street? Did we tell you?

That was my father, dressed in his ice-cream suit and wearing his new straw hat that he wouldn't take off, even in the house.

Did we tell you?

Yes, we said.

Oh, they told us. Yes. We looked with new respect at Paulie, who had done what he was told not to.

* * *

Did I really see that? Is that a real memory? Or is that just something I was told about afterwards? It could be something I was told. And yet I seem to remember it—I seem to see it clearly. But could I have seen it? It would have to have been in the summer that I was two years old; careless as my parents were, would they have let me play unsupervised in the street at age two?

I seem to remember my father saying afterwards: meaning Paulie: that child was doomed. I saw it in his face the day he got hit by the car. After that he wanted death. I saw it.

Truly. My father was a strange, sweet man: who could say things like that.

* * *

Anna was the middle one of my grandmother's five daughters. Five girls and three boys. Surviving, that is; a boy, the baby William, Bernard's twin, and a girl, Josette, died in a diphtheria epidemic.

My mother—in a rare instance of self-revelation, mostly she kept her thoughts and memories to herself—told me once about that epidemic.

* * *

My mother never got sick. In all her life, in all the part of her life that I was with her, that I could watch this, I knew her to have maybe two little colds. And even they didn't amount to much. A little sniffling for two or three days and a cold was over.

She said it herself: I never get sick.

There was always some anger around it when she said it. It was as though "getting sick" was a privileged position that had been denied to her.

Oh, well, you know that I never get sick . . .

And: *I never got to stay home from school. The others got to stay home sometimes, but not me.*

Let me see your tongue, Elizabeth, my mother would say.

And: Let me feel your forehead.

And then: You are not so sick, Elizabeth. You can go to school.

My mother's eyes, blue like my Grandma's eyes—in fact, she was the one who looked like Grandma, and she was the favorite daughter—my mother's eyes would seem almost to well with tears for a second when she said it: *I never got sick:* but then the tears, the bare hint of tears, would vanish, and my mother would again be the cool, cool person that I knew.

And in fact, you know, I came to believe that she did not feel anything, that she had no feelings. Honestly—it was a perfectly logical deduction for a kid to make from the evidence.

Remember the two children who were missing from the picture on my wall?—William and Josette?—the way they died was apparently typical of events in my mother's life.

Everybody in the family came down with diphtheria at the same time; everybody from Grandpa to the twin babies got it. Except my mother and my Grandma.

Can you see it?—the mother and the little girl working around the clock, days, nights, to keep the sick ones comfortable: well: to keep them *alive.*

There would have been ten sick and those two well.

No, wait, Mary was at the convent then, and Cyril was gone. So there would have been eight sick.

We moved all the beds that we could manage into the parlor downstairs, my mother told me. In her soft, cool voice. *We lined everybody up like in a hospital ward so we could take care of them easier.*

Doctor?

No, no doctor came. Well. My mother knew as much as any doctor knew in those days.

We did what we could to keep the fever down.

We did what we could to help them breathe.

We went from one to another and opened their mouths and scraped the awful white stuff out of their throats and sucked it away with a glass straw.

As much as we could.

Again and again.

My mother taught me how to do it. I don't want to, I said. You must, she said. *Or they will die.*

We gave them spoonfuls of her herb tea.

And broth. Whatever they could swallow. When they could swallow at all.

My Elizabeth . . . My good little nurse . . . my mother said.

But I got so tired.

And William died anyway. And Josette died.

Did she see them die? She must have seen them die. After a while, it might have seemed no great shakes. So later when it seemed to her that it was okay for a child to see anything, to hear anything, to be left out of nothing, might that not also have been for her a logical deduction?

I never got sick: I can hear the complaint in her voice now, many, many years later, when they are all eight of them dead of one thing and another, and my mother is dead too, my grandmother too, they are all gone, all, like it says in the Bible story, like grass, cut down.

One day I said to my Mama, when she was an old lady herself, and apropos of her then list of physical problems: At least you haven't got anything that you can die of. . . .

And she said: If I haven't got anything wrong with me that I can die of, how am I going to get out of here?

* * *

Anna was always odd one out; at any rate it sounds like that from the stories I have heard. And from my own observation; I took to Anna from the start, and Anna took to me.

You were the only one who was like me, she told me many years later: one day when she sat in a chair in the living room of the tiny house she lived in at the end with Cyril, who had never married, who stayed with Anna in quiet and apparently willing servitude.

Maybe Paulie would have been like me, Anna said.

If there had been a daughter, I imagine it would have been the daughter who stayed; but there was no daughter; and so Cyril stayed, a servant to Anna all his life.

Anna never forgave him for not being Paulie.

* * *

After Paulie died, Anna would talk and talk to my mother, and carry on like crazy.

Well, and *crazy* is what they said she was.

I heard her sometimes when they didn't think I was listening. I was that awful kind of kid who sneaks around and hides and stays quiet, so no one realizes that they exist, and everyone says things they shouldn't hear.

Why couldn't it have been Cyril who drowned? Anna would cry. Or Billy?

Shh, my mother would say. They'll hear. . . .

And they did hear, of course they did; children always hear.

I'd give God Billy and Cyril both, Anna said; if only He'd give back Paulie. . . .

I pray sometimes, she said. God, take Billy or Cyril, I pray. *Give back Paulie.* . . .

And: Oh, Paulie was my darling heart! How can I live without my darling heart?

Elizabeth, she would say: to my mother. You pray too. You ask Him for Paulie, you tell Him to take the others instead.

I can't do that, Anna, my mother said: shocked. You know I can't do that. . . .

* * *

My mother told me a story: that Anna had another suitor before she married Luke: young Lochinvar out of the west. He was not a Catholic. He was a perfectly nice person apart from that, and very good-looking, so my mother said, but *he was not a Catholic.*

So my grandfather—an old-world tyrant named Felix Ignatius, yes, honestly—put his foot down on Anna's heart, and declared that she could not marry her lovely boy.

I wonder what his name was.

Lochinvar?—but he never came to rescue Anna at the altar. No. No one did. No rescue occurred.

And Anna married Luke. Luke was declared by my grandfather to be a suitable match for his middle daughter.

I remember that Anna had a wind-up phonograph. She sat sometimes in the house by the river that Luke bought for her and played the phonograph: one song, over and over, and tears running down her face and splashing onto her hands.

Roses . . .

I give you. . . . ro-zes . . .

And hope their *ten* . . . der blossom*ing*. . . .

Why is Aunt Anna crying, Mama? I said.

Oh: she is thinking sad thoughts: my mother said.

Is she thinking of Paulie?

Maybe. Or maybe she is thinking of someone else that she wanted to marry once . . . she might be thinking of him. . . .

. . . *my heart disclo-zes*. . . .

* * *

Uncle Luke—I told you this—was a barber. I wore my hair then in a short Dutch-boy cut, and every once in a while, maybe every six or eight weeks, Uncle Luke would sit me down in a straight-backed wooden kitchen chair and cut my hair.

I can still feel the cold sharp scissors slipping gently, barely touching the skin, over my forehead, under my bangs, shaping my skull.

Snip.

Snip.

Go the scissors.

He was so gentle, so good and kind, my Uncle Luke.

I loved him in the same quiet way that he probably loved me, that he probably loved all the children, all the cousins, his own children too.

Anna? Who knows what he felt for Anna? Love? Maybe. Sure.

He cut all our hair. *Hairs,* we said. We were German, and *hairs* was the German construction. *Das Haar*—one single hair; *die Haare*— many hairs.

I can remember his face: ordinary, brown eyes, a baffled look, tentative smile: *What has happened to me? Can these really be my children? Paulie is gone. They say this woman is my wife. She doesn't want any more children. She hates this house. She wants a house away from the river. I can't buy another house. There isn't enough money. . . .*

* * *

Depression Days. There was never enough money. A couple of years after Paulie died Uncle Luke stopped being a barber and took a job at Grant Battery instead; where he could make more money. After a while he and Anna and Cyril and Billy moved into another house. But it was too late, of course. The horse was out of the barn. Paulie could not come back. God never sent him back, in spite of Anna's prayers. God would not make the deal she asked for. Billy and Cyril both lived for quite a long time. Well, and Cyril is still alive. He still lives in the little house that was Anna's last house, and far, far from the river. He is a taxidermist: that interest began many years ago, when he and my two brothers were little boys and laid trap lines out by the pole yards in North Minneapolis. They say the basement of the little house is full of stuffed animals: otters, mink, muskrat. Fox. They say he kept the best ones for himself, to stuff, and sold the pelts of the others.

* * *

When Luke was an old man, he had a stroke and had to be put into a nursing home—this was a family disgrace, we did not put our old people into nursing homes, we took care of them at home—they say that the stroke turned Luke mean, and he (they say) cursed God and Anna and everybody else, cursed life, and I thought: Ah . . . then there is a kind of justice after all, a kind of compensation, a kind of balance. . . .

I can't take care of him at home, Anna wailed, an old lady then herself. He's too *mean!* He's too *big!* I *can't.* . . .

My Uncle Luke *was* a big man, I suppose she couldn't have him at home. But we all said: thought: Well, that's Anna. She never *was* like the rest of us, was she? She never did care that much about family, did she?

* * *

None of us ever had to pay for Uncle Luke's haircuts. Of course. That was part of what family was about.

I still love to get my hair cut. I still feel, in any hairdresser's fingers, my Uncle Luke's fingers, my Uncle Luke's scissors, snipping, snipping, moving, faster than light, snip, snip, across my forehead: gentle, delicate, precise.

My personal belief is that Anna couldn't bear to touch him. She would have had to touch him a lot after he had the stroke, wouldn't she? If she had kept him at home.

But Cyril would have helped her. Cyril was Luke all over again. It could have been—what is that awful word they have now?—do-able. It could have been doable.

* * *

The river was the Mississippi, the Father of Waters, as they call it here. It runs through, or past, Minneapolis and St. Paul, the Twin Cities: one city on each side of the river.

The Father of Waters, the mighty Mississippi, one of the greatest rivers in the world, certainly the greatest on the North American continent. It flows from a shallow, narrow—you can wade across it, and people do, I did, just to say they did; and step across it at its source, a little spring bubbling up from the earth—it flows from a shallow narrow beginning to its destination in the Gulf of Mexico, the Mississippi Delta at New Orleans. On its way, bisecting the country North to South, many rivers join it—the Minnesota, the Missouri—until from a modest stream it becomes a broad expanse of water, in some places a torrent. In Minneapolis it is wide, but a quiet, patient, waiting river. It has—it says—all the time in the world. In the early days, it provided the power for the great milling industries that rose up in the Twin Cities, and made them prosperous.

The house that Luke bought for Anna was near the river. The young couple acquired the house during the first years of the Great Depression of 1929, a time when a lot of homeowners had to sell out because they could no longer make their mortgage payments, or keep up with the taxes. The house by the river was sold to Luke and Anna for a song, I would be surprised if it cost more than two thousand dollars.

Anna's sister Catherine and her girls lived in a house in the same block: that was how Luke and Anna heard about the house that was up for sale and came to buy it when Anna was pregnant with Cyril. Catherine had only girls, and they were perfectly well-behaved Good Girls, and none of them ever disobeyed their parents' edict in the matter of the river: *Never go near the river, never, never.* But Anna began to worry about the river.

We can't stay in this house, she said.

We have to find another house.

To Luke.

Beleaguered, Luke said: quietly: I can't do it right now, Anna. We'll move to a different house as soon as I can afford it. . . .

You're such a worry-wart, Anna, said Catherine. Don't worry so much. *I* don't worry. . . .

You have girls, said Anna, as a series of boys popped out of her Catholic womb.

What difference does that make? said Catherine. Just tell them not to play by the river.

The river had a tremendous pull. I feel it even now; I have always felt it. My own daughter and I lived about a mile from the river years later and we often took lunches and played in the sand on its banks: built sand castles and made sand castings, down where the showboat is anchored now, on the Washington Avenue side of the University of Minnesota East Bank campus.

I have walked across the covered bridge that joins the East Bank and the West Bank of the University, and have stood just in the middle and stared into the great flow and felt it wanting me.

Once, just at that spot, I consigned the body of a cat, killed I guess by a car, to the river, wrapped in a nice silk scarf and casketed in a shoe box. A black cat; I thought it was my own cat, Minnie, who had vanished, but Minnie turned up whole and healthy the next day, so it was someone else's cat that I gave to the river.

The river is part of the life of the Twin Cities: the cities' heart: you can't go far, or often, without seeing, or crossing, the great stream. Brown, muddy, enigmatic, not exactly a friendly river; an old, patient river, from the dawn of time.

* * *

Was Paulie Lochinvar's child? It is tempting to me to think so. Why not? It could have been, couldn't it? These things happen. Certainly Cyril and Billy looked like Luke, and Paulie looked like . . . well, not like Luke. Luke was of the earth. Paulie was from light.

* * *

One day: We are going to see Paulie.

I am so excited, I am skipping along with my hand in my father's hand and my mother is walking beside us carrying Arden Junior, who is just a new baby, only a few weeks old, maybe two months old.

I hate Arden Junior.

Be careful of your shoes, Joan, my mother says.

There is still snow on the ground, but it is dirty snow. Summer is far away, but the real winter is gone, melted.

I stop skipping and make my way carefully among puddles and mud-patches. I have on my white Mary Janes again. I have my white dress on too. Well, of course. We are going to see Paulie at last—of course I am all dressed up.

You'd better carry her, Arden, says my mother.

My mother's name is Elizabeth. Elizabeth is the name of a saint, and she is in The Book of Saints and Martyrs that Mama reads to me. Saint Elizabeth was important, like God's aunt or something. Like Anna is my aunt. Like Catherine is my aunt. And Irma, and Sister Elicia in Tacoma, Washington.

My father is all dressed up too, in his ice-cream suit. He is wearing his new straw hat. My mother says that it is too early in the season to wear the hat, but my father says he doesn't care, he is going to wear it anyway, he likes his hat.

Dressed for a wedding, he says. And I'm going to a funeral.

He picks me up and carries me over the rest of the puddles. Oh, nice, I am not going to get my Mary Janes dirty, so Mama will not be mad at me. And I get to hug this big marvelous Daddy. I feel very, very safe, and very happy.

I love you, Daddy, I whisper into his ear, which is right near my mouth.

He hugs me tight against his scratchy ice-cream suit coat.

We walk up the sidewalk to a big house.

Is this where Paulie is now? I say.

This is not the house where Billy and Cyril and Paulie and Aunt Anna live. And Uncle Luke.

No answer. Daddy only squeezes me harder, too hard, and I squeak like my rubber toy. I am squeaking like my rubber toy. Daddy, I say. Into his ear. And then he squeezes me even harder. He is not smiling at all. We go up the cement steps to the big door at the top and the big door opens by itself, like magic, and there is a man standing behind it, and the man bends over to us a little bit. Everything is very quiet. It is like in a fairy tale, like the magic castle, where everything happens.

Paul Dannheim, says my father to the man.

That is Paulie's whole name, I know that. Paul Joseph Dannheim. We all have to know our whole names and our addresses, in case we get lost. My whole name is Joan Elizabeth Theresa Shepherd. I live at 4351 Sheridan Avenue North in Minneapolis, Minnesota.

I am named for my mother and my grandmother and a saint named Joanavark.

The man waves his hand, pointing at another door.

There, sir, he says to my Daddy. He calls my Daddy Sir. Madam. He says to my Mama.

My Daddy sets me down onto my Mary Janes on the carpet.

We have to be very quiet now, Dolly, he says. My father calls me Dolly. I don't know why. My real name is Joan. We have to remember that this is a funeral, he says.

What is a funeral, Daddy, I said.

I told you before, he said. Your Mama told you. A funeral is when somebody dies. Don't talk so loud, he said. You have to be quiet at a funeral.

But where was Paulie? I held onto my Daddy's hand and looked around. Why. Up there in the front was Aunt Anna, sitting on a chair, and there was Uncle Luke, sitting beside her. Luke, that was a big saint too, somebody who actually knew Jesus.

And there was Grandma.

There's Uncle Luke, I said. There's Aunt Anna. There's Grandma.

I tried to pull away to go and talk to them, but my Daddy held onto my hand and pulled me back.

Shh, he said.

Mama handed Arden to Daddy. Then she walked right up to the

front of the room and put her arms around Aunt Anna and said something to her.

Aunt Anna started to cry, and then Mama started crying too.

Why are they crying, Daddy? I said.

Damned if I know, said my Daddy.

And then: they must feel sad. He said.

But why.

Because Paulie is dead. Said my Daddy.

Where is Paulie? I said. When are we going to see Paulie?

My father handed Arden to one of my Aunts, maybe Aunt Catherine. Then he picked me up again and carried me up to the front. There was a white thing like a pretty bed there, and Paulie—was that Paulie?—was lying in it. Is that Paulie? I said, and Shh, my Daddy said.

* * *

Why was Paulie just lying there? and why did he look so funny? He had his white suit on, that I remembered from the circle, and long brown stockings, and his hands were folded on his chest like when you pray, and there was a little white rosary twisted around his fingers, but his fingers looked so strange and his face looked strange too and the brown stockings looked like

Big sausages

And: Why are Paulie's legs so fat? I said.

* * *

He had brown stockings on, I said to Tildy at the get-together of family women that I told you about before. Why did he have brown stockings on? Why not white?

I don't remember brown stockings, said Til. I think the casket was closed on the bottom. Like they always are.

He had brown stockings, I said. I remember.

* * *

Why are Paulie's legs so fat? I said.

Mama came. Shhh, she said. You'll make Aunt Anna feel bad. . . .

And apparently I did make Aunt Anna feel bad, because she let out a great loud yell and slid off her chair and lay on the floor there and she made awful noises and Uncle Luke got down beside her and tried to touch her and Aunt Anna was a kind of a fat lady and when she plopped on the floor she made a large squish sound and

She hit Uncle Luke's hands away

She started screaming. Paul! Paul! she screamed. I can't bear it, she screamed, and she cried and snot was coming out of her nose like when you have a bad cold and spit was coming out of her mouth and Try to control yourself Anna said Uncle Luke and

Let Anna grieve, said my Grandma. Let Anna be.

I still needed to know why Paulie's legs were so fat. I still needed to know.

* * *

This is barbaric, my father said, to my Grandma. Take the little one out, said Grandma. Why did you bring her here? She iss too little to be here. My father picked me up and carried me to the back of the room and out of the room and out onto the street. For Christ's sake, he said: to himself, it seemed like. She's just a baby, what did they expect her to do? Kneel and say a goddamn rosary?

Listen, Dolly, he said to me. Out of the depth of dark recent experience, let me give you some advice: never marry a Catholic. They are barbarians. . . .

I hung onto his neck. What's a barbar, what you said? I said.

And: Daddy, why were Paulie's legs so fat? Why did he look so funny?

I'm going to take you across the street, he said, and buy you an ice-cream cone. How would you like that?

Yes, but. . . .

Daddy, why were. . . .

I'll tell you after the ice-cream cone, he said. But he never did tell me. And I forgot about asking after a while and the ice-cream with Daddy was good, I didn't get to be with Daddy alone very much any more because there was a new baby now, a little boy to—what Daddy said—carry on the name, and I dripped ice-cream onto my shoes and my Daddy got down on the floor in the ice-cream store and wiped them clean with his handkerchief and then he got up and showed me how to eat an ice-cream cone so it wouldn't drip, licking it first around the edge close to the cone and only taking a bite out of the top when I had all the drips licked off.

* * *

I did get the answer eventually. Maybe thirty years later I asked again, my mother this time, and my mother said: Why, his legs were swollen from being in the water so long.

Of course.

And what was wrong with his hands.

What was wrong with his face.

His hands were nibbled by fish when he was in the river all that time.

Said my mother.

I thought he had mittens on. I thought it was winter.

I said.

I suppose his mittens came off, my mother said.

It seemed that the mittens had stayed tied around his neck attached to idiot-strings (they called them that, yes!—Do they still?) that kids wore under their coats in those days, up the arms and across the shoulders; but they came off his hands in the water.

His nose was bitten off too. Fish will do that, you know; they'll eat off anything that sticks out. My ex-husband (from whom I have been divorced now for more years than I was married to him) for example had a wart on his elbow and every time we went swimming the fish would swarm to him and try to get that wart. He finally had it removed, it was such an annoyance.

My mother said: The undertaker repaired his fingers with wax, but they didn't look right, did they?

No they didn't, I said.

His nose too, she said.

I'm surprised you remember any of it all that long time ago, said my mother.

I remember, I said.

You were so little, said my mother.

* * *

They held an open casket funeral because Anna insisted upon it. The undertaker and the priest tried to reason with her, they say, but how could they put it to her? The flesh is eaten off your child's bones, could they have said that? His nose is gone? No, of course not. The body is not in a suitable condition for reviewal, that's what they would have said.

Don't say "body"! Anna would have screamed at them. *That's not a body, that's Paul!* I can hear it, absolutely. I knew her so well. I knew them all so well. They are all gone now, Mama and Daddy and Uncle Luke and Anna; even Billy; all dead themselves, so what does it matter?

Only to me. Only to that other child who still lives in me.

Maybe to Cyril, who lives alone now in the little house far from the river.

Maybe to Billy's children, Alix and Emma and Eloise. No saints' names there. We have wandered from our source.

Anna, they would have said, the body doesn't matter. It's the soul that matters.

I want Paul's body back! Anna would have cried. *God can keep his soul!*

Right, Anna. I'm with you. It was the body that I loved too and the little white suit and the perfect flesh and the hair and the dazzling, glowing face in the dark room.

I never forgave my mother, but I forgave Aunt Anna everything. Always.

* * *

I pieced together over many years the story of what had happened to Paulie, and when. It was for whatever reason important to me to know exactly when. Well, but it was important to me to know all that could be known. One piece my mother gave me—which was the only piece that in any way dated events—was that Arden Junior had been a newborn in her arms when she wandered up and down the river with Aunt Anna, both of them calling and calling for Paulie.

And Arden was born on February 1. So maybe Paulie drowned around the middle of February. Because they said he was in the water for six weeks, and they found him in March. So to say mid-February is cutting it fine.

* * *

My mother knew that calling to Paulie was hopeless—of course she did—but she did it anyway to placate Anna. Anna was entirely off her head. They say that she became really crazy during that six weeks when they couldn't find Paulie's body. A wild wail came into her voice then that never left it; all my life I heard that wail in her voice: the smallest things that she talked about, the most ordinary things, a walk around the block, the price of celery, a talk with a neighbor, became subjects for dirges.

You would have thought she was Cassandra calling out doom when she told about baking a pie.

* * *

So there they go, the two sisters, wandering up and down the river bank, the Mississippi, the Father of Waters, one of the sisters carrying a tiny new baby, the other mad with grief that her firstborn has been torn from her arms by this terrible river; calling and calling, the two of them.

Pauleee! Pau-au-au-leee! I can hear them, see their feet slipping and sliding in the wet-leaf-strewn melted-snow earth of February, of March.

Paulie!

My mother knows this is insane, of course she does. But she calls out because it eases Anna for her to do so.

He's alive, says Anna. I know he's alive. I feel it. . . .

My mother cleaves to reason, all her life. But where would he *be*, Anna, if he were alive?

Don't say that! Anna screams. *Don't say that! Don't ever say that!*

So they trudge and call and the baby in Elizabeth's arms grows heavier and heavier.

Here, let me take the baby, says Anna.

But Elizabeth won't surrender Arden. She is—she tells me this many years later—afraid of Anna.

She thinks Anna is so crazy that she would throw the new baby into the freezing water to be with the other one. So Elizabeth holds onto her own child, carries him up and down the river bank for hours, while Anna calls for Paulie.

* * *

I don't think Anna ever really got over it, said Myrna, Billy's widow, that day at the ladies' get-together. I think she always mourned for Paulie. She always wanted to talk about it. And she'd cry and cry.

She never talked about it to me, I said. Never.

I wonder why?

Maybe she thought you were too little, said Myrna. Maybe she thought you wouldn't remember.

Maybe, I said.

Did Billy talk about it, I said.

No, said Alix. My Dad never wanted to talk about it.

I guess I'm not surprised: I heard Anna's voice from long ago: wailing: You pray, Elizabeth. You pray that God will take Billy and Cyril, and send Paulie back. . . .

Jesus. Jesus.

* * *

Where am I, the little girl that was me, while all this goes on, this wandering on the river bank? And where are Billy and Cyril? Why, we are probably at Grandma's house, where Grandma lives with her youngest daughter, our Aunt Irma.

How can an aunt be a daughter? I puzzle about this. I am a daughter. But I am not an aunt.

I ask Grandma about this, but Grandma can't explain it. She tries, but I don't understand. Grandma doesn't talk very well. Grandma is from Germany, which is The Old Country. This is The New Country. Grandma came across the water on a boat. The ocean is a very large body of water. My Daddy told me that.

What is an ocean, Daddy.

An ocean is a very large body of water, Dolly. He says.

Body. Body of water.

But what I really meant to tell you here is that Grandma doesn't talk very well. They spoke another language in The Old Country, which is German.

The language in this new country is English. Our Grandma doesn't speak English even as well as I do. She does it a little better than Billy, but Billy is a *baby*. Not as small as Arden Junior, but still a baby.

But Grandma does not have to talk. Her face is old. She smiles a lot. Her eyes are blue. Her hands are kind. Wherever Grandma is, is peace, love, safety. Wherever Grandma is, is home.

* * *

When I was eight or nine, I had pneumonia. I actually had to be in a hospital, a notable and rare eventuality in those days. While I was in the hospital, my fever ran so high that a lot of my hair fell out, and what was left was allowed to become a tangled, matted mass. It probably wasn't the fault of the hospital nurses—nuns, all, at St. Mary's, the city's Catholic hospital—no, remembering what I was like as a child, I probably bit them when they came near me with a comb.

When I got home, my mother sat me in a chair in the living room and tried to comb through the mess. I begged her to stop, I cried, but she persevered.

I don't think pain impressed my mother.

But my grandmother happened to be at our house that day.

Stop this, Elizabeth, she said to my mother.

But Ma! I have to get the snarls out!

Nein, she said. She took out of her big black pocketbook a little pair of scissors and she cut every mat and snarl from my hair, freeing some hairs and snipping others, carefully, carefully; it took a very long time.

Finally: There, she said. Now you can comb.

To my mother.

But it's all uneven, my mother said.

Ja, said my Grandma. But it will grow again.

You do not understand pain, Elizabeth, she said. I wonder how can that be?

* * *

I can see my grandmother in my mind's eye now. I am an old lady now myself—*these things happen, dear, wait and see*—and I still see her holding Billy on her lap in the kitchen of the old house on Second Street, I see her holding a turning fork in her hand and turning over *fatigman* in the old black cast-iron frying pan.

I see her in the garden in the summertime, digging around the roots of the marigolds that grew under the wooden back stairs and round the outhouse.

Why do you dig around the roots, Grandma?

Ach, child, I haff to give them some air, *die Blumen*—the flowers, they need air, chust like you, Johanna. . . .

Johanna. She called me Johanna. Yo-hanna.

That is German for Joan. My name: Joan.

Which is feminine for John. *John:* from the Hebrew: *God is gracious.*

You can't get much better than that. For a girl's name.

* * *

I breathe air in and out through my nose for a long time, feeling the air go in and out, feeling me needing the air.

Then I try not to breathe in any air, to see if I really do need it.

Good Heavens, Johanna, you are turning blue! my Grandma says. Breathe, child. Breathe.

I *do* need air, Grandma, I say when I can speak.

My Grandma looks worried and she watches me to see that I keep breathing.

* * *

Paulie walked on the ice of the river in February that year, on what I later learned to call "rubber ice."

"Walking on water," I say to myself whenever I think of it, and I think of it often, probably every day, and I know that this phrase is totally inappropriate, bordering on blasphemy, and imputing Christ-like notions to Paulie; but he *was* my little white Christ, don't you see? so shining he was. . . .

And if he had worn brown that day in the circle, say, or green, would the memory be as sharp? Would it find its home in my heart like a white knife? Who can say? Who ever knows things like that? Life turns on such small occasions. I think of Kurt Vonnegut's beer can opener, and I shout: Yes! Yes! *that's* the way it is!

So Paulie walked on rubber ice, with his friends; they were all of course absolutely forbidden to try the ice, and as a matter of fact the river itself was forbidden to all of them.

Don't go by the river, Paulie. Danny. Roger. John.

Stay away from the river. . . .

* * *

For a while the other little boys—Danny, Roger, John—were afraid to come and tell what had happened. But finally one of them came to the house and told Anna that he had seen the ice break, he had seen Paulie slip under the ice.

* * *

When my own child died, about 25 years later, I chose not to have a public viewing. The only people who saw him before he was buried were his father and a friend. I couldn't go even for the funeral—I was too sick.

Aunt Anna talked about it for months, she wouldn't leave it alone.

Oh, Joan, she cried. Wailed, in that banshee wail of hers. Oh, why didn't you let anyone see your baby? Oh, why?

I did not want it, I said.

Oh, she cried, oh, I would have *loved* to see your baby, Joan! I would have *loved* to see him!

* * *

We were going to see Paulie.

I was so excited; that last time we saw him had been: when he was lying in that pretty bed and wouldn't get up, wouldn't get up: unsatisfactory.

This would be better.

Bound to be.

Grandma went out into the wonderful sunny day, big sun was jumping off the little yellow suns of the marigolds under the stairs

sun

Grandma

marigolds

oh wonderful day we are going to see Paulie.

My Grandma kneels down by the marigolds she has her blue apron on and she is careful to kneel only on grass not in the dirt she has a digger which she sticks in the dirt around one of the marigolds

What's that Grandma? *this is a trowel, child.* what are you doing Grandma? *oh, I am digging up this flower, Johanna.* why, Grandma? *oh, we are going to take this flower to Paulie . . .*

She marks a circle with the trowel around the chosen flower.

She pushes the trowel down deep along the circle marks, and then she pushes on the trowel backwards so that the flower comes up with its own bit of dirt around its roots.

Why are you doing it like that, Grandma?

Like what, Johanna?

Why don't you just pull it out like I pulled the onions out?

This flower is not like an onion, Johanna, an onion is to eat, but this flower we are going to plant again so that it will grow in a different place . . .

I must dig it up very carefully so that I do not damage the roots. She says. If the roots are too much damaged, the plant will not grow in the new place, it will not survive.

Not survive, not survive, not survive.

What is not survive, Grandma?

Not to live, Johanna, not to be alive.

Live.

Alive.

* * *

My Daddy has his straw hat on and he is wearing his ice-cream suit. I love his ice-cream suit. He says it is called an ice-cream suit because it is the color of cream and it has little red and green flecks in it like that nice kind of chocolate chip ice-cream and I say, But Daddy chocolate chip ice-cream has *brown* spots, and he says, red, green, brown, what's the difference, a spot is a spot, use your imagination Dolly, are you going to be like your Mama, with no imagination?

My Grandma says I have a very big imagination, I say.

Yes, well, says Daddy.

If your Grandma says it, it must be true.

My Daddy likes my Grandma a lot, I know that.

Your Grandma is a very great lady, he says. If your Grandma says something is true then it *is* true.

* * *

My Daddy took his hat off and laid it on the kitchen table.

Is that an ice-cream hat, Daddy? I say.

You could say so, he says. You could call it that.

Can I have it Daddy?

You can not have it, he says. You can touch it and you can try it on, but you can not have it. That hat is mine.

He goes out of the kitchen. The screen door swishes shut behind him with a little bang.

My Hat.

I think about it.

That hat is Daddy's.

The marigold is Grandma's marigold, and she is going to give it to Paulie.

This is something like the onions.

I pulled up the onions and they were Mrs. Erickson's onions and I didn't know they were hers, I thought if they were growing in the ground they could belong to anybody, and I pulled them up oh beautiful the shiny white balls and the lovely green sticks and the nice dirt and Mrs. Erickson was very mad at me she came over and yelled at my Mama and my Grandma was there too You have to teach this child some respect for private property, she yelled.

And my Grandma said She is chust a baby, she did not know. . . .

* * *

The hat was on the kitchen table and I picked it up and tried it on my head.

It was too big, it flopped around. It was a flat round hat with a flat piece sticking out all around it. Stripes of what looked like braids, like my Aunt Anna braided her hair, like my Mama braided dandelions for us, were stuck together in a hat shape, around and around.

How did they do that?

There was a little thread sticking out at the edge where the stripe finished.

I pulled at the thread a little bit.

It pulled loose in a wonderful zig-zag of white thread.

Oh!

I pulled some more.

More zig-zag.

More and more.

Suddenly the thread came loose, I had the end of it.

But.

Oh gosh. Oh horror. The hat was gone.

This might be worse than the onions.

I understood everything suddenly. Everything.

Without the thread there could be no hat.

This was an important thing! A wonderful thing to know! But I was pretty sure that my Daddy would not understand this.

I was pretty sure that he would only understand that he did not have his hat anymore. I tried to put the braid of straw back into a hat shape and I was doing fairly well with it, the straw looked sort of like a hat again, and then Grandma and Mama and Daddy came into the kitchen, and Mama was carrying the new baby who was not so very new any more but who was named after Daddy, Arden Quarles Junior.

There was a third name too, a saint's name, but nobody even remembered what that was after a while.

I hated that baby and I wanted his name and I knew that my own name was not good enough.

And Grandma was carrying the flower which was now in a little pot.

We're off! said my Daddy.

Where is my hat here it is he picked up the hat-shape and it fell apart into loops and loops of straw braid.

What the *hell!*

He yelled.

And then at me: What Have You Done To My Hat?!!

I was so scared, I saw that he really cared about that hat, but I didn't mean it, I didn't mean to do it, I didn't mean to make it fall apart, I just pulled the little thread with its little zig-zag points, one this way, one that way. . . .

My mother seemed to be holding her breath.

But:

Ach, said my Grandma. She didn't mean to do it, Arden. She iss little, she iss chust a baby. . . .

She's not too little to learn about private property, my father said softly. Whispered. Apparently this was too awful to even yell about.

Private property.

I knew private property.

I learned *that* with the onions.

This wasn't about private property, this was about pulling on a little thread, and how the thread made the hat stay together, and how the hat was not a hat without the thread. . . .

Yes, well, said my Grandma: not today. She will not learn private property today. This iss Memorial Day and we go to take this flower to remember Paul. . . .

Can I carry the flower, Grandma? I said.

No, Johanna, she said. You are too little to carry the flower.

You can carry the water, she said.

She took a glass jar out of the cupboard and filled it from a pail of water near the sink. She used a tin dipper and poured the water into the jar with the dipper and she gave me a drink from the dipper.

And when I stop and live in my tongue for a moment I can taste that water still, clean, sharp, cold, tasting of the earth, where it came from, the pump and the well under the stairs, and of the tin dipper.

Here, she said, you can carry this, and she put a cover on the jar of water and put the jar into my hands.

Iss this too heavy, Johanna? she said.

No, Grandma, I said: It's just right. . . . .

Just Right . . . the porridge in the story of The Three Bears was *Just Right. . . .*

My Daddy picked up the straw loops of his hat and threw them into the iron cook stove, the part where they lit the fire when Grandma cooked. Might as well get some good out of it, he said.

We all got in the car, which was a Model A Ford, I still have an old photo of that car, my mother is standing in front of it on her wedding day, holding her wedding bouquet.

We get into the car and Grandma and I sit in the back seat and she is holding the flower and I am holding the jar of water and in the front seat my mother is holding Arden Junior who has not yet begun to be called Sonny

and my father has no hat on and I am very sorry I spoiled the hat I am very sorry

Daddy I'm sorry, I say

Don't mention it, he says

Done is done, he says

but I am carrying the water and I am terribly proud to be doing that I am terribly proud that I am not too little to carry it and I hold it very very carefully so I don't drop it and so it doesn't spill and doesn't leak

What is the water for, Grandma? I say

The water iss for the flower, Johanna, my Grandma says. We will pour the water on the roots of the flower when we plant it, she says.

The flower cannot live without water.

She says.

Air and water. Yes. Okay.

An important thing then: carrying the water.

* * *

The car stops at the edge of a little road that does not go straight like the road by our house or by Grandma's house, but turns and curves quite pleasantly

it is more like the roads out in the country, which is where my Daddy takes us in the car sometimes on Sundays after church, but this is not the country this place is right in the city and it has a big fence around it and we drive past a gate made of big stones and I think this is beautiful the stone gate and the fence and the green grass and many little trees and some big trees and there are statues all around, I know what statues are, Grandma has a statue of Mary, who is God's mother, in the garden in the back yard by her house.

and the curving road is beautiful, and the blue, blue sky, I know that the sky is where God lives and I feel God very close today I could talk to him like I do sometimes if I have time but I don't have time I am carrying the water and that takes all the time

and we all get out of the car and we walk and I carry the water quite carefully only once I forget and I skip once *I am going to see Paulie!* and, Do Not Skip, Johanna, my Grandma says, only not meanly, just saying it, Do not the water spill, she says and I stop skipping and I walk along quite quietly carrying the water in the glass jar and Mama carries Arden Junior and Grandma carries the yellow flower and my Daddy carries nothing he just walks along with us and I know he is still mad about his hat I wonder if he will stay mad all day and we don't walk very far only a little way if I looked back I could still see the car quite near and then we come to a place where there is a little hill, sort of a hill, a little *tiny* hill, like I could make with the sand by the alley at home, not a hill like God makes and

Here we are, says Grandma.

I don't understand. Where? Where are we? And if we are *here*, then where is Paulie?

My Grandma kneels down and this time she does not have her blue apron on and she doesn't seem to care if she gets her dress dirty and she starts to dig a hole in the little hill. She has brought the trowel along—why! I didn't know she brought that, where was it, in her pocketbook?—and she cuts the grass out very carefully in a round circle and she lifts the grass away and sets it on the side and nobody says anything and a cloud comes over the sun and it is cold for a second and then the cloud is gone and it is warm again.

She digs the dirt out of the hole and she makes a pile of it on one side and then she tips the flower out of its pot and she sticks the flower with its own dirt around the roots, she sticks it in the hole.

I am simply fascinated, I love this planting business, I want to learn how to do this, I want to do the things that my Grandma does, and I want to be like Grandma and so I watch her very carefully.

She pats the earth down around the flower and it sits there just fine and it seems as though it will be all right in its new place and the sun shines on its little flower face and its face is like the big sun, a little sun, and

You can put the water now, Johanna, my Grandma says.

Pour it right around the roots.

She says.

* * *

I do what Grandma says to do. I kneel down and bend over the little hill, like Grandma did, down quite close to the flower, and I take the cover off the jar and lay it down on the grass and then I begin to pour the water right down onto the roots of the flower and the flower is like a bright yellow sun and I can see that there will be more suns, the flower has many more buds on it that can open up, if the flower *survives,* and the water pours with a wet, gurgling, pouring sound out of the glass jar and it pours and pours and

the water

goes

down

soaks

into the earth

and down

past the roots of the flower

and down

and down

and suddenly I know something.

The sun turns dark. The flower shrivels. The sky closes up and becomes a blue cloth that comes down very close and suffocates me so that I have no air to breathe.

Paulie is under there, I say.

* * *

Flashes: of memory.

Didn't you tell her about death, Elizabeth? my Grandma says.

Well of course I did, my mother says.

* * *

My mother lies.

* * *

I get the door of the car open I slam myself into the back seat, I try with my fingernails to claw my way through the leather, I want to *go into it*, I want to *go through it*, I want to

disappear

and I am screaming and screaming and I think everyone can hear me screaming except me I can hear nothing there is no sound at all but I can feel my mouth being open

a hole

a hole with no tongue in it

This is what death is then, death is being under the dirt, death is breathing dirt and not breathing air, there is no air to breathe under the dirt, will I be dead then too? Death is breathing water.

I will never see Paulie again and the dirt will cover me too the dirt covers me I lie with Paulie in the pretty bed under the dirt and my Grandma digs a hole for me and plants a flower and I pour the water and the water runs down into my eyes

into Paulie's eyes

the water runs down into the earth and runs down and

the marigolds

under the stairs

under the earth

all the people. All.

* * *

Ashes. Ashes. We all.

* * *

They took me over to Aunt Catherine's house the night that Arden Junior was born.

Feb. 1 it was—I know that now. Or maybe January 31, if he was born in the morning. Because I remember very clearly that it was night when I went to Aunt Catherine's.

Aunt Catherine's house—I see suddenly that I do not think of it also as Uncle Gabriel's house. I believe that is because the men seemed to count for very little in our family.

The women were everything.

They were all terrifically strong: Catherine and Anna and Grandma and Irma and Mary, who became Sister Elicia. My mother? Well, yes, in her different way; my mother too.

The men were just sort of *there*—the purpose of men was to provide a living for women and children. It did not matter very much what sort of *people* the men were; as long as they were "good providers."

Uncle Luke was a "good provider"—I knew that, I heard my aunts talking.

Uncle Gabriel was not such a good provider.

But good provider or not, it didn't matter much what kind of people they were.

My Daddy? Well. He was in a way the exception. It mattered to everybody what kind of person *he* was. To this day, my cousin Tildy says, Your dad was wonderful, a party was not a party without your dad.

But even he got drawn into the provider role. Even he, I think, took some of his sense of importance—and he did feel important, oh, yes, just as I do—from the fact that a woman had married him and that he was fathering children.

And our family lived in a house that we *owned*. It was truly Our House. It was not rented from somebody else.

Catherine and Gabriel and the girls: Dolly and Lollie and Tildy: lived in a rented house. I didn't know much, but I knew that. So: they took me to a rented house that I didn't visit very often, and that I didn't want to go to on this night, and they told me that I had to stay there—alone!—with people I didn't like very much, *because my mother was going to the hospital to have a baby*. . . .

Where was my Mama? What was happening to her?

I find myself wondering now, as I write this, why they didn't take me to Aunt Anna's house where I knew everyone and was perfectly comfortable; and in a sudden flash I understand that this birth had to have occurred right around the time that Paulie died.

It could have been that the whole rest of the family—Grandma and Irma and everyone—was rallied around Aunt Anna because of this death, and that was why I had to go to Catherine's house.

And that—I imagine—might also have been the reason I was so terribly frightened that night. The whole family would have been frightened, they would all have been in a state of shock—and then, into the maelstrom, my mother's second child was born.

* * *

They tell me I am going to have a little brother or sister when I wake in the morning. Why would anyone suppose that that idea would comfort me in any way?

Why would I want such a thing? In the first place, what *was* it? I was not entirely sure; except that it must be another person; and in the second place I had my cousins, I didn't need more people; if a little brother or sister was *people*, I didn't need any more, and I didn't want any more.

My cousin Dolly had "heart trouble." "Heart trouble" was a disease, and diseases were something you caught from other people. You got diseases from being near people who had diseases. And "heart trouble" was a very bad disease, I knew this because my Mama and Grandma talked about it sometimes and Grandma said how she prays for Dolly, and how she is afraid that Catherine and Gabriel "won't raise" Dolly. I don't know what that is, "won't raise", but I am sure it is bad, and I don't want to sleep in the same bed with Dolly because when I wake up in the morning I will have "heart trouble" and also a new brother or sister and they "won't raise" me, oh, no, they "won't raise" me. . . .

Eventually, of course, being smaller than these others, I am overpowered and put to bed beside Dolly; also—eventually—I fall asleep. When I wake up, I do not have "heart trouble"—(What do you mean, you haff caught heart trouble? says my Grandma later: little Johanna? You don't *catch* heart trouble, you just *haff* it. . . .) but I do have a baby brother.

I hate Arden until we are both adults. I hate Dolly even longer than that: only in the last ten or fifteen years have I seen that she is basically a fairly decent human being, doing the best she can, a little silly, a person given to uttering really dumb and devastating insults, with her big silly brown eyes wide—"For heavens sakes, I sure didn't mean anything by that"—but, like most of the rest of us, fundamentally a pretty good person who means well most of the time.

And they did after all "raise" her. Since she is still with us, probably about seventy-five years old by now, and as far as I know okay apart from sciatica—which isn't catching either—they must, you will agree, have "raised" her.

* * *

Myrna, Billy's widow—Billy died about fifteen years ago, of a pulmonary embolism, on New Year's Day, just two days after he received a clean bill of health from a doctor in his yearly physical; make what you will of that; I know what I think—Myrna said to me: You know, Alix has all the newspaper clippings from the time when Paulie drowned. There's even a picture of Anna down by the river, calling to Paulie.

I thought my heart would stop.

Can I—can I see them? I said. Some time? Not really wanting to. But yes, wanting to.

Ambivalence, they call what I have.

Not right away or anything, I said. But some time.

Sure, said Myrna. I'll call you. We'll get together.

* * *

When my Aunt Anna hobbled toward the end of her life, there did after all come a time when the doctor said she had to go into a nursing home. That happened because she had one day been trying to clean out a furnace grate in the floor of the little house she shared with Cyril, and she fell into the open grate and stuck there up to her armpits for many hours, until Cyril came home from his car-wash job and found her and got her out: banged up and bruised and black-and-blue practically all over.

Poor Cyril. He didn't want to let Anna go to the nursing home. What would he do with his life? then? But the doctor insisted. Good God, man, he said: she has diabetes, heart trouble, ulcers on her legs, she's half blind and half deaf and she's wandering in her wits. She can't be alone any more. I won't take the responsibility. Blah blah blah.

I went out to visit her in the nursing home in Robbinsdale where they put her: not often enough, but sometimes. My visits to her, I mean, did not occur often enough. Well. I hated to see her there, that was it. But I went anyway; sometimes with my mother and sometimes alone.

I took a friend along once when I went with my mother. After-ward: Your mother is jealous, the friend said. Of you and Anna.

No way, I said. My mother doesn't care enough about either one of us to be jealous.

Trust me, said my friend.

Once I went alone to see Anna and when I got there she was asleep. I didn't know whether to wake her or not. I sat quietly in a chair, not knowing, uncomfortable, and after a while she woke up, and moved on the bed restlessly, angrily, and said: Is someone here?

I'm here, Anna, I said: Joan.

Joan, she said. Come here where I can see you.

I came over to the bed and bent closer to her and took her hand.

I can't see you, she said.

I'll put your glasses on, I said, and did so: thick cataract lenses, this was long before lens implants were common. Settled the ugly black plastic frames on her nose, placed the bows properly on her ears.

Joan! she cried. In that clarion wail. How did it happen that she kept that young voice still in that old, old body?

Yes, it's me, I said.

Give me a kiss, she said. Reaching up her fat arms, flesh hanging off them as old women's flesh does.

I kissed her soft old cheek.

I always liked you, Joan, she said: cried. Sometimes I pretended you were my own little girl.

I know, Aunt Anna, I said. I always knew that.

You were like me, she said.

You were the one who taught me to sew, Aunt Anna, I said. When I was twelve. Do you remember?

I remember, she said.

I remember sewing a white dress for you when you were a little tiny girl.

She said.

I'm having an awful time here, Joan, she said. With my life. I wish God would take me. I pray to him all the time to take me.

He will, I said. Soon.

He won't, she said.

Do you know why? she said. Squawked.

No, I said. Why?

I offered St. Joseph my death, she said.

This is a Catholic thing, in case you don't know. In case you are wondering. You offer your sufferings, whatever they may be, to atone for the sufferings of Christ.

Maybe they don't do that any more, but they did in the old days.

I told St. Joseph—said Anna—that whatever death God had in mind for me, I would accept it.

She held my hand tight in the vise-grip of age.

I made a mistake, she said.

I wish I hadn't done it.

Take it back, I said.

I can't, she said. They don't let you take it back.

* * *

Once, when Anna was still living at home, in the little house where Cyril lives still, far from the river, we—all the women—met there for the get-together. There was me and Myrna and Tildy and Lollie and Dolly (who was home on a vacation, something like that, she was married at the time and lived in Milwaukee), and my mother, Elizabeth. Six of us, and Anna. Well. That was enough. That was respectable. A quorum. So to speak.

Cyril was there too; in fact, Cyril had made the lunch and was for that day an honorary woman. Almost as good as a woman.

Tildy—may God help us all—had (I think out of boredom and

dissatisfaction with her life; and why not?) Tildy had just become a charismatic Christian. Otherwise known as a Born-Again. Catholic, still, I think, but Born-Again.

She was in the stage where she was trying to convert everybody. Me.

Joan, do you know Jesus? she asked me once over lunch. Oh, I think so, Til, I said. No, Joan, I mean, Are You Saved By The Blood Of The Lamb?

Well, enough.

Look, Tildy, I said. You know I love you dearly, like you were my sister that I never had. But I would like to respectfully request that you just shut up about this stuff. If you don't, I won't meet you for lunch any more.

And I have to give Til credit: she did shut up.

That day at Anna's house, though, she said: Let's pray for Anna. Let's pray for Anna to be healed.

(I already told you the list of things that were wrong with Anna: diabetes, deafness, blindness, ulcers on her legs, congestive heart failure, etc., etc. I never knew anybody else with more things wrong with them. The doc certainly had a point when he insisted that she go into a nursing home.)

(If Til could have managed it, it would have been a really spectacular healing.)

Do you want us to pray for you, Anna? I said.

Oh, sure, she said, reaching her hand out to me.

I took it, held it.

Tildy got on her other side and took Anna's other hand.

Then everybody joined hands, my mother holding my hand, then Lollie, then Dolly, then Cyril, looking sort of sheepish, etc., etc.

Until we made a circle.

Ring around a rosy: I thought.

Til talked. Prayed.

Dear Lord. She said. Please look with mercy on your servant, Anna; etc., etc. On and on. A sing-song drone.

As Til prayed, Anna's face grew more and more peaceful. Happier and happier. Beatific, you could say. A goofy fat smile broke that dear old face pretty much from ear to ear.

When it was over: Oh, Anna said. Oh, that was almost as good as dying!

When I do die, she said, this is how I want it to be! with all my family gathered around me . . . and holding my hands. . . .

Afterwards, on the way home, my mother said to me: Do you think Tildy can heal people?

I think healings can happen. I said. I think miracles can happen.
But do I think Tildy can do them?
No, I said. I don't.
I don't either, said my mother.
And when the time came, in the nursing home, Anna died alone.

* * *

In my dining room, resting on my mother's old cedar chest, I now have the box full of newspaper clippings and other stuff from the time Paulie died; Myrna brought it over about a month ago.

I've looked at it all a couple of times: read the clippings, touched the things Anna saved for so many years.

Like Myrna said, there *is* a news photo of Anna standing by the river: not fat at all as I remember her, but slim and elegant, looking lovely and tragic in a fashionable cloche hat and a beautifully cut knee-length coat, with those tiny-heeled pointy-toed shoes that they wore in the twenties and thirties.

I think I am shocked to see her so carefully dressed.

What did I want her to wear? Sack-cloth and ashes? Yes, maybe.

And wouldn't *I* try to look as good as I could if I knew I was getting my picture in the paper? No matter what was happening?

Absolutely. I would.

* * *

There's other stuff in the box too. Letters from my Aunt Sister Elicia, Sister Mary Elicia, O.S.B., which is Order of Saint Benedict, about how all the nuns in the convent and all the children in the grade school in Tacoma, Washington, where my aunt was a teacher, were praying for Paulie to be found; then, after all hope was lost, by everybody except Anna, for Paulie's body to be found.

There's a stiff pair of leather mittens; I imagine they are the ones he wore the day he was drowned. Why else would she keep them in the box? There are no idiot-strings on them.

There's a lock of curly blond hair. Did she cut it off his head after he was found? I don't know.

There's dark brown hair woven and braided and tied into a Victorian mourning corsage: did Anna cut her hair when Paulie drowned and have it made into this? Who can know? now?

Who can ever know?

What *is* certain is that Paulie died; and Anna lived and I lived; after a fashion, both of us. Both of us living strange, rich, twisted lives, curled as we were around a drowned child's finger: nibbled by fishes, mended with wax.

I think: How do we do it? How do we ever manage it at all? All of us; how do we survive? How do we live from day to day on this hard planet—too hot, too cold, too dangerous?

The box—a Buster Brown box, do you remember Buster Brown, the little boy in the ads, with long curls and a starched white Peter Pan collar?—the box sits on my mother's cedar chest—Hope Chests, weren't they called?—that I have in my house now: uncomfortable, like an urn on the mantlepiece full of an uncle's ashes.

I had thought that when I touched that box, read those clippings, held those mittens, the sky would fall. Again. But it didn't. I am trying to be honest here. The sky didn't fall. Nothing happened at all. I felt nothing at all. The important thing was the memory: unassailable in my mind; not the facts, and not the artifacts.

One of these days I'll have to give the box back to Myrna; well, really to Alix, to Billy's daughter, who seems to value it. Hey. Anna was her grandmother, and dearly loved from all I can make out. Of course she values it.

* * *

Myrna tells me that when her girls were babies, Anna would keep a drawer in the kitchen full of relatively harmless objects, and when the ladies came over for a get-together Anna would seat them around the kitchen table, take out the drawer, place it in the middle of the table, and plunk the current baby into the drawer. The baby— old enough to sit up, I guess—would be entertained by the drawer's contents for hours, and all the ladies could watch the baby and eat and chat at the same time.

My gosh, I said to Myrna. That's absolutely brilliant. . . .

Yes, wasn't it? said Myrna.

I adored Anna, she said. So did the kids.

Myrna was a kind of an odd-man-out too; or at least was different from most of the family; I took to her the first time I met her, when she was nineteen years old and Billy brought her to my parents' twenty-fifth wedding anniversary party. Forty-five years ago now. Forty-five or so.

* * *

Alix has two little daughters, Kim, who is nine, and Pammy, who is seven.

Pammy hasn't spoken except to her mother and her sister for four years. She has what they call "selective mutism." She doesn't speak in school or on the school bus; or to anyone else, not even to her grandmother, Myrna, who cries when she talks about Pammy.

Four years ago, Pammy's daddy left his wife and his daughters: just up and left them, not a word, never a word since.

And something else strange happened at just that time.

Do you remember the news stories about the house in New Brighton, which is a suburb in the first ring of suburbs around Minneapolis? where the police figured out that there were at least two murdered bodies buried in the yard and they dug and they dug all winter, all over the yard, a big yard, a double lot, great for children, dug it up, breaking the frozen earth with jackhammers? You remember that, the news was full of it for weeks. It was about four years ago.

Finally they did find the bodies, frozen in the winter earth; and dug them up. With jackhammers.

Well, that was Myrna's house.

And Pammy stopped talking.

* * *

My life has always felt fragile to me, easily lost and by that fact precious.

Pammy's life feels that way to me too; and yours. I pray for Pammy every day; and I pray for you, as my Grandma taught me to pray: Take care of them all, Lord, I pray. Take care of Pammy and Myrna and Alix. Take care of my daughter Margaret, far away in London. Take care of Tildy, who is taking tap-dancing lessons—at her age!—and could quite easily break something. Take care of my brothers and their families. Take care of Nathan and Elinor in Atlanta. . . .

As if I thought the Lord couldn't find them unless I told Him where they were.

On and on. A long list.

Take care of me.

Honestly. Every day.

Sometimes I think I'm getting as nutty as Tildy.

And I pray for that baby on the bus. Do you remember that baby? That I told you about? Whatever became of her? Him? Did she—he—become a saint? Or a martyr?